PAYBACK'S A WITCH

"*Payback's a Witch* is the book I've been waiting for all my life. A sexy, funny, charming romp of a novel that scratches that witchy, autumnal itch just right. I read this story in one breathless, giggling sitting, and at the first fall nip in the air, I know I'll be reading it again. One of my favorite reads in years."

—Emily Henry, #1 *New York Times* bestselling author

"*Payback's a Witch* is like the first Halloween wind through the corn: brisk, breezy, and altogether refreshing. This is a sweet, charming read, absolutely designed to be enjoyed on a crisp fall evening. I want to go to Thistle Grove. My greatest regret about this book is that it isn't a five-season TV show that I can already sit down and just *binge*."

—Seanan McGuire, *New York Times* bestselling author of *That Ain't Witchcraft*

"A sexy, charming, and completely magical romance full of sparkling dialogue and loveable characters . . . Reading *Payback's a Witch* is like curling up with a big mug of cider on a perfect autumn day."   —Kerry Winfrey, author of *Very Sincerely Yours*

"No tricks, all treat! Lana Harper's debut *Payback's a Witch* is a compulsively fun read."

—Jacqueline Carey, *New York Times* bestselling author of the Kushiel's Legacy series

"[A] light, atmospheric, sexy sapphic romance perfect for [the] spooky season."   —Smart Bitches Trashy Books

"*Payback's a Witch* by Lana Harper had me under its spell from the first page. Readers will love this book that has all the ingredients for the perfect spooky read: hexes, ancient grimoires, and ghostly spirits running amok."   —Under the Covers

From Bad to Cursed

LANA HARPER

JOVE
NEW YORK

A JOVE BOOK
Published by Berkley
An imprint of Penguin Random House LLC
penguinrandomhouse.com

Library of Congress Cataloging-in-Publication Data

Names: Harper, Lana, author.
Title: From bad to cursed / Lana Harper.
Description: First Edition. | New York: Jove, 2022. |
Series: The Witches of Thistle Grove
Identifiers: LCCN 2021054420 (print) | LCCN 2021054421 (ebook) |
ISBN 9780593336083 (trade paperback) | ISBN 9780593336090 (ebook)
Classification: LCC PS3608.A7737 F76 2022 (print) |
LCC PS3608.A7737 (ebook) | DDC 813/.6—dc23
LC record available at https://lccn.loc.gov/2021054420
LC ebook record available at https://lccn.loc.gov/2021054421

First Edition: May 2022

Printed in the United States of America
1   3   5   7   9   10   8   6   4   2

Book design by Alison Cnockaert
Interior art: Starry frame © Tanya Antusenok / Shutterstock

To all the chaotic good (and neutral!) witchy readers,
the ones whose hearts belong in Thistle Grove—this one's for you.

From Bad
to Cursed

1

Deviously Done

THE THING NO one tells you about summoning demons is, sometimes you have to think outside the box.

I should know; I've been calling them up into my circles since I was a kid. My mother even encouraged it, as a slightly safer alternative to a way riskier burgeoning fascination with elder gods. (PSA, if you don't want your daughter developing an interest in the gnarlier chthonic entities before she can even ride a bike, maybe don't read her Lovecraft at bedtime. Seems obvious enough, right?)

The books go on about how summonings are supposed to be these disciplined, rule-bound affairs—and most of the time, they are, if you know what's good for you. The truth is, if you take sensible precautions, it's not nearly as dangerous as people think. And *such* a rush, too; the daemonfolk are interesting as the hells, pun intended. Sometimes they're inclined to share juicy secrets or ancient spells, the kind you won't find in even the oldest, dustiest grimoires. Other times they're so gorgeous it breaks your heart, or so horrifying that even a quick glimpse caught before you banish them is enough to leave you panting, heart battering against your ribs, blood boiling through your veins while your whole skin rolls with chills.

Shit, even when you play it safe, there's nothing quite like a demon summoning to make you feel alive.

Of course, there's always the odd time that even a pro like me fucks it up just a *wee* bit.

As usual, I'd cast my summoning circle in the warrens of the basement beneath The Bitters, in a chilly, cavernous room that had started out as Elena's third wine cellar—because who gets by with just *one* these days; certainly not my mother—and now doubled as my demonic lair. No windows, musty air that smelled like centuries-old stone and aged Bordeaux, witchlight sconces flinging trembling shadows on the walls; the perfect ambiance for such a conjuring. The summoning spell was already whipping through me like a tempest, my protective amulets glowing hot against my chest. Everything felt like it should, all systems go.

But as soon as Malachus began to coalesce, I felt a twinge of wrongness in my gut, an unsettling, instinctive awareness that something was *off*.

According to my research, Malachus was supposed to manifest as a brawny reptilian dude, macho and mindless to the max. The type of mostly harmless demon whose bark was way worse than his bite. I hadn't summoned in a while, so tonight was meant to be just a practice flex, easing myself back into the swing of things after a little break.

But the silhouette gathering in my circle was unmistakably

femme-presenting, on her knees and with her back to me, with the kind of ridiculous waist-to-hip ratio that would've put Cardi B to shame. A swoop of hair, black and glossy as moonlit water, curled around an even darker set of wings folded neatly against her back. I could see the wings' outline fill with a faint scrawl like one of my own sketches, a vague suggestion of feathers, before they sprang into a three-dimensional profusion of lush black down. And the scent that engulfed the cellar wasn't just the usual rank whiff of sulfur and brimstone, but something sweeter, more elegant and piercing. Jasmine, maybe, with a subtle patchouli twist. The kind of compelling perfume that made you want to follow someone around, drooling until they told you what they wore.

When she turned to look over her shoulder at me, with massive eyes the color of molten gold, my mouth went dry as dust. I couldn't be positive, having never seen one before—they weren't exactly a dime a dozen—but for my money, this sure looked like one of the former seraphim.

A fucking fallen angel, landed in my basement.

"Oh, Hecate's chilly tits," I whispered to myself, my heart plummeting even as a rising thrill swelled inside my stomach. "This is so very deeply fucked."

From what I'd read, the fallen were temperamental, ultra-wily, and very powerful—exactly the kind of unpredictable daemonfolk I do not fuck with as a general rule. But here she was anyway, which meant shit was about to get *extremely* outside the box.

She whipped around to face me in a single blurring motion, still on her knees, dainty little hands folded primly on her lap. Her fingers were tipped with vicious black talons, knuckles dusted with iridescent scales. She cocked her head, examining me with a sly intensity, the tip of a pink forked tongue peeking between her full lips. Then she smiled at me, wide and feral, a flash of onyx teeth capped with fanged canines *and* incisors.

Let me tell you, there's something viscerally unnerving about black teeth, especially ones as sharp as hers. I had a mounting suspicion that, unlike the real Malachus—wherever in the hells *he* was—this chick's demonic bite might be a lot worse than her bark.

A bloom of pure dread unfurled inside my chest, shooting down into my fingertips and toes like a falling star. Alas, the thrill-chasing part of my brain that often took the wheel at times like this downright relished it. So this wasn't going to be a lesson-learned type of moment, then, I noted to myself. No big surprise there; I'd never been much good at those.

"Ill tidings!" the demon said cheerfully, in a cross between a velvety purr and some gigantic gong struck directly between my ears. Gritting my teeth, I narrowly resisted clutching my head. When it comes to demons, a show of weakness is just about the worst thing you can do. "Whom do you serve?"

The rote of her greeting defused the tension just a hair. Demons always start with the ill tidings bit; it's what passes for good manners with them, part of some governing daemonfolk etiquette they can't subvert.

I drew myself up, putting on an imperious expression modeled after my mother's and doing my level best to avoid looking as rattled as I felt. When dealing with slippery entities from the netherworlds, throwing up a badass witch front tends to be at least half the battle.

"I serve my goddess, my ancestors, and above all, myself," I replied, the traditional response of an Avramov summoner. I don't know what the Blackmoores, Thorns, or Harlows say—in the highly unlikely event that a witch from one of Thistle Grove's other magical families has ever had cause to banter with a demon—but I'd bet my ass on some cheesy noise about serving the ultimate good, light conquering darkness or whatever, cue a stirring orchestral overture. Avramovs don't buy into any of that oversimplified, good-versus-evil binary shit. Like the ultimate pragmatists we are, we've always staked our claim firmly in the gray.

The problem was, now came the part where I was meant to bind this entity by her true name. Which was going to be a neat trick, considering I almost definitely didn't have the real Malachus in hand.

"And you, Malachus Azaranthinael, appear at my will and behest," I finished, crossing my fingers behind my back. Hey, worth a shot; maybe the lore was just supremely off base on how Malachus was supposed to look. "Which means you must obey . . . and be gone at once!"

"A fine sentiment," the demon crooned, with another of those awful, spine-tingling smiles. In a streak of movement, she was on her feet, naked and stupidly gorgeous, a curtain of black silk hair draped over thick curves and long, smooth limbs. Her skin glowed like a paper lantern, as if lit from within. Too bad we'd started off on such a wrong foot; she probably had some killer beauty tips. "If I were, in fact, Malachus Azaranthinael."

"If you are not, why, then, do you appear in his stead?" I demanded, trying to enforce one final shred of protocol before this already wayward train went careening completely off the rails. Demons weren't supposed to be capable of bending the rules like this; when you summon one by their true name, what you call is meant to be what you get.

"Because, as it happens, there *is* no Malachus," she said, still grinning like the void, honest-to-goddess little flames dancing in her golden eyes. Sounds like something right out of a corny cartoon, but it sure as fuck didn't *feel* cliché when the abyss was staring you dead in the face. Chills crawled under my skin, crept into my knees—the type of nerve-jangling bullshit I lived for, the reason I went all in on such reckless antics as this in the first place. "There is, and ever was, only me . . . and the lies of Malachus I tell to entice dim little deathspeakers like you into calling me up unbound."

I tried not to take being called dim *too* personally, and failed— to be fair, she had a point.

The books do tell you that daemonfolk lie easier than they breathe. By the sound of it, this one had invented a harmless-seeming demon as bait, embedded his name into the lore for gullible assholes like me to find, and then tied his summoning to herself, like one of those fugly deepwater anglerfish that dangle an alluring light for their unsuspecting prey. All of which meant that once she appeared in answer to a Malachus summons, she'd be yanked earthside without any bindings in place.

Damn, I thought, with a grudging pulse of admiration, *well-played*. Demons were tricksters down to their brittle black bones, and this one had gotten me good, fair and square.

"Deviously done," I said, with a little dip of the head, making one last gamble. You'd be surprised how vain some of these tricky fuckers are, and how hard they fall for a little well-placed pandering. "And when they ask me into whose clever trap I stumbled, what fearsome name shall I say?"

She rolled her huge eyes, rosebud mouth pursed in exasperated disdain, like, *Nice try, witch, but maybe get up earlier in the morning next time you try to put one over on me, eh?*

"My true name is only mine to know, but you may call me . . ." she said, appearing in a shivery instant at the circle's very edge, one fine-boned foot poised as if to step over it. "Davara Circle-breaker."

A tad on the nose? Perhaps. Ominous as fuck? No doubt.

In the spirit of optimistic experimentation, I raised my hands and flung a banishment charm at her, murmuring under my breath—followed by another, and another, a barrage of them. She stayed staunchly corporeal, her inky smile only growing, her smooth form betraying not even the faintest flicker.

"Oooh, Yaga's Baneful Banishment, how quaint!" she squealed, widening her eyes. "I have not seen *that* one in centuries!"

She pressed against the boundary, the air around her rippling like a mirage. The cellar trembled with the sheer force of her assault, little shock waves radiating out from the circle as her will flung itself against the barrier of mine, testing its give. My cluster of protective amulets had now turned searing against my chest, but even my fail-safe runes were badly outclassed. They weren't going to keep me from getting soul-eaten by something of her caliber, not if she managed to break free.

I stumbled, barely keeping my feet, my heart pumping double time as uncut adrenaline crashed through my veins. If the demon got through me, she'd run roughshod all over Thistle Grove before someone else—probably my own mother, *double fuck*—managed to lock her down and banish her. Then I'd never live down the mortification of not having managed to handle my own demonic business, not to mention whatever punishment the tribunal saw fit to impose on me.

That is, if I even lived long enough to worry about such things.

"Not today, bitch," I muttered under my breath, mind whirling as I thought on my feet, every nerve ending alight and crackling like a fuse. "I am *not* the one for this."

I arranged my fingers into a different kind of conjuring, clouds of vaporous black seeping from my fingertips and gathering around my hands. You never really got used to the feel of ectoplasm, not even after years of handling it, the sticky cold of it clinging like a noxious second skin. But my magic itself felt wild and slick inside me, a quicksilver torrent racing up my spine and roiling in my head—the very best feeling in all the world.

Then came a headlong rush of haunts, harkening to my call.

The demon blinked in sudden confusion as the whole jostling host of shades that called The Bitters home began materializing around her one by one. Given that my ancestral demesne was over three centuries old, and impressively haunted at that, there were a *lot* of them. A mosh pit's worth of hazy gray-scale forms, tattered and nearly translucent, trailing smudgy limbs and writhing hair as they pressed in against one another.

At first, they emanated only bemused annoyance, having been rudely yanked away from whatever ghostly business they'd been minding before I called on them. Then they noticed Davara Circlebreaker, still poised at the edge of my circle, a tiny wrinkle of concern now marring her smooth brow.

Their irritable rumbling abruptly changed pitch into a disgruntled hum—which escalated very, *very* quickly into the kind of bloodcurdling wail you could really only describe as eldritch.

The thing about summoning circles is, they're a one-way barrier, meant to keep things in rather than out—and the thing about ghosts of the restless dead is, they're territorial by nature, hostile to interlopers in their domain. I'd guessed that a trespasser like

Davara, one that belonged in this realm even less than they did, would read as the ultimate provocation. And despite the huge power differential between a first-tier demon and a bunch of un-ruly revenants, I was banking on strength in numbers, the way a furious swarm of ants can bring down an elephant.

As the throng of shades bum-rushed Davara, a roar of pain and rage thundering from the center of the circle once they'd closed in on her, I could see that I'd been right on both counts.

Then the shriek cut off abruptly in a massive flare of scarlet light as the demon finally called it quits on this entire earthside outing. Apparently the prospect of munching on a witch's soul and wreaking some small-town havoc wasn't worth the trouble of get-ting nipped to (un)death by a rabid spectral horde.

"Woooooo!" I cheered, yanking down a victorious fist as the light faded away, bright afterbursts still popping in my field of vision. "And that is how it's *done*, motherfuckers!"

The ghostly mob slowed in their maddened whirling, settling back to hover just above the dusty stones. Then they turned to fix the glowing craters of their eyes on me—a.k.a., the presumptuous scally who'd dragged them here against their will.

"Oh, fuck me," I groaned, the garnet at my throat throbbing as I flexed my fingers. "Okay, then. Let's go."

2

>)) ● ((⟨

Not Enough Heart

I'M NOT GONNA say I agree with Aunt Elena, because that would be treacherous," Letha said, sidestepping the hairy animatronic tarantula that leapt out at her, hissing, from inside the dark passageway leading out of the teenage witch's lair. "But let's say, just as a hypothetical, if you turned *my* house into a poltergeist nest for shits and giggles? I, too, might be a little spicy with you for a while."

My cousin was referring to the lingering psychic fallout from my improvised banishment. It had taken me all night to subdue my ghost militia, and even then the fix was only temporary. More than two weeks later, we still had knives embedding themselves in the ceiling, shadowy figures hovering over us while we slept, doors slamming open and closed in a syncopated rhythm designed to drive us all mad. Not to mention the way the mirrors distorted your reflection into a Munchian horror show when you were just trying to put on some fucking mascara. The kind of trippy shit that really got under your skin.

It had also scared my three cats half to death, not to mention the zebra finches, which was the part I felt the guiltiest about. Maybe it was my imagination, but even Elphaba the hedgehog struck me as a little nervy, not quite her easygoing, mellow self.

Suffice it to say, things between me and Elena had been . . . strained, ever since.

"Just because you're turning it into a hypothetical doesn't make it any less treacherous," I informed my cousin, summoning a witchlight to hover above my palm so we didn't have to fumble through the dark. We kept the entire haunted house space—a retro-fitted warehouse adjoining the Arcane Emporium, our family's occult megastore—glamoured with a fortification of the oblivion charm that cloaked all of Thistle Grove. Any normie visitor or member of the cast who happened to catch my spell would forget it within minutes. "Also, it wasn't for shits and giggles. I had to get rid of the demon *somehow*, didn't I? Even Elena's not such an agent of chaos that she'd be down with me unleashing an ancient big bad unto the mortal plane."

"A big bad *you* summoned in the first place, Issa," Letha pointed out with irritating logic. "For the aforementioned shits and giggles."

"Okay, fair. And I do wish Davara would've talked to me just a little before trying to bust out of the circle," I added, pouting. "I had so many pressing questions. Like, do first-tier demons naturally have such popping skin, or does she moisturize with, the tears of the damned or something? Do they all smell weirdly amazing, or was that just her? The kind of stuff that isn't in the books."

Letha shot me an aggrieved look. "Yeah, about all that . . . how come you didn't invite me to spot you? Davara Circlebreaker sounds like a snack. And maybe I could have helped, before things got that far out of hand."

I squeezed Letha's shoulder apologetically as we stepped into the next scene—then yanked her out of the way as a tear-streaked prom queen in ruffled fuchsia taffeta nearly barreled into us, fleeing a chainsaw-wielding prom king with disheveled feathered hair. A cluster of real visitors, cowering by a table scattered with severed hands, corsages, and a cut-glass bowl of bubbling "poisoned" punch, shrieked with terror before dissolving into panicky giggles.

As the prom king sprinted past us, muttering to himself, I appraised his shredded powder-blue tux and bloodstained Converse with a critical eye. Stylishly fiendish, sure, but also just kind of *dull* in a way I couldn't quite put my finger on.

"Trust me, she was on the too-evil side of evilly hot," I assured Letha. "Even by your standards."

"Well, she might've been an edge case. And now we won't ever know, will we." Letha fixed me with a baleful side-eye, which, given how big and hooded her dark eyes were, was *extremely* baleful. "Seeing as I wasn't invited."

"I'm sorry, angel. It'd been a minute since I summoned, and . . . I don't know. I wanted to do it solo, blow off some steam. Try to get my groove back."

Letha gave a grudging nod, her cool expression thawing just a touch. She knew I'd been in an indeterminate funk lately, though she hadn't pushed me on it yet. My best friend and second cousin wasn't the cuddliest of creatures, but she *was* rock solid, the kind of unflaggingly loyal boulder of a person you always wanted at your back. You'd be wise to avoid finding yourself downhill of

Letha, because in true Sisyphean fashion, she might roll right back down and crush you. But you could lean on her anytime you needed, rest against her with all your weight, and know she'd never budge an inch.

"Okay, so you get a pass this once," she allowed. "But if I miss another demonic calamity, harsh words will be spoken. Of that you may be sure."

"Understood. So, what do you think?" I asked her, surveying the murderous prom unfolding around us. Torn banners fluttered from the exposed pipes far above, ironically wishing the class of '83 a happy life. While the prom king chased the queen around, oblivious couples covered in varying degrees of gore swayed lazily to the discordant strains of a slow, macabre cover of "Sweet Caroline." Letha's set design was impeccable as always, detail oriented and maximally creepy; my assistant director had a real eye for elevating horror ephemera into an art form. "Is it still working, six months in?"

As artistic director of the Emporium's haunted house, I was responsible for everything from designing costumes to hiring the cast members, and this story line was my brainchild. The basic premise was that a teenage witch who was just coming into her power had been spurned by the prom king / quarterback / all-purpose popular dickbag. Fueled by rage, she'd cast a bloodlust spell on the whole town that had belittled her, turning everyone into murderous fiends. Kind of *The Craft* meets *Carrie*, with a twist—and way less menstrual blood, because, ugh, no thanks.

Besides the prom, other set pieces included the teen witch's bedroom (complete with a bloody pentagram, black candles, and a human sacrifice—all the tacky accoutrements a real witch would never stoop to using), a classroom in which a homicidal chemistry teacher terrorized his students, a day care full of evil munchkins running amok, and a cheer practice gone heinously wrong.

"I think this one was a win," Letha replied, with a nod that rippled the slick veil of her pink-and-purple-dipped black hair. Courtesy of her Japanese mom, Letha had the kind of shining, slippery tresses I'd spent my teens chasing with too many products and an elaborate straightening regimen before giving up the dream in my twenties. "Thematically consistent, but with enough variety to keep them on their toes. A lively palette, compelling audio, wet work decent but not overdone. A *vast* improvement over the circus of the damned, no question."

I frowned, chewing on a knuckle. "You don't think it all feels just a bit . . . uninspired?"

"Uninspired?" She glanced over at a tableau unfolding by the punch table, the teen witch cackling above a cheerleader caught in the thrashing death throes of the poison punch. "I mean, it's a little slapstick, sure, but that's part of the fun. Looks like the tourists are eating it up."

"I suppose." I nibbled on the inside of my cheek, trying to deduce what integral piece it was that I felt might be missing. "The narrative feels a little lackluster to me, that's all. Like there's not enough heart."

Letha tilted her head, flicking me a bemused look. "Unless you mean that literally—which, yes, no bloody ventricles currently featured in the program—I'm really not following, Iss. This is one of our most elaborate takes yet. And the reviews bear it out, too. Whatever we do next, we'd be smart to keep it along similar lines."

She was right; we'd noticed a significant uptick in ticket sales over the past six months, much more revenue pouring in from the haunted house than we'd seen in years. Part of it was the fact that, since Emmy Harlow had won the Victor's Wreath during the Gauntlet of the Grove last Samhain, the town's magic was no longer exclusively favoring the Blackmoores—Thistle Grove's wealthiest and most powerful magical family, and our primary competitors for immersive entertainment. As a result, the rest of us were finally getting our fair slice of the tourist pie again. And now that we were well into spring, we were considering a redesign for the upcoming Flower Moon Festival, a town celebration organized around Beltane, the pagan holiday that usually brought the most tourists we saw outside of Halloween.

I should have been stoked to launch into a revamp; there'd been a time when I loved nothing more than bringing a new horror story to life, especially the costumes for the cast. I used to lose myself for weeks in the design, even dreaming in fashion sketches, their flowing lines and throbs of color weaving through my delta waves as they stitched themselves into full-blown garments while I slept.

Managing the haunted house might have been my day job, but for a long time, designing those costumes had also been my joy.

Maybe the real problem wasn't that Fiendish Eighties Murder Prom didn't have enough heart; maybe the trouble was that *my* heart wasn't in it anymore. A thing I felt guilty enough about that I hadn't even mustered up the courage to share it with Letha, who knew everything else worth knowing about my life, and had since we'd been creepy toddlers together.

"I guess I'll have to talk it through with Elena," I said, suppressing a reflexive wince. I had a debrief and planning session scheduled with her at the Emporium right after the walk-through. To say I wasn't looking forward to a dialogue with my mother, especially in her role as Avramov matriarch, barely brushed the surface of understatement. "It's her call in the end, anyway. Maybe she'll want to keep a successful show in place for another season, make it easy on us."

Letha stopped dead, so abruptly that one of the ghastly dancing couples collided with her. She shot them a glare so concentrated and intimidating that they hastily sidled away, discarding any budding plans of drawing her into the scene. Maybe they recognized her as one of their bosses, or maybe it was just the intense Capricorn energy Letha exuded. Despite her filigreed features and general pastel-goth aesthetic, Letha had that effect on people, like one of those gorgeous tropical frogs that actually signal their danger with pretty colors.

"What is with you, Iss?" she demanded, turning back to me. "I know you've been going through . . . *something* for a while now. I also know you haven't wanted to talk about it, and I've been respectful of your space, like the exceptional human being I think we can agree I am. But we're just about reaching the outer limits of my patience here."

"Letha, come on. It's not that serious."

"Isn't it? Because you've been shambling around like some subpar clone of your former self for months now. I mean, seriously, *you're* suddenly not feeling Fiendish Eighties Murder Prom? *You* don't want to brainstorm shiny new ways to terrorize the tourists?"

"Could it be that I'm just tired?" I ventured weakly. "Possibly coming down with something?"

Her dark eyes narrowed beneath the swooping wings of metallic eyeshadow. "Isidora Avramov, I'm starting to think you've been body-snatched. Are we talking an astonishingly lame demonic passenger here? Because I will admit that a prophylactic banishment *has* crossed my mind."

I chuckled despite myself at the idea of Letha attempting to spring a stealth exorcism on me, like the world's shittiest surprise party.

"I'm still me, I swear on my witch's soul," I assured her, looping my arm through hers and tugging her toward the exit. "If I *wasn't* me, would I know to offer to buy you an apology Revenant 'Rita at the Shamrock Cauldron tonight, with extra pickled jalapeños?"

"Make that two 'ritas, plus several shots of Cazadores," she muttered, reluctantly letting herself be drawn forward. "And it had all better come with a detailed walk-through of what's going on with you."

"If not tonight, then soon, promise." I gave her arm a conciliatory little squeeze. "And it's really sweet, by the way, that you love me enough to throw a surprise banishment in my honor."

"Don't flatter yourself, cuz." A corner of her mouth twitched with the suggestion of a smile. "It's only because I may perish of boredom if I don't get the old you back soon."

Such a liar. Beneath the flippant facade, Letha cared about her loved ones with unparalleled ferocity, even for an Avramov, and "Blood is thicker than water" might as well have been our unofficial family motto ("We neither break nor bend" being the official creed). I knew she was genuinely worried about me, and if anything, the fact that I couldn't bring myself to open up to my own best friend and cousin about what was really going on made me feel even worse.

And even more of a traitor, to boot.

"Still," I said, letting her have this one. It was the least I owed her, what with the immensity of everything I was holding back. "It's the thought that counts. And you know demonic shit has always been my love language."

3

Cozy like a Straitjacket

AT LEAST THE Arcane Emporium still smelled like home. A sweet waft of incense and melting wax billowed around me as I stepped inside. Frankincense, myrrh, sage, and sandalwood burned all at once, in fragrant loops of smoke that hovered in the air like dragon breath. The vast showroom of what the younger generation had fondly dubbed Ye Witchy Walmart—to be used strictly among ourselves, unless you wanted to see Elena burst into flames while shooting hexes from her eyeballs—peddled everything from spellcraft supplies to spooky decor. Crystals winked from bins arranged along the central walkway, while aisles of racks and display cases stretched to either side, boasting besoms, staffs, and wands; censers, smudge sticks, and multicolored candles; pendulums, scrying globes, mirrors, and tarot decks; robes, dresses, and occult-inspired jewelry.

Above, bundles of drying herbs hung from rough-hewn rafters, courtesy of the "cottagecore, but make it massive" look Elena had been going for when the store was built nearly thirty years ago. An entire wall was dedicated to the Avramov Apothecary, its shelves lined with stoppered jars of milky green glass. We even had our own line of "spell-infused" cosmetics—glamour serum, bath bombs that glowed in the dark, that kind of cutesy crap.

Most of the specialty items were actually made by Avramovs, so we got to claim that our goods were not only artisanal and locally sourced but handcrafted by actual witches. Of course, none of it was going to do the customer much good if they didn't have real magic of their own to work with, but at least we were sending the tourists off with genuinely beautiful collectibles.

I lingered among the wares as I walked toward the back, pausing to sink a hand into one of the cool piles of obsidian here, rub the velvety trim of a robe there, trying to summon up the joy this place had once kindled in me so naturally. I'd loved it here once, with a little witch's territorial fervor. It had been my favorite place in the world, both the ultimate magical playground and my family's most important holding. Something that belonged to every last one of us—but especially to me, second daughter of the Avramov matriarch.

But now I couldn't resurrect even a pale ghost of the sentiment. If anything, the sheer familiarity of it all felt almost claustrophobic, itchy and restrictive as a straitjacket tightening around my chest.

The same damn music that always played—a blend of ethereal chanting and woodland sounds, like the soundtrack to a witchy spa—stalked me through the store, growing louder as I reached the row of curtained alcoves visitors could reserve for tarot readings or scrying sessions. I could hear whispers threading from two of the nooks, the soft, muffled sound of crying drifting from another. Though much of what we sold was Witchcraft Lite, intended just for fun, this was where we drew the line; an Avramov scryer never lied during a divination. When it came to telling fortunes, we sold only the naked truth.

My mother's office lay behind the last door to the left, just before you hit the gigantic storeroom in the very back. I hesitated in front of it for a minute, stomach quailing as my fist hovered over the polished wood.

Oh, come the fuck on, Isidora, I told myself. *It's just your mother. You are* not *this much of a wuss.*

When I bit the bullet and knocked, the door swung open for me of its own accord, with an ominous, creaking whine. *Oh, nice touch, Mother,* very *subtle.*

Inside, my mother's sanctum sanctorum was bedecked in aged wood and oxblood leather, its stained-glass lamps shedding an elusive light. Elena herself sat in a hobnail armchair behind a weathered executive desk, a wall of mahogany bookshelves looming at her back, carved with lobed leaves and prancing imps and stacked with rows of fat binders that contained the kinds of cryptic financial documents I did my best to never think about. A laptop and a printer, recent concessions to modernity, sat on her desk between a set of spiky brass candelabra. The air smelled of Elena's mints and the pipe tobacco she occasionally smoked, along with the spicy-sweet Dior Poison she'd worn since I could remember.

All smells that usually signaled comfort, instead of my current squirming anxiety.

"Isidora," Elena said, flipping the laptop closed with a neat click as I shut the door behind me. "Sit."

She twitched her chin at the wooden chair across from her

desk, a rickety thing that looked like something the miller's daughter had sat on while spinning straw into gold, designed to put anyone addressing Elena firmly in their place. I sat, doing my best impression of a circumspect employee. When your mother was also your boss, you couldn't really indulge in demonstrative sulking on the clock.

"So, your walk-through," she said briskly, resting her elbows on the blotter and interlacing her hands. "What did you and Letha think?"

So this talk was going to be strictly business, and not a more brutal dissection of my chaotic-disaster tendencies, I thought, the tension ratcheting down a notch in my chest. Business I could handle. I felt myself relax a bit as I launched into a recap, the buzz of nerves under my skin subsiding just a little.

"More or less what I thought, too," Elena said when I wrapped up, resting her chin on her linked hands, "when I went through yesterday. A sparkling premise, well-oiled execution . . . impressive work all around. Kudos to you and Letha for keeping it running so smoothly."

"You did a walk-through, too?" I said, not quite managing to keep the hurt from my voice, stomach sinking despite the compliment.

"It's not a reflection on your judgment, Isidora," she said with a significant pause, an unspoken (and unmistakably salty) "this time" hanging in the air between us. "I hadn't visited since the opening, and the stakes are high for us this year. With Igraine stepping down as elder and Lyonesse taking up the reins, the Blackmoores will want to make a show of force for the festival—which means they'll be doubling down on Camelot's offerings. And as always, they'll have their magic to their advantage. Unlike us."

I shifted in the uncomfortable chair, considering. While we used scrying spells at the Emporium, Avramov necromancy was *not* the type of magic you'd ever let loose on a haunted house, unless you wanted the thrills and chills getting a little too real for comfort. In contrast, the Blackmoores specialized in transmutation spells—the loud, glittery *Fantasia* shit so many people think of as conventional "magic"—which made them the ultimate illusionists. Their immersive medieval castle experience included several stage shows each season, combination acts of circus, musical, and real magic that tended to be infuriatingly spectacular.

And it made sense that the newly minted Blackmoore elder would go particularly hard this year, trying to prove that her family still ran this town on their own merits, even without the lucky talisman of the Victor's Wreath.

"Which means we'll just have to be that much better," I finished for Elena, feeling a flicker of the fierce competitive spirit our family passed down like an heirloom, the one that had kept our rivalry with the Blackmoores alive and kicking for so many centuries.

"Exactly, my *lisichka*. We've *finally* clawed some ground back from them, and I'll be damned if I give it up now," my mother said, sharp jaw setting with determination. "So let's blow them right out of their motherfucking moat, shall we?"

I burst out laughing, and she dropped me a sly little wink and a ferocious grin in return. For a moment, I let myself savor the leap of warmth between us, the easy camaraderie I'd enjoyed with her for so many years. She'd called me "little fox" since I was a baby, and I'd grown up hearing how much I looked like her; we shared the same soaring cheekbones, jade green eyes, and auburn hair, though mine was deeper and darker than her fiery copper.

But while I was very pretty in a freckled, weirdly wholesome way, my mother was gorgeous like a catastrophe, something you couldn't tear your gaze away from. Looking at her felt like staring into a fun house mirror at a far more impressive and self-assured version of myself.

It didn't help how temperamentally similar we were, impulsive risk-takers with mile-wide stubborn streaks, allergic to convention. I may not have been the family scion—that honor went to my older sister, Talia, next in line to be the matriarch—but of the four of us siblings, I'd always been the most like our mother. And for a very long time, she'd been who I wanted to be when I grew up. So what were you supposed to do when something that foundational stopped being true? When you suddenly stopped seeing eye to eye with someone who actually *had* the same eyes as you?

Possibly my recent funk was closer to an existential crisis than I'd given it credit for.

"So, let's hear your ideas," Elena went on, spreading her hands.

I took a deep breath, dragging myself back into the moment. "Well, we can't do anything eighties again, obviously. But since that played so well, I'm thinking we lean into the whole period piece aesthetic. Let's say . . . the story of two feuding vampires, as they go from lovers to rivals, something like that? A hate-love saga spanning continents and centuries, very macro."

Elena tilted her head from side to side, mulling it over. I knew she wasn't likely to go for a premise like this; it was too high-concept for her taste, less classic horror and more HBO. And since I'd had the idea for all of thirty seconds, I wasn't even totally sold on it myself. But I thought at least the wide variety of costuming involved might be a fun challenge for me. Something to wake me the fuck up a little, bring my floundering ass back to center.

"Sounds . . . unusual. And a little complicated, don't you think?" she finally said, tapping a crimson-tipped finger to her chin.

"A little, sure. But I'm confident Letha and I could pull it off."

Provided Letha didn't kill me with her bare hands for foisting a project of this scale on her without even running it by her first.

"Then again," Elena mused, "maybe unusual and complicated is just what we need this time around. And you've been running the haunted house for, what, six years now? Which makes you our resident expert on what works."

"Has it only been that long?" I glanced down at my hands, toying with my fingertips, the forced lightness in my voice not even fooling me. "Sometimes it feels like I've been running it since time began."

"I've been meaning to ask you, *lisichka*," Elena said, leaning forward over the desk with her eyes slightly narrowed, two slim lines sketched between her feathery copper brows. Back when I was little, always vying with Talia, Micah, and Adriana for her time, there'd been nothing I loved more than that look, the feeling of basking in the dazzling limelight of her attention. "You've seemed a little off-kilter, these past few months. I've been assuming you're in a bit of a rut, needing more challenge at work—and believe me, I understand just how stifling too much routine can feel. So, is this concept what *you* really want to do to shake things up?"

For a split second, I played with the idea of being fully honest with her, the way I once would've been without a second thought. *No, Elena, that* isn't *what I really want to do,* I would say. *What I want is to design* real *clothes, for* real *people. Not costumes, not Basic Witch Apparel for the fucking Emporium—but my own line of ready-to-wear.*

And what's more, I'd rather not be part of the Emporium at all, because this is what I want to do full-time instead. Start my own business, right here in Thistle Grove.

I could picture her face in high definition, as this revelation struck her like a slap. Shock melting into confusion followed by disbelief, before hardening into the bitter lines of betrayal as she grasped how dead serious I was. That I genuinely wanted to turn my back on what my family had built, and orient my professional life toward a path that had nothing to do with being a witch—or, worse yet, an Avramov.

Yeah, hard pass on that kind of honesty today.

"I'll go over the details with Letha," I said, swallowing down the prickling tightness in my throat. "We may still tweak it a little. But I do think it's the way to go."

4

Something Very Wicked

SPRING IN THISTLE Grove has always been my favorite season.

Each year, Hallows Hill became a purple riot, thistle flowers spilling from the banks of Lady's Lake and racing all the way down the mountain's flanks like a violet wildfire. The season came early, too, our first crocuses nosing up through the snow before January's end. By mid-February the sunshine felt like a balm, the trees in full, extravagant bloom. And there was Beltane to look forward to in May, the month of the Flower Moon—hence the town festival's name. Thistle Grove witches made an entire month of the holiday, with a series of celebrations kicking off at the start of April and leading up to May Day itself.

I get that fertility festivals celebrating the return of summer aren't supposed to be my vibe, Samhain being the much more traditional Avramov fare. But I've always loved flowers, and who can resist a holiday built around bonfires, feasting, and dancing around a maypole, with the excellent bonus of promiscuity thrown in? All entirely my speed.

More annoyingly, even I had to admit that the Thorns' rolling orchards looked particularly stunning in the spring.

Per tradition, the families had gathered at Honeycake Orchards for the ceremonial Beltane Crowning on the first of April—basically an audition to cast the May Queen, who, along with the Green Man of her selection, would lead both our private celebrations and the tourist-facing festival parade. I'd snagged a seat next to Talia, in one of the cushy folding chairs the Thorns had set out for their guests. Around us, the apple and cherry trees were laced with snowy blossoms, like a lingering ghost of the season past. Each fresh gust of breeze brought their petals spiraling down onto the stage that had been assembled for the audition, crowned by a massive arch of morning glories and azaleas. The flowers had been animated to sing an upbeat chorus as they twined adorably around one another—just the kind of unbearably twee shit the Thorns took such great and misguided pride in crafting.

The platform was currently empty save for Emmy Harlow, most recent Victor of the Wreath and my older sister's girlfriend, sitting toward the right as she waited to preside over the competition. Paired with the silvery dolman top she wore over sapphire velvet leggings and metallic espadrilles, the wreath gleamed on her glossy shoulder-length brown hair like a thoughtful accessory, a touch of vintage class.

She caught my eye as I glanced her way, flashing me and Talia a smile before schooling her features back into stern decorum.

"Your chick looks like she's about to adjudicate a war crimes tribunal, *sestra*," I mumbled to Talia through a mouthful of the lavender-laced goat cheese I'd scored from the snack table. I had to give it to the Thorns on this; they really knew how to feed their guests. "I know she's still cutting her teeth on the whole Victor thing, but she *is* aware this is essentially just a chance for the Thorns to show off, right, followed by a pleasant picnic lunch? The pressure isn't exactly on."

"Oh, let Emmy live, Iss," Talia said, giving me a not-so-gentle swat. "She just wants to get everything right. Haven't you heard all that shit about 'heavy lies the crown'? My girl takes her responsibilities *very* seriously . . . with, like, several additional helpings of gravitas on the side."

I snorted, rolling my eyes just a little. I'd gotten to know Emmy fairly well over the past six months—she and Talia were so high-key into each other that you rarely saw one without the other—and on top of rocking killer style, she was generally very cool. She was also exactly the kind of intense overachiever who'd put her all into judging an event fairly, even knowing that we wound up with a Thorn May Queen almost every year.

While the Green Man's role was mostly to stand around and look pretty, the spells the Queen was called upon to do fell squarely in the Thorn wheelhouse—the kind of green magic so incompatible with necromancy that most Avramovs didn't even bother attending the Beltane Crowning ceremony, much less auditioning. The smattering of family who'd shown up today were mostly here for the excellent spread. Even Letha had begged off, snacks and free booze not having been enough to combat the pervasive threat of cuteness overload.

"Don't look now," Talia said, elbowing me with a smirk, "but thine sworn enemy approacheth."

I followed her gaze to the second row from the stage, where

Rowan Thorn was flashing broad, apologetic smiles at people as he clambered over their knees with his long legs. Even though I'd known he'd be here, my shoulders rose toward my ears of their own accord, my hands clenching into fists in my lap.

It was remarkable how just the sight of his face could spike my blood pressure, like the mercury shooting up in an old-timey thermometer.

"You'd think he could've made it on time to an event on his own damn grounds," I muttered to her. "But *noooo*. Probably too busy delivering quintuplet foals all by himself, or saving a blind kitten from mortal peril. All in a day's work for Rowan Thorn, Wildlife Hero."

"Wait, for real?" Talia demanded in a lower tone. "I was just fucking around, but you're actually serious. So that whole workplace enemies thing is somehow *still* happening?"

"Wait, is this not my 'over it' face? Whoops, my bad." I bared my teeth in a manic leer, grinning until my cheeks ached. "How's this, better?"

Talia shook her head, venting a little sigh. "Iss, you know I'm the poster girl for grudges . . . *when* they're warranted. But in my experience, Rowan's one of the good ones. If it hadn't been for him, Emmy wouldn't be sitting up there at all."

It was true that Rowan had been part of a coup instigated by my sister—the vengeance pact between her, Emmy, and Rowan's twin sister, Linden Thorn, that had led to Gareth Blackmoore, prolific cheater and colossal shithead, losing the Gauntlet of the Grove to Emmy, the first real Blackmoore loss in centuries. I did have to give Rowan some slight credit for that, I supposed. Ideally so slight as to be invisible to the naked eye.

"Pretty sure you had a little something to do with that, too,

Tal," I said. "You did get a whole boatload of ghosts all up in you for your trouble."

The strategy my sister and Rowan had employed to take down Gareth in the final challenge, an unprecedented blending of Thorn and Avramov magics, had backfired—leaving Talia possessed by an entire horde of spirits for a night, until the family banded together to exorcise her. It had been a tremendous magical effort for all of us involved, and unimaginably torturous for Talia.

I *still* had nightmares about it sometimes, and I hadn't even been the one possessed.

"Worth it," Talia quipped, in the same blithe way she always dismissed having briefly been the human equivalent of The Bitters. "I do still get the odd migraine, but it's mostly like it never even happened. And you get what I'm saying. You worked at that shelter for a month, tops. Now that it's seventy million years later, don't you feel like it might be time to let things go?"

"It's been seven years, not seventy million," I informed her, before shifting my stare back to Rowan. The least I could do was chafe him with my presence as much as possible, make him uncomfortable in his own family demesne. "And it's not a grudge, it's an archnemesis-ship. Trust me on this, you'll grasp the difference when you have an archenemy of your own to loathe."

As if he could feel the hatred in my gaze like some kind of airborne venom—Mother and Crone, now *that* would be cool—Rowan paused in his passage and looked up, meeting my eyes.

We glared at each other, the distance between us seeming to thin and contract, pulsing like a heartbeat, as if our shared loathing were potent enough to actually distort the fabric of reality. He looked away first, shaking his head in a slow, huffy, can't-believe-this-shit way, a muscle twitching in his chiseled jaw.

At least the feeling was so reliably mutual, I thought to myself with a burst of satisfaction, like sinking my teeth into some tart, delicious fruit. I couldn't even pretend not to enjoy knowing that seeing me was guaranteed to also ruin his day.

"I guess if you *have* to have an archenemy, you could've done worse," Talia said, throwing me a sly, sparkling look. "He's definitely less Thanos, more Killmonger."

"Ugh, not the point, Talia," I said with a shudder. "So far beside the point."

Since I *wasn't* the blind kitten Rowan had likely just saved from untimely death, it wasn't like I'd ever missed how attractive he was. Back when I started volunteering at the Thistle Grove Animal Sanctuary, where Rowan was doing one of his vet school rotations, I'd more than noticed his smooth brown skin, absurd jawline, and heavy-lidded hazel eyes, all framed to perfection by coils of waist-length locs. He'd been twenty-two to my eighteen, which meant our paths hadn't crossed much in the witch community before I began volunteering. I remembered thinking that he looked like a superhero, the sexy-as-shit kind you'd actually want rescuing you—and then, ideally, backing you up against the nearest alley wall.

That was all before I discovered how thoroughly his garbage personality salted his game.

"I wish you'd just tell me what he did, already," Talia complained, shifting to look at me. Like our mother, my sister had one of those preternaturally incisive gazes, the kind of eyes that saw all the way down into the sketchiest recesses of your soul. "He came through for me, sure . . . but you're my *sister*. Whatever it was, you know I'd always back you up."

I took another bite of the aggravatingly sublime cheese, mulling it over. Only Letha knew exactly what had gone down between me and Rowan; I'd needed at least one trustworthy ally to share and savor all that secret, stifled rage. And it wasn't that I didn't trust Talia to take my side; of course I knew she would. It was just that the way things had played out was so fucking *embarrassing* that it almost hurt to tell.

But seven years had passed, and it *was* Beltane season—time for rebirth and new beginnings, all that fresh and dewy crap. Just because I felt so weirdly unmoored, so detached from my family for the first time in my life, didn't mean I couldn't take this chance to connect with my sister. Shit, maybe that was exactly what I needed to feel more like a real Avramov again.

"Okay, fine," I said, casting a privacy bubble around us as the competitors filed onto the stage. The air warbled a little as the spell took effect, wavering like a mirage before settling around us into a transparent dome that would seal off any sound we made. "But you can't tell *anyone, ses*, ever. Upon pain of agonizing death—inflicted by me, just to be absolutely clear."

"That bad, huh?" Talia grinned even as she gave a solemn nod, trailing a finger over her chest. "Cross my heart, hope to die, stick a needle in a cheater's eye. I vow to be silent as the grave."

I took a long breath, psyching myself up, as one of the twenty-odd competitors assembled on the stage stepped forward—a white Blackmoore blonde, one I only hazily recognized, probably called Gwenhwyfar or Blanchefleur or something equally abominable. Full lower lip pinched between her teeth, she began casting something like a floral cat's cradle, lacy curls of ivy and tiny periwinkle flowers dancing in a web between her hands.

Sweet, but nowhere near dramatic enough to cut it for a Queen.

"For starters, I didn't exactly *leave* the shelter," I said to Talia.

"Technically you can't get fired from something you're not even getting paid to do. But, turns out, you *can* gently but firmly be told to GTFO and please never come back."

"They gave you the boot?" Talia exclaimed, eyes widening. "Why the fuck would they do that? You're *amazing* with animals! You're like the everything whisperer."

"Not if you ask Rowan Thorn," I said, a fresh swell of indignation surging through me. "A.k.a., the shithead who wrote me up every single day I worked there. If I was the one doing the thing, you can bet your ass he had a problem with the way it was done. And he was a vet-in-training—it wasn't like management was going to take a lowly volunteer's word for it that he had some personal vendetta in play."

"But you were so into it," Talia argued. "You even hand-sewed those neat enrichment toys for the dogs, all on your own time."

"The peanut butter squeezies for the pups, yeah. Well, he straight up hated those. 'Not in accordance with shelter hygiene standards.'" I'd dropped my cheese plate on my lap to make finger quotes, imitating his gravelly, patronizing tone. My voice couldn't go that low, or that pompous, but the gist came through. "And then he didn't like how I interacted with quarantined animals. Or the high-risk ones. Oh, and let's not forget, the way I washed the food bowls and did the laundry. Apparently I managed to suck at even menial tasks."

The sense of injustice only gained fervor as I told the story, my eyes fixed on the stage. The next competitor, this time a Thorn, was growing a miniature tree around herself, its boughs and leaves intertwining with her own deep brown limbs and hair as if she were morphing into a dryad.

I had to admit, it was sort of pretty, *if* you were into that.

"That's such rancid bullshit," Talia snapped. "You're *always* the one doing the dishes after family dinner. Micah and Addie barely lift a finger, those utter ingrates. What the hells was his problem?"

"No clue. He was so constantly aggro, I might've been impressed—that takes *energy*, you know? But he just picked and picked on me, and never on any of the other volunteers . . ." I spread my hands. "Not that I could prove it, but it was clearly less my work ethic that was the problem, and more my last name."

"But he was so down to work with me," Talia said, shaking her head in bemusement. "Why single you out like that?"

"Just didn't like the particular cut of my Avramov jib, I suppose," I said, blowing out a frustrated puff. "And obviously I couldn't just let him get away with that egregious shit. I mean, consider the honor of the family name."

"Oh, fuck," Talia muttered, seeing where this was going. "You got even, didn't you?"

"You bet your ass." This part, I still enjoyed remembering. "By that time, I'd at least been around long enough to hear the rest of the staff giving Rowan shit about his squirrel phobia."

Talia sputtered, thick eyebrows soaring. "I'm sorry, his *what* now?"

"Right? Rowan the Wildlife Hero, terrified of the tiny buck-toothed banes. So, I thought, hey . . . why not a little squirrel hex?" I grinned at the memory, still proud of my younger self's creative take on wickedness. "Conjured squirrels popping up at the foot of his bed at night, following him to work, appearing at the water cooler. They were only conjurations, so it wasn't like they could *hurt* him, just make him jump. Although I did also make them a wee bit fucked-up, just for funsies. Red eyes, kinda fanged out. Heavy on the *Pet Sematary* vibe."

Talia was cackling now, arms hugged around her middle. "And I'm once again reminded why you're one of my favorite people. So why didn't you just *tell* me this, Iss? Surely you know I would've mostly applauded your deviousness."

"Because he caught me," I said flatly, the last of the joy dying down. "He trapped one of the conjurations. Theoretically I knew it could be done, but it's fucking hard. It hadn't even occurred to me that he might be strong enough to isolate a manifested entity."

"You saw him at the Gauntlet," Talia remarked, mouth tugging to the side. "Rowan's no lightweight."

"Well, I didn't know that at the *time*, did I?" I protested. "So, anyway, he brought it to the Emporium in a bespelled bell jar, told me that if I ever did anything like that again—or if I ever tried to volunteer at any other shelter that he knew of—he'd report me to the judiciary for practicing forbidden magic. And he'd have the evidence."

If found guilty of hexing, my punishment would've been up to the judiciary, of course, but it more than likely would have been at least a temporary banishment from Thistle Grove.

A flash of sheer rage streaked across Talia's face, more intense than I would've expected from her. As a rule, Talia tended to be a good bit more even-keeled than me—and in this case, some might argue that I'd sort of deserved the blackmail. But now my sister glowered at the back of Rowan's head, her eyes roiling with a dark, unfamiliar wrath.

"You should have told me when it happened, Isidora," she said, her voice lower than normal, a little roughened around the edges, as if she were struggling to control herself. "I could have backed you, when it was most needed. That's what family does for each other. You should know as much."

"I wanted to tell you," I said, still taken aback by her vehemence. My sister *had* always been protective when it came to me, but this was a touch over the top. "I just . . ."

Back on the stage, another contestant had stepped forward; about my age, Black and East Asian, her twists in a towering updo glinting with fine gold adornments. I recognized her as another Thorn, possibly named Holly. She was conjuring a floating braided tapestry of wild strawberries, tiny green leaves, and daffodils, shaping it into an intricate pattern like the filigreed outline of a flame. A symbol of the Beltane bonfire, the one the families would light on May Day itself.

And this wasn't an empty illusion, either, not like my hexed squirrels, but real and living greenery suspended in midair, fed by the life magic she was so deftly manipulating.

It was so compelling, so elaborately crafted and complex, that for a moment it sidetracked me into silence, my design brain hopelessly riveted. How was she managing to maintain so many separate threads? Was this one spell or a commingling of several? You'd need to draw this out in advance to prep, sketch it down to the last tendril, and even then . . .

"That's what family does," Talia said again, into my rapt silence. "Protects their own."

"I *know*, Tal, but it was mortifying. I let myself get caught—and by my archenemy, no less." I grimaced, wincing at the ignominy of it all. "Talk about amateur hour. It would've made me look so . . ."

My voice died in my throat—because the Thorn girl's wreath had begun dying, too.

The death started at the top, a traveling blight that blackened and then shriveled the curlicue of flowers forming the topmost lick of "flame." Then the rot raced downward, infecting each thread of her lattice, the tiny strawberries and frilly leaves withering into husks that rained onto the stage. All the natural noises of the day, the hum of birds and insects and even the shifting currents of the air, huffed out in a breath. The atmosphere itself seemed to shift perceptibly toward malevolence, like some encroaching doom from a parallel dimension had leaked into our own.

My heart leapt into my throat, and a fine, cold sweat broke out all over my skin, chilling me through. I was an Avramov, and one who summoned *demons* for a thrill—but I'd never been scared like this before, frightened far past the point of fun.

Then the rot leapt down into Holly Thorn's hands—turning them ashen gray, a black spiderweb flickering over her skin. The witch's eyes fluttered, all the color leaching from her face, and she crumpled onto the stage as if her strings had been cut.

A clamor of shrill alarm rose from the audience, chaos erupting all around us, people standing so abruptly they toppled their chairs.

And the blight didn't stop there.

As the competitors scattered from the stage, it surged up to kill all the flowers in the arch, the bright, pert blossoms curling into themselves as they withered. As annoying as I'd found their singing, I felt a sharp pang of regret to see them die this way. Then the blight rushed furiously outward from the stage, rolling through the grass like a lethal wave, leaving only charred stalks in its wake. It crawled up the nearest ring of tree trunks and blistered them, scorching their petals into twists of ash. The air around us filled with an acrid, peppery smell, like the aftermath of fireworks.

"Holy shit," I whispered, reaching out to clutch Talia's cold hand. She was gaping at the stage, her face so blank with shock she looked like one of those creepy porcelain dolls, the ones with lashes that fluttered over glass eyes if you shook them around. "Talia, what the actual *fuck* is happening?"

She stared for another moment, frozen and aghast, before snapping out of it.

"Something very wicked," she whispered back grimly, squeezing my hand as she stood to tug me along with her between the chairs. "Would be my guess. We have to get to Emmy. I need to make sure she's okay."

I flung a panicked look to the stage, where Emmy stood with her chair overturned behind her, her hands spread wide as she prepared to mount some magical counterattack. The wreath on her hair glowed a bright, unearthly blue, which surged down her arms and danced around her hands in blinding sparks before flowing toward the blight in sapphire waves. Even her wide, furious eyes had a cobalt tint to them, pulsing to some inner rhythm that likely attuned to Thistle Grove itself.

In my opinion, she didn't particularly look like she needed anybody's help.

Then Emmy's blue wave reached the blight, and it simply halted in its tracks, leaving a sharp line between the wreckage it had wrought and the jarringly flawless orchard that lay just beyond.

5

Cleaning House

"THE CURSE THAT struck the Thorn witch," Elena said, her voice ringing across the length of the Mandrake Salon, "has been confirmed to be a necromantic casting."

A murmur of unease rippled through the assemblage of Avramovs gathered in The Bitters' biggest hall. Standing shoulder to shoulder among the crowd, beneath the spear-tipped cast-iron chandelier that hung from the ceiling's embossed copper tiles, Letha and I exchanged grim looks. It had been two days since the blight at the Crowning ceremony, and the story had spread quickly to those who hadn't witnessed it firsthand. Last night, Emmy had convened the Thistle Grove witch quorum—the elders of the four families, their partners, and the scions—to determine a path forward. Unsurprisingly, the Thorns were considering the blight spell a personal attack leveled against one of their family—which would make it a crime of a magnitude that hadn't happened in our town for centuries.

And everyone in the community knew which of the families specialized in the necromantic arts.

"The Misbegotten Curse, to be precise," my mother continued, lips pressing together, fingers tented in front of her chest. "An Avramov silent contribution, with no record of ever having been performed on these shores."

Another unsettled whisper threaded through the crowd, feet shuffling over the red-veined marble of the floor. Misgiving curdling in my stomach, I glanced up at the massive gilded portrait of Margarita Avramov—our family's ancestor and one of the four original founders of Thistle Grove—hanging on the flocked maroon wallpaper above the fireplace. She appraised the crowd of her descendants with black and lustrous eyes, set in the kind of gorgeous resting-bitch face that could launch a thousand ships, probably mostly out of screaming terror. Our ancestor was descended from Baba Yaga herself, and it really showed; there was a good reason she'd chosen to identify as the Dread Lady Avramov.

A silent contribution meant that this curse was a spell that had been included in the Grimoire, the spellbook shared by the families as a magical resource, without Margarita ever having cast it first. A working so dark and malign that the Dread Lady herself hadn't even deemed it safe to demonstrate for her witch peers.

"Is the Thorn witch hurt?" someone called out.

"She is," Elena replied with a grave nod. "Nothing mortal, fortunately. Physically speaking, she's already on the mend. But her magic appears to be . . . impaired, to a degree we haven't yet fully ascertained. While the Misbegotten Curse is primarily intended to drain vitality, as it did when it subverted Holly Thorn's floral spell, its secondary intent is to strip another witch of their magic, render them defenseless." Elena gritted her teeth, unable to keep the strain from her face. "Which means that this interference with her magic was not an unforeseen or incidental effect."

A collective hiss of indrawn breath sounded in the hall like a struck match.

"Fuuuuuuck," Letha exhaled next to me, nostrils flaring, the equivalent of someone less composed shrieking at the top of their lungs and rending their hair.

"Fuck," I agreed quietly, a pit yawning in my belly. Because this was very, *very* bad.

It wasn't like the Thorns would turn to the normie police over a magical assault; even if that were a realistic possibility, that simply wasn't how things worked in Thistle Grove. The witch community tended to its own affairs, which meant we cleaned our own house, too. And short of inflicting mortal injury, the worst crime any of us could imagine was being somehow sundered from our magic, hence why so few of us ever left at all. Beyond town lines, the magic we drew from Lady's Lake—the wellspring that fueled our own innate talents for spellcraft—quickly waned, leaving us powerless.

The idea of losing my own magic was unthinkable, like living without a beating heart. I could only imagine how poor Holly Thorn felt in the aftermath of such a loss.

And anyone convicted of damaging someone else's magic beyond repair would be sentenced to permanent exile from Thistle Grove.

"Gabrielle Thorn and I will be collaborating closely on undoing its effect and salvaging Holly Thorn's talent," Elena continued.

"But there are no guarantees of success. The damage done to Holly may become permanent."

As if in response, the chandelier above us swung in a wild arc, like a pendulum gone rabid, while the dank, ghostly breeze that always wafted through the hall whipped up into a stiffer wind. The double doors slammed themselves open and shut three times in rapid succession, so loudly it made even my usually unflappable cousin twitch beside me, even as I nearly leapt out of my skin.

Groaning, I lifted a hand and murmured a quick and dirty banishing spell at whatever had hijacked the chandelier, in hopes that it would at least simmer down. After a minute, it grudgingly quieted, settling into a less dramatic arc.

Goddess-damned poltergeists just did not know when to fucking quit.

"The quorum is also launching an investigation, aimed at uncovering the perpetrator and bringing them to justice." Elena's glacial gaze skimmed the room, as if resting momentarily on each of us. If it left a pinprick trail of chills down even my spine, I could imagine the effect it had on everyone else. "According to the process laid out by the Grimoire for addressing magical infractions, the aggrieved family has the right to appoint their own investigator—and Elder Thorn has chosen his scion, Rowan Thorn, to head their investigation. As an independent third party, the Victor of the Wreath will review Scion Thorn's findings, and the judiciary will take it from there."

"But what about bias?" I hissed to Letha under my breath, unable to believe what I was hearing. I entirely trusted Emmy to see this through as fairly as humanly possible, but Rowan Thorn, investigating a crime committed against his own family, with *us* as the usual suspects? Not in a million years could he be impartial, with Avramovs in the crosshairs.

Though perfect neutrality likely wasn't what the founders had intended to begin with; they often tended to have some borderline barbaric, eye-for-an-eye notions on how witch business should be run.

"Of-fucking-course he'll want to pin it on us," I muttered. "He hates us."

"Well," Letha considered, tilting her head from side to side, "he at least hates *you*, specifically. So this should be interesting."

Up on the podium, Elena clasped her hands at her waist, her face turning even severer.

"I won't mince words here," she said in a low, ponderous tone. "With a necromantic curse at fault, the suspicion falls on us—as much as I don't believe *any* of our family would ever do something so atrocious, especially unprovoked. In cases involving such a strong presumption of guilt, the Grimoire allows the family under suspicion to participate in the investigation, to even out the scales. So I've appointed a coinvestigator of our own to collaborate with the Thorn scion."

"Gotta be Talia, right?" Letha murmured to me.

"For sure." I craned my neck, trying to find my sister in the crowd, but I couldn't spot her. "Our scion to match theirs. And they worked well together during the Gauntlet, so maybe he'll be more inclined to cooperate with her. Plus, Talia's always been . . ."

I trailed off as Elena's gaze landed on me with unexpected weight. An even more concentrated and unwelcome feeling of misgiving bubbled up deep in my guts, like some primordial gas.

Hecate's chilly tits, I couldn't think of a *single* good reason for her to be looking at me now.

"To represent our side of things," my mother announced, a touch of pride lighting her jade eyes, "I've chosen my daughter Isidora Avramov."

"I HAVE TO admit," Elena said, taking a sip of sherry, "I thought you'd be happier about this, *lisichka*. Aren't flawed yet brilliant supersleuths your area of special interest?"

I slumped in my musty armchair, fighting a powerful urge to drop my head into my hands. It wasn't like I would ever undercut my mother's authority in front of the entire family, so I'd plastered on a dignified expression and done my best impression of "dutiful daughter obviously down to represent the fam" until everyone was gone.

But after the crowd dispersed, I'd cornered her in the sitting room where she liked to take her aperitifs amid a dust-choked profusion of brocade, the dour-faced portraits of our ancestors keeping her company. Pretty much everything in the room had claw-and-ball feet, down to the looming curio shelves filled with a porcelain menagerie of skulls, snakes, and mythical monsters. A scaggy taxidermy wolf head, mid–furious snarl, presided over it all with glassy eyes.

It was, truly, a big stylistic mood.

"I'm not . . . *not* happy," I replied, lying through my teeth. "I just don't completely understand. My taste in relevant TV aside, why not Talia? She's the obvious choice. The Avramov heir, friendly with the Thorns, about as diplomatically minded as our family gets . . ."

"And partnered with the Victor, our ostensibly independent third party," my mother pointed out with an arched eyebrow, re-crossing her ankles over the tufted ottoman that propped up her bare feet, a little puff of dust billowing up around them.

Shit, I hadn't even considered that piece of things.

"This is looking very bad for us already; I'm sure you can see that," she continued. "We don't want even the suggestion of mis-conduct, not so much as a waft of foul play tainting the investiga-tion. Nothing to suggest that Emmeline Harlow might give any undue weight to our perspective."

"But Emmy and I . . ." I trailed off, having been about to say "are friends" but not quite able to pull it off, given that she and I had never spent so much as half an hour alone. "Know each other, too," I finished instead.

"We're Thistle Grove witches, Isidora," my mother said dryly, brushing off the objection. "We *all* know each other. More to the point, you're a mainline Avramov—and everyone knows how closely you and I have always aligned. If I can't appoint my scion to serve, then I want my choice of proxy to make clear how seriously I'm tak-ing this. Both the allegation itself, and our family's innocence."

I chewed on the inside of my cheek, unable to suppress a warm pulse of pride at being her choice. If she couldn't have Talia, my mother could have picked one of my aunts or uncles, even an older cousin—a more senior member of the family. But instead, she'd chosen me to represent our interests. Even with my poltergeisting antics, all my brash daredevil tendencies, I was still the one she trusted to do things the way she wanted them done.

Of course, she probably wouldn't have, had she known about my tangled bullshit with Rowan—but I certainly couldn't come clean about any of that now. *Hey, so, it turns out some of us do occasionally hex the Thorns . . . but only when they deserve it. Pinkie-swear it wasn't me this time!*

"So, you really believe it wasn't one of us?" I said, still thinking along those lines. Minor hexes aside, I couldn't imagine one of our own doing something as heedlessly destructive as the curse had been. But it was also true that we Avramovs could be a little . . . volatile, compared to the other families.

"Beyond a shadow of a doubt," she replied, fury flickering in her eyes like a spritelight. "We do as we will, yes—but we do *not* do casual evil. It's not to any of our benefit to alienate the Thorns, and that spell . . . it goes too far. Far beyond a misguided prank. Whoever did this, they must have intended the most serious kind of harm."

I could see how deeply it had rocked my mother; beneath her controlled facade, the idea that the family she headed had fallen under suspicion for something so abhorrent. And if I chose not to help her put it to rest, wouldn't that make me the most abysmal of traitors not once, but twice over? Someone who not only wished they could break away from their family's legacy, but also was not even willing to stand up for their kin when it came down to the wire?

Of course I had to do it. Even if it meant the misery of spending an indeterminate amount of time in proximity to Rowan Thorn. On the upside, imagining the appalled look on his face when he discovered who he'd be working with gave me a bright, electric jolt of pure delight.

This arrangement would not be without its perks.

"But if you're not comfortable with the responsibility, you need to tell me now," my mother said, those familiar twin lines appearing between her eyebrows as she leaned forward in her chair, rolling the dainty stem of her sherry glass between her fingers. "I haven't informed the Thorns of my choice yet, so there's still time to appoint someone else, as long as we're quick about it. It's in all our interests to have this sorted before the festival."

"Not at all," I said, making sure my face betrayed nothing but conviction. "I just wanted to . . . understand where you were coming from. And now I do."

She appraised me for a long moment, unblinking, her gaze so clear and keen it took all I had not to squirm under it. I pressed both hands to my thighs to keep my legs from jiggling nervously.

"Are you *sure*, Isidora?" she finally asked, brow cinching. "Because once I formally announce my choice to the Thorns, there'll be no going back."

"Absolutely sure," I said, girding my resolve. "If I'm the one you want for this, consider it done."

"My *lisichka*." She smiled then, warm and open, the way she only really did for closest family. "Of course you are."

6

Ground Rules

AND THAT WAS how I wound up at the Shamrock Cauldron, face-to-face with my archnemesis for the first time in seven years.

The quirky bar came across as a kind of friendly visual assault, festooned in sparkly, multicolored shamrocks and Halloween-themed string lights, a plastic skeleton in a leprechaun's green top hat leering in one corner—Dead Frederick, the Shamrock's unofficial mascot. I'd chosen the spot for its status as a popular haunt of Thistle Grove's magical community, a neutralish ground for our kickoff lunch. Their food was solid, if not amazing, but I'd always had a soft spot for Dead Fred, and the drinks had become pretty legendary since Morty Gutierrez had taken over for his dad.

I was going to need many of those drinks to get me through today.

Rowan sat across from me like a thundercloud incarnate, silent and baleful, threatening imminent rain. We'd been glaring at each other in dead silence for a good while now, since I'd purposely come in almost twenty minutes late as a power move. Either this had pissed off Rowan Thorn, (Supremely Punctual) Wildlife Hero, to such extremes that he couldn't speak, or we'd both come in determined not to be the first to break. We hadn't exchanged so much as a word in all those years; whoever conceded now was definitely going to be losing face.

Under the table, I recrossed my legs in an effort to keep my butt from going numb, smoothing my skirt back over my fish-netted thighs. I'd donned battle armor in the form of a bottle-green-and-black baby doll dress in a subtle print of snakes twined around roses, adorned with chiffon inlays I'd added myself. I had my chunky-heeled lace-up hiker boots on, along with all my protective amulets, spiked leather bracelets lining both wrists. It was a look I intended to read as "I could kill you in your sleep and look motherfucking stellar doing it."

Given the circumstances, it maybe wasn't the *most* productive take. But hey, it worked for me.

Slowly, without breaking eye contact, I lifted the copper mug of Witch's Vengeance to my lips and took a long, loud slurp from its straw, draining the peach-and-lemon whiskey smash down to the citrusy dregs. Shit, that meant I was going to need a refill soon; the idea of standing up felt like a tacit admission of defeat.

Fortunately, my next protracted slurp tipped Rowan past his breaking point.

He closed his eyes, lids flickering over them, drawing a breath so long and deep it actually tugged his crisp, sky-blue button-down taut over his broad chest. Of course even his fashion would be terminally straight edge. He did it a few more times, until I determined he was counting to four on both the inhale and the exhale.

A gratified glow fueled by pure pettiness lit just beneath my ribs. There's a certain special exhilaration in driving the object of your loathing to soothing breathing techniques.

"Oh, for fuck's sake, Isidora. Did I seriously come here just to watch you mess around with a cocktail," he finally said, more statement than question—he, of course, was allowing himself only coffee while on the clock. His voice was even deeper than my memory of it, richly textured and heavy on the bass.

"I don't know, Rowan," I replied with exaggerated patience, lacing my hands under my chin and tilting my head to the side. "*Did* you?"

His jaw tightened, muscle twitching under the skin. "You're the one who sent me an engraved invitation via a whole-ass raven, like some kind of evil sorceress who lives in a tower," he pointed out. "Instead of texting or calling like a normal human being. So why don't *you* tell *me*. I mean, for real, what the fuck was that red ink? Was I supposed to think that was actual blood? Because I hate to break it to you, but real blood doesn't dry like that."

"What can I say?" I spread my hands, the picture of innocence. "Couldn't find you in the phone book."

It wasn't that I couldn't have gotten his number, had I wanted to play it aboveboard. But, I'd figured, why not acknowledge that our forced collaboration was going to be inherently adversarial? Maybe even have a little fun with it?

Instead of responding, he laid his hands flat on the table and drew his lips through his teeth, one at a time, as if schooling himself into patience. His lower lip had the perfect amount of pout, finely cut but somehow still unabashedly masculine. It baffled me to no end why the Mother and Crone or the universe or whoever else was in charge of that particular department would have seen fit to bless him with it. A pompous, do-gooding (do-goodering?) ass of his caliber didn't deserve a gorgeous lip like that.

"Okay, how about this," he said. "*However* the message was delivered, I appreciate your taking the initiative to reach out."

Oh, so he was going to play the grown-up now? No, sir, not on my watch.

"My pleasure, really. I just assumed one of us would have to be reasonable and fair," I added placidly, putting a snarky little emphasis on "fair," just in case he'd somehow forgotten the sordid details of our history. "And reasonable individuals find a way to bridge the gap."

"Oh, because your people are *famously* reasonable," he shot back, eyes blazing. "And correct me if I'm wrong, but pretty sure it's *my* cousin who still can't feel her magic or her hands, just because she wanted to try out for Queen this year. Any part of that sound *fair* to you?"

We subsided back into silence, sinking into another glare even as my stomach twitched uncomfortably at the reference to Holly Thorn's damaged hands. Caught up in the whirlpool of our private animus, I'd momentarily forgotten what was really at stake here. No matter our history, what had happened to Holly wasn't ripe for jokes or playful debate. And she was Rowan's family, his blood—how would I be acting in his place had it been Letha hurt by one of *his* family's trademark spells?

I clenched my teeth, staring down at the table's pockmarked wood, where someone had scratched LIBBY + alexis ♥♥♥ into the pitted surface. Were our roles reversed, I was pretty fucking sure I wouldn't be demonstrating even an iota of restraint.

"I'm sorry," I finally forced out, meeting his eyes, though the words soured in my mouth. "You're right, that was . . . below the belt. I know this whole thing must be deeply fucked-up for your family."

His jaw actually dropped open, pure shock flaring in his eyes.

"Hold up . . . you're *sorry*?" he repeated, giving his head an incredulous little shake. "I'm *right*? Did Isidora Avramov really just utter those words in that exact order, or is this what it feels like to experience a psychotic break?"

I rolled my tongue along the inside of my cheek, my newfound benevolence draining away. Of course he couldn't even accept an apology gracefully, not when it came from an Avramov. What was I even thinking, offering him an olive branch? What had I thought he might do with one, besides sharpening it into a shank and trying to stab me with it?

"I have zero memory of saying either of those things," I said, giving him a bland stare. "Definitely all in your head."

He shook his head, huffing a laugh through his nose. "And she's back, folks."

"More like never left."

Still shaking his head, he plucked two laminated menus from the metal display holder, offering one to me. I pinched it from his grasp by the farthest corner, making sure our fingers didn't so much as brush. By the time Rowan gestured for Morty to take our order, I'd skimmed the offerings and made my pick.

"Cheeseburger with the works," I said to Morty as he drew up to our table, and shot him a warm smile. *Feast your eyes on what it looks like, Thorn, when I'm being polite.* "And a double order of the crinkly spiced fries."

"You got it, strawberry shortcake," he said, tipping me a wink before turning to Rowan.

The men I'd let call me a nickname like that—or who could pull off a noncreepy wink, for that matter—were few and far between, but Morty Gutierrez was easily one of them. Bright azure eyes, a tousled shock of dark hair, and what I could only describe as an "edgy eclectic" aesthetic, featuring eyeliner and dark nail polish paired with a variety of *Peaky Blinders*–inspired looks. I'd have made a move years ago, had Morty and my brother, Micah, not been a Very Brief Thing a while back. That being the case, however, the ick factor was *way* too strong.

"Same here, except Impossible Burger," Rowan said, giving Morty an easy smile. I grudgingly revised my estimation of him upward by a notch. Morty was the kind of broadly appealing genderqueer person who made some cishet dudes clutch the manly equivalent of their pearls—their balls, perhaps? But I didn't detect even a hint of any such implied judgment in Rowan's demeanor. "Side of vegan mayo, too, if you got it."

"Sure thing, boss."

Tossing us a jaunty salute, he turned smartly on his heel and headed back behind the bar, running a hand through his ruck of hair. Once he was gone, Rowan looked back at me, one eyebrow flicking up just the slightest bit, something suspiciously like a smirk tugging at his lips.

"Strawberry shortcake?" he repeated, with a careful lack of affect. "That what you're going by these days?"

"Do not take it upon yourself to get any cute ideas," I warned him. "For your own good. That's an extremely Morty-specific nickname, and I plan on keeping it that way."

"Wouldn't dream of gambling with my life like that," he assured me. "Just surprised, that's all. Wouldn't have pegged you for anyone's fluffy dessert."

Something about the way he said "dessert," combined with the forthright way he was watching me with those hooded hazel eyes, sent a weird, unexpected flush spiraling through my stomach, warm tendrils extending down my thighs.

The fuck, Issa? Remember who you're talking to. You hate him; he hates you. That is how this works.

"It's not, uh, not like that," I said, clamping down mercilessly on the feeling. "Morty's just . . . nice, to everyone. And he and my brother dated for a minute back in the day. So, you know, that's ultra-gross, just the worst kind of sloppy seconds. I would never."

I cleared my throat, painfully aware that I was babbling in a way that was very unlike me—and that Rowan realized as much, judging by the faint flicker of amusement in his eyes.

"Speaking of surprises," I barreled on, eager to put this moment far, far behind me, then kill and bury any lingering memory of it, "you eat burgers? With mayo?"

"Uh-huh." His eyebrows, dark and winged, a little jag like a lightning bolt missing in the left one, shot up. "Any reason I wouldn't?"

"I don't know. A burger for lunch seems somewhat . . ." I swayed my head from side to side. "Self-indulgent. And therefore not your brand."

"And my brand would be . . ."

I gestured demonstratively, as if it were obvious. "A vast and overwhelming aura of moral superiority, of course."

"Ohhhh, I see how it is." He gave a sage nod, pursing his lips. "Because I have a well-established sense of right and wrong— unlike some—you think that means I don't eat."

"I mean, I'm aware you need to eat to sustain your life," I clarified, ignoring the gibe. "I was just thinking more along the lines of healthful smoothies. Kale salads, tofu, assorted nuts and seeds. You know, the virtuous foods."

"I'm vegan, not a raw food influencer," he said, rolling his eyes. "Or a sugar glider. 'Assorted nuts and seeds'? Come on, now. Does that sound like food for a grown-ass man to you?"

"Hey, just giving you my impressions," I said, shrugging. "You are what you put out into the world."

His eyes drifted back to mine, suddenly shocking in their intensity, laced with a subtle but unmistakable distaste. "Bet you'd know all about that, though, right?"

The thinly buried past came roaring back up between us like some furious wyvern bursting out of its underground lair, spewing fire everywhere. There he went again, judging me, not just for my own actions but seemingly for everything, and everyone, I stood for. As if that were the only way he could see me—not a person but a figurehead, the avatar of a family he despised on principle.

My skin flushed hot all at once, and my hands tightened into fists where they rested on the tabletop, my lip curling with affront. So this was what they meant when they said something got your dander up; it felt more literal than I'd expected. There was a whole shit ton of anger dander happening right now, that was for damn sure. Such a copious amount of it that it might've been visible had we been sitting closer to the windows, swimming like a swarm of dust motes in the sunshine slanting into the bar.

I managed to keep from telling him to go fuck himself only with a massive effort, by mentally repeating, over and over, that I was doing this for my mother—that I was representing her, and my whole family by extension. That I wasn't going to let this condescending shithead goad me into misbehaving on our very first day.

"The reason I asked you here," I said icily, as if he hadn't spoken, "is to set some ground rules for this joint investigation."

"We already know the rules. They're in the Grimoire?" he said, that maddening upturn in his voice making it sound like maybe he wasn't totally sure I knew what the Grimoire was. Or, for that matter, whether I could even read. "Investigator for each family involved, independent third-party review, followed by a trial. What's there to set?"

"Rules for us, I meant," I said, grinding my teeth. "You know, the kind that'll keep us from killing each other before this thing is done."

"And here I thought as long as I didn't call you some kind of cake, we'd pretty much be good."

"That's just rule number one. Rule number two . . ." I leveled a stony glare at him. "We keep our stuff out of this, make sure it doesn't compromise this investigation. No dredging up of personal history allowed."

"And how the hell are we supposed to abide by that, exactly?" His eyes sharpened on me, that suppressed flicker of dislike growing more prominent. "If anything, I'd argue our . . . *stuff* has some very specific bearing on this case."

"And what's that supposed to mean?" I said, though I was starting to get an unfortunate inkling, a clearer insight into his hostility.

He flipped his palms up, cocked his head. "It means I happen to know that at least one Avramov isn't averse to hexing a Thorn."

This time the anger was closer to lava, boiling up through all of my cracks, blistering my skin as it spilled out of me.

"Listen to me, Thorn," I hissed through my teeth, both hands flat on the table as I leaned toward him. "Because I won't say this twice. There's a *major* fucking difference between a few conjured squirrels stalking you—"

"The word 'few' really does not mean what you think it—"

"*Some* conjured squirrels stalking you—and for very good reason, I might add—and a deathly curse with a name like 'Misbegotten.' I would *never* cast some heinous shit like that. Nor would anyone I know."

"Is that so." He glared at me, flinty, his chiseled features unyielding. "Then prove it."

"Talia was sitting right next to me at the Crowning," I snapped. "Why don't you ask her if she maybe noticed me casting a horrible death curse for absolutely no reason, in between snacking on goat cheese and gossiping?"

"Talia may be solid, sure. But she'd throw herself into traffic for you, or any of your other siblings, and everybody knows it—which makes her word meaningless in this case. So try again."

"How about *my* word, then?" I lifted my chin and cupped my hands in front of my chest, summoning up a tiny spark of magic to bear witness to what I was about to say. "I, Isidora Avramov, swear upon my magic, my undying witch's soul, and Lady's Lake itself, that I did *not* hex Holly Thorn with the Misbegotten Curse."

A sparking little thrill whorled through me as I finished speaking, like a twisting funnel of cinders, very warm but not quite painful. Giving a lakebound oath like that served as a magical verification, basically certifying that you were telling the truth, and it was invoked as rarely as possible. No witch would, or could, screw around with it—because if you did, you'd be gambling your magic away, along with everything that tied you to Thistle Grove and its enchanted lake.

It would be like severing every link to home you had. Every link to your deepest self.

A look of profound surprise skimmed over Rowan's face like a scudding cloud; so he hadn't been just trying to burrow under my skin. He'd really believed it might be me—and it shocked him that I'd been willing to do something so risky as taking the lakebound oath. Lady's Lake was unknowable, a font of magic beyond our understanding. You could never be absolutely sure what it would make of your intentions, how it might interpret a human witch's perception of truth. Swearing by it was an oath of last resort, and I'd been willing to take that risk, just to assuage his fears.

I hadn't thought I could possibly get any angrier, but apparently I hadn't quite hit my ceiling yet. I pressed my lips together so I wouldn't growl through my teeth, resisting a powerful urge to dart across the table and bite him right on his horrible smug face.

He nodded a few times, eyes clearing, as though he'd come to some internal understanding. "Fine, then. We leave our history out of this, as best we can. What else?"

"Rule number three," I said tightly, still struggling to keep my shit together, "we investigate everything as a team. Obviously, there are some . . . unresolved trust issues between us, which we'll need to manage—"

"Understatement of the damn century," Rowan muttered, but his lips twitched ever so slightly. My willingness to take the oath had bled off the most poisonous part of the rancor, leaving behind only a manageable amount of baseline animosity.

I could work with that—especially since I didn't exactly have a choice.

"You're not wrong," I agreed, relaxing a fraction myself. "So, for the sake of checks and balances, there'll be no going our separate ways to investigate and then reconvening. No shady lone-wolf bullshit of that nature. Whatever we decide to do, we do together."

"Always make sure to have your buddy with you!" he parroted in a singsong tone, like an overzealous kindergarten teacher.

A little laugh burbled out of me, totally unexpected. For the briefest moment, his expression lightened into something almost pleasant—something that let me imagine what he must look like when interacting with someone he didn't completely loathe—before he schooled his features back to a neutral chill.

"That's correct," I said, sobering. "For the duration of this investigation, you and I are buddies, in this together. Which leads me to rule number four—besides the two of us, no one is above suspicion. We should be prepared to look into all the families."

"Come again?" He scrunched up his face, peering at me askance. "You can't mean the Thorns, too."

"Oh, but I can."

He pushed his tied-back locs over one shoulder, ticking objections off on his fingers. "One, the victim is a Thorn, so, kind of a glaring problem with that philosophy right off the bat. Two, that spell was necromantic. A Thorn likely couldn't cast it even if they wanted to."

"We don't know that for sure. A very strong Thorn might be capable of it," I countered. "Affinities are just that—affinities, not built-in limitations. There's *always* a way to pull off a demanding spell, for a skilled enough witch. Like tying one to a powerful artifact, a talisman or something."

"Even in the very unlikely event that something like that could be done . . ." Rowan began, crossing his arms over his chest. I forcibly wrested my attention from how dense his forearms were. He even had powerful wrists, and large, tendon-ridged hands.

Probably all that slinging cows over his shoulder to run them to safety when barns caught fire. "What possible reason could one of us have to go all dark side like that, hurt one of our own?"

"People are tricky," I replied with a shrug. "You never know for sure what someone might be capable of."

"Spoken like a true Avramov."

"Believe it or not, the inherent complexities of human nature apply to Thorns, too. Even if most of you are, admittedly, nearly indistinguishable from walking stuffed animals ninety-five percent of the time."

This time, he was the one to laugh, a low, startled chuckle that grated out of him like sandpaper, surprising both of us.

"Walking stuffed animals?" he repeated with a slow shake of the head, a little not-quite-dimple forming to the left of his mouth. "*That's* how you see my family?"

"Basically animated Build-A-Bears, yes," I replied with a solemn nod. "Prove me wrong. All I'm saying is, maybe it was some kind of vendetta—a family member Holly really, *really* pissed off. Or maybe it was something equally personal between her and a member of one of the other families. Given how nasty a spell that was, we'll have to delve into all the possibilities."

Rowan surveyed me for another long moment, still on the brink of reluctant amusement, then nodded. "Okay, then. I'm pretty sure you're way off on that one, but in the spirit of cooperation, we'll do it your way. Anything else?"

I shook my head, leaning back to tilt my chair onto two legs. "That's it from me. Unless you'd like to contribute a rule of your very own to this endeavor?"

Rowan licked his lips in thought, drawing them through his teeth again. It was an extremely distracting habit, as contemplative expressions went. I wished he'd pick a different thinking face, mostly for my own peace of mind.

Then he leaned forward, clasping his hands on the tabletop, his expression growing almost stern, an aura of command I'd have found pretty damn compelling had it come from anyone but him.

"Rule number five," he said, voice low and resolute. "If it does turn out to be one of your own—"

"Except it won't."

"But if it *does*, Isidora." His hooded gaze shifted between my eyes, a clear and penetrating hazel, almost as incisive as Talia's and much more uncomfortable to endure. And there was something about hearing him say my name that kept rubbing me the wrong way. I jiggled my leg furiously to defuse the anxiety it evoked, trying to make sure I didn't give myself away by bumping the underside of the table with my knee. "You have to accept it, and not start some kind of ultimate family flame war. Burn everything down just to defend your own."

"Kind of a unilateral rule, don't you think?" I said, with more than a little edge to my voice.

"It's not. Because if it does turn out to be one of mine . . ." His eyes lit with a quiet fervor, an expression much more dangerous than anything I'd ever seen on a Thorn before. "You'd best believe I'll be first in line to march their sorry ass to court."

"Alright, then," I said, letting the chair's front legs slam back onto the floor. "I'll agree to shake on that."

7

The Scene of the Crime

THE BLIGHTED SECTION of the orchard looked even worse
than I remembered.

Before parting at the Shamrock yesterday, Rowan and I had
agreed that our first move would be to return to the scene of the
crime to see what we could find. He and his family had already
combed over it at length, of course, but Avramov ESP was much
more finely tuned than most. I'd be lending a uniquely fresh perspective.

"Do we really have call it that, though?" he'd complained,
furrowing his brow in distaste. "Sounds corny, somehow. Like
someone's been watching too much *CSI*."

"'Scene of the crime' *is* the accurate term. Don't you want us to
be precise about our investigative process? And excuse you, I have
not," I'd retorted. "If you must know, I'm an *NCIS* girl at heart. A
vastly superior show in most respects."

"Wouldn't know the difference," he said with a shrug. "Haven't had time to rot my brain with any of that crap in years. It's all the same, anyway. Dime-store candy for the eyeballs."

"What are you trying to say, that *all* of serialized television is beneath you?" I demanded, hands on my hips. "Or that you actually work so much you somehow missed the whole 'Netflix and chill' moment?"

The words had emerged before I'd had enough time to consider the unbearably awkward implications of referring to "Netflix and chill" and Rowan in the same breath. They hung glowing in the air between us, like a tacky neon sign without an off switch, glaring and inconvenient. Now how was I supposed to pretend I'd never even entertained the notion of Rowan as a sexual being, that the concept was innately alien to me?

Way to out yourself, Avramov.

"All I'm saying is, if you're gonna put something on specifically to *not* watch," he'd said, shooting me one of those forthright looks while I tried my damnedest not to blush, the barest hint of a smile ghosting over his mouth, "I'd rather pick something classier than *NCIS* to ignore."

Our closing exchange had left me with an uncomfortable, fidgety feeling I was eager to exorcise—even if that meant walking among the charred ruins in the orchard with no shielding in place, all my senses extended and vulnerable. Trying to pick up any wayward current I could, like a human dowsing rod.

Bad magic, the forbidden kind, tends to leave a blaring psychic stain; those of us who dabble in the darker pools learn that young. Avramovs are naturally receptive, keenly attuned to the vibrations of the other side, and given that we work with ectoplasm—the ghostly substance spirits are made of, a magical medium not particularly inclined to the light—we all get trained up in shield-work and psychic defense while we're still little. To practice murk-ier spells with any degree of safety, you needed to be able to draw lines around yourself, to cordon off your soul and body from what-ever dark thing it is you're courting. If necessary, to fling up tow-ering walls at a moment's thought.

The impulse was so ingrained—and the aura of wrongness hovering over the orchard so intensely awful, lapping against me like water tainted with foul algal bloom—that I had to actively fight the itch to shield up.

"Horrible, right?" Rowan said through a pained grimace as we walked the perimeter of the blackened patch. It looked like a tiny atomic bomb had gone off in the middle of the orchard, blistering it in a ragged, uneven circle. Stalks of dead grass crunched under our feet, the leached soil beneath it releasing puffs of acrid dust that burned in my nose. The place actually smelled like carcino-gens.

It occurred to me that Beltane and the Flower Moon Festival, along with the surge of tourists they would bring, were less than a month away. How were the Thorns going to heal their grounds in time for all those visitors to traipse through here? Would any-thing new ever grow in this blitzed space at all? The worst of the damage may have been done to Holly Thorn, but it wasn't con-fined to her—and maybe that had been by design.

It was something to think about, at any rate.

"Truly atrocious," I agreed. "I mean, I've seen some pretty grimdark shit in my day, not gonna lie. But this . . . this really sweeps it."

"Sticky as hell, too." He shook out his arms, as if the floating badness were adhering to his skin. "Just, absolutely disgusting.

I've taken like a thousand showers since it happened, and still feels like I can't scrub it off."

An incongruous image seared across my mind of Rowan under a pounding stream of water, droplets beading over his skin, clinging to taut curves of muscle, glistening in that little divot in his lower lip . . .

What in the hells was happening here, I wondered a little wildly, shaking myself loose of the intrusive thought. Maybe Letha was right. Maybe I *was* possessed, by an extra-horny succubus or something, or possibly Talia's teasing about hot archnemeses had somehow infiltrated my subconscious, taken root.

Because this could not *possibly* be my own brain at work.

"Are you getting anything?" Rowan asked, glancing at me over his shoulder as he strode toward one of the afflicted apple trees. Or former apple tree now; it didn't look like it was likely to bear anything ever again. "Besides the obvious. Fucked, bad, wrong, et cetera. Guess there's a good reason they called it misbegotten."

I'm getting visions of you naked in showers, does that count?

"Nothing yet," I said instead as I reached the tree, drawing up next to Rowan. Steeling myself, I pressed my hands against the chalky bark, stroking it until it crumbled roughly against my palms. Closing my eyes, I prodded at it with my mind, seeing where that might take me.

Sometimes things lingered inside trees, took solace in them—or infested them, depending on your view. The Witch Woods, the haunted forest that lurked behind The Bitters, was like that, colonized by ghosts who'd grounded their restless spirits inside the living wood. You could pull them up from within their new homes if you were both gentle and insistent about it, even talk to them if you were skilled enough. And even in the case of a spell rather than an entity, an imprint might have been left behind—something that could shed light on who the caster might've been.

But I could detect nothing special inside the tree beyond emptiness. An absence of life so complete it rang hollow to my psychic senses, like rapping your fist on a rotten log.

"Still nothing," I said, stepping back and shaking off my own hands like Rowan had done. Misbegottenness still coated my palms; the stuff really was both revolting and persistent. "It's just . . . megadead. Impressively not alive."

"No doubt about that," he said tightly, peering up with narrowed eyes at the tree's leafless crown, its newly stark silhouette. Its loss clearly pained him, even if he was loath to let me see how much.

Gauzy spring sun filtered through the bare branches, buttery and mild, gilding his face as he stared up at the tree. I'd never noticed that Rowan had freckles, a charming speckle of darker brown against the lighter shade of his skin. Not nearly as many as I did—my freckle-to-skin ratio was one of my most impressive personal achievements, even if I couldn't take full credit—but enough to smatter his bold cheekbones, the indented bridge of his nose. They softened his strong features, lent just a little boyish vulnerability to their chiseled superhero lines.

Worse yet, I didn't even hate them. Clearly I was going to have to redouble my efforts.

"Think we should take a scraping, check the bark out under a microscope?" he asked, flicking me a wry glance. "You never know. We might get real lucky, find a tiny reflection of the perp's face caught inside a splinter or something."

"I realize you *think* you're taunting me. But in reality, by mocking a beloved trope of the genre, you're admitting to having seen at least *one* episode."

"Wish I led the kind of blissful existence that'd let me opt out of them altogether," he said, giving a broad shrug. "But this is the world we live in. Catching an episode of *Not How Crime Investigation Works in Real Life: Insert Flashy City* is part of the social contract now."

"Hey, if you don't like it, I have an idea. You could always go be a recluse off the grid, somewhere far away," I suggested, flashing him a wide grin and two thumbs up. "I hear *such* good things."

"You mean, like, clear out and leave Thistle Grove to you?" He snorted, shaking his head. "Girl, don't hold your breath."

"Hope springs eternal!" I replied, gratified by the barest curl at the corner of his mouth. At the very least, Rowan Thorn wasn't coming out of this partnership without some appreciation of my comedic prowess. "On the upside, your weak mockery of an enduring art form has given me an actually interesting idea."

He flicked me a curious look, tilting his head. "Oh yeah? Does it involve calling in pseudodetectives with weird syntax and a penchant for mirrored aviators? 'Cause I hate to break it to you, but I don't think we're in the right zip code for that dude. You know, if his job even existed."

"A *real* idea, smart-ass," I corrected, magic coursing down my arms as I let a little cloud of ectoplasm begin gathering around my hands, a floating smudge of billowy black. Rowan's gaze snapped down it, growing a touch alarmed. "No need to look so skittish, Thorn. Not a single creepy squirrel shall be involved, cross my heart."

"Hold on, is that . . ." He squinted, cocking his head to one side and then the other, as if trying to catch an elusive sound. "An un-lawful dredging up of our history that I'm detecting?"

"Shoot." I pressed my mouth shut, widening my eyes. "I forgot that time."

He gave a somber shake of his head, in mock reproach. "Already breaking rule number two, and it's only our first day. For *shame*, Avramov."

"In my defense, I was goaded into it. No jury would convict me." I jerked my head at him, motioning him out of the ruined perimeter. "You'll want to step out of range for this, just to be safe."

His brow crinkled with more curiosity than concern, Rowan walked a healthy distance away from the blackened border of the spell's sphere of influence, resting his back against a living apple tree and crossing his arms over his chest. The tree's leaves sighed a little above him, as if it were getting the very best of hugs. A few of the lower boughs dropped closer to his head, rearranging themselves to give him more ample shade. He gave the bark behind him an absentminded pat, the way you might pet a horse's flank.

Shit, no wonder he thought he was the bomb; I wouldn't have put it past the tree to speed-grow an apple and then drop it into his waiting hand. Clearly far too much positive reinforcement in his life thus far.

Good thing he now had me to help him offset all that noise.

I took a few long breaths, centering and grounding as my garnet fired up, preparing myself for the casting. Then I began churning up more and more ectoplasm, winding its slick, ferny substance around myself like thread shuttling around a loom. The clear day around me disappeared into its funneling dark, as if I stood in the eye of a gathering storm, only a cornflower scrap of morning sky visible right above my head.

When I thought I had enough, I gave a quick, sharp *push*, sending it all whooshing out and away.

Like I said, bad magic leaves a stain. It also leaves behind something like a memory, a ghostly imprint of itself etched into the fabric of reality, like a drawing scored into glass—and guided by my will, the ectoplasm knew just which imprint I wanted it to reveal.

The glistening darkness settled swiftly into place, falling into the lines and crevices the blight had carved into the orchard's own memory of the day. Where the real-life stage had stood, a smoky black replica now rose instead—as though the ectoplasm were lending depth and texture to something that had been there all along, invisible, the way a dusting of powder reveals hidden fingerprints.

Ectoplasmic likenesses of the contestants stood gathered on the stage, a wispy black mimicry of the animated flower arch curving above their heads. And in front of them, a phantom version of Holly Thorn held a sooty tapestry suspended above her hands, like a photo negative of the flame wreath she'd woven on Crowning day.

A heady glow of satisfaction expanded inside my rib cage, warming my chest. I'd snared and resurrected the exact moment that Holly Thorn had cast her spell, and now I held it frozen in time, ready for my inspection.

I mean, talk about gathering evidence.

I glanced over at Rowan, ready to gloat—only to find him already staring at me, lips parted, an expression of awestruck fascination emblazoned over his face. For once completely stripped of judgment and disapproval, unclouded by hostility. If anything, he looked . . . *impressed*.

It took me by such surprise that my concentration briefly buckled, nearly breaking the spell. For a moment the entire reproduction rippled like a reflection dashed by a pebble, or a mirage wavering in high wind. Then Rowan's face smoothed out, the unabashed wonder disappearing as if it had never been at all. When he met my eyes, it was without a whisper of emotion, as if that rapt expression had been only a flight of fancy, a momentary illusion of his own.

That raging assboat couldn't even let me have this *one* little win.

Teeth clenched and my fists curled by my sides, I re-honed my focus and let the memory unfold. Dark Holly abruptly came to life, casting her spell until her tapestry began to die, turning a bright, overexposed white at the tip. The rolling blight—recast into a hideous pallor by the ectoplasm's reversed palette—ate up the ground, rushing toward and then around me; I'd positioned myself directly in front of the stage, about ten feet from where the audience had sat back when this really happened.

As I turned to follow its progress, the shadowy copies of the crowd scrambled to their feet and abandoned their seats in panic, shedding blurry contrails of ectoplasm. Freezing the memory in place, I walked slowly through their motionless figures, peering into the sea of aghast faces, trying to spot anyone who seemed suspicious. But all I could see was confusion and fear rendered in various shades of black and gray, people reaching for each other's hands or craning their necks in search of other loved ones in the crowd.

I even walked right by Talia and my own ghostly self, both of us still seated in shock, gaping at the stage. The hollowness on my sister's face was as unnerving as I remembered, and my own likeness rendered in spectral black was somehow even worse to see.

Turning away, I let the memory unspool again. Up on the

stage, Dark Emmy began to cast her counterattack, though the ectoplasm couldn't properly convey how bright that shimmering blue magic had been, like a host of sparks leaping off a welder's flame. Still, I saw it race toward the blight, carving its own path through the air like an opposing storm front until the two clashed.

But, wait . . . that *couldn't* be quite right.

Frowning, I paused the memory again, taking a long, slow lap while Rowan watched me from his apple tree, clearly perplexed but unwilling to interrupt. Then I ran it again, both forward and back, keeping a close eye on how much ground both spells had covered at the exact moment that the Misbegotten Curse had halted in its tracks. I even got on my hands and knees, bringing myself eye level with where Emmy's spell and the curse had pooled along the ground where they collided.

Or rather, where they hadn't ever touched at all.

"Holy fucking spaceballs, Batman," I muttered to myself. "Isn't that some shit."

"Isidora?" Rowan called out. "The hell are you playing at down there?"

"Oh, you know," I tossed over my shoulder as I straightened, dusting blighted grass off my legs. The spell collapsed around me, the ectoplasm melting into wisps, vanishing into the air. "Just cracking this whole thing wide open for us."

Then everything went sparkly, a shimmer of fireworks exploding behind my eyes as my knees gave way.

8

Time Dies, Too

"TELL ME AGAIN," Rowan said, tearing another hunk off his doughnut. "Exactly what you saw."

We were sitting in Honeycake's farmhouse restaurant, a charmingly rustic space inside a refurbished barn. Fresh flowers perched in hand-painted vases on every table, and horseshoes, embroidery, and framed pressed flora hung on the creamy yellow walls. I'd crashed hard after wrapping up the spell, and once I could more or less stand again, Rowan had hustled me here for an emergency sugar fix. He'd probably been afraid of having to give me mouth-to-mouth or something, and the deathly dose of Avramov cooties he might contract while saving me.

In hindsight, I really hadn't made the most of fainting.

"It wasn't Emmy's spell that stopped the curse," I said through a mouthful of sugary dough. Rowan had ordered me strawberries-

and-cream doughnuts, vegan cheesecake, and some kind of de-lightfully gooey peanut butter tart, just to be a thousand percent sure I wouldn't swoon on him again. I'd crushed most of it already, and would probably die of old age before the sugar rush wore off. "It never even touched the blight at all. The curse just . . . stopped. Entirely on its own."

"Which means whoever cast it also ended the spell, before it could do any more damage," Rowan concluded with a furrowed brow. "Of their own volition."

"Right in one," I said, pointing my fork at him. "I had been wondering if maybe, even though it *seemed* to be aimed at Holly, the curse was actually intended to eat up the entire orchard."

"Damn," Rowan muttered under his breath, lips thinning. "I hadn't even thought of that."

"And now you don't have to. Because if the caster had meant to do more damage, they easily could have—even with Emmy's spell incoming, they could've kept casting, going for maximum oblit-eration. But instead, they chose to stop."

"So Holly likely *was* the intended target, then. And the rest of the damage, just incidental." His voice took on a bitter tinge, nos-trils flaring with outrage. "Who gives a shit about a dead apple tree or three when there's scores to settle. Fucking *people*, man."

"It's looking that way." I trailed the tines through the lacy drizzle of chocolate and caramel syrup on my plate. Why did *all* their food have to be so fire? It really wasn't fair. "Cold comfort, I know, but at least it narrows things down for us a little. We're probably looking for someone who has a bone to pick with Holly—not someone with a generalized hatred for all things Thorn."

"That settles our next move, then." Rowan said, sliding his

water glass from hand to hand along the table. "Much as I hate to bother her about this while she's recuperating, we need to talk to Holly soon as we can."

"How's day after tomorrow work for you? Afraid I can't completely skip out on my actual work." The new haunted house wasn't going to design itself in time for Flower Moon, more's the pity.

Rowan drummed his fingers on the table, shooting me a covert look from under his brow. "I was thinking . . . how about you leave this one to me? My cousin's already been through the wringer, and—"

"And you don't want to put her through being interrogated by a heartless Avramov," I finished dryly, twitching up an eyebrow. "Relax. I know appearances might lead you to believe otherwise, but I *can* be gentle. And she is the victim here, the one we're both supposed to be protecting. I promise to go easy on her."

"Still, though. She might be more open if it's just family. I mean, wouldn't you be?"

"Maybe so, but that's not how this works. Rule number three, remember? No lone-wolf escapades. We did shake on it."

He appraised me for a moment, clearly trying to generate more convincing reasons to ditch me, before giving me a reluctant nod. Satisfied, I dived back into my desserts; after all this was over, who knew when I'd next have the chance to eat this stupidly delicious food. Depending on how this thing shook out, maybe I'd never set foot back in Honeycake again.

When I looked back up, he was still watching me, a complicated expression slanting across his face like a shadow.

"Spit it out, Thorn," I said, taking a long, icy swallow of lemonade. I'd already drained two glasses, but I still felt parched, a headache rattling around my temples. Manipulating that much ectoplasm really threw your electrolytes out of whack. "You're about to put me off my food."

He did his thoughtful face, lips drawn slowly through teeth as he stared down at the tabletop, clearly grappling with himself.

"I didn't know you could do that, is all," he finally said, meeting my eyes with such frank curiosity that I almost choked on my next swallow. So that was his struggle, then—maintain a morally superior distance, or admit he was actually intrigued by my magics most dark and foul. "What you did out there, with the ectoplasm . . . I never saw Talia do anything like that."

"My sister's very good at what she does." I twitched my shoulders in a little shrug, giving him a pert smile. "I'm better."

"But how did you know to try that?" he pressed. "Even if you are some kind of necromantic prodigy, conjuring up the ghost of an entire *day* is a pretty damn specialized application."

"Only if you think basic summoning and divining are the only things Avramovs can do," I countered. "But we're a lot more than just two-trick ponies. We can feel the other side, connect with anything dead and gone—anything at all that used to be alive and isn't anymore. And time dies, too."

"Ladies and gentlemen, time dies, too," he intoned in the moribund register of a *Twilight Zone* presenter, shaking his head in half wonder, half bemusement. "Are you even aware of how dead-ass creepy that sounds?"

"But also cool, right? Don't even lie."

"You *would* think that," he said, rolling his eyes. "So, what does it feel like to do it? Clearly wrung you out; you're still pale. Does it happen often, you passing out like that?"

I squinted at him, trying to determine his angle. Had I, all unwitting, turned into a sickly puppy? Was he actually demonstrating genuine concern for my health?

"I do try to eat more if I know I'm going to attempt something on that scale. So, no, I don't typically full-on swoon. But death magic is like that, always debilitating on some level. Can't really duck that part of things."

"And why is that?"

"Because I'm a living human being, soul included," I said, raising my eyebrows pointedly, "no matter how difficult you might find that to believe. And when it comes right down to it, life and death energies don't really play well together. The garnets we wear mediate some of it, keep us grounded. But there's always a price to pay."

"And you do it anyway?" he said, incredulous. "Even if it makes you feel like shit?"

"Of course," I said, in equally disbelieving tones. "It's my magic, my family's legacy. And trust me, any pain aside . . . it is always, always worth it."

"Then show me," he ordered, extending his hand across the table. "I want to see what it's like."

"Maybe learn to ask nicely, then. I'm not one of your underlings," I shot back, bristling, uncomfortably aware that a certain part of me kind of liked this bossiness.

"Hey, my bad." He smiled at that, a real, full smile—the first one of his I'd seen directed at me, possibly ever. It commanded serious wattage, generous lips curving over even teeth, his canines just a little sharp. The breadth of it crinkled the corners of his eyes into little fans and made them seem to glint an even warmer hazel, like a radiant light had been flicked on behind them. "Sometimes I come on a little strong, when I'm interested in something. Allow me to rephrase. May I, please, have a demonstration?"

I considered, swaying my head from side to side, trying to hide how much it threw me to see him smile at me like that, without holding back. "Since we're partners, I suppose you may."

I cast a furtive look around the restaurant; a handful of normie tourist families sat at the other tables enjoying their late lunch, but no one seemed particularly interested in us. Reaching for Rowan's hand, I turned it palm up and held it cupped between my own, trying to ignore the warm, masculine heft of it, the scratchy callus on his palm, the way it dwarfed both of mine. Raised veins ran over its broad back like ridges beneath the skin, and his nails were squared off and trimmed very short.

Rowan Thorn, shame and forsooth, had beautiful hands.

"Okay," I said, clearing my throat. "Now close your eyes."

He squinted at me, skeptical. "Uh, why would I do that?"

"Because seeing it will only creep you out, trust me. It's, like, some instinctive thing, reflexive. Always happens. Try to just feel it first, and then once you get comfortable, you can look."

He pursed his lips, mulling this over, then complied. "You're the boss, I guess."

Once I was sure he wouldn't reopen them, I sent a small wisp of ectoplasm dribbling into his palm, where it collected like smoke or a miniature black hole, hovering above his skin in a little spiral. At first, he didn't react at all, and I wondered if this was a historic moment in the making; what were the odds that any other Thorn had ever handled ectoplasm? Maybe we were about to bridge the centuries-old chasm between our families. Maybe—

Then a full body-shudder wrenched through him, and his hand jerked in my grasp.

"Oh, that is motherfucking foul," he said, face twisting with a toddler's pure disgust. He even stuck out his tongue, like an actual baby. "God*damn*. I cannot believe y'all do this on purpose. It's like . . . really cold, really slimy jellyfish? Crossed with something sticky? Ugh, *rank*."

"It does take some getting used to," I admitted, attempting not to feel offended on all of ectoplasm's behalf. Another part of my mind noted how interesting it was that he used "y'all" so naturally; though we had our Southern transplants, it wasn't something you often heard in Thistle Grove, or in Illinois at large. "And it does get easier once you're in the moment, actually casting the spell. You can open your eyes now, if you want. Just . . . try not to freak out."

"Your bedside manner could use some work, you know that?" Warily, he pried one eye open, peering down at the ectoplasm. It had crept up his wrist like a ghostly slug, extending questing little tendrils toward his forearm. "Oh, *shit!* What the fuck is it doing, Isidora? Why is it moving like that? Why does it look like it's going to *infest* me?"

"Dude, chill out," I snapped under my breath, stealing another glance at the other tables. The oblivion glamour would take care of anyone who happened to catch this display, but I wasn't trying to traumatize a random child with weird night terrors or something. "It won't hurt you."

"You absolutely positive about that?" he said through clenched teeth. "'Cause it sure *looks* like it might have some ideas. Nasty ones."

"It doesn't have any ideas, Rowan, given that it's basically ghost goo. It's not *alive* alive. Although I guess it is kind of sentient in the most basic sense," I admitted. "Like, I don't know, amoeba or something? Necromantic biology isn't really my strong suit."

"Cool, cool." Rowan resolutely shut his eyes again, holding himself so still he almost quivered in place, as if the ectoplasm were a venomous snake that might turn on him at any moment, sink fangs into his wrist. "Now make it go away."

I couldn't help it; I giggled just a little, biting my lip to stifle the sound. Rowan's eyes flew open for long enough to widen into an emphatic glare as he frantically jutted his chin toward his hand before closing them again.

"Isidora," he bit off. "Get. It. Off. Me. *Now*."

"Okay, okay, you don't have to yell." The ectoplasm vanished in a blink, its remnants wisping into the air. Rowan's entire body sagged with relief, his tense shoulders relaxing under the crimson plaid of his shirt, a huge breath gusting out of him. "There you go. Better now?"

"Don't know about better. I might need some time." He clenched and unclenched his hand experimentally, then wiped it on his jeans, grimacing. "Feels less like I need to gnaw off my own hand to get away, at any rate."

"Progress! And hey—now you definitively know it's not your cup of tea."

"Man, you can say that again." He surveyed me, running his tongue under his upper lip. "Thanks, I guess, for indulging me. Hard pass on *ever* doing that again, though. I'll stick with green magic all day, every day."

I crossed my arms on the table, leaning over them and fixing him with a challenging stare. "Are you really trying to tell me life magic feels that much better in comparison?"

"*Hell* yes, hands down. No competition whatsoever. Not even the same playing field."

"Fine, then, prove it." I extended my own hand, sliding it toward him across the table. "Go on, Thorn, turnabout's fair play. Show me yours."

His face scrunched with amusement, lips pressing together as he shook his head. "The sass mouth on you is really something else, you know that?"

"Oh, this is me just getting started." I wiggled my fingers in invitation, quirking an eyebrow. "Now quit stalling."

Rowan licked his lips, fighting a smile. Then, still shaking his head, he took my hand, lacing my fingers loosely through his. The warm, rough way his palm rubbed against mine sent a spark of pure electricity jolting down my wrist, nothing at all to do with magic; more like a certain kind of physics.

Or, let's be real, biology.

Just as I'd managed to quash the inconvenient feeling, he closed his eyes, and my hand suddenly warmed in his grip. The sensation unfurled from there, like butter melting under my skin, a honeyed heat traversing through my bloodstream. I could feel it traveling toward my heart, expanding through my arteries as it coaxed them open. Coursing through me, gentle but insistent, in search of something to fix or nourish.

It felt so wonderful I let my head tip forward a little, my eyes fluttering closed, a tiny sigh escaping my lips. Across from me, I could feel Rowan smiling to himself without even having to see it.

"Feels pretty good, right?" he said.

"It does," I admitted grudgingly. "*Damn* it."

"Hold still for a sec," he instructed me, his hand tightening over mine. "You've got a lot of mixed-up stuff going on. Let me see if I can just . . ."

A wave of intense well-being and clarity washed through me, as he somehow righted all the imbalance the necromantic magic had left me with in one fell swoop. My lingering headache faded, taking the rest of my fatigue with it. I felt shiny, scrubbed new—

and more than that, meltingly relaxed, like I'd just stepped out of a hot tub after the best massage of my life. With a banana bag of fluids and CBD thrown in for free.

When I opened my eyes, Rowan was full-on beaming at me again, looking entirely too pleased with himself, that maddening not-quite-dimple hovering beside his mouth. How could a *facial feature* look so self-satisfied?

"Gloating doesn't become you, you know," I informed him, snatching back my hand. "So you can stop making that . . . *face.*"

"What can I say?" he spread his hands, widening his grin an extra, obnoxious fraction. "I take pride in my work."

"And here I thought green magic was more about turning flowers into Harry Styles wannabes."

That startled a full-fledged laugh out of him, low and rich with a gravelly edge to it, all tumbled rocks and slow molasses. Shit, several genuine smiles *and* a laugh from Rowan Thorn, (Supremely Stoic) Wildlife Hero, all in one day? I was really breaking some personal records here.

"Not how I'd describe it, but fair enough, I guess," he said, still chuckling. "Though healing's always been more my speed."

"How does it work?" I asked, intrigued despite myself. "You can tell what's wrong with someone just by touching them? How much can you fix?"

"Yeah, it's like an instant diagnostic, pretty damned handy. But it can't fix anything deeply systemic, unfortunately. Not cancer, or any deadly germ once it's got a solid foothold. None of the major life-threatening stuff."

His face darkened for a moment, eyes dimming, losing that bright internal light. Then he ran a hand down his face, wrested himself away from whatever memory was troubling him.

"That's why I had to go to vet school, if I wanted to help really sick animals get better," he continued. "But the magic's still killer for the smaller stuff. Cuts, bruises, your basic metabolic imbalances. It can also speed healing along when it comes to broken bones—and give a little plain old comfort, if that's what's called for. Sometimes nothing beats that endorphin rush."

Given how good it felt, I could think of certain other, considerably less PG applications for the magic, not that I was about to bring that up.

"About the animating," I said instead, pivoting away before curiosity got the better of me. "This is maybe going to sound stupid, but did you . . . know those trees? The ones that died?"

"Nothing stupid about it," he replied, knuckling a hand over his mouth, his voice going a little gruff. "And yeah, I did. They were the only Pink Pearl varietals in the orchards—their apples are bright pink inside. Like a little miracle when you cut one open. Guess there won't be any more of those now."

"I didn't even know apples came that way," I said, tempering my voice with softness, hoping he could hear how sorry I was for his loss without me having to actually say as much. "Sounds special."

"They were . . . but we would've mourned any other ones just the same. I know all the trees on our land, every last one. That's what animating does, when it's done well. Gives voice to the dormant essence of anything alive, lets it communicate with us."

"So you're telling me those azaleas and morning glories in the arch just *wanted* to bust out into a bop?" I said, trying to lighten the mood a little. "Felt the rhythm deep down in their little floral souls? I always thought it was the caster directing them."

"Okay, there may have been some caster intent involved that

time. You *can* do that, if you want—my little sister likes to mess with the sunflower field that way, get it to sing certain songs. But also, flowers are just like that," he said with a shrug. "Big old attention hogs, always trying to steal the limelight. Trees, though, they're . . . deeper, more wisdom to them. Can't ever tell one of them how to sound."

"That seems nice," I said, unable to suppress a brush of uncharacteristic wistfulness. I'd never been up close to animated flora; they didn't, as a rule, react well to Avramovs. But I'd always wondered what it might be like, talking to a tree—especially now that I knew it would be the tree's own soul I'd be engaging with, not just the caster speaking through it.

That sounded like something I would very much want to see.

Rowan's eyes lingered on my face, a private conflict playing out behind them. Then he nodded to himself, as if he'd come to some conclusion.

"Think you'd like to meet one?" he said, lifting his eyebrows at me.

My heart rate picked up a little, thumping with anticipation. "Wait . . . really? You're serious?"

He shrugged a shoulder, pushing back his chair. "I'm gonna have to let you question my cousin, isn't that the deal? You may as well get to know a little something about us first."

9

> > > ● (((

You Smell of the Void

IN ALL MY twenty-five years of Thistle Grove, I'd never gotten
a proper tour of the Honeycake Orchards. It wasn't a thing
Avramovs *did*, much like a Thorn wasn't likely to stroll into the
Witch Woods uninvited, or enjoy a bit of light shopping at the
Emporium. Nothing prevented either of us from doing those
things, of course, and some of us probably did. It was just that,
historically speaking, our families had never been on such comfortable terms with each other. The opposing nature of our
magics—and mentalities—made for an awkward dynamic at the
best of times.

Now a flawless spring afternoon unfurled around me and
Rowan: a lapis-lazuli sky veiled in clouds of puffy tulle, trills of
birdsong weaving through the air. The sweetness of new grass
and budding flowers drenching every fresh ribbon of breeze. Com-
paring it to my family's very different holdings felt disloyal—but

it did give me a small pang to know that outdoorsy Little Isidora, in her slip-on fairy wings and sparkly Doc Martens, had missed out on all of this.

Even Rowan seemed more relaxed in the sunshine, shucking his plaid until he was down to a white V-neck tee that revealed muscle-corded upper arms, his button-down slung over one shoulder. He led me through the expansive store attached to the restaurant, where tourists could snag some of Honeycake's fruit, fresh-baked goods, cider, and wine. Then we strolled by the sunflower field and the stables, horses hanging their sleek heads over crimson stall doors, huffing at us inquisitively as we passed by.

I wanted to pet one of them with every fiber of my being, but Rowan was about to let me chat up one of his trees; I didn't feel like pushing my luck.

"And this is the 'haunted' hedge maze," he said with finger quotes as he led me into a warren of towering green that parted just ahead of us. The shrubbery was woven with animated flowering vines in a variety of colors, surging back and forth and bobbing their vibrant heads. "Biggest one in the Midwest, major tourist draw."

"Pretty neat trick, calling it 'haunted' when it actually *is* magic," I said, pointing at one of the fidgeting flowers. "I bet it drives the tourists nuts, not being able to figure out what makes them tick."

"And keeps them coming back, with friends in tow. Works out great for us."

As we walked, it became clear that the hedge maze would've vastly preferred not to be hosting me. Just as we were about to hang a left, an entire corridor abruptly thorned up, a web of sweet briar roses springing up like a prickly pink thicket right in front of us. They exhaled a delicious apple fragrance in our faces—in stark contrast to the shrill, chittering tirade they unleashed in my direction.

"Are they talking smack about me?" I asked Rowan, planting my feet more solidly and lifting my chin. "*Rude*. Hi, roses. I'm right here. I can *hear* you."

"I don't speak eglantine any more than you do," he replied, humor coloring his voice. "But that sure sounds like a bunch of trash talk to me. Unless you feel like throwing down today, why don't we take a different path?"

"Bye, bitch," I told the roses over my shoulder as I flounced away after Rowan to retrace our steps—even though I was the one who was leaving.

Technicalities.

"Don't let them get you down," Rowan said, fighting a smile as I sulked behind him. "Roses can be petty, and really self-involved. Like the poodles of flora."

"No need to bad-mouth elegant dogs just to excuse your mean-girl flowers," I told him. "I'll have you know poodles like me just fine."

"If you say so."

He was still smirking about it when we emerged from the hedge maze to traipse across a field strewn with buttercups and pink phlox, making our way toward the grassy little hillock topped by Honeycake Cottage, the Thorn elders' demesne. I'd never been out here before, and the scale of the house took me aback; the English Tudor wasn't anywhere near Bitters-level massive, but it edged close to mansion territory. The pastoral style made it seem much homier, though, the fieldstone chimney and half-timbered facade all draped with a curling crochet of ivy that rippled in the wind. Some of the mullioned windows held bright stained glass in a delicate design of flowers and bees.

"It's cute," I told Rowan when he paused at the hill's base to gaze up at it. "Looks like somewhere nice people live."

"That'd be my parents in a nutshell," he said, eyes softening with fondness. "Nicest people you'll ever meet."

A bolt of envy ricocheted through me at the uncomplicated love that lit his face at the mention of Aspen and Gabrielle. Rowan clearly didn't harbor any fraught feelings toward either of his parents—which was a lot more than I could currently say for myself.

He led me up to and around the house, by the fenced-in flower garden in the front and the vegetable patch out back, scallion shoots poking up from turned earth, next to orderly rows of tomato plants that had just begun to blush from green to red. We sidestepped down the hill, much steeper behind the house than on the other side, toward a tucked-in glen at the bottom.

"These are some of the oldest trees on our land," he told me as we stepped into a shadowy copse of trees at the bottom of the little vale. "The first ones Alastair Thorn planted when he settled here."

"And this," he added, stopping in front of a midsize hawthorn that occupied the center of the grove, "was the very first."

I wasn't sure what I'd expected; maybe something more along the lines of an imposing oak, hoary and magisterial. This tree was nothing like that. It was only about twenty feet tall, frothed with creamy white flowers that opened into tender pink insides, so dense they obscured the wide spread of its boughs. Rowan led me underneath its canopy, close to the slim brown trunk. Above us, the blossoms shifted against one another in a whispery rustle;

though the tree wasn't yet animated, somehow it felt like it exuded peace, an elegant and self-assured energy.

A kind of unshakable serenity I'd never found inside myself.

"This is what we call the orchard's heart tree," Rowan said, laying a hand on the trunk. "The first and oldest, as old as Thistle Grove itself. She knows more about this place than any of us could ever hope to learn."

I took a step closer, feeling unaccountably shy and even anxious, the familiar tingle of nerves jittering in my knees. What if this ancient, pretty tree didn't take to me? Chances were good it wouldn't, especially if it'd somehow been privy to my chilly reception in the maze.

If it's not a fan, you'll deal with it, I told myself, clamping down on the jitters. Not like it'd be anything new, being rebuffed by an animated plant.

But even so, I already wanted it to like me.

"Hey," Rowan said, touching a light hand to my upper arm. I realized I'd been jiggling one foot frantically in place, and with an effort, made myself stop. "Relax. It's not gonna be like the roses. This tree doesn't play like that."

He closed his eyes and set both palms on the trunk, a sparkling, jewel-toned wash of magic gathering around his hands. In its purest form, green magic apparently wasn't *only* green; within the emerald outline, I could see its ombré shift into a pearly pink and gray, like the inside of a shell, or the tender inklings of a new dawn. A color that would render beautifully in satin.

Then the tree inhaled, taking a long, deep breath above our heads.

It sounded like a crackling hiss, a bellows wheezing into life after a lengthy silence. All of the branches shook themselves at once as if in a massive stretch, sending a storm of stray petals spinning down onto our heads.

"Rowan of Aspen," the tree rumbled in a creaking voice with a distinct feminine timbre. Her lowermost branches extended toward Rowan, feathering over his face and chest in such a loving way that tears sprang to my eyes in a salty wash. I blinked them away hastily, before Rowan could spot them. "Sweet son of the orchard. I offer you shelter under my crown."

"Good to see you too, *mo chroí*," Rowan said, his own voice gruff with emotion, the last two words clearly not in English. Gaelic, maybe, a remnant of the family's Irish druid ancestry. "I brought you a guest today. Someone new, not of the family."

"And whom have you brought to see me?" The tree's attention shifted toward me—somehow almost tangible, despite the fact that she didn't have a face or eyes to turn my way. "Friend, or foe?"

The nervous tingle spread throughout my limbs, leaving me a bit light-headed as I waited to see how Rowan would introduce me—shit, at this juncture, I wasn't even sure how *I* would identify myself.

He stole a glance at me, clearly struggling with the same dilemma.

"Neither," he finally said, splitting the difference. "This is Isidora, of Elena of the Avramovs. A . . . partner, in a new endeavor. She's helping me sort out what happened over by the Pink Pearls. What caused the cull, the unnatural death."

The tree swayed some of her larger branches, as if in grim understanding. Then she extended the slimmer, lower boughs toward me, petals brushing suede-soft and ticklish over my face, the branches' sharp tips a rougher scrape. I held myself as still as I could, resisting the urge to break into a nervous giggle.

It felt, weirdly, like she was sniffing me.

"You smell of the void," the hawthorn concluded, in a halfway accusatory tone. But she didn't recoil, her branches still brushing over my face. It took me a second to grasp that she meant necromantic magic, and I bit back a silly impulse to apologize.

"I do," I said, standing my ground instead. "My family, we work with . . . uh, the void. Like the Thorns work with green magic. It's in our blood; it's what we've always done."

The tree pondered this for a moment, slow as sap, swaying her entire canopy back and forth in consideration.

"As someone must," she finally allowed, letting her branches droop onto my shoulders. "To keep the balance from tipping. Life chokes upon itself when there is too much. But it must ache so, to be filled with void. As it aches me when my outermost self grows brittle and dies of frost."

"It does ache, sometimes," I admitted, through a sudden lump rising in my throat. "But I—I wouldn't have it any other way."

"Then you bear a heavy crown with grace, Isidora of Elena," the hawthorn creaked at me. "Like a banyan, or a monkeypod. Your roots must run very deep and strong."

With that, she withdrew her branches from my shoulders, turning back to Rowan. I almost teared up again, at the abrupt loss of such an unexpected comfort.

In spite of everything, I'd loved having her touching me— approving of me.

"*They* smelled of the void, too," the hawthorn said, and this time her voice rang bleak and angry, nearly menacing. A rippling wave of goose bumps unfurled along my skin; the tree was clearly talking about the caster of the curse. "The one who made the death. But *their* void was a rot, an affliction, much older and colder than yours. Like a parasite that burrows under the bark, then sends its poison up into the sap."

I caught my breath, exchanged a meaningful look with Rowan—the shock on his face told me that the hawthorn hadn't divulged anything like this before. Maybe the Thorns hadn't even thought to ask it.

"Do you know anything else about them, *mo chroí*?" he asked, keeping his tone steady even as he balled his hands into fists, almost quivering with impatience. "Anything we could use to find them?"

"Nothing else, Rowan of Aspen," the tree intoned morosely, her leaves and flowers rustling with chagrin. "The deathmaker stood on soil too far away. The ends of me only barely felt them."

"Not your fault," Rowan murmured, patting the bark, though his brow crinkled with frustration. "Better that you weren't any closer to where the harm was done. And thank you for letting me know now . . . maybe you'll remember something else, in time. Either way, I'll be back round soon to see you."

"You are always welcome in my shadow, orchard son." The tree turned to me, somehow contemplative. "And you, daughter of the void . . . return sometime, when the sun is stronger, and sit beneath me for a spell. I will not mind."

"WHAT DID YOU make of what the heart tree said?" I said to Rowan, breaking our silence. We'd been walking along toward the Honeycake parking lot in the slanting light of late afternoon, each absorbed in our private thoughts. "About the 'deathmaker'? Cold, old, like a parasite?"

"Found it eerie as fuck, but that's about it." Rowan shrugged, mouth twisting to the side. "Didn't ring any other bells for me. You?"

"The parasite part . . ." I brought a fist to my mouth, nibbled at a knuckle. "It reminds me of *something*. But what, I have no idea. I'll keep thinking on it."

"I'll do the same, though I'm not getting my hopes up. Weird-ass shit being more your vibe, daughter of the void."

I rolled my eyes at the snark, but there wasn't any real barb or venom to it, nothing intended to genuinely sting. Coming from the hawthorn, that name for me had felt oddly benevolent, more offbeat compliment than insult, and I couldn't quite bring myself to take offense.

"She's a lot kinder than I expected," I said. "I didn't think any of them could talk like that. Or *know* things that way."

"Told you she was wise." A corner of his mouth curled. "And most plants can't talk, not the way the heart tree can. I mean, most trees are a lot more with it than flowers, but our hawthorn—she's on a whole other level."

"Why wasn't she animated when we got there?" I asked. "Like the hedge maze?"

"The maze has an animation spell permanently embedded in it, for the tourists' benefit—we charge it up every few weeks. But even though the maze is physically bigger, it's also a hell of a lot easier to maintain, takes way less juice. The essence of the vines animated there . . ." He whistled low. "Put it this way, they've got nothing on the heart tree."

"Do you ever just shoot the shit with her?" I wondered. "Like, ask her life advice?"

He chuffed a laugh through his nose. "Oh, all the time. You'd best believe *mo chroí* has *opinions.* Plenty of hot takes she's more than down to share."

"What does that mean? That name you keep calling her?"

"'My heart,' in Irish Gaelic. That's what Alastair Thorn named her, when he planted her as a bare-root tree." He grinned to himself, eyes cast down. "Sometimes I just call her the boss, too. I can tell she likes it."

"She does have that big guru energy," I agreed. "Chill, yet authoritative."

Rowan cast me a startled look, as if surprised I'd been able to pick up on the tree's vibe at all; maybe he thought all Avramovs were entirely aura-insensitive, when it came to plants.

"Mm-hmm. Sometimes we even run orchard decisions by her, just for perspective. Like, lately we've been trying to go even more sustainable, now that cash flow's steadier again."

This reminded me that Thorns were in the same position as we were—since the Blackmoores had stopped using the Victor's Wreath magic to divert tourist flow exclusively to their own holdings, the orchard's finances had likely stabilized just like the Emporium's.

It was very cognitively dissonant to think of our families as having such clear commonalities, in addition to our glaring differences.

"But, man, it's been rough to try and do that while keeping profits up," Rowan went on, rubbing a hand over the back of his neck. "Recapturing energy from waste can be so expensive. And sometimes *mo chroí* will be like, 'Hey, slow your roll; real progress takes time. It's okay if everything doesn't happen all at once.'" He shook his head in slow wonder, lips curving. "Hard to beat that kind of long-game thinking."

"I get it, though," I said, nodding. "Fashion's like that, too. It's *much* easier and cheaper to be fast about it. The brands that really care about the environment, they make incremental progress toward being sustainable. Upcycled fabrics, lab-grown leather, cool cutting-edge shit like that. Stuff that doesn't become affordable overnight, but is a step in the right direction."

"And that's something you care about?" he said, incredulity suffusing his tone. "Sustainability in fashion?"

Spiky irritation lanced through me, from the top of my head down to my toes.

"Why wouldn't I?" I snapped. I cared about it so much, in fact, that a central part of my clothing-line dream was how to make it not only sustainable, but even positively impactful—not that I was about to share any of that with him. "I *do* live on this earth, same as you. Of course I care about the environment."

"Hey, no shade," he said, holding up his hands. "I was just curious. Lots of people don't exactly lose sleep over their carbon footprints. I didn't realize you were into that, is all."

"Well, I am," I said, a little mollified. "Though I'll admit it's been baby steps, especially when it comes to meat. I mean, I have six pets, and I love them all to bits. It's not like I don't know eating animals is fundamentally wrong. But ugh, I also love burgers something fierce. And bacon, and chicken tenders. And creative combinations of the above."

"So did I, way back when, and I'll be the first to say that it's a struggle to maintain. But you gotta start somewhere, right? Weaning yourself off animal products is a process."

"For sure," I said, nodding sagely. "You don't get to cultivate moral superiority overnight. It's more of a long-term commitment to the brand."

Rowan snorted, but let my ribbing go. I rubbed my goose-bumped arms as we neared my car, wishing I'd brought a jacket. I hadn't planned to stay this long, and so close to dusk, the days still turned brisk, with a noticeable nip to them. Rowan clocked the movement, his hand twitching toward the plaid slung over his shoulder as if to offer it to me—before thinking better of it, letting his hand fall back to his side.

So we weren't even at that level of courtesy yet, I thought, with a queasy twist of ache. Not that I needed any man to give me the shirt off his back, but it would've been . . . nice, a companionable gesture between two people who were working together. A tacit show of good faith.

Probably we'd never get there, and for the best; no use in forgetting who we were, or where we stood with each other.

10

))) ● (((

Spring Meets Storm

I SPENT THE NEXT day holed up in my studio at The Bitters, brainstorming the new haunted house.

Around me, Pigma Micron pens were strewn everywhere, along with nubs of the Prismacolor pencils I liked for the washes of color in my designs. Work surfaces were barely visible, buried under a splay of fabric swatches in dozens of hues and textures. Scissors and needles, sequins and beads, tinsel and half-buried sewing machines glinted from underneath like hidden treasure. I liked to sit on the floor to start, with my sketch pad on my lap, kind of like meditating in the eye of a craft-store hurricane. All that external creative chaos somehow exerted a calming effect on the hectic scatter of my psyche.

When it came to developing a new concept for the haunted house, I always began with the costumes, letting the story line particulars flow outward from there. And vampires feuding across the centuries should have given me a whole phantasmagoria of inspiration: frilly baroque masterpieces, austere Victorian gowns, a little freewheeling flower child action to rep the seventies. All manner of promising visuals to get the juices flowing.

But today, my mind kept straying insistently contemporary. For women, flowing asymmetrical pieces in silk and linen trimmed with lace, hand-painted in intricate florals of cream, rose, and green; kind of an ultra-fey bloomcore aesthetic. For men, I found myself gravitating toward much edgier, sharper lines, mixed media in different shades of black and gray.

It was a weird vibe, very budding spring–meets–thunderstorm, a clash of opposites—but I found myself really feeling it, excitement swirling in my chest.

It took me longer than it should have to realize that I was riffing on green magic and necromancy, orchard and void. I was designing based on me and Rowan, only gender flipped.

"Well, this is . . . a choice," Letha pronounced as she peered over my shoulder, the paper bag dangling from her hand wafting appetizing smells. She'd shown up just in time to discuss set design over lunch; Letha tended to be her most productive self over food. "I mean, I'd personally fuck with some of this—but must admit, I'm not really getting 'vampiric glamour over the centuries.'"

"I know," I moaned, dropping my face into my hands. "It's all wrong for that. But it just keeps coming out like this. Save me from myself, cuz, for I am lost and adrift."

"The muses do be a bitch sometimes," Letha muttered as she dug into the bag for clamshell containers of salad and fragrant garlic naan rolled up in tinfoil. "What if we ditch the whole centuries aspect, then? That would've been a leap for us, anyway. We could stick to more of a haunted woodland theme instead, as your spirit is so clearly craving. Or like . . . city versus forest, somehow? Possibly that's why they're feuding in the first place, defending their respective territories?"

"I'd have to get Elena on board if we changed direction like that," I said, reaching for my kale Caesar. No sesame chicken strips this time, even though they were my very favorite at Leaf Laugh Love, and I was already mourning the absence of all that umami. But, baby steps; if Rowan Thorn could ditch meat, then so could I. "But she seemed more flexible than usual, this time around—she basically left it up to my discretion. I think she'd agree if we made the case."

"Well, I don't wanna go all Damoclean on you, but the sword's swiftly dropping, cuz," Letha pointed out, arching a pierced eyebrow. "We need our theme nailed down by end of the week, at the very latest. Or I'll be really screwed for time."

Letha maintained an impressive inventory of set pieces from over the years, housed in several giant storage units at the edge of town. But even superhumanly talented as she was—and a total force at managing her minions—she'd need time for her own design process, all the repurposing she'd have to do in addition to churning out brand-new decor.

"Let's say definitely a strong woodland component, then," I said, the idea expanding in my mind, gaining detail and dimension. "But more *Avatar* than Witch Woods, creepy beautiful. Lots of big, complicated flowers, strange fruit, trees with animatronic faces. To lull the visitors into a false sense of wonder, before everything goes mega-twisted."

"Now we're talking," Letha said, flashing me a sweetly evil smile as she jotted down notes in her angular scrawl. "Oh, yes, I can vibe with this."

"So, you get cracking on that, and I'll keep mulling on the city aspect. We can hammer that out a little down the line."

We bounced more ideas off each other as we ate: what different parts of the forest might look like, the kinds of jump scares and lower-key, stealth freakishness they could generate. I felt almost excited, a fluttering echo of the electric thrill I used to catch from brainstorming a new theme—enough to make me borderline optimistic.

Maybe I really *had* just needed some time to get back into my old groove again.

"I have to ask," Letha said, putting down her fork. "Before the curiosity crushes me. Where is this whole concept coming from, Iss? I'm feeling it, don't get me wrong, and I think we can really spin it out. But it's a wee bit crunchy for our taste, no?"

"It's because of Honeycake," I admitted, pressing fingers to my temples. "I spent a long day there yesterday with Rowan, getting our investigation underway. And it's kind of creeping into my head. They have this hawthorn there, what they call a heart tree. You can talk to it—and I mean *really* talk, none of the cutesy, shallow shit you usually see during Thorn ceremonies."

I described the heart tree to Letha, the sense of peace and stability it emanated, the aura of sweeping kindness, a universe of wisdom in the roots beneath its soil. She hadn't spent much time at the Thorn orchards either, so I walked her through a virtual tour of the farmhouse restaurant and the stables, the maze with its rude roses, the barn full of darling baby animals that I'd caught only a passing glimpse of but was dying to return to for a cuddle. The way Honeycake Cottage looked like the most harmonious demesne out of all four family holdings, like something delicately grafted into our world from some enchanting storybook.

And not the brothers Grimm kind that our own family tended to emulate.

"You really liked it there, didn't you?" Letha said, eyes narrowing. "Almost seems like you're crushing on the place—which I find very confusing given how tragically vanilla it all sounds, but sure. Either way, this has to be the sparkiest I've seen you in ages."

"Believe me, no one's more surprised than me. But it did feel nice to spend some time there. Roses with attitude and the whole blight thing aside, the whole place felt . . . more welcoming than I'd've expected."

"And what of your reluctant collaborator?" Letha asked, deftly peeling a blondie out of its plastic wrapper with her long coffin nails, polished a galactic swirl of blues and purples and smattered with zodiac signs. Letha had the kind of high-glam witch nails lesser beings only aspired to in their dreams; I still wasn't sure how she worked with her hands as much as she did without ever dinging them. Possibly protective spellwork was involved. "Still monstrously heroic, I'm assuming?"

"Oh, he continues to be an abomination," I assured her—even as my mind offered up the charming way Rowan's eyes crinkled when he smiled, the gravelly edges of his laugh, the glowing wonder in his face when he watched me cast my spell. The intoxicating way his magic had surged up into my skin and dipped below it, the swirl of warmth it left behind.

As if in rebuttal, the more rational part of my brain dredged up his revulsion toward ectoplasm, his incredulity at the idea that I might care about the environment, the fact that he hadn't even been able to bring himself to offer me his shirt when he saw that I was cold. And the current of distrust for me that always swam just beneath the surface of his eyes, like a silty undertow. As if he saw me mostly as the catalyst of chaos, the kind that was not only destructive but tacky to boot.

And he didn't even know about me and the demons yet; I could only imagine how *that* might go over.

No, no matter how much I liked his family's orchards, there would be no further common ground found with Rowan Thorn.

"But you know me," I said to Letha as I snagged my half of the blondie, my resolve solidifying. "I always make it work."

11

Pisces Never Forget

HOLLY THORN LOOKED like someone keeping it together only by sheer formidable force of will.

She sat across from me and Rowan at one of the glossy high-tops at Whistler's Fireside, a gastropub I'd been to only a few times since it opened a couple of years back. It wasn't really my scene—too "Victorian gentleman's cave meets artisanal brewery" for my taste, the kind of place a time-traveling dandy might wet his whistle—but it was a big hit with Thistle Grove's trendier crowd. Holly had asked to meet us here for drinks, instead of any-where on Thorn grounds. So maybe it was her favorite, too, or at least comfortably distanced from the magic that had hurt her. And the magic she had lost.

This time, Holly's black-and-brown braids swam loose around her shoulders, glinting with gold cuffs. Her makeup was layered and impeccable, the tangerine gloss on her lips picking up on the orange tigers splashed across her bell-sleeved navy romper. She looked spectacular, especially for a witch who'd been struck down by a malicious curse just over a week ago.

Or, she looked like someone who hoped that seeming bullet-proof might make it true.

The details gave her away. Her hands wrapped around the cut-glass tumbler so tightly the knuckles strained the skin, as if that anchor were the only thing keeping her from spinning out into dust. And below her orange manicure I could see faint marks on her hands, a spiderweb of ashy pallor the blight had left behind. If you looked closely enough, every so often you could catch the scarring *pulsing*, in a way that made her hiss in a breath each time it happened.

"It hasn't completely stopped hurting yet," she said, flashing me a weak smile when she caught me noticing. "Gabrielle and your mom, they've been working with me every day, trying to help. And it *is* much better than it was."

"But pretty fucking awful nonetheless, I'm sure," I said flatly, feeling a solar flare of fury at whoever had done this to her. Her hands were damaged, her magic broken, and she was still sitting here so tightly pulled together, putting a hopeful spin on things.

The injustice of it made me want to burn everything to cinders.

Next to me, I could almost hear Rowan grind his teeth. He'd been emanating low-grade rage ever since we sat down, like a dense planet with too much gravity, but I could tell he was intent on keeping it in check for Holly's sake.

"Yeah," she said, closing her eyes for a moment. When she opened them again, they were dull and bleak, dimmed with fatigue. "Awful, and exhausting. To be honest, the jacked-up magic thing, not being able to cast . . . it's a lot worse than the pain. I keep reaching for it, and each time it's like smacking face-first into a wall in the dark. Like being lost inside your own house at night."

"That sounds like the worst kind of nightmare," I said, my stomach tumbling at the thought.

"It is—except I can't even wake myself up." She thumped a helpless fist against the table, grimacing. "This is the first time I've been out since it happened; I've been taking PTO from the day care where I work. They don't want me 'sick' around the kids, anyway, so they're being pretty good about it. But sitting in my house was getting to me, too, listening to myself think and think in circles. And I . . . I'm sorry, Row. But I couldn't go back to Honeycake either, not yet."

"Don't even apologize," Rowan said fiercely, reaching out to brush his fingertips over hers. Clearly wanting to grasp her hand, but knowing that might only hurt her worse. "We're here for you, Hols. It's whatever you need to feel comfortable."

I started at that, almost doing a double take. I'd known that Rowan was objectively kind, at least to other people; I'd just never *seen* it, not like this. But right now, he was pure earnestness, good intentions distilled down into knowing exactly the right thing to say.

Holly nodded shakily, her eyes glossing bright with tears. "I don't know about comfortable just yet. But . . ." She looked around the bar, a small smile tracing over those determinedly bright lips. "I'm feeling less like the walking dead just now, being here. Which is *something*, at any rate."

"Whatever it takes to get you there," Rowan said, the corners of his mouth tightening. "Whatever you want, that's what goes. Just keep that in mind when we start, okay?"

They sat together for a moment, his fingers fanned over hers, heads bowed toward each other. I'd forgotten about the Thorn empathic bond, the way they could pick up on one another's feelings as if their emotions transmitted across a private radio frequency. A far gentler rapport than what we Avramovs shared with one another. If I fell, I knew with unshakeable certainty that my family would always catch me, too—it just might not be the softest of possible landings. We didn't tend to tread this lightly with one another's emotions, or take anywhere near this much care. It had simply never been our way.

But maybe, sometimes, knowing you'd be caught with such tenderness when you stumbled could make you feel a different kind of safe.

I sat quietly next to them, trying not to feel like a trespasser on their moment, maybe even guilty by association with necromantic magic. Then Holly lifted her head and took a final sip of her drink, clearly steeling herself.

"So," she said, gaze shifting decisively between me and Rowan. "Let's do this. What can I tell you that might help?"

"Why don't we start with your impressions of the day," Rowan said. "Any weird shit, bad juju you picked up on. Anything at all you noticed that might've struck you as somehow off."

Holly shook her head, smooth brow cinched. "That's the thing, though. There wasn't anything like that at all, as far as I can tell. Mostly I remember being nervous as hell. I *really* wanted to be Queen this year; you know that, Row. I'd been practicing my floral repertoire for months, and I was thinking it could happen for me this time."

"It would've happened," I said firmly. "Your spell was badass, blew the others right out of the water. Such impressive design, crazy intricate. If you ask me, you had the crown in the bag."

She flashed a smile at me, wide and dazzling, a glimpse of a family resemblance to Rowan that I hadn't caught before.

"Thank you. It did turn out pretty, like my better practice runs. Before my turn came round, I was mostly focused on the other competitors—running comparisons with what they had going, trying to rein the jitters in. But then once I started casting..." She looked past us, her face softening with the memory; Holly Thorn clearly loved her magic every bit as much as I did mine. "Everything else kind of faded into the background. I had to keep a bunch of separate threads up at once, which didn't leave a lot of room for nerves—or for staring at the audience."

"And it's not like you were expecting anything bad to happen," Rowan added. "Course you wouldn't've been on high alert."

"Right." She rolled her eyes, made a wry little face. "Ancient curses weren't exactly top of my mind. My bad, I guess. Next time everybody gets a game-time stare down, just to be on the safe side."

"We do our job right, there won't be any next time," Rowan assured her. "What about when the spell took hold? You notice anything then, besides the obvious?"

"You mean, besides the fact that it hurt like a bitch?" she said dryly. "'Cause that part surely did not escape me. I could feel it sort of *stealing* my spell. Sucking the life out of it, turning it all dry and dead. It was like when we were kids, lighting paper scraps on fire to see how long you could let them burn before it hurt too much. Except I couldn't let go."

"Wait, Thorn kids go through the fire-starter phase, too?" I exclaimed. "I thought playing baby pyro was an Avramov thing!"

"It's a *kid* thing, Isidora," Rowan said, with a slight eye roll. "Everyone does dumb shit like that, before they grow some judgment."

"Hey, maybe we're just late judgment bloomers," I said, shrugging. "Mine could crop up any day now, who's to say!"

That stole another smile from Holly, though more restrained this time. "From where I'm sitting, good judgment might just be overrated. My whole life's been about clean living—and look where it's gotten me."

"What happened to you was *not* your fault, Hols," Rowan said. "I know you know that. Sometimes you just can't predict how some messed-up motherfucker might react to something you did. But I do have to ask—can you think of any reason someone might be angry with you? Mad enough to pull some whacked-out shit like this?"

Holly twitched her fingertips along her tumbler, tracing its delicate etched pattern as she bit at the skin below her lower lip in thought.

"As far as I know, no one out there's feeling *that* type of way about me," she said, but I could see how her poise faltered, her mouth quivering a little. "Though, I guess . . . well, this isn't anyone else's business, and definitely not something I planned on advertising. But I *was* seeing Gawain Blackmoore for a little while."

All my internal alarms sounded at the mention of Blackmoores, especially the notorious Gareth's little brother. I could feel Rowan's reaction beside me, a subtle shift into a state of even higher alert.

It wasn't so much that Blackmoores were inherently nefarious; in the more distant past, Avramovs and Blackmoores had even considered themselves allied. But in the years since, they'd attained something of a reputation for underhanded fuckery. They'd spent a long time in possession of the Victor's Wreath, throwing their weight around Thistle Grove in a variety of obnoxious ways—and it was Gareth Blackmoore's blatant two-timing of my own sister and Linden Thorn that had precipitated the vengeance plot, and his family's ensuing fall from Gauntlet grace.

"You were seeing him, as in, the past tense," I noted. "Is that right?"

"Yeah, we're done now. He was just . . . too much. Clingy, possessive, wanting things to happen way too fast. And I was feeling weird about it already, because of what happened to Lin. Not that Gawain must be shady by definition just because his brother's a dog, but you know how it is." She shrugged, spreading her hands. "Learned behavior. And when folks are *that* suspicious of their partners, it's usually because they're the ones with the skeletons."

"So you were the one who broke up with him?" I asked, just to confirm.

She nodded, eyes clear and resolute, obviously not regretting her decision one iota. Good for her.

"It wasn't worth the nonstop drama; that's just not my style," she said, tipping her head to the side. "I like my relationships calm, clean, reasonable. And I wanted to be single anyway, for Beltane. I hadn't really been looking for anything serious to begin with when we got together back in February, and he *knew* that. Guess I still should've anticipated how dramatic he was going to be about ending things. It being Gav's default setting and all."

"Sounds like a charmer," I said sourly. Probably a fucking Pisces man. In my experience, male Pisces were *always* the ones with too many overflowing feelings, forever foisting them on everyone else in the vicinity.

"So he flew off the handle when you told him you were done?" Rowan said, jumping back in. A muscle had started leaping along his jaw, the same one that interacting with me tended to provoke. The one that functioned like a gauge, indicating he'd had it up to here with your garbage.

Only this time it was the thought of Gawain Blackmoore inciting it, not me.

"Oh yeah, in a major way." She nodded, braids swishing, the bar's vintage Edison bulbs glinting off their cuffs. "I was like, 'Settle down, my dude, this is not that serious.' It hadn't even been a full two months! But he was all, 'How could you, this was gonna be special, I was about to fall in love with you.' Acting like I was some wanton temptress leading him on, instead of someone who'd been up front with him from the very start."

"*About* to fall in love with you!" I spluttered through a sip of water. "Oh, that's classic. And then you *dared* interfere with the trajectory of his feelings. The tragedy of it all."

"I know, right?" she said, scoffing through her nose. "I mean, he's nice to look at, and he could be a good time—but still, such a damn clown. I didn't even know what to say, so I just cut off communications after that, went radio silent. I was hoping he'd wear himself out, move on."

"Pisces *never* forget," I muttered darkly.

Holly burst out into giggles, sweetly pitched and musical, the kind of mood-enhancing laughter so harmonious to listen to that it actually made you happy. No wonder Gawain Blackmoore had been so captivated by her; not only was she gorgeous and funny and clearly smart, but even her laughter was optimal. Holly Thorn was a stone-cold catch.

Under different circumstances, I could almost see us becoming friends.

"He *was* a Pisces!" she said, looking delighted, her burdens momentarily set aside. "And I'm an Aries, so, obviously a doomed fit from the start. But how did you even know that?"

"I have a checkered history with them myself," I admitted. "On the upside, now I can sniff one out a mile away. Never get taken unawares again."

"Maybe once this is all over," she said, still grinning at me, "you could share some of that knowledge with me? I could use a solid detection method for the future. You know, weed 'em out before they can take root."

"I'd be more than happy to," I promised, thrilled that I'd lightened her mood even just a little. "In the spirit of fire sign solidarity."

When her laughter rang out again, I could feel Rowan's eyes settle on me. I glanced back at him, already steeling myself for that undercurrent of disapproval—but for once, there was nothing like reproach in them. Instead, they were warm and unguarded, glowing with that internal light I'd seen only once before.

If I hadn't known better, I might even have confused that warmth with gratitude.

12

))) ● (((

Parallel Universes

T O MY SURPRISE, Rowan wanted to stay at Whistler's once Holly left. To debrief, he said, while the conversation was still fresh in both our minds.

To my even greater surprise, he suggested we do it over drinks, which he was even willing to snag for us from the bar. We ostensibly had a server, but the place had filled up to the gills as night fell, and we'd seen neither hide nor hair of him for at least twenty minutes. I didn't even really remember what he looked like, besides the kind of overwrought facial hair that made me never want to come here in the first place. The waitstaff at painfully cool venues like this always had that Schrödinger's cat quality, like they existed both in insufferable HD and only as figments of your imagination at the same time.

"Sure," I'd agreed, a little nonplussed, feeling like I'd been spirited away to a strangely conflict-free parallel universe. "Dirty martini for me, please. With blue cheese olives, if they have them."

Rowan had made a very expressive face at that, but refrained from comment. A short while later, he resurfaced with a nicely murky-looking martini for me, and a double scotch for him.

"Cheers to our first interview, I guess," he said, clinking his lowball against my glass and only barely scrunching up his nose as I swigged back a briny sip. "Or is there different *NCIS* terminology for it that I should be using?"

"No, you're right on," I assured him, sliding one of the olives off its toothpick with my teeth. Rowan's eyes flicked to my mouth, presumably revolted that I'd befoul good alcohol with pickled fruit. I offered him the toothpick, amused by how adamantly he shook his head.

"More for me," I said with a shrug, popping the other two olives in my mouth and following the chewy bite with another delicious swig. The bartenders here really knew their way around a dirty martini; I might have to give Whistler's another chance to win me over.

"I'll never understand the dirty martini hype," Rowan said, suppressing a shudder. "Like, let's all be real about it. You're basically just chugging olive juice."

"*Highly alcoholic* olive juice," I corrected. "Also, it's salty and delicious. Unlike your double order of bug spray."

He looked possibly more offended than I'd seen thus far, shoulders bunching in defense of his scotch's delicate sensibilities.

"This is an eighteen-year-old Macallan," he argued. "Smooth as hell, tastes like woodsmoke and elegance in a glass. You can't beat this depth of flavor."

"What are you, an aged hedge fund manager?" I retorted.

"Also I can smell it from here, and it smells like overpriced Raid. Bet it tastes like it, too."

He cocked his head at me in mock concern. "You spend a lot of time drinking Raid in your day?"

"Oh, yes," I said, giving him a solemn nod. "When I wasn't burning my fingers to nubbins, most of my childhood was dedicated to swilling bug repellent. You know us Avramovs. When it comes to living on the edge, they start us young."

"'The edge' being the poison control center, I guess. Does explain a lot about y'all's many problems."

But I could see him struggle against a smile as he raised the glass to his lips, taking a long, slow sip, letting the scotch linger in his mouth before he swallowed it. I found myself wondering how it would taste on him, before I banished the thought with extreme prejudice.

"There's that 'y'all' again," I pointed out instead, clearing my throat. "You don't hear it much around here. What's that about?"

"I went to college and vet school in Virginia," Rowan said with a shrug. "Guess it just grew on me."

"I hadn't realized you spent that much time away from here," I said, feeling an unexpected stab of wistfulness at the idea. I'd never been farther than fiftyish miles from Thistle Grove myself, and never for more than a few days or so.

"That's where my mom's side of the family's from," Rowan elaborated, smiling at the thought of his relatives. "The Watts clan. Even before I went for school, Linden, Lark, and I used to spend whole summers down there sometimes, in Charlottesville, with my grandma Ramona."

"That's a long time to be away from magic," I said, balking a little. That was how it worked for Thistle Grove witches; our talents were inextricably bound up with the town and the lake. The more time you spent away, the weaker your magic became. It would spring back readily once you came home—Lady's Lake didn't hold even a prolonged absence against you—but I still struggled with the notion of willingly letting the gift of your magic slip away, even if the loss was only a temporary one.

"It was worth it, for those summers," he said with a shrug. "I loved every minute of it. Peach cobbler, sun tea, sitting out on the porch all evening watching fireflies . . . you know, the whole Southern deal."

"Wouldn't know, I've never been," I said shortly, leaving it at that, without tacking on the silent (and pathetic) "or anywhere else, really."

The smile faded as he shifted in his seat, face falling back into serious lines. "So, sounds like Gawain Blackmoore's our next stop. What'd you make of all that, what went down between them?"

"Shouldn't I be asking you that?" I pointed out. "You're the one whose twin sister has history with an even bigger bastard of a Blackmoore."

"Yeah, that's the thing. I'm trying my damnedest to keep from jumping to conclusions," Rowan said, jaw setting, "seeing as I still occasionally give thought to busting up Gareth's smarmy-ass face. So it's not like I have the coolest head in town when it comes to Blackmoore men. That said, it doesn't sound to me like he's a piece of work on Gareth's level. You?"

I considered it, swirling my drink. Gareth's little brother had been a year ahead of me in high school, and while I wasn't sure what Gawain was up to these days, back then he'd held a certain niche appeal—if pouty pretty boys who wrote inscrutable song lyrics about the beauty of entropy happened to be your bag. I recalled a general air of overwrought preciousness, and *vast* over-confidence in his own musical abilities. There may have been a cover band involved, bankrolled by his parents and given way too much airtime at school events.

"You never know," I said. "He sounds super high-touch, on top of being a poster boy for white, rich, and privileged. And if Holly cut him off right after they broke up? He might've convinced himself she deserved some real hurt over that kind of slight."

"Blackmoores *are* strong as hell," Rowan said thoughtfully. "If anyone besides one of yours could pull off a curse like that, it'd be one of them."

I considered emphasizing—mostly for the record, and only a little nastily—that Holly hadn't mentioned anything at all to implicate my family. If anything, the bread crumb trail was leading squarely away from us. But I didn't feel like spiking things, not when we were getting along so unusually well.

"And wouldn't it make sense," I said instead, "if it *was* Gawain, that he'd purposely choose a spell that would, by its very nature, cast blame on another family?"

"Sure. Like you said, people can be all kinds of sneaky."

It was almost like he didn't want to fight with me, either, for a total wonder. Possibly we really had slipped sideways together into some parallel universe.

One in which we somehow weren't natural enemies.

"Should we pay Camelot a visit tomorrow, then?" I asked, rolling the glass stem between my palms. "I'm free in the afternoon, if you're game."

"Works for me. I'll reach out to Lyonesse, let her know we're coming."

"Doesn't that tip our hand, though? Giving them advance notice like that?"

He smirked at that, shaking his head. "This is the real world, not one of your shows—and Camelot's Blackmoore turf. I'm not trying to go traipsing in there and disrespecting their elders. You and I, we're playing by the rules. That way, no one can take it upon themselves to second-guess anything we turn up."

"Okay, I do see the logic. But I still resent it."

He motioned to the server—who'd finally reappeared in all his mustachioed glory; who the hells went all-in on a handlebar in this day and age?—for another drink. I hadn't even noticed that Rowan had already drained his double scotch, drinking at a pace I wouldn't have expected on a weeknight, especially not from him. At our first meeting at the Shamrock, he hadn't even ordered anything stronger than coffee.

But, admittedly, tonight had a different vibe. A shimmering filament of something I couldn't quite identify.

I swigged the rest of my martini and hastily ordered another before the server could vanish again. No way was Rowan Thorn going to be outdrinking me; it would upset the natural order of things, set the cosmos itself askew.

"I forgot to ask, did you want anything to eat?" Rowan said after the second round arrived, cocking an eyebrow at me. "My treat."

"I'm good. Also, why are you being so nice to me?" I demanded. "It's making me antsy. Like maybe you secretly have a hit out on me or something."

He took an amused sip, taking his time before he replied. "Come on, out of the two of us? You'd be way more likely to have those kinds of connections."

"Fair enough," I conceded. We probably *did* have an assassin or two lurking somewhere in our family tree. "Still doesn't answer my question."

He shrugged, a loose, rolling movement that shouldn't have been half as compelling as it was. "Maybe I'm just being polite."

"Come on, Thorn," I said, just a little scathing, mostly to distract myself from the way my eyes seemed to have become magnetized to those broad shoulders. Maybe that second martini hadn't been the smartest of calls. "When have you ever done 'polite' with me?"

He winced a little at that, as if it were a low blow instead of the simple truth.

"The thing is," he said, drumming his fingers on the table, casting me a piercing look from under lowered brows, "I saw how you made my cousin laugh. The way you distracted her from all the miserable shit she's dealing with. You didn't have to do any of that for her, but you did. So, thank you for that."

"You're welcome," I said, a little stunned that he thought this was a gesture worth remarking on. What kind of callous person did he think I was?

"And Holly," he went on, licking his lips before taking another long swig, "she's *amazing*. Not only is she a killer caster, but she's just . . . one of those rare people who thoroughly excel at life. We're talking dead-ass hilarious, considerate, kinder than anyone you'll ever meet. Works with high-needs kids, and is just infinitely patient with them."

"She does seem awesome," I agreed, warmed despite myself to hear him compliment her. I kind of doubted any of my cousins would fanboy over me in such an enthusiastic, wholesome way; Rowan and Holly seemed to genuinely get each other. "I really liked her. I was even hoping I'd get to be friends with her, after all this is behind us."

Rowan nodded vaguely at this thought—as if the idea of friendship with me weren't, under normal circumstances, the kind of thing he might not wish on his worst enemy, much less a beloved cousin. I snuck a look at his glass, which was already close to empty; maybe I wasn't the only one whose judgment was on the verge of impaired.

"She doesn't want us worrying about her," Rowan said, dropping his chin, his voice dipping so low that I leaned over my crossed forearms to hear him better. It put me close enough to him to better appreciate how the bar's muted light lit his downcast face, falling over bold jaw and cheekbone, highlighting the soft yet precise cut of his mouth. It made him look not only like some modern angel, but also more vulnerable than I'd ever seen him. Neither hero nor archnemesis, but the solid dude my sister probably saw him as, grappling with a profoundly awful situation.

"But she's still in a lot of pain," he continued, lifting his eyes back to mine with an effort. "And terrified to boot, scared she'll never get her magic back the way it was."

"I would be, too," I half whispered, afraid he might withdraw if I got any louder. "I mean, who wouldn't be?"

"Man, it fucking *kills* me that she has to go through this," he said, and this time his tone was so raw it rocked me. That explained the uncharacteristic drinking, then; he was still badly shaken by what he'd felt from his cousin. "I keep asking myself, why her? No one deserves this less than she does."

I knew exactly where he was coming from—because I really *had* liked Holly. She wasn't just a symbol anymore, the inciting event of my collision with Rowan, an unfamiliar Thorn witch whose injury had catalyzed this entire unfortunate cascade. But rather someone I vibed with on a personal level, a person I genuinely wanted to get to know.

My feelings could never compare to Rowan's, of course, but the fact that someone had done this to her made me furious, too.

"We're going to get to the bottom of this thing," I told Rowan, inching my hand a little closer to his on the table without quite touching it. "And when we do, we'll find the total waste who did this to Holly, and haul their wretched ass straight to Emmy's doorstep. Possibly after just the *tiniest* of beatdowns. I won't tell if you won't."

He looked back up at me, eyes lingering on mine, shifting back and forth between them before he let his gaze drift down to my mouth. This time, the intent behind the look was unmistakable, and I could feel heat gathering under my skin like smoke.

In this parallel universe we were temporarily inhabiting, Rowan Thorn was thinking *thoughts* about my mouth.

"Well, look at you," he murmured, a faint smile playing on his own lips. "With your warrior face on and everything. I may just about believe you."

"You'd better," I said, still feeling several degrees too warm. "For I do not fuck around, not when it comes to shitty hex-slinging bullies. *Almost* worse than a dude Pisces on a bad day."

Rowan chuckled, a low, caramelized sound that sent all that collected heat spiraling straight to my belly. I was playing with the worst kind of fire here, and I knew it—but when had that ever stopped me before? When had it ever done anything at all, besides making me want to keep blazing my way down trails marked "forbidden"?

For me, the forbiddenness usually tended to be the point.

"Pisces-shaped chip on your shoulder aside, that was a cute bit," he said, the chuckle still warming his tone. "How'd you guess about Gawain, anyway?"

"Didn't guess, but knew," I replied, with a one-shouldered shrug. "Like I know you're a Taurus beyond a reasonable doubt."

He reared back a little, mouth dropping open. "Okay, how the fuck did you do that? There's no way you know my birthday!"

"Goddess-given talent. Yours is easy, anyway—you display all the relevant attributes. Intense stubbornness, an even keel, your standard Taurus slow-boil temper. A boatload of basic decency."

"Wow, you're gonna throw in basic decency?" he echoed, lips twitching. "Careful now, before you trip and give me a compliment."

"Plot twist," I said, singsong. "Turns out I can imagine worse things than accidentally saying something nice to you."

He mimed shock, widening his eyes and rounding his mouth into an exaggerated O. "Wait, have we met? I'm Rowan Thorn . . . and while we're at it, what's *your* sign?"

I tilted my head back and forth, considering, my lips tucked slyly behind my teeth. "Get us another round, and maybe I'll let you guess."

13

All the Signs You're Not

To MY ABSOLUTE delight, Rowan Thorn, (Wasteyface) Wildlife Hero, utterly blew at the zodiac.

"Wait, wait, no, I got it!" he cried, slipping sideways in his seat a little before righting himself, hooking one foot around the chair leg. We were four drinks deep—which, for Rowan, meant more like eight—but he somehow managed to make even impending sloppiness look close to charming. "Scorpio!"

I exploded into laughter, dropping my forehead down onto my crossed arms.

"You've clearly never met a Scorpio in your whole entire life if you think that's even remotely possible," I said once I'd gotten myself mostly back under control. "Try again."

He scrunched up his face, fumbling for his glass with one hand. "Wait, which've I already said? Uh, Cancer—"

"That was a definitive no."

"Virgo—"

"*Hells* no, OMG. How are you so amazingly terrible at this? There's only twelve options to pick from!"

"But did I say Sagittarius already?" He squinted at me with one eye like, *Gotcha pegged!* "Because that feels right."

"I mean, warmer. But since I'm not currently dancing topless on our table before jetting off to Thailand for some spontaneous me time, you can safely assume that one's a no."

"Oh, is *that* what they do?" He tipped his chair back onto two very precarious legs and rocked it back and forth, raising his eyebrows. "Damn, that sounds kinda fun. Gotta get me a Sagittarius chick one of these days."

"Why?" I demanded, "so you can escort her off the table and lend her your shirt, then get her safely tucked in at home with a glass of water and two Aleve on her nightstand?"

"Come on, now, give me *some* credit." He draped his arms over the table and fixed me with a devastatingly lazy grin, his eyes shimmering with too much booze and that enticing inner candlelight. "I would, at least, chastely kiss her cheek good night before I let myself out."

I rolled my eyes elaborately. "Ever the consummate gentleman."

"And do you know what gentlemen get for their trouble?" He laid his palms flat on the table and leaned forward with great gravitas, giving his eyebrows a rakish wag. "*A lady's number.*"

"As if you wouldn't do it anyway, just because it's the right thing to do."

"Maybe so. But—you know, as a vet—I *also* know when not to look a gift horse in the mouth."

While I puzzled over what that was supposed to mean, he gazed off to the right for inspiration, then refocused on me, lifting a triumphant finger. "Okay, how about . . . Gemini!"

"Are you just saying random signs now? Resorting to the process of elimination?"

"Why not? If I can just figure out all the signs you're not . . ." His eyes fastened on mine, both dark and radiant, glossed with liquor. Gazing into them gave me the same heady, stomach-tumbling feeling I sometimes got when I stared up into a sky chock-full of Thistle Grove's diamond-dust stars. "Maybe then I'll know what you are."

My breath caught a little at the avid, almost hungry way he was looking at me. As if he meant some deeper kind of knowledge than what could be readily diagrammed onto a star chart.

"What I am is way too tipsy for a school night," I said, much more glibly than I felt, my face swarming with renewed heat as I looked around for the server to bring us the check. Tonight seemed to have morphed into something much more intense and enjoyable than I'd expected; I could feel that forbidden path beckoning more brightly each minute that I stayed, as if it were lit by signal fires. And I could sense myself leaning dangerously into it, becoming increasingly tempted to stay the risky course, better judgment be damned.

But for once, I was going to at least try to do the right thing. See how that looked on me, for a change.

"So maybe let's both head home," I finished, both relieved and bummed out to see Handlebar heading for us with check in hand. "Before we turn into pumpkins."

As was often the case, I somehow became much drunker as soon as I set foot outside.

A chunky half-moon floated above the rooftops of Yarrow

Street, wisped with a fine film of cloud like bridal lace. The night air hit me like a shot of floral-infused liquor; Thistle Grove in spring smelled of enchanted garden, so heady with jasmine and sweet pea and creamy freesia you could almost taste petals and pollen dissolving on your tongue. And being drunk always made me feel like my sense of smell had been dialed up to eleven.

"Whoa," I mumbled, closing my eyes as my head swam like a flipped water globe, awash with glitter. "So, yeah, I will *not* be driving myself home this evening."

"Want me to call a car?" Rowan asked, swaying only just a little himself. The light shed by the faux gas lamps that lined the street picked out the variegated browns in his locs, dipping them in gold. "We could share."

"I think I'll just walk the spinnies off; it's not that far to The Bitters. And it's such a gorgeous night."

He frowned. "Still, it's late. Even in a town like this, you never know."

"While I'm flattered that you'd fret over a lady's safety, this is me you're talking to," I said, letting demonstrative billows of ectoplasm swirl around my hands. "I've gone for walks this late before. And around these parts, *I'm* the one who goes bump in the night—or hadn't you heard?"

"Not doubting you can take care of yourself," he said, showing me his palms. "But if it's all the same, I'd still rather walk with you. I'll just call myself a car from there."

"Suit yourself. I don't mind the company."

When I fell into step with him, he reflexively took the side that would've put him closer to traffic, had any existed on the town's pedestrian main drag. Around us, Yarrow Street lay placid as a pond, unusually quiet and still even for this late on a weeknight.

Besides our reflections in the windows as we passed, I saw nothing stirring all the way down its length. Not a flicker of movement, either outside on the cobbles or from within the darkened storefront glass.

It felt as though we really had stepped into an alternate dimension, a pocket of space-time that had folded itself around us like a bubble before pinching closed.

"You know, for someone who puts so much stock by chivalry," I said, darting a look at Rowan's swooping profile, emboldened by all the martini coursing through my veins, "that they'd give a drunk Sagittarius the shirt off their back . . . you weren't so quick to do the same for me back at Honeycake."

Rowan stopped dead in the street, so abruptly I nearly stumbled over my own feet as I turned to face him.

"Come again?" he said, brow wrinkling.

"I was cold," I said, trying not to sound too drunkenly petulant, even though the memory still made my feelings twinge. "Out by the parking lot, when we were walking back from the heart tree. You saw me shiver, went to give me your shirt. Then you didn't."

"I didn't . . . *oh*," he finished, as the recollection dawned. "Isidora, that's not—that isn't what happened. Not at all."

"No?" I said lightly. "You didn't decide, 'Shit, let the Avramov just suck up the chill? It's only *Isidora*, after all. What's the harm if she gets a little cold?'"

His face softened, went gentle in an indefinable way that undid me a little, made me cross my arms over my chest.

"I thought you wouldn't want it," he said simply. "That it'd offend you, maybe piss you off, if I even offered it."

I swallowed hard, so thrown that for once, I had no idea what to say. Because I believed him. This sounded not only plausible, but like he might have had my likeliest reaction pegged. I probably *would* have overreacted, launched into an offensive by reflex.

"Probably," I admitted, forcing myself to meet his eyes. "But I still wish you'd done it, anyway."

Rowan's gaze shifted between my eyes, growing somehow even more intent, gaining a keen focus that turned my insides to a liquid sear. He took a step toward me, followed by another, until we stood closer to each other than we'd ever been before. Close enough that I could finally smell him, something I hadn't even realized I wanted to be able to do. His was a clean, rich blend of soap, cedar, and citrus, mingled with the alcohol on his breath.

Rowan Thorn smelled like the best of Beltane, fragrant bonfires and spiked lemonade, day-drinking in spring sunshine. All my very favorite things.

"How do you even do that?" he murmured, his voice dipping into a rumble, so deep I could almost feel it vibrate within the confines of my own chest.

"Do what?" I said, just a little shaky.

"That," he exhaled, reaching out to barely cup my cheek, touching me so lightly I felt the heat rising from his hand more than I felt the touch itself. I froze in place, lips parted, afraid that if I even breathed, all of this might go away, evaporate. "The way you make it look so goddamn *cute* when you're being impossible."

"I'm sorry?" I tried, almost trembling with the effort to stay still even in the face of this total revelation. That Rowan Thorn thought impossibility—impossibleness?—looked good on me. "Wait, no. Not sorry."

"Well, maybe you should be." Now his eyes looked like someone had lit an entire furnace behind them, like the hazel might give way to a flood of molten gold. He skimmed his thumb down my cheek with an achingly light touch, only a graze, before letting it hover right beside my mouth. "Because it makes me want to kiss that look right the fuck off your perfect little face."

"Dare you to try," I whispered, throwing all my noble intentions straight into the fire.

Someone else could take it upon themselves to behave tonight— because I was personally done with pretending to be good.

We didn't kiss, so much as collide with intent. Rowan let out a low, raw sound, somewhere between a moan and growl, closing the space between us in one rough step. My back pressed hard against the glass of whatever storefront we happened to be standing near, and *What if we fell through* blazed thrillingly across my mind just as his mouth covered mine. His lips were, fuck, *ridiculously* soft, lush and pliant and demanding. Amazingly—impossibly—they felt even better than they looked.

Maybe the rules for that kind of thing were different in this other universe.

His hand curled around my chin, tilting it up toward him, his thumb stroking my lower lip even as he kissed me, his other hand sliding tight behind my waist. I twined both arms around his neck, slipping them beneath the warm weight of his hair.

Tall as I was, he was a lot taller than me; I had to crane my neck against the glass to properly meet his mouth. When my lips parted, his tongue swept against mine, a liquid heat that sent a flashfire of lust roaring down my abdomen and curling between my thighs. In response, an absurdly helpless little moan came surging out of my throat. The kind of needful sound I wouldn't have been caught dead making in front of Rowan Thorn even in my own imagination a few hours ago.

The effect it had on him was instant; a ragged breath jolted from his lips, exhaled hot into my mouth. He went so hard against me I had to swivel my hips to accommodate him, draping my leg over the outside of his thigh, looping my foot around his calf. We fit together like we were made for it, his heat hitched up right against mine.

"Goddamn, Isidora," he groaned against my mouth, dragging my lower lip through his teeth. "How do you feel so fucking perfect?"

When he kissed me again, I thought I might melt right out of my torn jeans, pool directly onto the pavement like some dirty porno version of the Wicked Witch of the West.

He tasted strongly of scotch—which I apparently liked a shit-load more than I'd been led to believe—but beneath that he was also somehow sweet, a burnt caramel taste like butterscotch. Each time his lips remolded to mine, tongues surging together, I tilted my head farther back to give him better, deeper access. Both his hands had slid down to grip my ass, fingertips digging in hard enough that it almost hurt, just the way I liked. Grinding me against him in a slow but urgent rhythm that matched the cadence of our mouths.

The kind of ravenous kissing I would never in a million years have expected from Rowan Thorn, Wildlife Hero (and Utmost Gentleman).

When he pulled back, it was to draw my earlobe into his mouth, teeth sinking in until I let out a soft cry in that same help-less pitch. He kissed the sensitive spot right beneath my ear, trac-ing nibbles down to where my jaw met my throat, until the whole left side of my body rolled with tingles.

"So that's what you like," he murmured against my skin, his voice so rough it made my insides twist. "That, right there."

"That's my, um . . ." I caught my breath as he gave the curve of my neck an open-mouthed kiss, chills spreading through my chest, my hips writhing against his. "That's my favorite spot."

"Oh, but I bet you've got others."

I let my head fall back, the glass taking all my weight, wondering giddily what would happen when it finally gave way behind us. The center of me throbbed with lust, the kind of clenching desire that felt like caving in, like imminent implosion. I was so dizzy with the soap-and-citrus smell of him, his heat in my mouth and pressed against my pelvis, that when shrill laughter rang out from somewhere close, it took me a second to comprehend just what in the fuck was happening.

"Heeeeey!" some asshole bellowed from up the street, half falling on his shambling way out of Whistler's. "Why don't you get a fucking roooooom, pervs!"

"Why don't *you* come over here and say that to my face!" I roared back at him, as if this made any sense at all.

The drunk dipshit let loose another bray, then stumbled off in the opposite direction, flipping me off over his shoulder.

When I looked back up at Rowan, my cheeks abuzz with fury, insides still molten with need, I could see that the spell—the one that had transported us to this parallel universe in the first place—had broken like a fever.

For a moment he stared down at me through a haze, desire and confusion still filming his eyes. Like he'd sleepwalked here by accident, and come awake much too close to my face. Then he all but lunged back into the street, away from me. Something like panic darted across his features, followed in rapid succession by concern, consternation, and then full-on regret.

That anyone should look like that after kissing me made me feel like a black hole had opened inside my chest. Roaring and insatiable, sucking everything around it into a compact core of pain.

"Isidora," Rowan said, dragging the back of his hand over his mouth, as if to wipe me off. "Shit, I . . . I'm so sorry. I should not have done that."

"You have nothing to be sorry about," I said tightly, pushing away from the glass and wrapping my arms over my aching chest. "I *was* here, too, last I checked. Pretty sure I kissed you back."

"But I'm the one who started it, and that—that should not have happened." He shook his head, lacing both hands behind his neck. "We're working together, and that all was just, fuck, unprofessional beyond belief. And beyond that . . ." He trailed off, as if unsure how to finish, a grimace twisting his face.

"You can't be seen making out with an Avramov," I finished for him, still hoping against hope that he was going to tell me no, of course something so stupid and hurtful couldn't be the case. "Not when you have a reputation to maintain."

He said nothing, but that muscle in his jaw jumped in the streetlight, giving him away.

The hole in my chest yawned, aching so badly that I pressed a hand against my sternum, trying to will myself into believing this wasn't that big a deal. It had been an unfortunate mutual accident, that was all, I told myself as I turned away from him. Those happened sometimes, especially when too much drinking paved the wrong path—and then lit it up with flares, until it looked like an enticing adventure instead of a horrible mistake.

"I get it," I said, with a brusque nod. "And no need to worry; I won't be telling anyone about this."

"Isidora, wait, that's not—"

"Do *not* come after me," I tossed over my shoulder as I struck off toward one of the side streets, where I'd be able to call myself a ride, get the fuck away from him as quickly as I could, and then scourge my memories of this night with napalm. Just in case he was still inclined to follow, I emanated a wake of ectoplasm until it hovered behind me like a dangerous, trailing cape.

I'll show you a tower-dwelling evil sorceress, you sanctimonious prick.

14

)) ◗ ((

Not Here for Bridges

I WOKE UP WITH a brutal hangover, black hole residue still clogging up my chest. The very last thing I wanted was to see Rowan that afternoon, much less present the Blackmoores with a united front—so it came as a massive relief when he begged off first, while I still lay languishing in bed. Ostensibly some emergency had cropped up at work, and he couldn't make it today. Probably some newborn chinchillas had lost their mom, and needed his tender loving care.

Oh, I'm so sure *that's what it is*, I thought witheringly as my phone pinged with a follow-up text rescheduling us for Sunday; I tossed it aside and yanked my comforter back up to my chin. No doubt this had nothing whatsoever to do with not wanting to face me in the sober light of day, my lips still bee-stung from last night's mistake.

But whatever; at least this way I got to keep my dignity intact, look like the one who'd been ready to soldier on for the sake of investigative integrity. And by the time we headed over to Camelot on Sunday instead, I'd have scrubbed my brain clean of the lingering memory of Rowan's hands, the searing imprint his mouth had left on my lips and neck, the tantalizing way I'd been caught between him and that glass.

Shit, it wasn't like I didn't have *years* of experience making poor choices when it came to lovers. I'd dated more than my fair share of normie locals and folks just passing through, along with a Harlow and even one of the more distant Blackmoore cousins—all of them nothing like Rowan, but straight from central casting in either their classic bad-boy bullshit or generalized emotional unavailability. On the upside, picking myself up and dusting myself off was now a thing at which I excelled, due to so much practice.

Eventually, compelled by starvation and raging thirst, I got up to drag my sad carcass downstairs to the kitchen. As I roamed the halls in my fleece-lined bathrobe, The Bitters seemed to loom around me, even more sinister than normal. Its antique bronze lamps guttering and leaping like flicking tongues, the long corridors stretching out somehow too far into the distance, like an optical illusion. Above the peeling dark wood of the wainscot, the frayed edges of the velvet wallpaper rippled like the house's breath, weathered floorboards creaking before I even stepped on them. I didn't dare to sneak a glimpse of myself in the foxed mirrors that hung on so many of the walls, stubbornly listing sideways no matter how often we adjusted the frames.

The house still felt . . . *strange*, uncanny even by its own weird standards.

And at some point, I became aware of a presence keeping pace with me.

Hairs standing at attention on my neck, I closed my eyes and focused, murmuring a gentle summoning spell as my garnet throbbed against my throat. When I opened them, Lottie, the head chambermaid, drifted beside me, white cap askew on her curly mop of hair, her signature moue of disapproval conspicuously absent. Lottie hailed from a bygone era when the Avramovs had actual help—hard as that was to imagine nowadays—and she usually manifested only to cuss you out and judge you (*very* harshly) for failing to perform some household task to her exacting standards.

But today, she looked more haggard than reproachful, a glint of trepidation shimmering in her eyes.

She shouldn't be here anymore, she rasped at me, in a querulous tone that I felt more than really heard, registering it in some specialized corner of my brain. *Madam's dudgeon runs too high and waspish, too riled up for the rest of us. We keep trying to chase her off, but no . . . she's a pigheaded old thing, she is. Too damned stubborn to leave us be and go.*

She? I thought to myself, my heart swooping in my chest; maybe this could explain the source of the prolonged haunting. The only "she" that I could think of who hadn't belonged at The Bitters was Davara Circlebreaker—and given how cunning demons could be, it was possible that, just maybe, she had never really left at all.

"Is it one of the daemonfolk, Lottie?" I asked her, keeping my voice scrupulously calm. Shades were skittish by nature, easily chased off by too much need. "Davara Circlebreaker? The fallen that I summoned, that you and yours helped me banish, uh . . ." I almost always bungled it when it came to antiquated units of time, but they played well with ghosts. "Several fortnights ago?"

Lottie stared at me, thin lips parted, fear and confusion drifting across her careworn face as she slowly shook her head. Then she broke apart, fragmented into coils of gray like dying smoke.

So much for ghostly help, I thought wryly, continuing down the hall once it became clear she wasn't coming back.

Down in the drafty kitchen, Talia stood by the humpbacked beast of a gas stove in socked feet and polka-dotted black pajama shorts, whipping up some chocolate challah French toast for herself. Our sister, Addie, was already at school, Elena wouldn't be stirring until at least eleven, and Micah was nowhere to be seen, probably at a sleepover with one of his rotating partners. My brother thrived on poly anarchy, with so many members and shifting rules that his relationships basically comprised their own unruly nation-state—one in which he somehow always came out ahead. I'd have lost my mind within a month of juggling that many people's feelings, so maybe Micah had some kind of innate resiliency (and time management skills) that I lacked.

At least the sight of my sister cooking was comfortingly familiar, reliably like home.

"Morning, sunshine," Talia said, glancing up from the cast-iron skillet to note the storm brewing on my face. "Whoa, what befell *you*?"

"Rowan fucking Thorn befell me," I pronounced darkly, slumping into a chair. "Among other things."

Talia's face tightened for a second, lips thinning, and she paused with her spatula in midair as if she were about to say something. Then we both jumped as all the drawers in the kitchen slid out in a cascade, before slamming themselves shut at the same time with a thunderous rattle.

"Hnnnnghhhh," I groaned, dropping my head back onto my arms. "Stupid poltergeist. You can miss me with your bullshit today, you hear that?"

"You'd think it'd have settled down by now," Talia said, still sounding a little spooked. "Whatever's hanging around, it's worse than spectral bedbugs."

"I know, I know. I just ran into Lottie, and even *she* complained about it. It's got her jumpy, too—enough that she didn't even ride my ass about dusting the dining room rafters."

"So what did she say it was?"

"She didn't. Just complained about how the mystery entity is harassing the rest of them. But I'll do another round of banishments this weekend, promise." I dragged my hands through my hair, blowing air through my lips. "When I'm closer to human again. Pretty sure I'd projectile barf if I tried to cast much of anything today."

"I wasn't trying to press you, Iss. Not in your sorry state, anyway; that'd be plain cruel. Care to elaborate on what happened last night?"

"Posthumously, maybe," I mumbled, massaging my temples. "Good news is, my death seems imminent. So you won't have long to wait."

"Lucky for you, my French toast is actually a resurrection spell soaked in butter. And this slice has your name on it. Want some OJ, too?"

"This world does not deserve you, *sestra*."

With a glass of fresh-squeezed juice and half a chocolaty slice of toast in me, I started feeling marginally better. Once she deemed me less likely to bite, Talia set her cutlery down on her plate and met my eyes.

"So, how's it going?" she said, tilting her head. "The investigation, I mean. And I ask mostly out of professional curiosity, seeing as I'm the one who should've been doing it."

"I wish you were," I groused. "You'd probably already have it in the bag. But we *are* turning up some interesting stuff."

I filled her in on what I'd seen in my necromantic re-creation of that day in the orchard, what the hawthorn had told Rowan and me, the upshot of our chat with Holly.

"Old and cold, like a parasite with its poison," Talia repeated, reaching up to rub her upper arms, which were stippled with goose bumps. "Too fucking macabre. You know what's weird . . . I wouldn't have put it exactly like that, but that's kind of what it felt like to me when I was possessed. But you wouldn't think an ani-mated tree could understand enough about necromantic magic to even be able to sense its presence, much less identify it."

"She understood enough to call me a daughter of the void," I said with a shrug. "I thought it was more interesting that it wasn't Emmy's magic that ended the spell, that the caster stopped of their own volition. Like they weren't trying to take the whole orchard out once Holly fell."

"And a Blackmoore as a prime suspect . . ." Talia lifted her chin, pale eyes turning cold. "I wouldn't mind seeing one of them go down for this. Especially if the bastard's trying to frame us."

"I'll fill you in after we talk to him. And I know I don't have to say this, but . . . this stays between us, right? No letting anything slip to Emmy?"

"You know I would never, sis." Her face settled into stern lines, an unyielding echo of our mother I didn't normally see in Talia. "This is strictly a family matter. And at times like this, family comes first."

The heaviness in my chest stirred, compounded by guilt—that was how *I* was supposed to feel about our family, too. But when I rummaged around for any such sense of uncomplicated devotion, all I found was confusion, laced with a little resentment. It didn't seem fair, somehow, to demand that kind of unthinking fealty, to be so uncompromising. From what I'd seen, that wasn't what the equally tight-knit Thorns expected from one another. What if I wanted just a little of that kind of latitude from my own clan?

Shit, why couldn't *anything* in my life be simple anymore?

AFTER BREAKFAST, I refilled the zebra finches' seed mix and water and made sure Elphaba the hedgie had a fresh nest of paper shavings before I retreated to my studio. Since I wasn't a white male genius fueled by cultivated anguish, I didn't tend to be at my most creative when mired in angst. But even with my stomach full of challah, that heavy feeling in my chest just wouldn't let up, clamoring for an outlet.

What if, I thought, curled up in the bay window with a sketch pad in my lap, beads of light spring rain crawling down the misty panes. Phedre and Imriel, my two black cats, sat together by my feet, purring in unison, while Moirin the Persian blue lounged on the floor below. Moirin was usually thick as thieves with Talia, despite technically being my pet, but all three of them had been sticking as close to me as possible since the poltergeist activity began.

What if, I asked myself, tapping my pen to paper, *the forest vampire clan with all their pretty, ethereal garb were actually the villains—judgmental fuckers who wouldn't cut their darker brethren a damn break?* And maybe the others weren't hard-edged city dwellers at all; maybe they were the denizens of a vast, abandoned cemetery next to the forest, so large and labyrinthine that it was almost a city unto itself. A graveyard that housed some trapped ancient evil, of which they were also the guardians.

And what if that evil got loose somehow, seeped into the forest, and tainted it, even as the guardian clan strove to contain it? As it tore its way through the woods, it would twist everything that it encountered, turning trees and flowers into monstrous things—infuriating the forest clan, who blamed the cemetery guardians for their failure, even though they'd done their utmost to prevent this horror from happening.

If I did it right, the macabre cemetery-dwellers would be the ones the visitors wound up rooting for.

It was a compelling concept, lending itself to all kinds of subtly creepy shit alongside the bigger scares. And I could see Letha running with such an expansive narrative, integrating the kind of immersive detail that would allow visitors to wander off and explore the haunted house on their own, delve into the side stories for as long as they wanted until they felt like rejoining the central story line.

The thing was, the conceit just didn't quite work with vampires. What in the hells were they all doing living in far-flung forests and abandoned cemeteries anyway, places that most living people tended to avoid? Vampires, by definition, needed to be somewhere they could hunt.

So maybe they weren't vampires. Maybe they were witches, from rival families.

I groaned at myself, at the painful obviousness of this ploy, even as the story grew legs, began galloping around my head. Shit, why not snatch inspiration wherever I could find it? So what if the villainous forest witches were obviously Thorns, the dark yet valiant cemetery dwellers clearly Avramovs? Not like the visitors would ever know.

And if a Thorn should ever wander in there and grasp the bigger picture, recognize themselves being vilified . . . well, so much the better.

I wasn't here to build any bridges. Rowan Thorn had made sure of that.

15

The Carnival of the Darkest Hour

LATE THAT NIGHT, the revelry invitation slid under my door like a sigh.

It was accompanied by the lightest of knocks, so insubstantial it might as well have been delivered by a shade. The kind of knock that would draw the attention of someone barely dozing or already awake, but not jar you from deep and restful REM.

Our late-night revelries were meant to be impromptu frolics, not disruptions or obligations. You were always welcome to sleep right through one; no one was going to come banging on your door to drag you downstairs.

But I had been awake and stewing, still mired in hurt and resentment, so I'd have heard it sail over my threshold even without that whisper of a knock. Heartbeat quickening with anticipation,

I scrambled out of bed, already wondering what Talia had dreamed up for us. Because ten to one, this revelry was Talia's handwork. Though Elena occasionally caught the whimsy to host one of her own, my sister was the mastermind behind most of our witching-hour parties.

Padding over on bare feet across the chilly floor, I bent to scoop up the invitation from where its corner had wedged under my door—dense black cardstock, inscribed with silver calligraphy. I summoned a tiny pearl of a witchlight, so I could read it without even turning on a lamp.

Revelries were an entire mood, and darkness was a major part of it.

Your presence is requested in the Wolfsbane Salon for an evening revelry, it read. *Please consider arriving in your finest carnival attire—though, as ever, pajamas will suffice.*

So we had a theme tonight, I thought, grinning to myself. Definitely Talia.

Fifteen minutes later, I rolled into the Wolfsbane Salon decked out in every sequined item of clothing I owned—a rainbow crop top I usually saved for Pride, over a silver miniskirt split by a black lightning bolt, and black combat boots splattered with gold glitter. I also had on a festive little headdress I'd bought at an actual carnival—a glossy magenta party hat with a sheer pink veil that fell over my eyes, like a cross between a fascinator and a trashy bachelorette tiara.

It clashed ridiculously with my hair, which only made it work even better.

The salon swirled with calliope music, in minor key harmonics that would have sounded not just pleasantly macabre but outright melancholy if they hadn't been underpinned by such a sick beat. It was almost a touch *too* cool, which meant Micah had probably chosen it; my brother's Spotify was a painfully hip space. There were no overhead lights on, of course, only points of candlelight. Enough to pierce the dark, but too few to create more than a dim, diffuse glow. The effect was of isolated spheres of light that seemed to bob like separate little galaxies against the salon's pervasive gloom, as if in mimicry of the veil itself. Dim shapes passed in front of the light like shadows, there and then gone, as The Bitters shades whisked around the room, drawn by the activity and the music.

With a few notable exceptions, like Lottie the chambermaid and the random Carmelite nun who haunted part of the attic and loathed the world at large, our demesne's ghosts loved our revelries.

Talia met me at the door, in a clinging body-con dress with her face painted like a harlequin's in black and gold. Emmy hung on her arm like her equal and opposite, her dress white to Talia's black, her face paint reversed. Sometimes, the two of them could really stand to be less cute together.

"Welcome to the Carnival of the Darkest Hour," Talia intoned with dramatic grandeur, the capitalized words unmistakable. She pressed a caramel-laced negroni into my hand, my favorite of her cocktails. "Dance, drink, mingle freely with your fellow mortals of a darker bent. Also there's popcorn and funnel cake, courtesy of me, obviously. And possibly some edibles, though you'd have to ask Micah about that."

Generally, given their late hour and spontaneous nature, these gatherings were limited to Avramovs—often it was just whoever of the family happened to be staying at The Bitters besides the five of us. But there was certainly no rule against partners attending, and Talia must have sent out her invitations widely tonight, probably using a dispersion spell to deliver them to guests outside of our demesne; there were at least forty people milling in the darkness behind her. Over Talia's shoulder I could see Letha and her girl-friend wearing black flower wreaths, Mardi Gras beads, and beaded flapper dresses in a very loose interpretation of "carnival." Micah had his latest throuple in tow, all three of them swathed in at least a dozen multicolored feather boas, shedding plumage everywhere.

Our cousins Cleo and Selah were here, too, their Afros glam-oured cotton-candy pink and turquoise, respectively, studded with hairpins shaped like shooting stars. Both they and their boyfriends wore gigantic party glasses and wielded huge sparklers, using them to scrawl hypnotic shapes in the air.

"Hey, Issa," Emmy added through giggles. "Just chilling with your extremely low-key master of ceremonies over here, don't mind me. *Love* the top."

"Forever 21," I admitted in a stage whisper. "But if you tell anyone, your remains will never be found."

Emmy was still chortling as Talia lunged forward and snatched me into a tight one-armed hug, brushing a kiss over my cheek. I'd probably be smeared with her gold face paint now, too, but hey, it'd only help me get into the spirit of things.

"Tonight's for you, okay?" she whispered into my ear. "So go forth, and please enjoy the entire fuck out of yourself. I know you need it."

"Thanks, *ses*," I whispered back, engulfed by such a flood of love for her that it felt overwhelming, impossible to contain.

After that, the revelry felt like they always did: a dark, delight-ful pandemonium, floating outside of space and time like some interstellar oasis. The hours and minutes shrinking and elongat-ing as they wheeled by us like a wayward flock of birds, until they lost most of their meaning and became only fleeting notions. Until the idea of tomorrow felt like legend, some mythical thing none of us would ever see. The rest of our lives would be spent right here, joyfully stranded in this liminal space. This dome of perfect night we'd carved out for ourselves, that smelled of powdered sugar and caramel.

"Darling," Micah said to me, when I wandered over through the darkness and the hovering drifts of eerie music to dance with him and his. "Darling," I replied breathlessly, exchanging air-kisses with him, letting him twirl me around and around until I went so dizzy he had to catch me against him, steady me as I stumbled. My brother smelled like so much weed that I could practically feel the contact high seep directly into my bloodstream. Weed generally wasn't my thing—my tweaky nervous system wasn't wired for it—but tonight I felt so easy and mellow that it seemed apropos.

At some point, Adriana joined the fray, her dark brown hair braided in some impossible way she'd probably learned on Tik-Tok, a slew of crystal pendants hanging around her neck, both her clothes and skin covered in glow-in-the-dark handprints. She'd been holding court in a corner of the salon like our very own Gen Z fortune-teller, giving fake tarot readings so purposely ludicrous that they made her "clients" howl with laughter.

I'd even seen Elena with tears of laughter running down her cheeks, and it took a lot to make our mother lose her vaunted cool.

"Bitch, don't you have school?" I asked Addie, a running joke between us. Addie was a stone-cold prodigy, the smartest of all of us by far, and a model student when she actually deigned to attend her classes. Her teachers were in such collective awe and terror of her that they mostly let her get away with showing up only when she felt like it.

It was probably easier—and safer—than mounting a resistance.

"Bitch, don't you have a life?" she retorted, grinning at me, her teeth a sharp flash in the dark.

"You're the resident scryer; you tell me."

She peered closely at me, the glitter of her eyes like twin stars suspended in the darkness.

"No evidence found of one," she concluded. "Just sewing needles and hedgehog litter, and birdcages with their little doors askew. And is that . . . oh, *dear*. The shade of a severely deceased pizza in your back seat. You should really probably exorcise that shit ASAP."

"And if I don't?" I asked, playing along.

"It'll expand to monstrous dimensions, and then terrorize the town," she told me cheerfully. "Think *Cloverfield*, but with extra cheese."

If only Rowan could see me now, I thought with a malicious glint as I laughed and danced with my little sister, spinning her around in circles. Shades drifting fondly around us like breezes enrobed in temporary flesh, passing so close their icy nearness met our skin with welcome cool. Brushing against us like ghostly kittens.

As if they loved us, too, like we were as much a home to them as The Bitters was itself.

As much as I'd seen the Thorns support one another, there was no way in all the hells that they ever delighted in each other quite so immersively as this. Like they'd made a whole separate world together, a rabbit hole writ cosmically large. A capricious realm that molded itself to them with such exquisite and perfect strangeness.

One that belonged to them entirely.

16

The Blackmoore Me

TWO DAYS LATER, before I was due to meet Rowan at Castle Camelot, I stopped by the Emporium for a quick consult with Elena. She often spent Sunday mornings poring over the monthly financials with Talia, and I'd been hoping to get her sign-off on my new-and-hopefully-improved concept for the haunted house.

"Oh, I love that. Fiendishly clever," she said once I wrapped up my summary, bright, mischievous interest glimmering in her eyes, "and *just* the right amount of brutal. I do enjoy seeing art imitating life, when it's done well—and I have no doubt that you and Letha will do the conceit justice. I take it you drew at least some inspiration from your collaboration with the Thorn scion?"

"You could say that," I replied sourly. Over by the mahogany bookshelf behind Elena's desk, where Talia stood on her tiptoes in search of a particular binder, my sister's shoulders stiffened. "Speaking of, I did wonder if dunking on them wasn't the most . . .

diplomatic tack to take, given the circumstances. You know, in the event a Thorn finds their way into the show once it's open, maybe gets their panties in a twist."

"A doubtful proposition," Elena said with a blithe shrug. "They don't truck much with horror; I can't see one of them paying for the privilege of experiencing it. But even so. Veiled reference though it clearly is to what's happening between our families now, your premise is also entirely true, isn't it? On the whole, their family *does* tend to find ours . . . objectionable, at the best of times."

"To put it mildly," Talia muttered over her shoulder, yanking the binder out of its slot so violently that the entire sturdy bookshelf quaked.

"So why not use the medium you have to present a different point of view?" Elena finished, reaching behind her to give Talia's arm a quelling little squeeze. "I don't see any problem with it. By the time you open, I have no doubt your investigation will have exonerated our family, in any case. And if the Thorns still choose to take exception to a little bit of pointed art, well . . . such a lack of both imagination and self-awareness will be on them."

I nodded, Elena's confidence flooding through the raw fissures in my chest like some healing ointment. Despite the welter of my own conflicted thoughts, it felt so good—so necessary—to find myself back on the same page with her. To feel like we were cut of the same cloth again, even if only for a moment.

The revelry had soothed my spirit, too, reminding me of just how deeply I belonged to and with my family. But my mother's enthusiasm and approval went even further, somehow, made me feel more stable than I had in weeks.

"How do you do it?" I asked her, my hands knotting into fists on my lap. "Collaborate with Gabrielle Thorn every day to work on helping Holly? Doesn't that soaring moral righteousness ever grate on you?"

Elena tilted her head back and forth consideringly, her foxy hair catching the light from the stained-glass lamps like fluid sparks.

"Not so far, no. For one thing, Gabrielle's not nearly so dogmatic as her son," she said mildly, spreading her hands. "Remember, she married into magic, rather than growing up here like Rowan has. The notion that we're the Dread Darkness personified isn't ingrained in her in such an incorruptible way. I find her company very enjoyable, actually. She's quite a bit more irreverent than many of them, when she feels like showing her edge."

"Rowan must take after his father, then," I muttered—though in fairness, Aspen Thorn had never been anything but scrupulously polite to me. But that played right into the Thorns' holier-than-thou attitude, didn't it? That they were just *far* too kind and upstanding to be openly rude to us was part of their whole shtick. "Because I can tell you for a fact that he isn't half as tolerant as Gabrielle. Pretty sure he thinks we all might be worse than any actual forces of evil that walk this land. Or that *I* might, anyway."

Talia dropped the binder down onto Elena's desk with such a forceful thump that it rattled the spiny candelabra set.

"Pardon me, my fellow demonic empresses," she snapped, the words vibrating with pent-up rage. "I have to go use the little succubi's room. Maybe open some portals to the hells on my way back, check in on our infernal domain. Let you know how it goes, 'kay?"

With that, she wheeled around and marched out the door, not *quite* slamming it closed behind her but leaving no doubt that this would have been her preference.

Once she was gone, Elena and I exchanged bemused looks.

"What's gotten into her?" I wondered, scrunching up my face. "The demonstrative flouncing off is usually more in my wheelhouse. Seems like she's been a little keyed up, lately."

"I'm not sure what's troubling her," Elena admitted, her eyes drifting back toward the door, those delicate worry lines marring the milky skin between her brows. "For one thing, I don't think she takes kindly to the idea of an intransigent Thorn disrespecting her sister, even if he does happen to be a former ally. And to be clear, *lisichka*, neither do I. But your collaboration is a necessary evil, and I find that these misunderstandings often tend to resolve themselves. And if they don't, well, you know what they say."

"What do they say?" I asked, the corners of my own mouth tugging up in response to the arch wickedness that flitted like firelight over my mother's face.

"Wiping the floor with an obstinate man is the very *best* revenge," she answered with a sly flourish. "And once you delve to the bottom of this mess on your own devices, I doubt he'll ever condescend to you again."

BY THE TIME I met Rowan at Castle Camelot, I was feeling much more composed. In the wake of the revelry and my conversation with Elena, the void in my chest had mostly subsided, filling with a fresh groundswell of resolve. I was going to crack this case wide open, as the best possible way to stick it to Rowan Thorn.

Even though they'd had advance notice that we were coming, the Blackmoores had parked us in Camelot's gigantic theater until Gawain saw fit to make himself available. Unlike the Renn Faire kitsch of the rest of their medieval castle—all snarling gargoyles and looming suits of armor tucked into every corner—the theater was more classically majestic, a grandiose space clearly intended to inspire awe as a backdrop to the shows. A waterfall chandelier hung from the dome-vaulted ceiling, dripping with icy crystals, a gold-flecked mural of the Knights of the Round Table painted above it. Rowan and I had been seated in one of the velvet-curtained balconies—hey, at least they were *pretending* we were VIPs—while a matinee performance of *Merlin and Vivien* unfolded below.

As town legend had it, the Blackmoores were descended from Morgan le Fay, King Arthur's mythical sorceress, and they sure as shit never let anyone forget it.

"Do you think the Lady of the Lake *actually* wore a sequined bodysuit under her robes?" I wondered aloud to Rowan as the sorceress let her robe slip from her shoulders, emerging all aglisten from an actual pond built into the stage. "Seems anachronistic, but what the fuck do I know."

Rowan shot me yet another uneasy glance. He'd been peering at me warily since we arrived, trying to puzzle me out. I'd settled on a strategy of killing him with oblivious kindness—acting as though That Forsaken Night had never even happened, as if nothing between us were amiss at all. The exact opposite of what he might be expecting from a spurned Avramov.

It was working *wonderfully* so far, in terms of keeping him off balance.

"Merlin seems to be feeling it," Rowan finally said, with a shrug. "Which is probably what counts."

I gave a thoughtful nod, gazing down at the stage, where the extremely statuesque Vivien was sashaying toward an equally hot

Merlin, intent on seduction. Airborne coils of water snaked all around her, gleaming as if illuminated by different hues of light: a twilit plum, the silver glaze of moonlight, the liquid gold of setting sun. While some of the show relied on mundane special effects, parts like this were clearly magic—not that the audience, or likely even the normie actors involved, would ever realize as much. Because they had no reason to suspect that this *was* real magic, the oblivion glamour wouldn't kick in, either, which meant they'd all remember every last sensational detail.

It was annoyingly ingenious on the Blackmoores' part, even if they were taking some serious liberties with Arthurian legend. For one, I was pretty sure the wizard Merlin and the fabled enchantress of Avalon hadn't looked like CrossFit enthusiasts who moonlighted on a CW show.

"They do have solid chemistry," I agreed. "And at least she can really sing. He's kind of half-assing it, but then again, I guess this *is* the matinee."

We lapsed into silence, watching the spectacle unfold. Merlin and Vivien had launched into a sexy duet, a glittering wave of sparks streaming from the wizard's gnarled staff and entwining with the enchantress's watery ribbons as the two circled each other, much to the audience's delight.

Something *very* visually dramatic was going to pop off when they finally locked lips, I knew it in my bones.

"Isidora," Rowan started, voice gritty with discomfort, "about the other night. I just wanted to make sure we—"

"Dude, we're cool," I cut him off, turning to toss him a bright, empty smile. "Really. Don't spare it another thought. We were drunk, it was dumb, end of story, okay? Let's neither of us worry about it anymore."

Rowan surveyed me, clear hazel gaze shifting between my eyes, looking so genuinely distressed that a shadow of that hollow ache in my chest leapt up again. *He doesn't actually care about how you feel, remember? He's just making sure you don't go rogue on him, derail the investigation.*

"Alright, then," he said, shooting me an uncertain smile before turning back to the stage. "If you say we're cool, we're cool."

Fresh pain flared in my gut that he'd let it go so easily, before I squashed it into oblivion. This was the better path, I told myself. How much worse would I feel if I let him see how badly it had hurt me, to have had him pull me close only to shove me away with such determined aversion?

Avramovs didn't roll weak like that, not if we could help it.

A few minutes later—just as the sexual tension on the stage built to a crescendo of epic proportions—a Blackmoore flunky costumed as a medieval squire appeared from the double doors at our backs to usher us to our rendezvous with Gawain. We rose to follow him, me pausing every few feet to twist over my shoulder, just in case Merlin and Vivien might finally be making out.

"This timing blows. I can't believe we're missing out on the smooch to end all smooches," I groused to Rowan. "Cheated out of our money's worth."

"I mean, we didn't actually buy any tickets," Rowan muttered back, a corner of his mouth flicking up.

"*Hardly* the point."

We trailed the squire down stony corridors, Blackmoore pennants of black and gold strung up along the walls, following him up winding staircases until we reached the castle's topmost floor. He swung open a heavy wooden door clasped with iron hinges, and beckoned us through before melting away. I felt a tiny burst of envy that the Blackmoores could afford to hire actual gracious attendants, while *we* had Lottie's testy shade popping up from cracks in the grubby Bitters tiles to hector us about our sloppy regrouting skills.

Truly, this life wasn't fair.

Even though we were clearly in one of the castle's turreted towers, the sleek office beyond the door seemed like it had been lifted from some entirely different venue—possibly a skyscraper housing an expensive law firm. The floor was creamy rose marble, the walls adorned in (deathly dull) abstract pieces in muted pastel shades. An airbrushed, poreless blonde sat behind the massive executive desk that occupied the center of the room, in a charcoal Alexander McQueen pantsuit with the kind of flawless structure that made my hands itch with want—not to wear myself, but to make. This was Nineve Blackmoore, the middle child of the Blackmoore main line and Gawain's older sister.

Gawain Blackmoore himself sat in a black leather swivel chair beside his sister's desk, his knobby ankle propped up on his opposite knee in that thoughtlessly obnoxious manspreading way. He was as angel-faced and pouty as I remembered, with ultramarine eyes and long, sunny blond curls swept back from his high forehead like a lion's mane. He wore distressed jeans and a blue blazer, over a white tee silk-screened with a smirking gray scale Prince holding out a magenta rose. A gold signet ring and a pair of bespoke navy Sperrys completed the entire grating look.

Beside me, I could almost *feel* Rowan chuckling silently, deep inside himself—and I couldn't blame him. I was having a very hard time determining what Holly might've seen in this ridiculous hothouse orchid of a bro besides the pretty face.

"Mr. Thorn, Ms. Avramov," Nineve said, giving us a polite but clipped smile. "Sorry to keep you waiting. Gawain had an artistic crisis to manage with one of the cast."

"Our Sir Pelleas is being a bit of a prima donna," Gawain said, widening his eyes for emphasis and raking a hand over his curls, careful not to muss them too much. "Frankly, I've had it up to here with his nonstop bullshit. The way that gasbag carries on, you'd think all of Broadway's out there just *mooning* over his—"

"Gav," Nineve broke in, with a barely perceptible eye roll that instantly made me like her more. "I know he's been very frustrating to manage. Believe me, we *all* know. But let's not get carried away."

Closing his eyes, Gawain brought three fingers together in front of his forehead and slowly drew them down to hover over his navel, sucking a deep breath in through his nose like he was striving for some elusive serenity.

"You'll have to excuse me," he said on a long exhale. "It can be so hard to set all that noise and junk aside and just *be*, you know? Sometimes I think, hey, maybe it would actually be so great for my mental health to take a step back, instead of composing *and* directing our entire repertoire . . ."

So the angsty high school front man had grown into an equally high-strung Andrew Lloyd Webber wannabe, in charge of Camelot's entertainment. It all made a terrible kind of sense—I was basically looking at the Blackmoore me.

And it was not a pretty sight.

"*Never*, Gav," Nineve protested, wide-eyed, and this time the sarcasm was so plain I couldn't believe her brother didn't catch on. Hey, maybe the Blackmoores weren't *all* bad.

"Oh, you know I wouldn't, Nina," he assured her, mollified. "I'm just so fucking exhausted, beyond burned out . . . and it's only going to get worse, with the festival coming up. Anyway, woes for another day, right? And you two—you're here about Holly."

The offhand way he made this proclamation somehow implied that he'd been the one to summon us, like we'd appeared at his behest instead of the other way around. A prickle of irritation lodged like a burr just under my skin.

"Actually, we're here about *you*," Rowan corrected flatly, clearly just as annoyed. "And your relationship with Holly. Which makes me wonder why you're in the room at all, Ms. Blackmoore."

"Because I serve as in-house counsel to Blackmoore Enterprises, Mr. Thorn," Nina replied with another brisk snapshot of a smile, there and gone so quickly you couldn't be totally sure you hadn't imagined it. "An enterprise that Gawain happens to be an integral part of. It's just out of an abundance of caution, you understand. Feel free to pretend I'm not even here."

"This isn't some normie criminal investigation," I broke in. "And we're not the police—you *know* that isn't how this works. We'd prefer to talk to Gawain alone."

Another crisp smile, nude lip gloss flashing over small, even teeth, a combative flame flaring in her dark brown eyes. She was a tame, predictable kind of pretty, but that unexpected flash of spirit brought her tidy features close to beautiful.

"To my knowledge, the Grimoire doesn't prohibit legal representation in situations of this nature," she said, still in that unruffled tone. "Which means you have no authority to request that I excuse myself. Given that my brother is willing to proceed only with me in the room, I suggest that's what we do. So why don't you both take a seat?"

Rowan made a disgruntled sound deep in his throat, but caught my eye and gave a little nod. This was clearly not a fight we were going to win; arguing would only waste what time we had with Gawain.

Once we'd sat down in the sleek chairs, I took the lead. "Let's start with you telling us about your relationship with Holly, Gawain," I said.

"There's no *relationship*," Gawain retorted, mouth twisting with disdain. "We dated, it wasn't working, so we broke it off. That's it, *fini*. Not much to tell."

"Not exactly how we heard it," Rowan said, rocking his head from side to side. "You sure Holly wasn't the one to end things?"

"And this matters how?" Gawain huffed, squinting at us. "What are we, still in high school? Who gives an actual fuck about who broke up with whom?"

"Someone burned Holly's magic right out of her at the Crowning," I said, anger leaping into my tone, "and whether or not she gets it back is still up in the air. So the answer is, *we do*."

Gawain paled at that, eyes flying wild between us. "So she *is* hurt!" he burst out, rasping a hand over his blond stubble. "I keep trying to call her, just to check in, see how she is. But all I get is stonewalled. I've been losing my mind over it, and she can't even be bothered to pick up the phone, so much as shoot me a text . . ."

"Sounds like maybe there *are* still some feelings there, after all," I suggested. His affront at the fact that Holly wouldn't deign to call him back seemed real, but it could be veiled guilt, or even just a flat-out act. "On your end, anyway."

"It's not just on my end—what we had was *real*," he insisted, jaw set stubbornly. "I don't care what she told you, how she's spinning it now. You don't just shut off emotions like that, like a spigot. Even if you're an utter fucking ice queen like Holly Thorn."

Wow, the Pisces *was* strong in him. He probably had the sign as an ascendant, too; it would explain a whole lot. And if he was still this pressed about how things had fallen out between them, it would give him something that looked much like motive.

Rowan shifted in his seat beside me, radiating that restrained aura of gravity-like menace, obviously sharing the same line of thought.

"Wait," Gawain said slowly into our silence, splotches of color mottling his face. "Are you—are you seriously suggesting that I might have done this to Holly? That I might have *cursed* my own ex with a necromantic hex, for breaking up with me? Shit, *you*— you're an Avramov! This is the type of screwy garbage you all get into, not us!"

"Watch yourself, now," Rowan cautioned through his teeth, a muscle twitching in his jaw—and in spite of everything, it made me just a little happy to see him come to my defense. "And while we're at it, how did you know Holly might be hurt? Saw it happen, or just heard about it?"

"Okay, yeah, I was at the Crowning. Along with just about every other witch in Thistle Grove. But I mean, come on. You *must* know what my family is to this town. Who the hell are either of you, to accuse me of some completely batshit thing like this?"

"Easy, Gav," Nina said, spreading one small hand flat on her pebbled leather blotter, clearly aware that *Do you even know who I am* wasn't her brother's best look. "I know talking about this is upsetting for you. Understandably so. But how about we all take a beat? Ms. Avramov and Mr. Thorn are only aiming to get to the bottom of things—and at the end of the day, isn't that what we want, too?"

After a moment, Gawain nodded, working his jaw from side to side, like he was used to taking stage directions from his big sister.

In the window behind him, lightning carved across the leaden sky, pulsing in irregular rhythm like some monster's heart shuddering to life. It had begun pounding rain, the kind of melodramatic deluge Thistle Grove only mounted every once in a rare while.

I'd bet my last red cent that this corny asshat relished the effect.

"Right, right, yeah," he said, still nodding furiously, some of the color fading from his face. "Sorry, yeah. I just . . . I'm a really passionate person, you know? And I despise it when someone paints me in the wrong light. Having a vibrant inner life is not a *character flaw*, last I checked."

"Why do you think Holly would misrepresent the situation to us?" I asked, trying to take my cue from Nina and keep my tone nonconfrontational, handle this touchy softboi with kid gloves.

"Why don't you ask her that—or better yet, ask Juniper Thorn," he sniped. "Holly's best friend. She was forever in Holly's ear about us . . . making me look bad, telling her to break things off with me. Ten to one, bitch was just jealous of what we had, of anything Holly had that she didn't. So why don't you go see about what *she* was up to when shit went down."

Rowan and I exchanged fleeting looks. We knew exactly where Juniper Thorn had been when the curse struck Holly, because she'd been one of the other contestants on the stage—and not only that, but Juniper was also the substitute who'd been chosen by Emmy to take Holly's place as May Queen. Which suggested that there might actually be something to Gawain's flailing accusations.

On the other hand, Holly hadn't mentioned her best friend at all when we spoke to her, or even brought up Juniper's involvement in her decision to end things with Gawain.

"Are you suggesting that Juniper might've had a reason to hurt her own best friend?" Rowan said, making no effort to keep the disbelief from his tone. "And not just friend, but cousin?"

"What I'm suggesting is, you go harass her instead of me," Gawain said, crossing his arms over his chest. "Because I'm done here. Nothing more to say.."

"If that's so," Rowan said, playing our sleeve ace, "I assume you'd be willing to take an oath upon the lake. Just to verify what you've said."

"Oh, the hell I would," Gawain snapped, temper flaring again. "I wouldn't swear a lakebound oath to verify my own damn name. No fucking way. You have no right to ask me to do that."

"What my brother means to say," Nina broke in smoothly, steepling her hands, "is that such drastic measures don't seem to be called for yet. And our family will back Gawain in this regard—a lakebound oath is a substantial risk for any witch to undertake, given how unpredictable we all know the lake's magic to be in its assessment of truth. Otherwise the oath would have been invoked much more often than it has been in our history."

"But you do agree that the Grimoire vests us with the authority to make a request like this," Rowan countered, lifting his eyebrows, "in pursuit of whoever did this."

"And should you and Ms. Avramov fail to make further headway in your investigation, we would be open to reconsidering," she replied. "But at the moment, Gawain will—*respectfully*—decline to swear."

Nina must have seen this angle coming, to be able to shift the burden onto us so deftly—making it look as though our own failure to flush out the culprit were driving us to make such an unreasonable demand. But she was also right, to a degree; taking the lakebound oath *was* a massive ask. We couldn't force Gawain to take it, and we also couldn't consider his refusal as evidence of guilt. Many entirely innocent witches would choose to duck it just as he had, unwilling to make even the most minor gamble with their magic.

"Then we won't take up any more of your time," Rowan declared, dusting off his thighs and standing. "But like you said. Need be, know that we'll be back."

Gawain shot us a sulky stare, eyes at half-mast, having transitioned into petulance.

"Whatever, man," he said, slumping in his chair. "I didn't do anything to Holly. And if you're going to talk to her again, or to Juniper, please do convey that I don't appreciate their slandering my good name."

I stood to follow Rowan to the door, tipping Nina Blackmoore a wry little salute. She'd played this like a pro, and you couldn't really blame her for protecting her own, even if her whole family kind of blew.

"I really like your Lady of the Lake, by the way," I tossed over my shoulder to Gawain as I turned toward the door. "I mean, that bodysuit, à la early 2000s Britney? *Super* authentic, almost to a fault."

The last thing I saw before the door slammed shut behind us was the deeply satisfying shade of puce creeping up his face.

17

Snakes of Cold Breath

Lark Thorn's studio—A workspace she shared with the owners of the Silver Cherry, one of Thistle Grove's pricier jewelers—was on Hyssop Street, only a few blocks away from the Emporium. But until today, I'd never been inside. From the whisper-dainty pieces always on display in the windows, bathed in warm pools of light, I'd figured it wasn't really my style.

"Are you sure this detour is the right call?" I asked Rowan as we walked up to the store, its name dashed across the glass door in calligraphic silver foil. We were huddled together under a single black-and-gold umbrella we'd grudgingly picked up at the Castle Camelot gift store, its spindly frame thrashing above our heads. I wasn't loving having to stand so close to Rowan, the humidity in the air whetting the soap and citrus of his scent, but the alternative was getting drenched.

"Shouldn't we be going straight to Juniper," I continued, "what with First Dew happening tomorrow?"

Holly's apartment had been warded to the hells and back by all four of the families, and she hadn't strayed far from it during her magical convalescence. But she was holding firm on attending First Dew, even if she couldn't preside over it as Queen. Given how central the ceremony was to our pre-Beltane festivities, and the fact that it was one of our more sacred rituals to boot, it seemed beyond cruel to deny her the chance to participate. Especially when she should have been the one leading it.

Of course, the elders would all be on high alert, along with a rotating guard of Avramovs on the lookout for any necromantic castings. But there was always the risk of the caster seizing the opportunity to at least take another shot at her.

"Let's be clear, I'm nowhere close to buying Gawain's ripe bullshit," Rowan said, shaking his head. "And even if it was Juniper—she already got what she wanted, right? She's Queen instead of Holly, so the risk of any further bad shit going down tomorrow is minimal."

"That's true, I guess."

"But like you said, rule number . . . whatever it was. We investigate everyone involved, even Thorn suspects. And before we do, I want all our ducks in a row—including whether it would've been possible for Juniper to pull off something like that hex at all, with help."

"And your sister can clue us in about this?"

"Bespelled amulets are Lark's jam," Rowan said, breaking into a smile at the mention of his little sister. "Or a part of it, anyway. You'll see."

He shouldered the door open, with me scuttling in behind him as he snapped the umbrella shut and turned to shake it out over the threshold. Trust Rowan Thorn, (Exceedingly Considerate) Wildlife Hero, not to drip inside a nice establishment. Maybe he'd be equally considerate of me if I were more a pretty herringbone tiled floor, less an aggravating Avramov.

Inside, the store was empty, weekend browsers deterred by the downpour. Paper cutouts of silver cherries and stars dangled on wire strung from between the twinkling recessed lights. Like the window display, the jewelry in the cases was filament fine, meant to be intricately layered. The kind of ultra-delicate accessories I rarely wore myself but could see pairing with some of the statement-piece clothing I wanted to design.

One of the velvet mounts on more prominent display held three silver necklaces nested inside one another, the chains so slim their loops seemed more shimmer than shape, each adorned with the very tiniest of pendants. A beetle, a bee, and a crescent moon curved around a flower, all set with a minuscule gemstone.

"That's one of Lark's," Rowan said, drawing up behind my shoulder. "Pretty amazing, right?"

I bent to inspect the pendants more closely, marveling over the held-breath finesse, their exceptional delicacy. It seemed almost impossible that human hands could have made something so small and fine, especially without magic involved.

"It is," I said, my breath fogging the glass. "She's really talented."

"More like a hopeless workaholic with no social life to speak of," a warm voice interjected from behind the counter. "Easy to make neat stuff, when you do literally *nothing* else."

I looked up to see Rowan's little sister slip in through the door that led to the back of the store, shooting us a bright smile. Lark Thorn was dark-skinned and pretty, a softer-looking version of her mother, Gabrielle. Her cheeks were high and round, hair twisted into complicated cornrows drawn away from her dewy face before spilling down her back. She wore a tasseled marigold caftan slipping off one shoulder, her skin radiant against it, and tiny earrings marched all the way up her lobes. Her nails were a creamy yellow, subtler than the dress, some of them accented with harlequin patterns in ruby and gold lined with black.

After Gawain's visual nonsense, just looking at her was like a palate cleanser.

Rowan slung a possessive arm around her neck as she stepped out from behind the counter, yanking her close to press a kiss on the side of her head. She looped her own arm around his waist, grinning up at him. I felt a sharp pang of envy at such easy closeness, the effortless camaraderie.

The kind I used to have with my own family, especially my mother.

"Wouldn't kill you to work a *little* less, kid," Rowan said, beaming down at her. "Maybe we'd get to see more of you over at the cottage. But now that I see what you've been getting into over here, I gotta admit, it might be worth missing a family dinner. Or three. Or four."

"Okay, ouch. I've been the worst, I know. Will you tell Mama and Dad I'm sorry?" Lark said with a penitent pout, making puppy eyes at her brother. "I'd tell them myself, but last time I canceled on them, Mama's texts had that kind of *tone*, you know? Like she loves and supports me unconditionally, but if I don't start showing up more I still might just get myself disowned."

"Stop it. I may be the firstborn, but you know her baby can do no wrong. Just go all out for Mother's Day. She'll forgive you so fast your head'll spin."

Lark chewed on her lower lip, flicking up a thick eyebrow. "You know, that's not a bad idea. Maybe I *will* make something special just for her." Her gaze shifted to me. "Sorry, that's probably way too much family talk for you. On the phone, Row said you two needed a consult on amulets . . . for your investigation, right?"

"You know it," I said. "Specifically, whether an amulet could be enchanted to contain a necromantic hex like the Misbegotten Curse. So that even a Thorn could wear and trigger it, even if they couldn't cast a spell like that on their own."

"Interesting." She gave a thoughtful nod, eyes narrowing. "I do some of that kind of work, in my Thornspell line; it's all jewelry infused with magic. I mostly stick to the healing cantrips, though, which you'll know Thorns can work with no issue anyway. But I do beauty glamours sometimes, too. The Blackmoore type of stuff that's much harder for us to cast."

"What kind of glamours?" I asked, intrigued. We sold cosmetics allegedly imbued with spells like that at the Avramov Apothecary, too, but none of it actually worked.

"Oh, you know, fun, whimsical things. Necklaces that'll change your eye color for a night, or make your hair and eyes all glowy, give you a little of that je ne sais quoi for a date," she said, dancing her shoulders playfully and widening her eyes.

"And you sell them not just to witches, but to normie buyers, too?" I said, a little taken aback. The legitimately occult objects and apparel we peddled at the Emporium were magically inert— meaning they *could* be used for spellcraft, but only by someone who had the necessary talent and skill. Beyond telling fortunes, it had never occurred to us to sell real, active magic.

"Yeah, but with a catch," she said, dark eyes sparkling with mischief. "I sell it exclusively out of this storefront, never online—and all of it only works within town lines, subject to a tweaked oblivion glamour. So whoever buys a piece can use its spell here, but they'll forget what happened as soon as they leave town. At most, they'll remember it as a very vivid dream they had while they were here. You know, the kind that feel like they really happened."

"Wow, smart take," I said, nodding along. "And what a freaking treat for a normie buyer, no matter how much of it they remember. Great way to broaden your customer base."

"Pretty economical, too, while I save up enough to hang my own shingle. That's how my arrangement with the Cherry owners works; they're super into the 'gimmick' of carrying enchanted jewelry made by a 'real witch' from a town founding family," she said, making playful finger quotes. "So they let me work in their studio space for free . . . as long as I'm also cool with working the counter a few shifts a week, like today."

"My baby sister the entrepreneur, turning her side hustle into a career," Rowan said affectionately, not a trace of resentment or disappointment to his tone. "What a trip."

"So you're not planning on sticking around here?" I asked, wondering why this conversation was suddenly making me so anxious, jitters buzzing in my joints, zinging into my toes and fingertips in a familiarly unsettling way.

I hadn't had a panic attack in years, though they'd been a frequent occurrence when I was younger. But now I could feel one brewing, on the periphery of my awareness. My nervous system gearing up for it, the way you could smell a bad storm coming long before the sky turned a dangerous green.

"Oh, no way. I never intended to limit myself by catering only to witches," Lark said, beckoning us to follow as she headed back toward the door behind the counter. "It's fun, for sure, but that wasn't ever the dream. I have an entirely separate mundane line, too, my Larksong pieces. Just normal, pretty jewelry for normal, pretty humans. That's the stuff I push everywhere online, sell via all the socials and Etsy and Local Eclectic. The space I want to *really* make my name in as a designer."

With Rowan at my heels, I trailed Lark into the brightly lit storeroom-slash-studio at the back of the store, the walls lined with storage racks and rows of stacked plastic containers, soldering supplies neatly laid out along the metal worktables. As we followed her to one, my mind still wheeling and my lips a little tingly, I realized what my problem was.

Stumbling across common ground I hadn't expected to share with Rowan's sister.

Lark designed magical items, yes, but she wasn't affiliated with Honeycake Orchards at all, like so many of the other Thorns. And even though she made spell-imbued necklaces, she was actively pursuing her bigger, deeper dream—a future as a designer operating within the mundane world.

The exact thing I desperately wished I could do in fashion, without letting down my family.

"And your parents . . . they don't mind that you're not part of the Honeycake business at all?" I asked her, trying to make it sound like a casual question. "That you're working to build out a full-time non-witch venture?"

"Oh, I'm sure they'd love having me underfoot all the time, Mama especially. But, *mind*?" She scrunched up her face, like, *How ridiculous.* "Of course not. They seem pretty damn proud to see me out here, chasing what I love more than anything."

I opened my mouth to ask a follow-up question, only to realize that Rowan was staring at me again, with that off-putting intensity threaded through with confusion. As though I were an increasingly challenging puzzle he was hard-pressed to figure out.

"So, about curses in amulets," I said, hoping this turn might guide me back to solid ground, head off the monsoon building inside me. "What can you tell us? For starters, do you think you could make one?"

"Honestly, I've never even thought to try," she said, with a broad shrug that reminded me of Rowan's own mannerism. "Why in the world would I ever mess with any of that?"

"Would you be comfortable trying now, sis, while we're here?" Rowan asked, setting a hand on her shoulder. "Just to see how far you get?"

"You mean, embedding an *actual* curse into an amulet?" she said, her face tightening with reluctance. "Even if it turns out I can, I'm not sure that's safe. Or, frankly, something I want to do at all."

"We wouldn't even need to trigger it," I assured her. "If we go with a necromantic hex—a much less nasty one than the Misbegotten Curse, of course—I should be able to *feel* whether it would work, without having to set it off. And we'll make sure to safely dispose of it afterward, of course."

Lark scraped the inside of her lower lip with her teeth, dark eyes troubled.

"Row?" she finally said, her gaze shifting to her brother. "You sure about this? It's still a malignant working, meant to cause harm. You know we don't do that, ever."

"The way I see it, the intention is what matters—and it'd be for the good," Rowan said, giving her a firm nod. "And Issa, she's a stone-cold necromantic badass. Like a heavyweight champion at all that dark shit. Anything goes wrong, you can trust her to contain it, protect all three of us. You know I wouldn't ask you to do this otherwise, if I didn't think she had your back."

I nodded, as if I weren't rocked to my core to hear Rowan vouch for me this way, with such sincere trust. He was doing it only to reassure his sister, put her mind at ease before she cast something that would take a heavy toll on her both physically and morally. But I knew him well enough by now to know that no matter what, he wouldn't lie to her—which meant his confidence in my abilities must be genuine.

It was weirdly nice to know that my reluctant partner had stumbled his way into some legitimate respect for my magic.

"Okay, then," Lark said, her face clearing. "That's what I needed to hear."

She scraped back one end of the bench tucked beneath the table and slipped in front of it, tugging it under her as she sat. There was a partitioned wooden box set out in front of her, filled with little plastic ziplocks. She plucked one out of its nook, peeling the bag open and dipping her fingers into it to fish out a tiny gold locket on a chain.

"This one's already hopeless, anyway," she murmured, inspecting it with a wrinkled nose before she let it pool in her palm. "Came out a little too wonky even for intentional asymmetry. May as well put it to some use."

She folded her long fingers around it, closing her eyes. I could feel the rising hum of energy gathering around her, the cloud of nonspecific magic she'd summoned up.

"Can you walk us through what you're doing?" I said quietly, not wanting to interrupt her flow too much.

"Yeah, no problem. Right now I'm just pooling magic into the locket," she said, brow furrowed with concentration. "Drawing as much as I can from the lake and infusing it into the gold. Like with metalsmithing, it's always better to have a surplus than a scarcity; if there's any magic left over once I'm done shaping the embedded spell, it'll just flow right back to its source. Whereas if I came up short, I'd have to purge the gem, start all over again. Waste of time, and a significant pain in the butt."

Rowan and I waited in silence for her to finish, the thrum of gathering magic like static electricity, buzzing against our skin. I usually loved the way magic felt before it was given shape, the vibrant, living potency of it, but right now it only amplified the unpleasant judder of my nerves. I bounced from foot to foot, shifting my weight, trying to bleed off some tension as Lark worked.

"Okay," she finally said, opening her eyes. "It's full of juice. What do you want me to try to do with it?"

"Do you know the Serpentinus Hex?" I asked her.

That particular hex was in the first tranche of nonlethal curses listed in the Baneful Workings section of the Grimoire—which made me think that even a Thorn might have stumbled across it in their studies of our shared spellbook, if they had any curiosity at all about the dark side. If cast properly, it would summon up a chunk of ectoplasm, enough to hatch a clutch of ghostly snakes you could then sic on an enemy. They weren't real serpents, but they were eldritch as fuck and they *could* bite, in an awful way that infused the victim with bone-chilling terror and nightmares instead of venom.

In hindsight, given the hideous panoply of vengeance tools at my disposal, Rowan should've thanked his lucky stars I'd stuck to creepy squirrels.

"Ugh, really?" Lark complained, screwing up her face. "That one's *horrible.*"

"It's actually not that bad, as curses go," I said with a shrug. "But at the same time, it's demanding enough that I think it'll be telling, whether or not you're able to embed it."

Lark nodded, rolling her shoulders as she psyched herself up for what was sure to be an unpleasant experience. While Thorns could theoretically cast necromantic spells, it was so miserably difficult for them—running so counter to the natural bent of their own magical talents, and so foreign to their do-no-harm philosophy—that the extent of their limitations wasn't even completely clear. What was more, Lark had probably not only never done anything like this, but also never even thought about it.

And when it came to shaping magic, thought mattered most of all. It was the needle that sewed the spell into its final shape, looped with the bright and pulsing thread of the caster's will.

Eyes closing, Lark started slow, murmuring the words under her breath in a halting tone. I would have used my hands much more to get things going, modulated the working with movements of my fingers—necromantic magic responded beautifully to that kind of sculpting—but clearly that wasn't something that came naturally to her.

"Snakes of cold breath, serpents from death," she chanted, and I was relieved to hear her place the emphasis on the right syllables, landing hard on that sibilant hiss. "Born to sow terror, to reap in stealth. To bite dread into those who creep against me, until these same rue and repent . . ."

It did sound wrong as all the hells, those baneful words carried in Lark's sweet voice. But she'd gained steam, started funneling real effort into the casting, a fine sheen of sweat rising on her temples. I could tell she was a talented witch, nearly as strong as her brother, from the meticulous finesse with which she worked even this unfriendly casting that she'd never handled before.

But as she launched into her seventh recitation, I could hear a ragged catch in her breath, her eyelids fluttering with strain. The spell was wearing on her, and badly—even though she was only embedding it, not casting it outright. Rowan made a distressed sound low in his throat, moving as if to set a hand on his sister's shoulder. I caught his elbow and drew him back, shaking my head. You broke the flow of a necromantic hex to absolutely everyone's peril; it wasn't the kind of working that brooked interruptions well.

By the time Lark reached the twenty-seventh and final recitation, sweat was streaming down her neck, darkening the cheerful yellow of her dress. Her entire body trembled with strain, the soft lines of her pretty face drawn stark with revulsion.

The spell itself clearly *felt* wrong to her, somehow viscerally bad.

"There," she breathed, opening her eyes, which were now cloudy and threaded with red, as if she'd pulled one all-nighter too many. "I think . . . damn, I think I did it. I think that awful thing is really in there, all pent up."

She thrust the locket at me with a shaking hand, opening her fist almost before I had a chance to catch it, obviously desperate to be rid of it.

"You okay, sis?" Rowan murmured to her, setting both hands on her shoulders. "You need anything?"

"I'll be fine," she said, letting out a whooshing sigh, her throat working as she swallowed hard. "But that—we are *not* supposed to do that, okay? Maybe no one's supposed to do that, but definitely not Thorns. It felt . . . ugh, like being stuck inside a waking nightmare. Like holding a handful of maggots or something, except in my mind. If I hadn't had the buffer of the locket between me and . . . and *it*, there's no way I could have even come close to pulling it off."

I wrapped my own fingers around the locket and closed my eyes, reaching inside it with my mind. I could feel the necromantic vapor swirling within, woven into a precise, smoky lattice, a pattern that I recognized as the correct shape for this spell.

"But you did finish it," I said grimly, opening my eyes. "It's in there, alright, ready to rock. Which means Thorns *can* cast hexes, as long as they're embedded in amulets."

18

Not in This Alone

IN ROWAN'S CAR, I rested my temple against the rain-lashed window, my mind feeling like a hot-air balloon snared by a tornado, helplessly awhirl.

"Did you need me to stop by a pharmacy?" Rowan asked, darting a look at me. "Grab something to tide you over?"

"Thanks, but no. I can wait until I get home."

Even though we'd driven in separately, I'd asked him for a ride back to The Bitters, citing an oncoming migraine as an excuse. I *did* feel too shaky to drive, like my rising tide of panic might escalate too fast once I was back behind the wheel, threaten to swallow me up.

When Rowan offered a healing spell, I'd declined, claiming that I didn't want to impose.

What I *really* didn't want was him peering inside me when I felt like such loose-spun chaos. Even if what was wrong with me wasn't physical, who knew what weakness he might sense in me that I didn't want him to know?

By the skeptical look he'd shot me as I climbed into his immaculate, eco-friendly Nissan—pine scented, and conspicuously lacking in any of the snack wrappers and empty soda cans that rolled around the shadowy wells of my own car—he wasn't totally buying my migraine bit. But he was also too distracted by what we'd learned to press me further, clearly ruminating as we drove. Gripping the wheel too hard, face dark with the knowledge that one of his own could have cast a curse on Holly after all.

But all I could think about was Lark, and her gorgeous, pristine designs. She was really doing the thing, living her most creative life, the way I only dreamed about for myself—and felt racked with guilt for even dreaming. That she was doing it meant it *could* be done, if you were brave enough, or if you had your family's unconditional love and support behind you.

Would I ever have either of those things? Would that kind of life ever happen for me?

The turmoil and confusion spiraled ever tighter, concentric circles with less and less white space between them, crowding out any rational thought and leaving behind only electrifying panic. An iron band constricted around my head, and my entire body crawled with nerves, a twitching, restless, terrible feeling that burrowed deep beneath my skin. Demanding that I run, that I move, that I not let myself be trapped, Or Else.

I only realized I was hyperventilating when I heard Rowan repeating my name with growing concern, his voice a distant warble that reached me as if from a tunnel's length away.

"Isidora?" he was saying, eyes flicking between me and the slick windshield. Rain rolled down the glass, branching and dividing, forming patterns that seemed somehow sinister, like cryptic glyphs. "Issa . . . damn it, Issa, what is going on with you? You feeling okay?"

The panic crested then, crashing into and over me, a towering wave that closed over my head while a sickening column of fear spiked from my guts to my brain. If I didn't get out of the car, I was going to die; I knew it in the deepest parts of me. My skin would split apart and my essential self dissolve like dandelion seeds blowing into the winds, never to be recaptured.

I *had* to escape before that happened, to get away from here.

"Pull over," I rasped through my teeth, my mouth dry as sand, my whole body quaking. "Now. I need to get out."

"But we're on the road, it's *pouring*—"

"*Now*, Rowan," I half keened, pounding one weak fist against the window.

He snuck another look at me, then gave a tight nod. "Alright, I got you. Hold on a sec, okay?"

As he pulled onto the shoulder, wet gravel spraying from the tires, I became dimly aware that we were on the road that bordered the Witch Woods, the forest that sprang up behind The Bitters and curved along the eastern edge of town. Through the whipping curtains of rain, it loomed like a patch of living night, a spiky tangle of evergreens broken by gnarled sycamore, black tupelo, and oak. As a kid, I'd spent as much time in those woods as I had roaming The Bitters itself, as if the forest were my own backyard, and now it beckoned to me like home. Like somewhere safe I could hide, to ride out my own inner storm.

As soon as the car rolled to a stop, I flung the door open, tumbled out, and took off toward the trees.

The land inclined steeply away from the road before flattening out, and I nearly lost my footing as I skidded down the drop before breaking into a headlong run. Cold rain drenched me in an instant, a downpour so heavy it felt like a needling weight dumped onto my head and shoulders.

"Issa!" I heard from behind me, followed by the sharp slam of a car door. "Issa, wait!"

"Just *stay* in the car, Rowan!" I flung over one shoulder, rain whipping into my mouth, plastering my hair across my face. I spat it out, raking one hand through its soaked length to fling it to the side. "Please, just leave me alone!"

By the time I reached the tree line, my flats were so full of water that it sloshed disgustingly around my toes. I paused for just long enough to step out of them, leaving them where they lay. They were a favorite pair, electric-blue suede patterned like snakeskin, and now they'd be ruined. But I had much more pressing things to worry about, like whether air would reach the bottom of my lungs ever again.

As soon as I stepped into the Witch Woods, the rain cut out as if someone had changed the channel on the weather.

The crash of it remained, battering the canopy above my head. But the tree crowns interwove so tightly, lacing together like puzzle pieces, that they barely let any water stream directly down. What little made it through leaked only along the trunks, sluicing down into the thirsty mat of branch-strewn forest floor.

I stopped for a second to catch my breath, heart pinging painfully in my chest, gaze raking over my surroundings in search of somewhere I could go. Being in the woods was good, much better than the car, but it wasn't quite enough. I wanted something closer to shelter, something to hold and ground me until I clawed my way back to myself.

Just beyond the outermost thicket of trees, I spotted a tremendous sycamore, its dense roots bulging up from the ground to form little niches like alcoves as its base. A downy layer of ferns grew inside each, soft and inviting as a featherbed.

Exactly what I needed.

With a grateful moan, I stumbled over to the tree, lowering myself on jellied legs into one of the nooks, my back pressing against the chilly trunk and my arms propped up on the roots. Then, safe as I was going to be, I drew my knees up against my chest and dug into them with my chin, my body quaking with fear and cold, eyes welling with furious tears.

Why was this happening to me again, and why now? I'd thought I'd outgrown this awfulness years ago, my body's own betrayal of itself, the warp and weft of me unraveling with terrifying speed. Was I really still this weak, this much of a scared little girl, that I couldn't even manage my own emotions when they ran too high, get myself in check?

What made it even worse was that we Avramovs were supposed to be storied rebels, for fuck's sake, rampaging warriors, not huddled, whimpering prey. This sorry show of panic and self-pity wasn't how we handled ourselves. We were strong; *I* was strong. We inspired fear, commanded respect. Like our family creed proudly proclaimed, we neither broke nor bent.

But no matter how I repeated this mantra to myself, I couldn't fend the panic off, force it to loosen its taloned grip.

"Issa."

My gaze flew up, arms locking tighter around my legs. Rowan stood in front of me, rainwater beading his face and hair, dripping from his hands where they hung by his sides. His face a study in pained tenderness.

Hot shame flared in my gullet, simmering at the base of my throat, that I'd allowed him to see me this way.

"I t-told you to stay in the car," I croaked, dropping my eyes.

"Like I was really gonna leave you out here by yourself." But there wasn't any real admonition in his tone, no sharpness to the rebuke. Just mild disbelief that I'd expected him not to chase me down. "Who cuts out when their partner's having a panic attack?"

My eyes snapped back up to his, at the utterly calm way he said the words. Like what was happening to me was just like any other normal affliction, no worse than the migraine I'd claimed.

"H-how did you kn-know?" I forced through chattering teeth.

"My aunt Wisteria gets them sometimes," he said, dropping down onto his haunches, eyes clear and warm as they met mine. Even in the forest's gloom, I could see the sparkling rain that had gathered on his lashes, spangling his lids. "Feels like she's having a full-blown coronary every time it happens, has to lie down flat to ride it out. She's the toughest old lady I know, but it can be scary as hell for her. She does take meds for it, though—you happen to have any on you?"

I gave my head a brusque twitch of a shake. "I don't . . . no. I don't have any."

I'd thought about it, of course, back when this had been a more frequent problem. But seeking out that kind of help would have meant admitting I wasn't up this challenge, not fit to conquer it myself. In what I realized was a profoundly stupid way, the idea of being so weak had seemed worse than the panic attacks themselves.

"Got it." He drew his lips through his teeth, one by one, bouncing a little on the balls of his feet. Like we were just chilling here together, having a casual little meetup on the sopping forest floor. "In that case, how about a hug?"

A shocked giggle burbled out of me. "*Excuse* me?"

"You heard right." He spread his hands, lips curling in a half smile. "What's happening to you is partly your nervous system fritzing out from being dialed up too high, drenched in a whole flood of cortisol. Calming hormones can help regulate the response. And hugs release oxytocin, if being held isn't too uncomfortable for you."

"Rowan Thorn. Are you seriously offering to *hold me* right now?"

"Only if you think it might help. Has it helped before, having someone support you through it?"

"I . . ." I trailed off, teeth clicking together. "I have no idea. Never tried it."

Of course I hadn't. It wasn't like I'd ever have let my mother or one of my siblings see me reduced to this, much less ask them to hold my hand as I fumbled my way through an unraveling. Not even Letha, who knew everything else worth sharing about me, had known about this in any real detail, beyond the simple fact that it sometimes happened—and that when it did, I much preferred to be left alone.

And how much worse to ask Rowan Thorn of all people—who'd pushed me away right after kissing me, who judged me so harshly for the sheer fact of my Avramov blood—to comfort me now?

But he'd already seen me diminished, melted into a helpless mess, which meant the harm was mostly done. And I was so *cold*, chilled right down to the marrow, the panic still clattering through my bones like a skeleton dangling in a draft. The idea of arms locked around me, a solid, warm chest at my back instead of rough bark, sounded so comforting it made my stomach clench with want.

I couldn't blow apart like dandelion fluff if someone held on to me.

Unwilling to say the words, I just nodded, scooting forward on my butt to make room for him.

Some layered emotion scudded across his features—satisfaction, maybe, mingled with relief and something oddly like gratitude—before he climbed over the exposed roots and eased in behind me, long legs bent to either side. Once he'd settled in, I slid backward, resting my back against his front. Slowly, with infinite care and caution, he wrapped his arms around me. When I went tense, my spine drawing taut, he waited until I relaxed to draw me closer, tucking my head under his chin.

"Okay to use magic, too?" he murmured into my sodden hair. "Won't fix this, but might help warm you up, at least."

I nodded shakily, licking my lips. When the surge of heat and healing came, lapping at me like warm water from every point of contact with him, his closeness, the rock-solid stability of both Rowan and his magic, was so soothing it made me want to weep.

And so I did, tears sliding down my cold cheeks, because what was there to hold back anymore? He already knew I wasn't what he'd thought. That for all my thrill seeking and wild shenanigans, at the deepest core of me I wasn't brash or brave or bold.

Far from it.

"I hate this," I said through a sob, reaching up to wrap both my hands around one of his wrists. "All of this. I just . . . hate it so fucking much. That it's like something alien inside me that I can't control. That it makes me feel so weak and stupid and small."

He gave me a little squeeze, hitching me up against him. "Must be tough like I can't even imagine, to feel like you have an enemy living inside you," he said, his warm exhale fanning against my ear. "But that you can come through for yourself, find the other side . . . Issa, listen. That makes you *strong*, not weak. Strong as hell, in fact."

LANA HARPER

I laughed again, a flat, bitter sound like wet coffee grounds. "I don't know. Not exactly feeling the vanquishing warrior vibe over here. Closer to *pity me*."

"Maybe so. But." He shifted our positions a little, making us both more comfortable. "You let me help you, and that's a major thing. And if I may point out, your teeth have stopped chattering. Which means you're already on the tail end of the adrenaline spike."

"You're not half-bad at this, you know," I admitted. "This doctor thing."

"Size of my student loans, I damn well better be *phenomenal*," he said, so dryly it startled another laugh out of me. He was right; if I could laugh, then I *was* feeling better, and much more quickly than it usually took to bounce back from an attack. Normally I couldn't muster up any real humor or positive emotion to buoy me up for at least the rest of the day.

"And you don't even have people training," I observed. "Impressive improv, there."

"Oh, you know, just a little off-the-cuff human medicine. Long as we don't tell anyone, my DVM license should be safe."

"Well, I won't tell if you won't. Pinkie swear."

A whisper of a laugh, exhaled into my hair. "End of the day, we're all living beings, right? And everything alive just wants to feel like they're not in this alone."

19

Of Dew and Flowers

I OPENED MY EYES long before dawn to the buzz of First Dew energy pressing all around me.

After Rowan had dropped me off the night before, I'd gone to bed before nine, drained by the lassitude that always came in the wake of a panic attack, that sense of psychic weights dragging at me from the inside. My sleep had been dark and dense and fuzzy as wool wrapped around my eyes. And though I'd been afraid that I'd still be shaky for today, and sticky with the shame of having been so weak in front of Rowan, all I felt now was the fizzy excitement of Beltane approaching.

Warm and golden, like the first filaments of sun heralded by the dawn.

It was still early enough that beyond my bay window, the sky had barely begun to lighten to a less impenetrable blue, which meant I had some time to soak it in. I lay in bed for a while with my eyes closed, just savoring that heady, thrumming buzz, like some tremendous chord plucked somewhere far beyond the human register. It swept aside all my accrued concerns: my worries about the investigation and the unknown caster of the curse, the increasing muddle of my feelings about Rowan. Even the ponderous prospect of my own future.

First Dew was an ode to joy, a day to set heavy things aside.

Then I got up to wash my face and put on a totally marvelous amount of makeup, way more than I usually wore. I flicked my eyeliner into dramatic wings, painted a trail of little purple flowers flecked with silver that wound across one cheekbone and around my temple. I plaited half my hair into French braids that I pinned up in a wreath, letting the rest spill down my back. Then I anointed all my pulse points with the special blend of cherry, almond, and hibiscus oil our family used only for this ceremony, before slipping into my lace-trimmed charcoal kirtle and shrugging on my mulberry robes. Gray and purple, the Avramov colors we always wore for covenstead holidays.

When I examined my reflection in the mirror, which remained clear and normal—maybe even our pain-in-the-ass poltergeist was taking the day off—what I saw was effervescence with just a touch of the sepulchral. Like a bright flourish of wildflowers that grew beside the grave.

Days like this, I fucking loved being a Thistle Grove witch. And even more so, an Avramov.

Right on cue, three brisk taps came at my door. I opened it to find Talia and my mother waiting for me, kitted out very similarly except with much smokier eyes (because, of course). Talia held a green pillar candle and Elena a ceremonial copper goblet, its rim engraved with prowling wolves and a snake twining around the stem.

"Happy Dew, my daughter," she said, offering the goblet to me, a tiny smile on her vermilion lips.

"And to you, my mother," I replied formally, leaning forward to exchange kisses with her. Then I took a sip, a lush blackberry mouthful tanging with lemon and meadowsweet—spring wine that the Thorns made for us all, for which only the family elders had the recipe. Despite the fruity flavor, it had some serious kick to it; it lit up my empty stomach like a shower of bonfire sparks, giddy little wisps coiling up to my head.

Did I mention that part of why I loved Beltane and its lead-up was all the day-drinking that went on? Because that *certainly* factored in.

Talia lit my candle, the fat lavender pillar I had tucked in a pocket of my robe, with her own flame. I whispered a little spell over it, ensuring that it wouldn't gutter even if it met a breeze.

As I fell into step behind Talia, the three of us drifted down The Bitters halls to collect Micah next. My little brother had gone so heavy on his eyeliner that the moss green of his eyes all but glowed, especially against his black stubble and fair skin. Then we scooped Addie, who at sixteen was *technically* supposed to take the smallest sip, but instead slugged back two healthy chugs, knowing she wouldn't be getting any (aboveboard) access to the rest of the wine today.

"Adriana," Elena chided, in what was supposed to be a reproachful tone but didn't quite make the cut.

"The cup slipped," Addie said, a sly curl to her smile as she fell into step, bringing up the rear of our mini procession. "Beg forgiveness, Mother."

"Sure you do, kitten. Very convincing."

With a fond eye roll, Elena led us onward, flinging open The

Bitters' double doors with a flick of the hand. Together, the five of us glided down the weedy driveway, to where the rest of the Avramovs had already pooled along the speared black gate that surrounded the demesne. Candles flickering in their hands, waiting for the five of us mainline Avramovs to take our places at the lead.

Our procession wound through Thistle Grove, first through the quiet residential neighborhoods of colonials and Cape Cods that ringed downtown, then over the cobbles of Myrtle, Hyssop, and Yarrow Streets where they converged to form Thistle Grove's town square, bronze statues of the founders presiding over every corner. There, we joined the stream of the other three families, clad in their own ceremonial robes, candles in hand.

Though I couldn't see her from where I stood, I knew Juniper Thorn, the alternate Queen, would be at the line's head, crowned in flowers and with a huge empty chalice in her hands. The Green Man she'd picked would be beside her, holding two candles for both of them.

Above us, windows were flung open by the town's early birds, or those curious enough about First Dew to bother setting their alarms to catch a predawn candlelit parade. The normie population was well aware of the day; they tended to assume we were a bunch of Wiccans celebrating some obscure pagan holiday, which wasn't *that* far from the truth. If anything, the First Dew procession only added to the town's mystique when it came to tourist draw, the same way that the Flower Moon Festival capitalized on Beltane itself.

Once we reached the base of Hallows Hill, the procession became more like a group hike. Normies often hiked up here, too, but for occasions like this, the Blackmoores cast a repelling glamour over it, one that thwarted anyone but witches. It lent the hill a slight wavering shimmer, a mirage well known to locals and considered a natural phenomenon.

Though the trek could take it out of you, depending on which route you took, on First Dew we always followed the slower, gentler path that circled our little mountain, twining around it like a rope. As we climbed, the sun began to melt over the horizon, spilling gold and tangerine and raspberry into the barely lightening sky. When we reached the mountaintop, Lady's Lake appeared in front of us like a mirror of the breaking dawn, the scarlet blaze of sunrise dipped into its royal blue. Thistles crowded all around its banks, the flowers' own reflections forming a spiky outer ring, like a rippling purple frame for the reflected sky. The mountaintop grass shimmered with so much clinging dew it looked like the lingering aftermath of yesterday's rain, even though I knew this wasn't the case. This was just what always happened on this day.

An abundant springtime dew as magical as Lady's Lake itself.

The procession circled the lake, keeping a dozen feet back from the banks. When we'd all found our spots, our candles held in front of our hearts, the sky still ablaze above us, Juniper stepped forward toward the water. I recognized her now, from the Crowning ceremony; she was the budding dryad, the Thorn girl who'd grown a miniature tree around herself.

Followed by the Green Man—a slim, dark-haired white guy I didn't recognize, possibly a Harlow—she walked clockwise around the lake until she'd reached its southern point, the cardinal direction that corresponded with the element of fire. As spring festival, Beltane was all about the return of light and heat, with fire at its very heart. Elation glowing on her face—she'd gone with a glossy purple lip and gold-and-yellow eye, a look that popped against the muted neutrals of the druidic Thorn robes—Juniper lifted her elaborate floral headdress off and flung it up high.

"May spring land sweet upon this, our lake!" she cried out as it flew up, her Green Man following suit by lifting the two candles to the sky.

The crown scattered above her like a floral explosion, petals flying every which way—before freezing into a mosaic that hovered over our heads. As she held the flowers suspended, she also drew that precious dew from every leaf and blade of grass, sucking it up into faceted, swirling trails that crisscrossed one another like a shimmering fountain above the lake. They webbed between the floating petals, both reflecting and distorting them, glinting pink and red and yellow and blue. A kaleidoscope of spring.

Better, more spectacular, than the best fireworks you could imagine.

There was an artistry to this display, a finesse; it looked different every time it was done. And while I appreciated the beauty of Juniper's spell, a part of me panged at how stunning it might've looked with Holly at the helm. I couldn't see her in the crowd, but I knew that wherever she stood, she must be feeling a much deeper version of this same ache. Because these should have been her flowers and her dew, this spell her magic.

This should have been *her* spring.

Then Juniper dashed apart the spell. As the petals tumbled, drifting down toward the water, the dew pearled together into a sparkling sphere that floated over to Juniper. Hovering above her empty chalice, it released a slow and gentle rain, until the last of it had pooled inside the cup.

Juniper brought it to her lips for the ceremonial first sip, shivering a little as she tasted it. First Dew had a special zing, both fiery and sweet, like Everclear might if hard liquor ever tasted like something wonderful.

After she offered the chalice to the Green Man for a sip, they shared a light and grazing but seriously lengthy kiss; while the ultimate communion between the Queen and the Green Man was usually symbolic, these two *clearly* had some history. Then Juniper turned to hand off the chalice to the nearest Thorn. From there, it would make its rounds to everyone, the invigorating dew inside not running out until the very last Thistle Grove witch enjoyed their sip. Its effects lasted for days, sometimes weeks; it took care of minor pains, cleared your mind, even left behind sweet dreams.

Even in this, Lady's Lake took care of us.

20

More Than Just Good

AFTER THE CEREMONY, the day had bloomed a bright corn-flower blue, a dazzling sky with only wispy afterthoughts of clouds. Letha and I had rushed to raid the huge picnic table set out in the shade of the pine and spruce that ringed the lake, decorated with flower-and-candle centerpieces over a blue-and-white-gingham tablecloth. Once we were stuffed with the mini pies and the vegetarian baguette sandwiches the Thorns had laid out—as usual, they'd signed up to bring Honeycake food, which always worked out best for everyone—we snuck away together to sit under one of the trees. Far enough from the lake and the merrymaking crowd for a little privacy and chill.

"Much as it pains me to admit," Letha sighed, wiggling her bare toes in the grass, "I don't entirely hate that music."

One of the Thorns had animated rows of thistles along the water, like a floral sound system. The flowers were nodding their purple heads and crooning crystalline jams with a very Melanie Martinez meets Florence + the Machine vibe. The water amplified their acoustics, lending them an otherworldly timbre that floated in unpredictable ways, as if invisible fae sopranos were sneaking up behind you to whisper every other lyric right into your ear.

"Same. We could go dance, if you want," I offered, tilting my head back against the trunk. A grassy breeze wafted over my face, perfumed with pine needles and the cool scent of the lake, along with the incensey smell I always associated with magic itself.

I'd had two glasses of spring wine on top of my mouthful of first dew, and I felt like most of my blood had been swapped with slow rivers of warm honey. I hadn't realized how much I needed this break, the simple space to bask in magic and relax, to release all my worries for a day. My entire body felt physically lighter, untethered, closer to air than earth. Trending toward the sun, and eventually, that ultimate Beltane flame.

"Maybe later," Letha murmured, closing her own eyes. "This is too nice, to just sit for a while. This last week has been madness, I tell you. I've finally got the entire design nailed down in storyboards, and I am *tired*, cuz. That said, the Forest of Perdition is going to rock, and I also have all these baller crypts and tombs planned for the side stories in the Cemetery of the Forgotten. Gorgeous, and unsettling as all fuck. I think you'll love it."

"*Nazdravye*, cuz," I said, lifting my goblet of spring wine to clink against hers. "Thanks for working so hard. I appreciate your big, beautiful brain and all the fruits of its labor. I'm going to be nailing down the story line scripts and character sheets this week, and then the casting should be a snap; you know all the regulars will try out again. I think we're actually in good shape."

"No jinxing, but that deserves a double cheers," Letha said, raising her glass to mine again. "And with you juggling the investigation, too, no less. I know you can't spill the deets, but I'm dying for any info. So feel free to dispense whatever crumbs you see fit."

"Well," I said slowly, parsing how much was okay to tell her—and how much I wanted her to know, when it came to Rowan. "The suspect roster is growing, for one. We still don't have a real handle on who might've done it, but we do know that no one's out of the running . . . not even the Thorns."

"Despite it being a necromantic hex?" Letha exclaimed, with a mock gasp. "Well, fuck me sideways. What a twist."

"Right? Very intriguing. And more surprising yet . . ." I looped a lock of my hair around my finger, cheeks growing warm. "It turns out Rowan Thorn can be less than abominable, when he tries."

Letha twisted toward me, fixing me with her patented piercing stare. "Please to clarify."

"He's kind," I started, pushing past the reluctance; this was my best friend asking me to open up to her, as gently as she knew how. I wouldn't be doing either of us any favors by shutting her out of this, too. "And he has this . . . earnestness, when it comes to dealing with people, that I used to find completely obnoxious—mostly because he was such a committed dick to me—but am now reconsidering. Loath as I am to admit that I might've been wrong about him."

"Isidora Avramov," Letha said, eyes narrowing. "Cousin mine, and fondest friend. Has some dirty deed gone down between the two of you, and you've been holding out on me? And do not play coy, because I know you know *exactly* what I mean."

Now my cheeks felt like they were spontaneously combusting, which was a trip; for a redhead, I'd never been all that prone to blushing, mostly because very few things actually embarrassed me to that degree.

"We *may* have made out once," I admitted, stifling the urge to hide my face. "After a few drinks too many. And it was . . . well, it was totally fucking hot, much to my astonishment, until he remembered what a sinister force of darkness he was kissing and lost his shit a little. So, bad decision all around, okay, nothing new there. But then yesterday I had a—an unfortunate reaction after one of our meetings. Got too worked up, just kind of spun out a little. And Rowan . . . he took care of me, like it was no big deal. And, Letha, ugh, I *liked* it."

"Wait a minute." Letha stared at me, a slow, inexorable delight spreading across her face. "You have the actual hots for Rowan Thorn, Wildlife Hero and archnemesis. You do, don't you? You do! Admit it!"

"Let's not get carried away. I've made out with many an inappropriate individual in my day, which you of all people should know."

"Perhaps, but you sure as shit didn't sit there all gooey-eyed, turning *colors* over them." Letha started laughing, a high-pitched giggle that quickly escalated into her trademark infectious cackle, rarely heard in the wild. "Wow, this is—when you think about it, it's actually *too* good. I'm experiencing what may well be unprecedented amounts of joy. The comedy is exquisite on every level."

"I'm so glad you find my travails this amusing," I told her, taking a pointed swig of wine. "I do live to entertain you."

"Sorry, I can't hear you over the sound of overwhelming irony," Letha deadpanned, cupping a hand around her ear. "Is there such a thing as an irony explosion, do you think? Maybe an avalanche? I mean, this much of it *must* be a safety hazard."

"You're my cousin, and I say this with love. But you truly are the alpha Capricorn."

"You bet your ass I am. Is that supposed to be some kind of shade?"

A shadow fell over us, and I looked up to see Rowan Thorn himself, standing in front of us like an accidental apparition, swathed in his family's green-and-brown druid's robes with a hazelwood staff in hand. How had I not even realized he was left-handed? A bemused wrinkle deepened between his eyes as he took in the two of us, Letha lost in throes of laughter and me with my cheeks righteously aflame.

"Um," he said, rubbing his chin, nonplussed gaze shifting between the two of us. "Am I interrupting something?"

"Noooooo," Letha said through cackles, widening her eyes. "Your timing, sir, is what one might call *impeccable*."

He shook his head a little, like, *What is* with *this chick*, and then turned to me.

"I was wondering if I could catch you for a minute," he said, clearing his throat. "Maybe go for a quick walk?"

A prickling thrill ran through me, equal parts embarrassment and anticipation. But better to see what he wanted now, I told myself, than to add yet another layer of confusion and complexity between us, to trip us up when we returned to our investigation.

And while it might have been the First Dew vibes, the sensual Beltane buzz that would only grow stronger as May Day itself approached, it hadn't escaped me that Rowan looked even more enticing than usual. The sunshine dappling through the trees drew out flecks of honey in his eyes, playing across that sweet sprinkling of freckles on his nose and the flawless contours of his mouth, the bold line of his jaw.

Shit, I *wanted* to take a walk with him. Letha could just suck up all the extra irony.

"Sure," I said, scrambling to my feet. "Lead the way."

SOMETHING ABOUT THE flood of magic that spilled from Lady's Lake distorted geospatial perception. While Hallows Hill itself stood only about five hundred feet high, the lake on its summit seemed much bigger than it should have been, and the woodland that ringed it far too wide. You could walk for what felt like several miles up here, even though such dimensions should have been impossible.

Which meant, I thought, as I followed Rowan deeper into the trees, that even with all four families gathered by the lake, we were about to be very much alone.

"Have you seen Holly today?" I asked him, just to break the ice, even though the silence hadn't really felt uncomfortable. Birdsong floated from the boughs, the rustling canopy of leaves like antique lacework above our heads, sequins of sunshine filtering through the gaps. The Hallows Hill forest felt like the opposite of the Witch Woods in every respect: luminous and sweet, indefinably sacred. There was nothing here to fear. "It must be a hard day for her."

"Yeah. She's been putting on a brave face, like she does," Rowan said, jaw tightening. "She doesn't want to bring Juniper down, and the dew helped lift her spirits some. But I can still feel her struggling."

"What a generous person." I wrapped my arms around myself, shivering a little despite the warmth of the day and the electrifying dew in my own veins. "I'm not sure I could rise above things that way."

"Don't sell yourself short, now," he said, flicking a sideways glance at me. "I've seen you be kinder than many, too . . . and stronger, to boot."

I looked down, smiling to myself, at the deft way he'd acknowledged what had happened between us yesterday, while leaving it up to me whether I wanted to talk about it or just let the whole thing drop.

"Speaking of kindness," I said, eyes still on the ground. "I didn't get a chance to thank you. For what you did for me, yesterday."

"No thanks necessary. Anybody halfway decent would've done the same."

"Well, no one's done it for me before," I said, shrugging. "Though, to be fair, I also haven't given anyone the chance. Usually I have other ways of dealing with it, before it gets to that point. The anxiety, I mean. And then the panic."

"Mind if I ask what you do for it?"

I hesitated, steeling myself. But in for a penny, in for a pound; Rowan had already seen me at my weakest. He might as well understand the rest of it.

"It may sound completely counterintuitive, but I find if I can give that extra adrenaline—or cortisol, whatever it is—other outlets, it's manageable. So I do . . . risky things. Skydiving, bungee jumping, even just driving too fast. Your more run-of-the-mill thrill seeking." I gritted my teeth, took the plunge. "And, sometimes, I maybe summon demons."

Rowan stopped dead, turning to face me with a dropped jaw. "I'm sorry. Can you run that by me again?"

I paused along the path, too, forcing myself to hold his shocked eyes without cringing. "You heard me. Netherworld entities, daemonfolk, the ones you've heard about in stories, or read about in the Grimoire. I summon one, roll with it for a while, and then banish them. Catch and release, kind of, ha."

"Uh, don't take this the wrong way, alright?" he said, rubbing the back of his neck, letting his staff take his weight as if he actually needed the support. "Because I'm not trying to come across as some judgmental dick. But I'm gonna need some serious help understanding how *summoning demons* helps keep your anxiety in check."

"I don't fully understand it myself," I said with a shrug. "But I think it's partly a matter of control. If I can call up these insanely powerful, terrifying, unpredictable entities, bend them to my will, get them to show me or tell me things . . . it means *I'm* the strong one after all. The one capable of control. And it reassures me to know that. The rush of it all helps me relax, too, after."

Rowan considered this, eyes shifting back and forth over my shoulder as he struggled to gauge how potentially unhinged I might be.

"Okay, I can see that, maybe," he said. "Demonic endorphins. Damn, it still sounds completely wild. But I do get that it can be grounding, to master something powerful. I feel a little like that on my bike, sometimes."

"Bike?" I repeated slowly. "Like, as in, *motorcycle*?"

A wide, brilliant grin split his face, and he nodded. "Yeah, my Kawasaki. I mean, it's no demon—goddamn, I cannot believe you do that—but that thing's a beast, for real."

"Now I'm going to need a moment." I shook my head, my own jaw agape. "I'm having the hardest time imagining Rowan Thorn, (Supremely Responsible) Wildlife Hero, riding a fucking Kawasaki. A horse, maybe, let's say even a spicy stallion, but not—"

A low, surprised chuckle rumbled deep in his throat. "Hold up—*what* did you just call me?"

I clapped my hand over my mouth, eyes widening. "Shit, sorry," I mumbled through my fingers. "I did not mean to say that out loud that time."

"*That* time?" he repeated, eyebrows lifting. "You mean to say you go around calling me 'Wildlife Hero' in your head, just on a regular basis?"

"Yes?" I hazarded. "Not trying to break rule number two, but it's a snarky holdover from our shelter days. You know, back when you made it your mission in life to torment me for no good reason."

"No good reason." He laughed again, this time more openly, and with genuine disbelief. "Isidora Avramov, you are truly a piece of work for the ages—and I swear, I say that fondly. Is that *really* how you remember it?"

"Uh, it's how it *was*, dude," I retorted, blood heating. "Do you not remember how it went? I showed up every day, and according to you, screwed up every single thing I did. Handling the animals—"

"Because you wouldn't follow safety protocols!" he cried, flinging up his free hand. "You can't just be trying to pet a nonsocialized feral cat on a whim! That's not just some bureaucratic prissy shit. It's for your own protection, with the shelter's liability in mind. Same goes for handling a sick, contagious puppy, just because *they're lonely.*"

"Roscoe *was* lonely!" I shot back with equal fervor, planting my hands on my hips. "The parvo wasn't his fault! And I always, always made sure to wash my hands and sanitize after a cuddle. I would *never* have put the other animals at risk."

"And knowing you now, I'm sure you took precautions," Rowan said, lowering his voice to a calmer register. "But those rules were in place for a reason, and you were a volunteer who refused to follow them. Intentions don't matter in situations like that; they can't. You've gotta be able to see that."

"So maybe I was a little emotional about it," I allowed. "Eighteen-year-old me wasn't known for her impulse control. But what about the rest of it? The dishes, the laundry . . ."

"Issa," he said, even more gently this time, and I belatedly noted that he'd only called me by my nickname once before, during my panic attack. "I don't remember you signing up to do any of those tasks, *ever*. You only did them because a supervisor flat-out made you if you were gonna be allowed to spend time with the animals—which is all you ever wanted to do. Even though shelter hygiene and animal health, they both *depend* on all that other stuff getting done, too. And when you did deign to do an actual chore, it was, like, rage work. No one wanted to be around that."

I *did* have some dim memories of clattering bowls around with much attitude and stomping demonstratively around the washing machine, feeling hugely put-upon that I was wasting time cleaning things while forlorn caged animals waited around the corner, in dire need of snuggles.

"I'll admit I probably wasn't the most diligent about the other tasks," I said with a grudging nod, crossing my arms over my chest. "And in hindsight, policing me on top of your other actual duties must have been really annoying for you, and for everyone else. But, Rowan, I was eighteen, and I loved animals more than anything. I was *so excited* to be there. Are you saying it was all on me? And you couldn't have handled any of it differently?"

He heaved a deep sigh, broad chest rising. "That's not what I'm saying. I could've sat you down, had a real conversation about it instead of just writing you up; that's not really my style, anyway. It wasn't like we'd never had a well-meaning but clueless volunteer before. And then you could've decided to clean up your act, or not. So it's on me that we'll never know how it might've gone instead."

"So why didn't you?" I said, pulse picking up, sensing that we were finally boring down to the crux of the matter, the bloody, beating heart of our history. "Why didn't you just talk to me?"

He worked his jaw from side to side, flicking his gaze away from mine before meeting my eyes again.

"Because you were an Avramov," he said softly, the cords of his neck flexing as he swallowed. "And I didn't think any of you belonged around animals."

I closed my eyes for a second, the injustice of it beating inside me like a pair of thrashing wings, outrage shooting through my veins even as my stomach wrung itself like a rag. It felt so unfair, so wrong, to be seen in this terribly reductive way, like I could never be more than my necromancy. Death magic that I belonged to, that I *loved*, that, yes, I would have chosen for myself again and again.

But for all that I adored it, it was *not* the sum total of me, the only thing I could possibly amount to.

And I'd be damned if I let Rowan or anyone else define me that way.

"So, I have six pets, all of whom I rescued . . . and you think I don't deserve to be around animals?" I finally said, when I could trust myself to speak again without my voice betraying me by breaking. "Because of my family's magic, magic I was *born* into? Do you even realize how horrible that sounds? How—how prejudiced?"

"Uh, Isidora, *of course* I do," he said, spreading his hands, a new undertone of harshness to his voice. "Last I checked, I was still a Black man living in America. Thistle Grove is special, yeah, but it's not actually on a different planet. So believe me, on the whole, I am very familiar with the concept."

I nodded, chastened, chewing on the inside of my cheek—
because Rowan shouldn't have had to point that out for me at all.

While Alastair Thorn had been white, he'd married a Black
woman, and the majority of his contemporary lineage identified as
Black, biracial, or multiracial. And while much of my own family
was white, we definitely weren't homogeneous, either. Back when
we'd emigrated from the Urals, a number of Margarita's closer
cousins had been of Eurasian ancestry; since then, the freewheeling notions of partnership many of us subscribed to meant lots of
half siblings, often of wildly varying racial makeup within the
same branch of the family. I'd grown up with five mixed-race first
cousins, and my uncle Anton, Elena's second-youngest brother,
had a Black father. At the very least, I was aware of the kinds of
pressing concerns some of my own close relatives had to contend
with that I didn't, the very real dangers they faced that would
never haunt me in my daily life.

At the same time, the fact that the Thorns' green magic was
generally accepted within our witch community as much more
"respectable," glowier, and more wholesome and delightful than
my family's necromantic bent was also a reality baked into Thistle Grove life. But given the diversity of my own lineage, I still
should have known better than to even imply something so ridiculous as Rowan being unfamiliar with prejudice.

"Of course you are," I said, ducking my head. "That was very
stupid of me to say. I . . . should not have put it that way."

Rowan leaned his staff against a nearby spruce, then wrapped
both hands around my upper arms.

"Let's back up," he said, heat radiating from his skin to mine.
"Obviously, the two things aren't comparable, not by a long shot.
Your life, for instance, has never been in danger because of any

prejudice of mine. But you're not wrong, either. I judged you un-worthy to be there from the start, because of your name. Because of the kind of magic that your family works. And, Issa . . . I'm sorry. That was wrong of me. And not just wrong, but dishonor-able. The kind of wrongheaded shit that should be beneath any good person."

I couldn't have imagined how gratifying it would be to hear those words from him, the satisfaction of knowing that even if I'd been a misguided nuisance—and much more of an entitled asshole than I'd let myself admit—that he knew he'd wronged me, too. And that he was willing to right it now.

But it still wasn't quite enough.

"So, what about the other night?" I asked him, insides quailing. What if his interest in making amends didn't extend to this? "When we were, you know, making out outside of Whistler's. And it was like you were so into it . . . until you suddenly remembered who I was, exactly who you were kissing. And then it became re-pulsive to you, to be with me that way. Somehow unacceptable."

Rowan winced, gritting his teeth. "Yeah, that's . . . that's on me, too. Only thing I can say for myself is, I was drunk as shit, Issa—which I don't do all that often to start because, as you saw, I don't handle myself well. And I was getting all tangled up be-tween what I actually felt and what I thought I should be feeling. So I panicked, in just about the worst way possible. But that's no excuse, I know. Hell, it's not even much of an explanation. I'm just saying, I know I hurt you . . . and I am sorry for it, if you can ac-cept that."

"Then I guess I'm sorry, too," I said, relaxing slightly into his touch. "For all that crap I pulled at the shelter. I should've done the chores like everybody else. I should've respected quarantine and, I guess, the rules. And I *definitely* shouldn't have unleashed hellish squirrel vengeance on you."

"Yeah," Rowan said with a half laugh, that radiant grin creasing the skin around his eyes into those lovely fans, light leaping into his irises like a magic trick. "That *was* fucked-up. But man, I do have to hand it to you . . . you got me back good. I was jumping out of my skin for, like, a week before I figured out how to nail one of those little fiends."

"I still can't believe you're scared of squirrels."

"For the record, I am *not* scared of them." He pulled a face. "More like, I don't trust them. One time I saw one strolling down Myrtle, holding a foil-wrapped burrito in its little paws. How the hell does a squirrel acquire a whole-ass burrito, I ask you?! You can't tell me that's not uncanny as hell."

"Yeahhhh," I said slowly, pressing my lips together. "No fear or trauma there *at all.*"

He rolled his eyes, mouth twitching, the not-quite-dimple cleaving by his mouth. "My point is, that hex didn't come to play. So, respect."

"Like I said back at the orchard," I replied, giving him a coy little tilt of the head, hyperaware of the way my heart rate had kicked up. "I'm very good at what I do."

"Yeah, you are," he said, holding my eyes. The atmosphere between us abruptly shifted into something slippery and sultry, shimmering with heat. I could feel the slight tightening of his grip on me, the warmth of his hands where they pressed against my skin. "More than just good. Especially when you're being impossible."

21

Bred into Darkness

I T FELT LIKE the whole forest held its breath around us. Reality itself coming to a full stop that trembled like new leaves, wavered like mist against our skin. Then we leaned in toward each other in seamless tandem, as if we'd been given the same choreography.

Our lips met just as his arms wound around me, his hands sliding down the backs of my thighs to draw me against him and then hoist me up, my legs wrapping around his hips. I'd been picked up like this before, but I was tall enough that things could get ungainly fast, if not devolve into straight-up comedy.

But Rowan held me with ease, as if carrying me through a hallowed forest was second nature, effortless as the way my mouth clung to his.

Then we found ourselves in a clearing, a small space nestled in the trees, open to both sunlight and breeze. The air smelled warm and sharp, of sunshine falling on grass and wildflowers. There weren't many thistles here, but the velvet green was scattered with zinnias and daisies, cosmos flaring between them like hot-pink sparklers. Rowan set me down on a smooth stone, one of many such boulders strewn throughout Hallows Hill without any obvious provenance. Polished and flat-topped, perfect to perch on or to use as altars, depending on your intent.

I'd been up on the mountaintop countless times, but I'd never found my way here before.

It was like we'd landed in the perfect slice of spring, a hidden Beltane enclave that Hallows Hill had offered up for the two of us alone.

Appropriate enough for two people with such a penchant for discovering alternate dimensions where they could coexist.

I could feel the stone's sun-drunk heat seep through my robes and into my skin, a shadow flitting over us as a bird winged by above. Rowan pulled back from me, cupping my face in both hands, thumbs sliding over my cheekbones as his hooded eyes drank me in.

"Does it break rule number one," he asked, a slow smile spreading over his full lips, "if I tell you that you actually taste like strawberry shortcake?"

"Seeing as we just busted rule number two to bits, I'll let it go this time. But only because you're making it sound like something nice."

"Because it is . . . and damn, so are you," he said, a shade of marvel to his voice, palm curling warm around my nape. "Issa Avramov, you are not at all what I expected."

"Hope you like lots of surprises, Rowan Thorn," I whispered, widening my eyes as I drew my lower lip through my teeth. One of my hands slid around his neck while the other feathered down his abdomen, dipping lower to fondle him. "They're kind of my calling card."

He made a low, incoherent sound, eyelids sliding to half-mast. Then he drew me hard against him, my hand still trapped between us, his mouth seizing mine in a deep, demanding kiss. Desire slammed through me in an instant, a bright pulse of it, buzzing through blood already galvanized by first dew. I could feel a wave of tingles roll through my skin, all the way up to my scalp. I cupped the hard contours of him with my palm, slipping my hand down his muscled inner thighs in a slow caress. He moaned into my mouth, stroking the line of my throat and the length of my collarbone, before sliding his palm lower to cup my breast.

I never wore a bra or panties under my ceremonial garb; it just kind of killed the free-and-witchy vibe for me. And when he found my nipple, rolling it deftly between his fingers as his breath turned harsh and jagged against my mouth, I let my head fall back. His lips landed right on the sensitive hollow of my throat below my garnet, trailing molten kisses all along the lace trim of my dress. Then the sharp edge of his teeth sank into the curve of my breast, where it spilled above the bodice.

I made a little mewling sound deep in my throat, my insides clenching, legs tightening around his hips. He paused for just a second, fingers hooked under the dress's trim, glancing up at me for permission. The intentness of his eyes—their hazel smoky with desire, foxed like scrying-mirror glass—took my breath away. Because this wasn't like the heedless chaos of the other night. This was just him and me, wanting each other badly but deliberate in our desire, neither of us unmoored or drunk.

I couldn't remember the last time I'd felt this aware of my own physicality, of the nerve endings bundled right under my skin, the electricity leaping from one to the next. The hot surge of blood lapping just beneath.

And all of it wanted him.

"Yes," I said on an exhale, leaning back to lie against the stone's flat top as he drew the bodice down. "*Fuck*, yes."

My back arched against the stone as his mouth settled over my nipple, sucking and nipping at me hard, the heat and wet of his tongue driving me wild. His other palm pressed flat against my sternum, gentle but unyielding, while the bottom half of me lay pinned between him and the stone—which meant no escape, nowhere to flee. The idea of it, of being trapped in this high-pitched pleasure, elevated my desire to a completely new plateau. My hand tightened around his neck, nails sinking in, and I heard myself whisper his name into the wind.

His other hand skimmed down my leg, twitching my robes aside and flicking up my dress. Deft fingers trailed up my inner thigh and then dipped between my legs, making me gasp, my hips writhing of their own volition.

"Oh, *there* you are," he breathed against my skin, with a vast, ravenous relief.

Like he'd been looking for me, for *this*, his entire life.

His fingers parted me, light but absolutely sure, stroking my clit in a slow, deliberate, delicious cadence. My mind went buttery soft, all glittery and gold-dipped, like the swirling patterns of sunlight scrolled along the insides of my eyelids.

Then the day *shifted* around us, without warning, tipping like a scale.

Another witch might not even have felt it, not right then, the edge of some malevolence traveling toward us, like the blackening burn of flame racing along curling paper. But I was an Avramov witch, born and bred into darkness, the real *something wicked* in "something wicked this way comes." This kind of magic swam like living shadows in my blood.

And I could *feel* this darkness rampaging through the sweet fizz of the air, monstrous in its incongruity.

"Rowan," I said, my voice still slurred with desire, but some new note of caution in it made him freeze against me. "Wait. Something . . . something's happening."

He pulled away, propping himself up on one hand, body still hovering above mine. "What do you mean?" he asked, brow furrowing. "I don't—"

Then a wave of pure malice rolled through our little dale and ripped every wildflower out from its roots.

I scrambled up to sitting, yanking my dress back up, setting a hand on Rowan's shoulder as he moved to stand in front of me. For a moment, the flowers simply floated above our heads, trailing the sad tendrils of their ripped roots as they dipped and wove around one another, almost in a mockery of the mosaic Juniper had floated above the lake.

A perversion of the First Dew ritual itself.

Then they withered all at once, bled of all their color—and snapped together, coalescing into a grotesque skeletal *face*. A skull-like thing, with empty eyes that were only open holes of sky and a giant maw lined with ragged teeth like stalactites. Ribbons of dead flowers, stems, and roots writhed all around it, thrashing like Medusa's snaky hair. The hatred emanating from it was so powerful it seemed almost *pungent*, like an acrid stench.

A malignant intent that I could feel homing in, focusing on Rowan even before the thing spoke his name.

"*ROWAN THORN*," the skull blared, in a harmonic roar that made me think of newly turned grave dirt and depthless black. A gaping, hungry darkness stripped of stars. "*YOUR WITCH'S SOUL IS FORFEIT, SOON TO BE MY FEAST!*"

"Hecate's chilly tits, that's . . . that's a Death's Head Hex," I said under my breath, heart bucking in my chest—then I leapt off the rock, bodily shoving Rowan aside. "It's—Rowan, *get down!*"

Without thinking too much about just what in the actual fuck I was about to do, I shouldered my way in front of him, pushing him back so hard that he stumbled against the stone. Then I planted my feet firmly and lifted my hands, a billow of ectoplasm rising around me as my magic surged to meet my call. The Avramov sentries must have felt this casting, too; but they'd be closer to the lake, where everyone else was gathered, their protection focused on Holly and the rest of the Thorns.

Fuck me, we really should have given some more thought to wandering off on our own.

But we hadn't. And now there was only me to stand between this awful curse and Rowan.

Rowan was saying something—screaming it, really, trying to be heard above the Death's Head's deafening roar—but I had no energy to spare for listening to him. Instead, I began funneling everything I had into the shape of another curse. Not a defensive working or a banishment, because I didn't have the first clue how to undo a Death's Head Hex, so I wasn't going to waste time trying. Instead, I went on the offensive, preparing a working of my own to cast against this abomination.

And as it happened, I already had one almost at the ready.

It had been barely twenty-four hours since I'd felt Holly embed the Serpentinus Hex inside the locket. If I'd had the amulet on me,

I could have triggered it with a thought, but it was safely back at The Bitters, in the wooden chest that held the worst of our talismanic arsenal safely inert, like the magical equivalent of a Faraday cage. But the shape of the spell—the clever, nasty lattice of it that I'd sensed inside the locket—was still graven on my mind. Its words right within reach.

All I had to do was cast it.

Teeth gritted, I raised my hands and began. Hissing the chant to myself as the Death's Head let loose another shriek and came tearing toward us, a warbling darkness distorting the air in its wake.

A tangle of ghostly snakes materialized in midair between us and the floating skull, as if truly born from cold breath. They hung like massive black ropes of scale and smoke, so icy the air around them glittered with suspended frost. For a moment they only hovered, writhing around one another. A churning, glossy knot so bad and wrong it triggered every dormant prey instinct in my brain and made the bottom of my stomach drop out.

I'd made them with my own will—technically they were a part of me—but they scared the shit out of me all the same.

Then they lunged toward the floating skull, jaws unhinged and curved fangs bared.

I could actually *feel* the bite as it happened, their fangs sinking in as they attached to the apparition, pumping it full of their monstrous venom. Nightmares and rage and insidious terror.

So I'd been right. You *could* wield a curse against a curse this way, like an improvised weapon.

My skin crawled from temples to toes, teeth chattering like they might shatter. Sure, I'd summoned demons, made some creepy squirrels do my bidding, but all that was child's play compared to this. Practically benign, just mischief with a little edge.

I'd never had *anything* like this kind of evil channeled through me before, baneful magic pounding through me like poison, the tang of blood and bitter almond souring my mouth.

It felt hideous and magnificent all at once, hurtling through me like the very darkest blaze, a towering black inferno building in my bones.

A kind of permeating wrongness that was even more danger-ous for how easily it could've felt right.

But the Death's Head was baneful magic, too, and many, many orders above the Serpentinus Hex. The dead-flower skull bellowed thunderously as the snakes latched on to it, tossing itself back and forth, trying to dislodge them. A few lost their hold and flew off as it thrashed, hissing like teakettles as they evanesced.

With each droning roar and shake, more and more flew off, until only three or four were left, clinging for dear life. They'd done some damage, I could see that much; bits of the skull floated in loose, unraveling tatters, skeins of dead flowers crumbling off before they fell, leaving ragged holes behind. But most of it still remained, aloft and ravenous, its empty eyes fixed on Rowan. Its loathing reaching toward him like psychic tentacles.

It was stronger than my snakes, there was no doubt about that. They'd never be able to bring it down on their own.

There was only one thing left I could think to do, a desperate, reckless shot in the dark.

I let the Serpentinus Hex drop all at once, the lattice unwind-ing in my mind as I released the spell. The remaining snakes disappeared in a breath, melting away into nothing. But all the raw magic I'd summoned to cast them stayed, like a captive sea swelling inside me. A pool of dark potential waiting to be shaped to my will, to leap to my next bidding.

Eyes drooping with the effort, every tensed muscle in my body quivering, I carefully wove a brand-new pattern, knitting it into a massive net—then flung it over the Death's Head like a snare.

Seizing it by force, and trying to transmute it into my *own* spell, a casting that I could control.

In theory, this wasn't impossible. You could take over someone else's working, wrestle it under your power, and make it your own. But spells of the Death's Head's magnitude took on some autonomy, something resembling semiconsciousness; they knew their maker, their point of origin, and they actively resisted this kind of subversion. You had to be stronger than the other caster to overpower their will, and incredibly deft and ruthless about it, too.

Under different circumstances, I wouldn't have had a chance in all the hells of twisting a working this complex into something of my own. But I had Rowan at my back to think of, Rowan to protect.

And for once, I was going to be the kind of ironclad Avramov that neither broke nor bent—but for someone else's benefit.

As soon as my snare settled over the skull, I could feel the shape of the trapped spell itself, the hex thrashing wild beneath it like an electric eel. As I coaxed and bullied the curse, imposing the net of my will onto it, I felt each of its dreadful contours as if they'd become a part of me. Hate built up inside me, thick and viscous, stratified like melted candle wax. A chorus of sly, insinuating whispers hissed in my ears, urging me to give in to my inner darkness, to do my very worst. I could feel how profoundly the Death's Head despised Rowan—and not just him, but *everyone* of his blood. Every green-magic practitioner who'd ever wronged an Avramov, put us down, or stood in our way somehow.

Winding all the way back to Alastair Thorn himself, Irish druid and master wielder of life magic, the Thorn founder of Thistle Grove.

And beneath the rage, I found something even more confounding, a twisted take on an almost noble impulse. The spell thought it was doing me some kind of solid. Protecting *me* from Rowan.

That was the final hook I needed, like a clasp I could latch on to, to bring the spell under my control. With a resounding psychic snap, the curse came fully under my dominion, a thrashing hydra of deathly fury over which I now held sole sway.

With a scream that built from the very base of my belly, ripping out of my throat like something barbed and alive, I dispelled the Death's Head Hex, exploding it into cinders that rained down over both of us.

Then I collapsed, crumpling like something broken, tears streaming down my cheeks. So utterly exhausted and depleted I felt like my cells might swim apart, like my entire body might collapse into formless goo.

The witch formerly known as Isidora, now a puddle of primordial soup.

I was chuckling weakly to myself through the salty gush of tears when Rowan's arms slid around me, one behind my back, the other under my knees.

"Issa, Issa, *talk* to me," he was repeating over and over, a raw desperation clinging to his tone as he lifted me, the ends of my robes trailing over the flower-scattered grass. "Please. I just need to know you're gonna be okay."

"I don't know . . . *what* I am," I slurred, my head lolling against his shoulder. "But, Rowan, we . . . I think we were wrong."

22

A Thorn's a Thorn

I HAD ONLY THE foggiest memories of slipping in and out of consciousness as Rowan brought me back to the lake, followed by a babble of distraught voices my addled brain wasn't capable of parsing—except for the faint memory of my older sister's voice.

"Give Issa to me, Rowan," I thought I remembered Talia demanding, a low, insistent danger to her tone. "She needs to be with family now."

"With respect, Talia, I can't do that," I recalled him saying in return—and his own tone had been a reflection of the words themselves, respectful but adamant. "She may be your blood, but she's also the person who just almost died trying to keep me safe. So until we get her back home, the last thing on earth I'm about to do is let her go."

They'd gone back and forth, but she hadn't been able to sway him, and as much as I loved my sister, I'd been woozily glad for it. Rowan had been the one I wanted taking caring of me.

Then there'd been the jostle of him carrying me all the way down Hallows Hill, my head nestled in the warm crook of his neck, the soap-and-citrus smell of him seeping into me like a balm. The spell's poison still circulated through my veins, bitter and corrosive as a contaminant, like something that could etch itself permanently into the fabric of my being. Maybe even shape me into something else, something I very much didn't want to be. I would've been terrified of it, had it not been for Rowan. The safety of his arms around me, the low thrum of his voice reverberating against my ear, brought me back to myself every time the fear threatened to overwhelm.

I trusted, somehow, that Rowan wouldn't let it hurt me now. Just like I hadn't let it hurt him first.

He'd held me until I was safely back at The Bitters, being tucked into bed by my mother and sisters. Only then had he finally loosened his hold, given me over to their care. I remembered a last tight squeeze of my hand, his lips skimming my forehead. A whispered "I'll see you soon, alright?" before I sank into sleep like a stone plummeting toward the muck-riddled bottom of a lake.

I slept for days.

There were fathoms of dreams, nebulous and harrowing. Like tunneling through cold molasses, swimming in an entire pool of sticky ectoplasm. Those sly whispers returned to curdle in my ears, whispering their silky, malicious taunts into the folds of my brain. I wandered barefoot through barren fields while dead flowers rained on me from nightmare skies; black and gray roiling with rust-red clouds that rushed to the horizon in fast-forward.

Flickers of the Death's Head jittered at the very edges of my vision, always just barely out of sight. When I grasped at brief snatches of wakefulness, I could feel myself alternate between tooth-chattering chills and searing heat, as if the last of the baneful magic were burning through me like a fever.

It'd be just my luck to catch a shitty case of bad-magic mono, on top of everything.

When I finally woke fully, it was to twilight outside my window, the room pooling with the kind of melancholy blue light that makes everything seem sad. My mother sat curled up in my armchair under a tasseled throw, face softened by sleep, her copper hair a tangled mess. Without her customary lipstick, she looked almost like a stranger, sweeter and somehow unfamiliar, younger and less austere.

I lay there for a minute, unmoving, basking in that sense of comfort and safety that stemmed from simply knowing a parent was there, watching over you while you were sick. Apparently it never got old, no matter how old *you* were.

As soon as I shifted with a rustle of bedding, easing myself up against the headboard, Elena's eyes flew open—like she'd been on alert even in her sleep, keyed to the slightest movement from me. Emotions chased one another across her face—fear, anger, and distress, before gratitude and relief overtook them all.

"*Lisichka,*" she said on an exhale, the throw falling from her lap as she stood. "You're awake. How are you feeling?"

I frowned, tilting my head back and forth, testing my limbs with little jerks and twitches. Most of me felt slack and achy, but more or less okay. But when I poked tentatively at my magic, a small spike of pain lanced through me. It wasn't terrible—more like a raw soreness than a full-blown wound—but it also wasn't something I'd ever felt before.

"I'm okay, I think," I said a little shakily as she sat down at the edge of the bed, smoothing the covers over my legs. "But my magic feels off. Is this . . ." I paused, biting my lip, almost afraid to say it out loud, lest it come true. "Do you think this is like what happened to Holly?"

"No, sweet," she said with a brisk shake of the head, and I sagged with relief. "You overspent yourself, that's all; you've been sleeping for almost three days. Completely normal, given the circumstances. You're not accustomed to handling baneful magic of that caliber. It took much more of a toll on you than anything you might've worked before."

"So I could still cast if I wanted to?"

"Of course. But it would hurt, and drain you even more. Another few days or so of rest, and it should all be back to baseline; not to worry."

Her face softened even further in the room's blue light, her jade eyes suspiciously glossy as she brushed a wisp of hair out of my eyes. Without eyeliner and mascara, her lashes were much lighter than my own brown, a downy gold that made her seem disconcertingly vulnerable. She must've been seriously rattled to forgo her battle-armor makeup while she watched over me.

"What you did for the Thorn boy . . ." She shook her head, pale lips parting. "Isidora, that was nothing short of a marvel. A feat of heroism. I'm not sure that even *I* could have done it."

"No way. I don't believe that for a second."

"Well, you should," she said tartly, sounding a little more like herself. "And you should be damned proud of what you did for

Rowan Thorn. He'd owe you a blood debt for it—had that spell not been yet another necromantic hex. And an even worse one than the Misbegotten Curse, at that."

"Shit," I whispered, mind racing as memories surfaced, what I'd felt from the curse when I took it over. The raw hatred that had fueled it, its wholesale loathing of the Thorns. "This is looking even worse for us, isn't it? And, Elena, I think there's something bigger at play than we considered. Something weirder. I think—"

She held up a hand. "Let's wait until Emmeline gathers all the elders before we get into it; everyone will want to hear this from you. No need to exhaust yourself telling it all twice. She asked that you and Rowan report to her as soon as you woke up. If you're up to it, we should visit Harlow House tonight."

"Is there time to eat first?" I asked, suddenly aware of the bottomless pit that my stomach had warped into. I could hear it gurgling very insistently under the covers. "I think I might be starving in a literal way."

"Of course," Elena said, smiling. "Talia's been dying to ply you with her various broths. She could barely settle down while you were sleeping—she took more bedside shifts than Micah and Addie combined, fretting over you. I could barely convince her to get some rest herself."

As if on cue, a light shave-and-a-haircut knock came at the door, followed by a creak as it swung open to admit my sister.

"I heard you two talking," she said, looking so wan you might have thought she'd been the one sick, her bleary gray eyes shifting between me and Elena as she leaned against the frame. "But I . . . I wasn't sure if you were up for more company."

"You're not company, you're you," I said, patting the free space next to me. "Come sit, *ses.*"

Talia's uncertain gaze flicked back to my mother, making sure; I couldn't remember when I'd last seen her so tentative. When Elena nodded, Talia flashed us both a weak smile, then came to perch on my other side, setting a light hand on my stomach. Her dark blue nail polish was peeling, the cuticles ragged from being nervously nibbled on. It rattled me even more than the sight of her peaky face; she'd always kept her nails pristine, even when we were little. Out of the two of us, I'd always been the nail biter.

"I'm so glad you're okay, Iss," she said, her voice splintering, and I realized with something like horror that she was close to tears. I'd once seen Talia step on an actual rusty nail in The Bitters attic without shedding a single tear; it took a *lot* to bring my steely sister to that brink. "You were pretty out of it, so I don't know if you remember, but I'm the one who found you and Rowan, right after it . . . it happened. Emmy and I'd gotten into it a little by the lake, and I was walking by myself in the woods to cool off, and then I—I saw you two. I saw the end. What it took for you to bring that thing down."

"You and Emmy were *fighting*?" I asked, thrown. Not that couples couldn't disagree, but as far as I knew, Talia and Emmy's honeymoon phase was so all-consuming and harmonious that they barely even got into spats—much less the kind of argument that would've driven my sister to walk alone on First Dew, of all days.

Maybe there was trouble brewing in paradise; it would certainly explain why Talia seemed so much more on edge these days.

"It was just some stupid tiff," Talia said, waving my concern away, though I could see from the way her chapped lips tightened that it hadn't been anything so minor. "Please don't worry about that. I'm just—I'm *so* sorry, Iss, I feel so guilty. Like I failed you, somehow. I wanted to be the one to bring you back home, but Rowan was back on his hardheaded man bullshit about it; he wouldn't even begin to listen to reason. But you're *my* sister, and I should have tried harder, I should have—"

My bedroom door abruptly flew open and slammed itself shut so violently that a rain of plaster flaked off the jamb, making all three of us startle.

"We really must do something about that vermin soon," Elena muttered darkly. "This is getting far too out of hand."

"I know, I know," I groaned, closing my eyes and letting my head drop back against the pillow. "As soon as I'm better, I'll have another whack at it, I promise. It's just been one thing after another, and I haven't . . ."

Elena rested a quieting hand on my solar plexus, right above the place where my sister had set her own.

"I said 'we,' my love," she pointed out. "You might have invited this pestilence to our doorstep—but it's in our home now, which makes it all of our responsibility. So *we* will handle it, together. The way we handle anything that dares to cross us."

UNLIKE THE OTHER families, the Harlows occupied only a relatively modest holding. Theirs was a spacious colonial in a normie residential neighborhood, oak shaded and pretty but entirely mundane except for them. Their library was barely a third of the size of the one at The Bitters, though much cozier and more comfortable, the bookshelves a gleaming chestnut, an intricate Turkish rug in cream and dusty rose spread over the Chantilly parquet. A punched-tin lighting fixture shed soft light over everything, boosted by a collection of mismatched vintage lamps. Not a single taxidermied wolf head or crystal skull lurked anywhere.

Elena and I were severely out of our element.

We all sat in sunken leather armchairs and couches, with Rowan beside me on a love seat, the two of us the center of everyone's attention. He'd given me a crushing hug when I arrived, and even now our arms rested warmly alongside each other. Like the team we clearly still were, if not like two people who'd been about to get seriously busy on a mountaintop before a necromantic curse cockblocked us.

Fuck, I really did have the very *worst* luck sometimes.

Emmy cleared her throat and clasped her hands in front of her chest, green eyes sweeping over us. "Thanks, everyone, for coming tonight on such short notice," she said, gaze landing on me. "Especially you, Issa. I . . . hear that you've had a rough recovery. How are you holding up?"

I clocked the slight hesitation in her voice, the swallowed mention of Talia; maybe they still weren't quite back on solid ground.

"I've been better," I said, with a half shrug. "But I'm in one piece, magic intact. So, could've also been much worse."

"And she didn't let that thing so much as touch me," Rowan added, shooting me a warm look, eyes glinting amber in the library's mellow light. "I'd say we caught a lucky break, all things considered."

Emmy nodded, shifting her attention to Elena. "Elder Avramov, could you tell us more about the curse Issa dispelled?"

My mother's composed expression didn't change, but I could see the ripple in her long throat when she swallowed.

"It was a Death's Head Hex," she said, voice measured but tight. "A necromantic spell. But this time, one intended to . . .

obliterate its target, beyond merely their body and their magic. To eradicate their witch's soul. Make sure none of them was left, even after death."

The Thorn elders went rigid where they sat, almost in tandem. Both their faces turned hard, suffusing with a quiet, stony rage. The small swarm of honeybees that hovered around Gabrielle Thorn—the only Thistle Grove witch whose green magic was strong enough that it attracted its own ever-changing retinue of followers—changed pitch in their buzzing, alighting protectively on her long braids. Aspen Thorn reached over to take his wife's hand, folding it between both of his and setting it on his lap.

"Why would such foul magic even exist?" he asked Elena, revulsion icing his normally warm baritone. "I have to assume it's yet another Avramov original."

"It is," she said, hands tightening on the curling wooden armrests of her chair. "And it exists because, like the worst of our repertoire, it's a form of necromantic battle magic. Violent and pernicious by design—not just reprehensible, but monstrous. But please consider, Aspen, that it grew out of a time when Avramovs had very powerful enemies who wished them harm."

"Except our family doesn't wish yours harm," Gabrielle retorted, dark eyes flaring. "And yet this is the *second* time we've been hit with one of these nasty, hateful workings. You can't even try to tell me this isn't personal, Elena."

"We aren't saying that," I jumped in before Elena could reply, a buzz of nerves zinging through me. My very own swarm of bees, only mine happened to live on the inside. "The opposite, in fact. The Death's Head Hex was *absolutely* personal. I know because I felt it once it came under my control. The caster—and by extension, the spell itself—hated the Thorns. And it specifically wanted to take Rowan down."

On the way over, I'd struggled with whether to mention that the spell had also thought it was protecting me, before deciding against divulging as much. For one thing, it made no sense; I very clearly hadn't been in any danger from Rowan. For another, that kind of motivation seemed like something that would shift the guilt so squarely onto the Avramovs—who else would feel so strongly about me besides one of us?—that Emmy might decide to focus further investigation exclusively on our family.

I couldn't let that happen. So for the moment, for better or worse, I was keeping mum.

"Then why target Holly the first time around, with the Misbegotten Curse?" Gabrielle demanded.

"I think that might have been an accident," I said, glancing over the assorted elders as a new silence fell, the tension between us all pulling tight as strung wire. "And that Rowan has been the true target all along."

At that, James and Cecily Harlow, Emmy's parents, met my eyes with pained expressions, concern scrolled across their kind faces. The Blackmoores, on the other hand, were clearly present only for formality's sake. From Lyonesse's pearls and politely bored expression, to the glances her husband, Merritt, kept sneaking at the phone in his khakied lap, everything about the pair emanated cool hostility, presumably that we'd had the temerity to drag their son into this fray. Their aloof demeanor also somehow suggested that this assembly was mostly a tedious waste of their time. Possibly they had dinner plans they were eager to get to, or maybe Merritt had a literal horse in some race that he needed to keep close tabs on.

Nothing could be less surprising than the fact that this pair of self-absorbed tools had managed to produce the likes of Gawain.

"Back when Rowan and I examined the orchard," I went on, "I used an ectoplasmic divination spell. A way to re-create the events of the day, based on the place-memory of what had happened there during the Crowning. I didn't think much about it at the time, but I saw how close Rowan sat to the stage—almost directly in front of where Holly stood when she performed. And a finicky, demanding spell like the Misbegotten Curse . . . If the caster was nervous or distracted in any way—or if they were some distance from the gathering—it would've been hard to control. To target properly."

"So let me get this straight. You're saying whoever it is that's targeting my son might've just *fumbled* an entire curse?" Aspen stared at me, aghast, running a hand over his close-shorn salt-and-pepper hair.

"Jesus," Gabrielle muttered next to him, shaking her head. "What a shame for our poor Holly. What a horrible, awful shame. So why didn't they just stop, once the curse latched on to her by mistake?"

"I'm not sure," I said, meeting her eyes with an effort, because this next part was even worse. "But I do think, given that the caster seems to have a bone to pick with the Thorns at large . . . once it got going, I think maybe they figured, what the hell. A Thorn's a Thorn."

Aspen burst from his seat in an explosive motion, beginning to pace around the room.

"How can you even say something like that?" he spat, turning to fling a blistering look at me. "And then tell us we shouldn't blame you and yours? You worship death and decaying things like we do everything green and alive—and somehow you even manage to be *proud* of yourselves for that kind of travesty. So who *else* would feel such an ugly way about us, besides one of your lot?"

"Aspen," Gabrielle said in a tempering tone. "Easy."

"Yeah, Dad," Rowan echoed quietly, lifting an entreating hand. "Let's just take a beat here."

With his other hand, he reached for my own, lacing his fingers through mine where everyone could see them.

Gabrielle's lips parted, her eyes flicking rapidly between our joined hands and faces, her expressive features running an entire gamut of emotions as she considered us. My own mother looked stunned, for once uncharacteristically and completely taken by surprise. Last she'd heard, Rowan and I had been at the starkest of odds, and I hadn't had the chance—or, let's be real, the inclination—to tell her otherwise.

I dropped my own gaze, equally taken aback by Rowan's show of support—and even more astonished that he'd align with me this way, so openly. I didn't even know what he and I were just yet. But here we sat, a Thorn hand in hand with an Avramov, possibly for the first time in Thistle Grove's history. Apparently all you had to do to get a little love around here was vanquish a soul-grubbing death monster for a dude.

Who knew!

"Believe me," Rowan went on, giving my hand a reassuring squeeze, "I get where your head's at, Dad. But Issa deserves better. If she hadn't been there, I'd be six feet under right now. Shit, I'd be *worse* than dead; I'd have had my soul eaten right out of me. And it took everything she had to keep that thing from ripping into me, I saw that with my own eyes. So just . . . sit down, Dad, please. Let's decide how to handle this, together."

"He's right, Elder Thorn," Emmy said with quiet conviction.

"You have every right to be outraged. But we do need to work our way through this as a collective, before anyone else gets hurt."

Aspen stood for another moment, almost vibrating with tension. Then he gave a clipped nod, storming back to the couch and dropping down beside his wife, who set a hand on his knee and gave it a tiny pat.

"Alright, then, son," he said wearily. "What do you suggest we do?"

"Exactly what we've been doing so far," Rowan replied. I could feel him tense beside me, anticipating his parents' response. "Issa and I keep investigating, until we get to the bottom of this thing."

"*Absolutely* not!" Gabrielle exclaimed, her bees' frenetic buzz taking on an even more irascible pitch. "Let you keep putting yourself in harm's way, after we damn well nearly lost you? Not a chance, baby. Not a snowball's chance in hell."

"Mama, I hear you, I do. But think about it. Would I be any safer sitting around at the orchards, twiddling my thumbs? Who's to say that whoever's behind this wouldn't just stalk me there, put you all at risk?" he demanded, hot gaze shifting between his parents. "Issa and I have already done the legwork—and she's proven she can protect me, probably better than anyone else could. Together, we have the best possible shot at flushing this bastard out. You *know* it's true."

"Rowan . . ." Aspen started heavily, dragging a hand down his face. "Son. What you're asking of us—"

"No, Dad," Rowan cut him off, brusque. "I don't even want to hear it. No goddamn way am I rolling over and playing dead. This twisted asshole wants me? Then they can come get me—but not if Issa and I find them first."

For a moment, an entirely silent discourse transpired among

the three of them, a wealth of looks so heavily laden with meaning and emotion that they might as well have been speaking some private, telepathic language. Shit, maybe they were; maybe the Thorn empathic bond ran that much deeper than the rest of us ever thought.

"Okay, then," Gabrielle finally said with a curt nod. "It *is* your call, baby. Depending, of course, on what Emmeline decides."

Emmy inclined her head thoughtfully, relacing her hands on her lap.

"I see the logic there, too," she said to Rowan, flicking an apologetic look at the Thorn elders to be siding with their scion against them. If memory served, Rowan's twin sister, Linden, had been Emmy's childhood best friend; it probably pained her to go against their wishes, if she'd grown up that close with them. "It's very risky, using you as bait like that, but from a strategic standpoint, it's a solid countermove. If both of you are willing to continue, then I'm inclined to allow it. Issa? Where are you on this?"

"Oh, I'm in," I said, almost before she finished speaking. A smile caught at the corner of Rowan's mouth, his hand tightening on mine. "All the way. Whatever it takes."

"Then it's decided." Emmy sighed, grim resolution settling over her face. "But we'll have to take other precautions. The Dance of the Maidens, for one . . . as much as I hate to do it, that'll have to be canceled this year, or at the very least, postponed. We can't give this assailant another invitation to lash out."

I should have seen this hit coming, but somehow I hadn't, and it landed like a gut punch. The Dance was my favorite of the series of Beltane celebrations. At midnight on the day it fell, the May Queen would lead our coven's female-identifying witches up Hallows Hill in a whirling dance, like some maenad parade illuminated by tiny bonfires lit all along the trail. Up on the mountaintop, the male-identifying witches of Thistle Grove would be waiting to receive us under a star-strewn sky, with more spring wine and flower wreaths and skinny-dipping in the lake.

A lot of delightful shenanigans went down on Dance night, and folks tended to let loose even more so than during the other celebrations. If the perpetrator seized the opportunity to try to attack Rowan again—or, in his absence, one of the other Thorns— we'd all be caught with our pants down (pretty literally) even if we instituted patrols the way we had for First Dew.

Fat lot of good they'd done us, anyway.

"Ugh, that blows," I muttered, dropping my forehead into my free hand, digging into my temples with my fingertips.

"But it's the right call," Emmy said, with the unshakable confidence that had lent her an air of gravitas far beyond her years since she'd become Victor of the Wreath. No matter how she might have felt, my sister's partner always gave off the impression that she had everything well under control. "We'll all miss it, but we'll manage—safety first. How long will it take you to get back on your feet, Issa? I don't want you two forging ahead with this until you're back to full steam."

"At least a week or so, I think," I said. "I'll take it easy until I'm a hundred percent again. I wouldn't put Rowan at risk, getting back out there before I know I'm back to full strength."

"Then that's settled." Emmy rubbed her hands together, then fixed me and Rowan with an unswerving gaze. "Just one more thing. Issa, Rowan, going forward—you have my permission to use whatever level of force is necessary to keep you both safe. Nothing's out of bounds, not anymore."

23

Bad Apples

I SPENT THE NEXT five days slowly getting my feet back under me, feeling incrementally better every morning and doing my best not to overtax myself. Every time I got antsy, I reminded myself that Rowan's safety hinged on my full recovery; playing the stoic hero and pushing myself too hard now would only put him in danger down the line.

Instead, for the first few days, I mostly stayed snuggled up in bed or curled in my bay window with my tablet, finalizing the story lines, character summaries, and costume designs for the haunted house, and ordering the fabrics and materials I didn't already have. I wasn't up to making most of the costumes myself the way I normally did, but I had a solid local network of tailors, cosplay enthusiasts, and makers to tap into. So while I did craft the more elaborate costumes for the two leads once I felt strong enough, for the first time since I'd started running the haunted house, I outsourced the construction of the rest of the designs.

I'd have expected to feel like I was letting my family down—but if anything, it was a tremendous relief not to feel overwhelmed. To not have to pretend I thrived on every aspect of bringing this new story to life.

Once I had that squared away, I asked Letha to organize remote auditions that I could just call into from home. We both already knew who our most dependable and talented actors were, particularly the ones who'd be perfect as the leads; once we had the hero and heroine of the cemetery-dwelling witches and their forest clan nemeses cast, everyone else fell into place. While I continued to rest, Letha put her final touches on the set design and oversaw a series of rehearsals. She'd also supervise our soft opening—a fully costumed run-through free for the cast's family and friends as a fun perk for the actors and a chance to show off before their performance really mattered—slated for three days from now.

And in ten days, we'd be ready to hit the ground running for the Flower Moon Festival.

With the haunted house mostly locked down, my thoughts kept returning to the details of Rowan's and my case. Drifting back to what little we knew, swirling like a murmuration.

Now that we knew Rowan was the true target, it was clear that most of our initial investigation had led us down dead ends. Our conversation with Holly wouldn't have given us anything useful to go on; the same went for our visit to Castle Camelot. While we had established beyond a reasonable doubt that Gawain Blackmoore was a certified turdbucket, his soured relationship with Holly and the suspicion he'd thrown on Juniper Thorn had now become largely irrelevant. And while we'd learned from Lark that a Thorn could conceivably cast a hex if they were using an amulet, the idea of something as huge and baneful as a Death's Head Hex successfully captured in a bespelled object strained even my credulity.

But we did know one thing for sure. The heart tree at the orchard had felt the caster and their intent.

But their void was a rot, an affliction, much older and colder than yours, she'd said to me, after she called me a daughter of the void. *Like a parasite that burrows under the bark, then sends its poison up.*

While I still wasn't sure what that could mean, the words conjured up a miasma of hatefulness, a malicious intent that fit with what I'd felt from the spells, especially the Death's Head Hex. And it made me wonder why the caster would have chosen those particular workings in the first place, out of the many less ghastly curses detailed in the Grimoire. Why would they have opted for such difficult and demanding spells, ones that relied on and channeled the caster's own hate and caused such tremendous, terrible damage?

Maybe that had been Rowan's and my mistake. In criminal investigations, the advice was often to start with the money, follow wherever it led.

So maybe, in our case, we should have started with the spells. Followed the magic itself.

"At least y'all are consistent with your choices," Rowan said wryly as I led him into the Bitters' vast and gloomy library two days later.

I shrugged, glancing around at the cobwebbed rafters that

disappeared into darkness high above us, the scrim of dust furring most surfaces, and the collection of macabre curiosities that served as bookends, including a pair of preserved vipers with shards of black quartz set into their eye sockets. Most of the time, I paid next to no heed to The Bitters' pervasive creep factor. To me, its eerie warren of nooks and crannies, the hazy smudges of the shades who disappeared around each corner just before you rounded it yourself, simply felt like home.

"Spring cleaning does not appear to be among your priorities," he added. "And every single room I've seen so far looks like it was literally designed to be as haunted as possible."

"Well, it kind of was," I said with a shrug, pulling the library's double doors closed behind us with a wheezy creak. Rowan didn't even realize how unusually quiet it was around here; I was the only one home today, and ghostly activity had been minimal. The speared chandelier in the foyer had barely even budged when Rowan crossed the threshold. "We like being surrounded by shades, you know that by now. Margarita did come over from Russia, so there's that, too; the decadent gloom aesthetic might actually be in our genes."

"Charming family trait, for sure."

"And *you* try maintaining a gigantic old pile like this without an entire staff at your beck and call," I finished, ignoring him. "We're all busy, okay? We clean when we can."

He held up his hands. "I'm just saying, good thing none of y'all have a dust mite allergy."

"Even if we did, it wouldn't stand a chance against our bone-deep stubbornness and powers of denial. Better than Claritin."

He was still chuckling and shaking his head as I led him to the ancient, clawed-up rosewood table—how it had gotten gouged by talons in the first place being a question for another day—where I'd already lit the swooping brass candelabra and laid out some of the tomes I thought might come in handy. Turning them up had been a chore in itself; any organizational principle that might once have been imposed on our books had long since fallen by the way-side. Unlike decadence and gloom, a sense of meticulous order wasn't exactly an Avramov dominant trait.

"You sure you're up to this today?" Rowan asked, eyes running closely over my face as he lowered himself into one of the wing-back chairs. "Wouldn't want you taking on too much too soon."

"I feel almost back to normal," I assured him, my cheeks heat-ing at his concern, the warmth in his eyes that had nothing to do with any clinical scrutiny. We hadn't spoken much while I was recovering, beyond touching base on how I was feeling; the deli-cate connection developing between us clearly wasn't the type of thing either of us wanted to discuss over text. It felt too tissue-paper fragile to talk about when we weren't face-to-face. "And we only have a week to go before Beltane and the Flower Moon Fes-tival. We need to get this in the bag."

"As long as you promise to keep listening to your body. We can take breaks anytime you need."

"I hear you, doctor." I popped off a crisp salute. "Though, I will say, I'm feeling pretty sturdy on that front. And it's not like we'll need any casting for what we're doing today, anyway."

Brow furrowed, Rowan gazed down at the books I'd strewn across the table, bound in black or oxblood leather, their covers crackled and peeling. "What are you thinking we'll find here, anyhow?"

"So, most of Thistle Grove's magical records are over at Tomes and Omens, right?" I began.

Emmy's father, James Harlow, served as the families' official record keeper, as the Harlows had done since the founding of the town. Records of the town's witchy history, along with the original Grimoire that had been penned by Elias Harlow, Thistle Grove's first founder, and a variety of other magical books were kept at the Harlow bookstore under lock and key. All of us had access to them, of course—but any requests had to be approved by James and his understudy, Delilah, one of Emmy's cousins.

"All of them, possibly, except for these," I said, gesturing at the books on the table. "These come from the Avramov secure archive. A repository for the kind of info that we'd prefer to keep in the family, if you know what I mean."

"Gotcha." He nodded, a sardonic quirk to the corner of his mouth. "The really shady shit best kept close to the chest."

I shrugged like, *You're not wrong.* "Obviously, the families' collected spells are listed in the Grimoire. But we also keep a separate book that sheds more light on our contributions: the spellsmith who crafted each spell, the circumstances around its creation, whatever other relevant history we happen to have."

Though witches rarely considered the origins of the spells we cast, magical workings didn't simply materialize out of thin air like preexisting artifacts, fully formed. Instead, each spell was a made thing, crafted by spellsmiths—witches with a particular affinity for inventing rituals that were especially creative and effective vehicles for manifesting will. While all of us could theoretically make spells, like any other learned skill, some of us had more natural talent for it than others.

Much more in some cases.

And the Avramov spellsmiths who'd invented the Misbegotten Curse and the Death's Head Hex would have been in a league of their own. A dastardly league, to be sure, but impressive all the same.

"We have records like that, too," Rowan said, nodding. "But they're over at Tomes along with the rest. No reason to keep the details of a healing spell private, right, if someone wants to learn more about it."

"That tracks. Unlike, say, a grotesque necromantic curse that should never be unleashed upon this realm ever again."

I drew the most timeworn of the tomes toward me, gingerly cracking its cover. It poufed out such a comically large billow of dust that it took all I had to suppress the sneeze tickling in my sinuses; I wasn't going to give Rowan the satisfaction. Eyes watering, I traced my fingertip down the yellowed table of contents until I found the Misbegotten Curse, flipping to the listed page.

Beneath the title, there was a bloodcurdling woodcut of a man caught mid-horrified scream, his pale face riddled with the same branching tracks that had webbed Holly's hands. Wavy lines radiated from his head, presumably the artist's whimsical depiction of his magic whooshing away.

"Lovely," Rowan said dryly.

"Like I said," I replied, my own nose wrinkling. "This one's not intended for public consumption. So you won't see much holding back."

I skimmed the entry, which was in Russian, like many of our older records had been before we'd formally (and begrudgingly) made the switch to English. Luckily, unlike some of my relatives, I'd been fascinated enough with the family legacy to bother learning the mother tongue while I was in high school, and I still had a working knowledge of written Russian. Enough, anyway, to get the gist.

"A necromantic working, intended to, uh . . . blanch, maybe, the vitality of whatever it is aimed at," I read aloud, translating messily as I went, "and drain thine enemy of their arcane strength and prowess."

"Sure as hell got the job done, then," Rowan said, an edge creeping into his voice.

My stomach twisted at the thought of Holly; she'd fallen to the back of my mind, but I hadn't forgotten her. "How is Holly doing?" I asked, looking up from the page.

"Better, actually," he said, the tightness in his face easing up a touch. "Whatever my mom and yours have been working on with her, it finally seems to be kicking in. She has some control of her magic again, and it looks like those scars are fading."

"Thank the Mother and Crone for that," I said softly, relief flooding through me, tinged with guilt that it was taking us so long to bring her attacker to justice. "I'm so glad for her. But I wish we had something, *anything*, to show her."

"She knows we're doing the best we can," Rowan said, sliding his calloused palm over my hand. "Alright? All we have to do is keep going."

I nodded, throat still a little tight, then looked back down to the page. "Okay, so . . . it lists the mountain town where the curse was first used—an Avramov stronghold in the Urals, it says, which makes sense. We were kind of witch royalty back then, dope-ass castles and all, before the general populace started thinking it maybe wasn't super cool and safe to have a bunch of wealthy necromancers running shit."

"Can't really blame them."

"Looks like this was in the mid-1600s, during a skirmish with the Volkovs. They were another witch family, and not exactly a friendly bunch, pretty hell-bent on driving us into the ground. And . . ."

I skipped down to the bottom, where the spellsmith in question was usually credited with the spell.

"It was crafted by spellsmith Valentina Avramov," I finished, cold riming my belly, snaking icy tendrils up to my ribs. "Margarita Avramov's youngest sister."

"Okay," Rowan said slowly, gaze shifting between my eyes. "So why are you making that face, talking about her?"

"Because based on family legend, she wasn't, um, a very nice person," I said, clearing my throat. "A bad apple, even by our . . . relatively accommodating standards."

I remembered story hour with Elena by the crackling library fireplace, my mother leading the four of us down the long-dead branches of our family tree in her sonorous voice, like some kind of psychopomp. Once we'd discovered our many-times-great-aunt, we'd clamored for Valentina tales; she'd sounded like a quixotic villainess ripped from a horror story, too impossibly badass and gory to actually exist.

Basically catnip for a bunch of spooky kids like us—especially since, with the buffer of all those centuries, you didn't have to consider any of that horror being *real*.

"Wow." Rowan sat back in his chair, looking a little haunted. "That's the stuff of nightmares right there. I mean, damn, what does an Avramov gone bad even look like?"

"I'm gonna choose not to take offense, only because you're right. From what I know, no one was particularly thrilled when she immigrated to come join Margarita here in Thistle Grove."

I remembered that Valentina had been a battle mage, and a wickedly ruthless one at that. A person with the kind of temperament that would've probably come in much handier when a bunch of berserker Volkovs were trying to raid your castle and steal your oxen or whatever than when you were building a new home for yourself alongside other witch families with more peaceable dispositions.

I ran my fingers through the unruly mass of my hair, massaging my temples with the heels of my hands.

"From what Elena's said about her, she was especially shitty about having to share territory with the Thorns," I went on. "According to her, magics like ours and yours were never meant to coexist, much less occupy the same territory. That's how she thought about land, sounds like. Very Settlers of Catan—and she did *not* want to be sharing that good grain and lumber with all of you."

"So, all-around shit-stirrer and hater, got it," Rowan said, pursing his lips with contempt. "Probably someone we'd be looking into pretty hard if she were around today. But seeing as she'd've punched out a cool three hundred years ago, I can't see how she plays into this. Unless she's got a living fan club you know about?"

I couldn't see it either . . . and yet. The way the spell itself had despised all Thorns, tracing all the way back to Alastair himself, the way it had thought it was somehow protecting me from Rowan . . .

It sounded exactly like how my diabolical pit viper of an ancestress might feel if she were around today.

"Yeah, no," I murmured, stumped, as I flipped back to the index. "I'm not aware of any Valentina stans hanging around, that's for sure. She was kind of hard-core, even for our more fringe elements. Why don't we see who was behind the Death's Head Hex? That might shed a different light on . . ."

FROM BAD TO CURSED

I leafed through the book to the curse's entry, my voice dying in my throat as my eyes landed on the bottom of the page, and the spellsmith attribution for the Death's Head Hex.

"Valentina Avramov," I croaked, meeting Rowan's eyes in shock. "Sixteen fifty-seven. It's her, Rowan. It's her, *again*. That cannot be a coincidence."

"Not necessarily—not if she authored a whole mess of spells," he pointed out. "That's possible, right?"

"It's easy enough to check, at least."

We spent the next two hours huddled over the pages, riffling through them just quickly enough to determine how many witches had contributed to the Avramov magical repository. The answer was dozens. Many of them seemed to be full-time spellsmiths, their stamp marking the vast majority of our collected spells.

And out of all of them, only these two were by Valentina Avramov.

"Why the hell would someone choose the only two of her spells in the Grimoire to cast?" Rowan asked, rubbing at his chin, face turning both distant and stormy as he considered the implications. "That's making a statement right there. I might be the primary target, yeah . . . but that's also saying, 'All Thorns, beware.'"

"And, Rowan . . ." I took a deep breath and closed my eyes for a moment, at war with myself.

What I was about to say was tantamount to choosing sides, a declaration that I was committing my loyalty to our team, to Rowan's and my investigation rather than my own family. It felt terrifying, like the ground was splitting open beneath me, yawning into a chasm that I now straddled with each foot very precariously planted on either side.

But I had to do it, anyway—because somehow, along the way,

we really had become a partnership. I owed this much to Holly, and to him.

"This book is private, accessible only by one of the family," I forced out, feeling like my rib cage might be imploding. "Only an Avramov could possibly know that those two spells were Valentina's handiwork. So if the choice is intentional, which it has to be, then it means . . ."

I trailed off, biting down hard on the fleshy inside of my lip, unable to complete the thought.

"Then the caster has to be one of you," Rowan finished for me, face turning taut. "We're looking for an Avramov with a grudge, after all."

24

Water like Milk

As it turned out, the American sequel to Valentina's Russian saga only cemented my great-aunt's status as an avatar of chaotic evil.

After a little more digging through the books I'd found, we discovered that a few generations back, one of my great-uncles had taken it upon himself to compile a detailed biography of every known Thistle Grove Avramov, starting with Margarita herself. Valentina featured in it prominently, from the vicious carnage she'd wreaked upon the Volkovs and various other pretenders to the Avramov claim back in the Urals, to her equally turbulent time in Thistle Grove.

Which she'd mostly spent throwing down with Alastair Thorn.

Rowan and I took turns reading the passages to each other, increasingly intrigued and appalled. Their feud seemed to have begun with Alastair's fixation on blocking many of the Avramovs' most "prestigious" necromantic curses from being included in the Grimoire, which at the time was still being compiled by Elias Harlow. There was no place for such vile magic, Alastair declaimed, in a community of witches who were intending to share peaceful, bountiful, beautiful magic with one another—not creatively gory ways to fuck each other up beyond recognition.

Valentina, in turn, took this as a personal affront, a vendetta against the Avramov heritage, as well as a hopelessly naive take on preserving the safety of the town. What if the same kinds of ruthless enemies she'd faced down in the Urals ever darkened their door, she wanted to know. Was Alastair planning on knitting a gate of brambles around the town, possibly growing them some precious poinsettia bouquets as his idea of defense?

More importantly, she argued, these spells were our family's hard-won legacy, and in their own way they *were* beautiful— macabre, horrifying works of art that demanded much more of a caster than whatever feeble workings some "bone-knitter with an affinity for clamorous flora" could pull off. In her view, such spells should have been honored for the astounding magical achievements that they were, not erased for all time because some lily-livered Thorn couldn't stomach their existence.

The two arrived at an uneasy truce only after tremendous pressure from all four families to quit their bitching, which had clearly become the kind of pervasive downer no one else wanted to tolerate. In the event that Thistle Grove ever wound up needing magical protection against some invading force, Alastair grudgingly allowed a limited number of necromantic curses to be included in the Baneful Workings section of the Grimoire, including the two of Valentina's that had been used against Holly and Rowan. But the rest of her arsenal would be retired forever—not even included in our private archives—and forgotten to history. Her descendants would never have the chance to resurrect the very worst of her spells, her darkest legacy.

I couldn't even *imagine* what those other spells must have been like if the Misbegotten Curse and the Death's Head Hex had been the least terrible of them.

Things seemed to simmer down after that, though the Thorn founder and my ancestress remained at odds their whole lives. Trees caught strange, warped blights on his property when they shouldn't have; Alastair forbade his most talented healers from ever treating ill Avramovs. The kind of obnoxious tit for tat in which no one functionally won.

The bad blood between our families had begun with the two of them.

"The way I see it, Alastair had a point," Rowan said, leaning back in his chair, arms crossed over his chest. "Even offensive and defensive magic can be aboveboard. Why include any of those screwed-up spells to begin with, when they're intended only to do maximum harm? I'm not seeing the alleged 'artistry' in that."

"I do see his take, and I mostly agree," I said. "But I also get where she was coming from, to a certain degree. The way Alastair framed it, her magic—and Valentina herself, kind of, by association—had no right to exist. For her, it probably came down to not wanting to be forgotten, or her contributions diminished. Especially by a man."

"Not that I'm ever down for misogyny, but that's kind of a tall order when you're all about that blood spatter," Rowan commented. "Seems like *that* part would've been Alastair's biggest problem with her, not the fact that she was a strong, independent woman."

"I'm not defending her, but in her mind, she probably saw herself as a protector of her people, a boon to her family. Plus, it's fair enough to want to be able to defend your new town, in case someone ever rolled up to your door, threatening to blow your house down. Something with which she had ample experience, sounds like."

Rowan tipped his chair back to the floor with a gusting sigh. "We could debate this all day, but fact remains, your gnarly-ass auntie's dead and gone. So how do we figure out which of your family's out here trying to stage some kind of revival? And what exactly is their issue with me, anyway? Could there be some racist bullshit brewing here that we need to factor in?"

"Unfortunately, I don't think we can definitively rule that out—but it'd be pretty intensely fucked-up, considering how many mixed-race Avramovs are around today. And if the caster's emulating Valentina for whatever reason, it makes that angle even more unlikely."

"Why's that?" Rowan said, mouth twisting. "You can't tell me she doesn't sound like some superpowered Karen to the nth degree, the kind who'd be the shittiest of racists if she were alive today."

"Oh, a thousand percent. But she and Alastair were both as white as it gets—like, I'm pretty sure they were both redheads. The daywalker ginger kind of white. Race wouldn't have played into their feud to begin with."

"But Rebekah Thorn was Black," he pointed out. "Alastair's wife."

"Right—but Valentina died in her late middle age," I countered. "And if I remember my Thistle Grove history, Alastair didn't even marry Rebekah until a little while later, after Valentina's death."

"Right, that's true." Rowan sighed, lacing his hands behind his neck. "Guess it's time to start asking your people some hard questions, then."

I heaved a sigh of my own, so deep it felt like I'd wrenched it from somewhere around my pelvis. A wave of fatigue washed over me at the idea of interrogating every single one of the hundred or so Avramovs in Thistle Grove until we rooted out our modern-day bad apple. Technically we could start with the Avramovs who'd been in attendance at the Crowning—but curses *could* be cast remotely if you were talented and skilled enough. The caster could've been elsewhere in the orchards, out of sight of the ceremony. And all of us had been up on the mountain for First Dew.

We had our work cut out for us, and then some.

But what other choice did we have? I could approach my mother with this new information, of course, but would her guesses be any better than mine? Not to mention the minefield I'd be stepping into, starting a conversation on Avramov culpability with her in light of everything I'd been holding back.

Given that I hadn't even told her about me and Rowan, I could see how it might look to her like I'd switched sides, become exactly the sort of turncoat she most despised.

I slumped over the table and plopped my forehead onto its pitted surface, the tang of centuries-old varnish stinging my nose.

"Guess so," I mumbled into the wood. "Fuck, I hate everything about this. Also, I realize this is a minimal concern, but I'm so bummed we don't even get to have the Dance of the Maidens this year. The Dance is my *favorite*."

"Which part?"

I swung my head up with an effort, draping my forearms on the table as I focused on him. "What?"

"Which part of the Dance do you like best?"

I thought about it, propping my chin in a palm.

"The skinny-dipping in the lake," I finally decided. "I mean, I love all of it, honestly. But after the dancing and the wine, you know how it always looks like there are *way* too many stars? And all of them are in the lake, too, when you get in, glittering all around you in the water? It's definitely the swim for me."

Rowan drew his lips through his teeth, one after the other, in that thoughtful way of his that seemed to set off a swarm of fireflies right beneath my skin. I could practically feel myself glowing, watching him do it.

"So, I can't promise you quite that many stars," he said, a slow smile tugging at his lips, that not-quite-dimple creasing by his mouth. "But if you're free this afternoon, meet me at the orchards and I'll see what I can do. Not like we'll be getting anything else done today, anyway. I can tell you're beat."

"You're talking about . . . swimming? At the orchards?" I stared at him, stymied. "I can usually hang with the non sequiturs, but I'm not catching on this time."

"Let's just say you're not the only one who can bring the surprises." He pushed back from the table, a sly gleam sparkling in his eyes. "Just come with a swimsuit, and leave the rest to me."

"ROWAN THORN," I said, jaw agape, shrugging off the bathrobe he'd loaned me when I arrived. It was one of his, oversized and freshly laundered, but also laced with the faintest hint of his own clean, citrusy scent. "Where in all the actual hells are we?"

Rowan and I stood barefoot on mosaic tiles, rough-hewn stone arches supported by wooden rafters soaring above us. We'd climbed even farther down from the basement of a small, nondescript administrative building near the orchard's farmhouse restaurant—and now, a series of interconnected pools spread out in front of us like steaming canals, separated by pillars and half walls of that same coarse stone. There was so much softly glowing water that it gave the impression of one massive pool, divided into many alcoves and partitions. The warm air smelled of humidity and chlorine, along with a faint, familiar tang of sulfur that I would never have expected to find near the Thorn demesne—though I doubted that here, it had anything to do with demons.

And there were dozens of tiny votives lit everywhere, glimmering in every corner, their flames dancing in the satin surface of the water. As close as I was likely to get to swimming in the sea of stars that Lady's Lake became on Dance night.

"Welcome to the Honeycake hot springs baths," Rowan said with a sweep of his arm, flashing a dazzling slice of smile at me in the dim light. "Open only to family and close friends. And today, reserved for the two of us."

"So, your family's been hiding an underground Roman bath crossed with a sex club spa beneath your orchards this whole time?" I demanded, still astonished. This kind of frankly sensual decadence was *not* in line with anything I'd ever expected from the Thorns. "This looks like the kind of place you need to be formally inducted into, by someone extremely rich and depraved. And you just . . . *have* it? For use at your leisure?"

"Well, the hot springs have always been here, yeah," he clarified. "But obviously, we've added to them extensively. A lot of these pools are artificial, with different temperatures. There's even a cold plunge, if you're feeling bold."

He shucked his own bathrobe and hung it on one of the hooks set into the blocks of stone. Whatever I'd been about to say promptly evanesced from my brain, evaporating like steam.

Above his navy swim trunks, his torso was both dense and defined as it tapered to his waist, his shoulders impossibly broad.

His was the kind of heavy muscle that came from a lot of physically demanding labor, and looked powerful without seeming bulky just for show. Over the topography of muscle, his skin shone taut and dark and smooth in the candles' wavering flames, like a canvas meant for moving light and shadow. I couldn't stop myself from staring at him, my eyes following the hard slabs of his chest, the ridges of his abs. The sharp V that plunged into his swim trunks like an enticing delta.

Fuck, even his *calves* were jacked.

He let me watch him, a faint smile hovering on his lips. His own heavy-lidded gaze so intent on my bikinied body that I could practically feel its weight as it dragged along the curve of my hips and dip of my waist, the long lines of my legs. I'd worn my favorite suit, lacy black triangles that set off the cinnamon-freckled pallor of my skin and the auburn tumble of hair coursing to the small of my back. It also matched the glossy dark polish of my nails.

It was possible that I'd thought this look through way too intensively. But then again, I'd spent a lot more time than *strictly* necessary dwelling on being close to naked with Rowan Thorn.

"Seems like you might be thinking some things," he said, voice gravelly and tinged with just a little humor. Eyes still charged, galvanic with that pent-up hunger. "It's like I can almost hear them."

"I was, um," I said, blinking fast, struggling to formulate words. "Just thinking you should probably never wear a shirt again."

He chuckled, taking a few steps closer to me, close enough to graze his fingertips down my arms. All the fine hairs on my body stood at attention like lightning rods, as though the whole of me had been electrified. I could feel my breathing quicken, turn into shallow little sips that ended at the very base of my throat, right above my pounding pulse.

My garnet rose and fell with each inhale, feeling heavier than usual, colder than the surrounding humidity. I wished I could take it off, but for an Avramov, that was almost never safe. That was how Talia had become so badly possessed back during the Gauntlet; hers had broken during a challenge, leaving her defenseless to sustained psychic attack. And there were desperate shades everywhere, likely even in a pretty place like this.

Something about this thought nagged at me as I grazed my fingers over the garnet. But it disappeared before I could grab hold of it, flitting away like a minnow darting off into the water.

"Why don't we get in," Rowan suggested, the liquid gleam of his eyes shifting between mine, hunger leaping in them. "Before we just . . . don't."

"Good call, yes." I nodded furiously, all but lunging toward the nearest pool like maybe I literally needed it for fire-extinguishing purposes, to put me out. "Because that would be a shame."

As soon as I set foot into the water, its silken heat parting around my skin, I realized that it really *would* have been a shame to miss out on this feeling. The heat of it was perfect, blissful without being overwhelming. Even the texture felt somehow different from regular water, closer to milk, swirling in velvety circles as it lapped against me. I walked farther in, as deep as the pool went, trailing my fingers over its rippled surface until I sank down to my haunches, letting it close around me to my neck.

"Your water," I moaned, tipping back my head to let my hair expand, losing all its weight, "is *amazing*. And you can tell everyone I said so."

A laugh rippled out of him, raspy and rich, echoing off the stone.

"An Avramov endorsement, for real?" he teased. "No one'll ever believe I got one for free."

"Oh, I may yet charge," I assured him, pushing off from my toes to lift my legs and float on my back. "Remains to be seen."

Water filled my ears, the soft underwater shush of moving currents. I closed my eyes for a moment, letting it leach the lingering aches from my body, suck the strain from my muscles. I could feel Rowan's own shifting movements as he took a leisurely lap, swimming away and then back toward me before flipping onto his back, too. We floated side by side for a long while, our bodies only just bumping each other, until his fingers brushed mine. Our hands entwined loosely as if of their own accord, fingers threading together. He tugged me closer, then pulled us both back up until we bobbed in front of each other, toes just grazing the tiles.

I slicked my hair back with my free hand as I met his eyes. Water had beaded all along his pulled-back locs, shimmering along his hairline and over the bold planes of his cheekbones. It reminded me of how I'd imagined him wet from a shower, what seemed like forever ago; apparently some fantasies did come true.

We watched each other for a minute, not speaking. Smiling just a little, feeling the tension grow between us like the thin skin of an expanding bubble.

"I never really thanked you," he said, eyes locked on mine, their hazel deepened to a rich honey brown by the low light. The moving reflection of the water played over his face like diamond facets. "For, you know. Saving my ass entirely, without any regard for what might happen to you. I don't know about how Avramovs roll with blood debts, but to me, that's a pretty big deal."

"Not a problem," I assured him. "The fallout has been a drag, for sure. But it was also an experience, and I'm generally all about those. Plus, don't forget I owed you one."

"What?" He canted his head, brow knitted. "What for?"

I ducked my chin, suddenly feeling a little diffident. "That day in the woods. The way you took care of me. I realize I never even explained why it happened in the first place, and that . . . that seems like something you should know."

"You never owed me an explanation, Issa. Whatever went down inside your head, that's your business."

"But I *want* it to be your business, too," I insisted, looking back up at him, realizing just how true that felt, the tenderness of this new softening inside me. I'd never felt anything like this compulsion before, not with anyone else—to have someone see me fully, ragged fault lines and all. To stand so vulnerable and exposed, to take a step toward them with no promises or guarantees between us.

And yet still feel confident they'd be right there, waiting to meet me on the other side with hands extended.

"I want you to understand," I admitted. "It doesn't feel like an obligation, like something uncomfortable or scary, to share that with you—and I can't tell you how amazing that is to me. How incredible."

"Then it's a gift to me, too, that you feel safe enough." His fingers tightened around mine, tugging me the slightest bit closer. "And I would love to hear it."

Our hands still joined, I rotated in the water until I had my back against his front, his arm wrapped around my slick middle; I couldn't quite bring myself to be facing him as I said this. He pulled us both to the edge of the pool so he could lean against it as he tucked me closer to his front. I relaxed into him, tipping my head back to rest on his shoulder. A flutter of nerves brushed across my throat and chest like moths, at the magnitude of what I was about to say.

But Rowan's arm around me, his sturdy muscle and bone against my back—the sheer solidity of him like the best anchor I could imagine—laid them to rest.

"I don't want to work for my family anymore," I whispered, though with the ambient echo, even those low words bounced accusingly around the room. "I used to, I think. I remember loving it, not even that long ago. But now it's like this constant weight I drag around, knowing it's not the life I want. Like I'm living inside a trap."

I waited for the poisonous betrayal to set in, the sense of having shot a dart of treachery at my family that I could never recall. But there was only a slow sense of peace, so startling and unexpected that it stopped me in my tracks.

The last thing I'd expected was for this to feel easy. But it did with him.

When I didn't go on, Rowan took a breath, chest expanding against my back.

"Okay. What *do* you want to do, instead?" he prompted.

"I want . . . to design clothes," I said on a rushed exhale, feeling an almost miraculous unfurling, a spiraling sense of wonder at saying it out loud. Only I'd heard those words before, and only ever inside my own head.

My stomach unwound, as if I'd been holding it clenched for longer than I could remember, a deep sense of relief radiating from my navel. It felt so good, so much better than I'd expected, to tell someone that truth.

"Start my own ready-to-wear fashion line," I continued, gaining steam. "I have this thing for unusual but versatile pieces— clothes you can easily wear to work under a blazer, but then also rock out in later. Hidden cutouts, leather inlays, lace detailing, even very delicate spikes and chains. Office drone to badass queen, in just one layer."

He chuckled against me, a low rumble I felt through my skin. "Probably leave the 'office drone' part out of your future PR, I think that may not go over so hot. But I love the sound of the rest of it . . . feels very you. Like you could make it beautiful."

"And I want it to be as eco-friendly as possible," I went on. "That's the other part of it, the sustainability. Because that *is* important to me, Rowan, it always has been. I know it doesn't sound very Avramov of me to be into preserving the green, but it's true. And I know it's possible; I've seen brands like Reformation do it. Incorporate it into their practices from day one."

"Even better, then. Sounds like you know exactly how you want to play this out. So, what's holding you back?"

"My family," I admitted, my throat tightening a little. "My mother, especially. There's this unspoken expectation with her, that we all work together. That our professional lives should be bound up with the Avramov legacy, somehow. Because what could be bigger, more important, than that? Than elevating our family name?"

"The thing you actually want to do," Rowan said, as if it were obvious. "Your purpose. By definition, that's worth more than what someone else expects of you."

I huffed out a sad laugh. "If only it were that easy."

"What's hard about it?"

"Look, I don't know what it's like between you and your parents . . ." I started, then trailed off, realizing I did know.

I'd seen it in the affectionate light that lit inside Rowan's eyes every time he talked about his family, that private inner sunrise that seemed to encompass all of them. I'd seen it in the way they accepted his decision to continue investigating with me, despite their own deep and completely reasonable concern for his safety— because they recognized the decision as his. I'd seen it in the way that Lark seemed confounded by the idea that her parents might take issue with her choice to break away from them, to pursue a dream that had nothing to do with Honeycake, with her being a Thorn witch.

"Scratch that," I said instead. "I *do* know what it's like with you and your parents. They clearly let their kids be their own people; it's like they can't even imagine holding you back in any way. And my mother . . . she's one of my favorite people, my closest friends. But she's also who I modeled myself after pretty much my entire life. So the idea that I could disappoint her so deeply now, by telling her I want to go off and do my own thing—a thing so far removed from what she wants for me . . ."

I shook my head, biting my lip hard. "It's crushing, Rowan. It's the most scared I've ever been. And let's not forget you're talking to a chick who fucks with demons to blow off steam."

"So that's why," he said softly, skimming a kiss over my wet hair. "Why the visit to Lark set you off like that."

"Yeah." I took a shuddering breath. "Because she has everything I want, basically. Her own dream, *and* her family's approval. The permission to go after it without letting anybody down." Despite myself, tears prickled in my eyes at how wonderful that must feel. How liberating. "The whole package, the exact thing I can't imagine myself ever having."

"That's a lot to carry," he said. "A serious burden. Have you thought about talking to your mom about it?"

"I've been too chickenshit to try," I admitted. "Because once it's out, there's no taking it back, you know? What if it ruins everything between us, and I lose my mother? My . . . my friend?"

Silence stretched thin between us, forming a fine, slim veneer like porcelain.

"Look, you know I can't tell you what to do," Rowan finally said, fissuring that fragile quiet. "And I wouldn't ever want to, because it's not mine to say. But my take on it is, can you afford *not* to take the chance? Because I don't think you can, Issa. I don't think you're built to be this unhappy, when you know you're meant for a different path. And you can't turn your back on a calling like this—from what I've seen, it's just not in you to limit yourself like that. So far as I can tell, there's no easy way out on this one."

"Damn it," I murmured. "Should've known there wouldn't be a Door Number Three."

"In my experience," he said with a husky chuckle, "there rarely is, when it comes to the difficult shit."

"Someone should really speak to a supervisor about that."

"Still looking for that direct line to management myself."

We lapsed into another silence, but this one had a different quality to it. A diffuse kind of shimmer, the sort of sparkling quiet that let you sink into sensation. The slick feel of Rowan's skin against mine where we connected above the water's surface, the smooth commingling of our legs beneath it.

The way he had begun to stroke my left hip in slow, delicious circles.

"What is it that we're even doing here, Rowan?" I asked him, the words slipping out of me before I could check myself. "You and me, I mean. *This.*"

Another low rumble of a chuckle reverberated through his chest and into me.

"I'm down for this to be anything you want, Issa. So why don't you tell me what that might be."

I turned inside the circle of his arms, to face him again.

"I think that depends," I said, my eyes roaming his clean-cut features, lingering on the fine flare of his nose and the crisp indent beneath it. Those unfairly perfect lips. "On whether you really lit all these candles for me. Or did you have your berobed sex-club attendants do it, before melting tastefully back into the shadows?"

"Did it myself, of course. If you're gonna be outsourcing your grand gestures, then why bother?" He cupped my face, brushing his thumbs over my cheeks before trailing his fingers down my neck. "So, I thought, one for all those stars you won't get to swim in at the Dance this year. Or one for each of your freckles, take your pick. Whichever you like better."

I sputtered a little laugh, tilting my head to grin up at him. "I don't know if you've noticed, but I'm at least ninety-eight percent freckle. I think you may have missed a few."

His eyes slid down my chest, the hunger in them leaving behind a sear I could feel on my skin, like a traveling flush.

"Maybe I just haven't had the chance to get a real good look at you," he said, a smolder catching in his voice, eyes falling to half-mast. "Take a proper reckoning."

I stepped back incrementally, just enough to open some space between us. Enough for cooler air to rush into where we'd been joined, raising a stipple of goose bumps where it met my skin. And enough for him to be able to skim his gaze down my entire torso, to the dip of my navel, the rounded swell of my lower belly, the jut of my hips under my skin.

Lips drawn through his teeth, he traced lines between my freckles with a fingertip, charting constellations, connecting one to the next with the slicks of water that pearled my skin. He skimmed over my breasts and down my ribs—then slid both hands down to my waist, tugging me against him. I could feel the taut bulge of him press hard against me, grinding into where I was already swollen and sensitive even though we hadn't so much as kissed yet.

"You're right," he said, a hoarse rasp that plucked at my insides as if they'd turned into high-strung chords, his darkened eyes snaring mine. "There'll be a lot more candles next time."

"Then that's what I want, for starters," I said, my heart feeling like it might punch through my ribs. "Just to know for sure that there's going to be a next time for us. That you're not going to suddenly re-remember my last name, and then change your mind about wanting this. Wanting me."

He winced a little, biting the inside of his cheek. Then he wrapped one strong hand around the nape of my neck, drew me a little closer.

"Okay, I deserved that. Would it help you to know that I already told Linden about us?" He smiled just a little, stroking the back of my neck. "And you do not go to your twin and best friend if you're on the fence about someone. That's the rule."

I rocked back a little, genuinely surprised. Talia and Linden had grown pretty friendly as they schemed against Gareth during the Gauntlet, and I knew from my sister just how close the twins were, how real with each other. Gabrielle and Aspen might have had an inkling about us, from the demonstrative way Rowan had taken my hand at Harlow House—but Linden knowing felt like an admission on a completely different level.

I hadn't even admitted to my own sister how I was beginning to feel about Rowan, so one could argue he was actually quite a bit ahead of me.

"She's stoked about you, too," he added, grinning. "Especially likes that you won't let me stay on what she refers to as my 'preachy bullshit.' I think you'd be surprised by how much you two have in common, when it comes to keeping me on my toes."

"You know what, that *does* help."

"Good. And here's the thing—what you may not know about

me yet, but that I hope you'll come to trust," he murmured, those warm eyes agleam on mine. "Issa Avramov, I do promise you this: I never make the same dumbass mistakes more than once."

Then he pulled me into a kiss.

It was tentative at first, a slow, interrupted graze, catching and releasing each other's lips, the sides of our noses brushing as we inhaled each other's unsteady breath. He deepened it only slightly each time, the sharp edge of his teeth sinking lightly into my lower lip, followed by the flickering heat of his tongue sweeping against it. And yet even only easing into it, I wanted him like I'd never wanted anyone, desire coursing through me like molten metal, scorching and savage.

Bursting through any barricades I still had left, razing them to the ground.

I wanted every inch of him pressed up against and inside me, the hard lines of his body bringing mine to yield.

As if he could feel my desire rising to meet his, he flipped us around so that my back was pressed against the tiles. Then he stood up in the water and lifted me, setting my butt on the pool's edge, my legs wrapping around his hips.

The next kiss consumed us both, a deep and sweeping rhythm, a slick entangling of tongues and lips. I could feel him unlace my bikini top behind my back, tug it out from between us and let it drop, my bare breasts pressing against his chest. Then his hand wound in my wet hair, looping it around his wrist—and he pulled gently, arching my neck, other hand at the small of my back. Lowering me until I lay back on the heated tiles, each pressing a diamond imprint into my skin, only my legs skimming the water where he still stood.

When his mouth met my goose-bumped wet skin, my hips bucked against his of their own volition. He nibbled and sucked at me, setting fire to every nerve ending as he palmed the soft swell of my breasts, rolled and tugged at my nipples, drew each hard into his mouth and flicked his tongue over them. Then he trailed lower, dragging mouth and tongue and teeth down the tender flesh of my sides and lower belly. A silken, scorching path emblazoned down to my hips.

When he traced his tongue along the sensitive seams where my pelvis met my legs, I thought I might die of how sweet it felt, how overwhelmingly and almost painfully delicious.

"Goddamn, Issa, the way I want you . . ." he groaned against my skin, biting at the inside of my thigh until I let out a low, urgent sound. Every time his wet hair brushed against me I jumped a little, oversensitized. "To taste and feel you, to give you fucking everything . . ."

"Then give it to me, Rowan," I demanded, high-pitched and strained. "I'm right here. I'm waiting."

With a low, inarticulate sound, he unlaced my bikini bottoms and swept them to the side.

And then there was nothing but the hot slick of his mouth melting against me, demanding and deft. Gliding along me in darting flicks and slow circles until my cries rose into half-strangled little screams, bouncing back to me from the rough stone all around us. I could feel myself building, my head grinding against the tiles, my nails sinking into his shoulders, my heels digging into his back. I wanted more and closer, and then even more, until I couldn't stand it any longer.

When I finally tipped over the edge, sparks showered the insides of my eyelids. A spiral of pleasure tore through me in rippling waves, all pinpricks and honey, with such intensity that it bordered on pain. I was still caught up in it when Rowan slowly pulled back and straightened, tugging me up with him, drawing me closer to the pool's lip until I sat on its very edge with him standing between my legs.

"Shit, I don't have a condom on me," he groaned against my mouth as we melted into another kiss. I could taste myself on him, and it made me lose what scant breath I had left. "I could go—"

"I'm on the pill," I assured him hastily, still trembling against him, my brain feeling like it was free-falling through a sky full of fireworks. "I'm good if you are. And I haven't . . . I haven't been sleeping with anyone else. So we're safe."

"Oh, same here, thank *fuck*," he breathed inside my ear, arms locking tight around me as he angled himself. "'Cause I might've straight up died if we had to stop."

"I would've brought you back for this," I assured him. "Forbidden magic or no. And not even felt bad about it for a second, trust."

He was still laughing against my mouth as he slid into me in a slow, sure thrust, my head falling back with a sharp gasp.

It was even better than I'd imagined it—and I'd spent a lot of evenings mapping out the mental terrain of how this might feel. With me perched on the very edge and legs wrapped around him, the angle of our joining was nothing short of mind-blowing. A dizzying grind of heat and thrust and straining fullness that I couldn't have designed for a better fit.

What kind of spell was this, I wondered giddily, that Rowan Thorn of all people felt like he had been made for me?

We rocked against each other, harder and faster, my arms locked around his neck and teeth sunk into his shoulder, both of us moving with that intuitive rhythm. Like our bodies recognized each other's in a way neither of us could have predicted; like everything we'd ever said or done with each other had been part of some prescient prelude. The groundwork laid for this aching, stunning perfection.

We came within breathless seconds of each other. Me first, panting and moaning into his ear, and then him, with a half growl of a groan and a full-body shudder that only drove me over the edge again.

A long while later, still entwined in shaky-breathed languor, an afterglow that felt like falling dusk, Rowan gently gathered my puddle of limbs and tugged us both back into the water's warmth. I wrapped myself around him like a koala, head nestled into his neck. Arms and legs wound around his middle, my butt resting on his lifted thighs as we floated together.

"So what are the odds," I mumbled into his neck, once I felt like I had the energy to speak again, "that we might ever get to do this in an actual bed? Seems like the stars have not aligned for us thus far. Not that I'm complaining."

"What do I get if I fix that up for us in short order?" he said into my hair. "Like, today?"

"My eternal gratitude," I assured him. "And round two, possibly."

"Oh, don't you start underestimating me now." I could hear the smile in his voice. "You'd best believe there'll be at least two more rounds, before the sun even sets on us."

"That may be the best threat-slash-promise anyone has ever made me. Which is *really* saying something."

"Stick with me, Avramov." He nipped at my earlobe, grinning against my cheek. "I'm only just getting started."

25

Red Wine and Raven Feathers

"TELL ME ABOUT the ghosts," Rowan said.

We were draped over each other, in the queen bed of the suite Rowan had snagged for us last night after we emerged from the baths. The farmhouse restaurant also served as a B and B for orchard visitors wanting a longer stay on the premises; our room was on the topmost floor. This morning, the window was still flung open—we'd wanted to smell spring air even in our dreams, not that we'd done much sleeping—and pale, early sunshine filtered in, the sheer white curtains just barely billowing. An overzealous bird was doing way too much under the eaves outside, singing with such extravagant bravura you'd think it had something to prove.

The perfection of it all stumped me a little; I frankly wasn't sure I knew what to do with this much happiness. I'd never really had to handle it before.

"What about them?" I asked, stirring in our messy nest of rumpled sheets and pillows, cuddled up against his chest.

The bed was a disaster, which tracked, given that Rowan had more than kept his promise/threat to me. I'd woken pleasantly achy, sore from the best kind of exertion. We'd already been talking for hours in a meandering conversation that took us every which way, like a long, unguided tour of a city you'd never visited before but somehow already halfway loved.

Like we'd been dying to dive into each other this entire time, and now there was nothing left to hold us back.

"I have a lot of material on that front," I added, "so you'll need to be more specific."

"I guess I want to know what it's like," he replied slowly, curling an arm around my neck to draw me closer. "To talk to them the way we talk to plants. What do they feel? What kinds of things do they want to tell you? I just keep thinking . . . it must be so goddamn sad for you, to have to interact with them."

"Sometimes it is. But it's rarely only that. Shades tend to retain the most powerful emotions from their lives—echoes of the feelings they can't bear to let go of. The clinging unresolved stuff that keeps some of them here when they should have passed beyond the veil. Love, jealousy, guilt, rage, occasionally a very powerful sense of obligation . . . in my experience, those tend to be the most common."

"So you're saying most people don't choose to hang around after they pass."

"Definitely not." I gave a little shiver. "Fortunately for those of us who can talk to them, too, or we'd be mobbed. Even as it is, if it weren't for our garnets, none of us would have any peace at all. Shades are already pretty much everywhere."

Rowan stiffened under me, swallowing. "Everywhere, like, even here? Even right now?"

I breathed out a laugh against his warm chest. "Is this a question you *really* want me to answer? I assume you're planning on sleeping again, without imagining a bunch of invisible ghosts chilling by your bedside every night, staring down into your face."

"Oh, damn, you're right. I am so sorry I asked." He gave a little shudder beneath me. "That's a visual I didn't need in my life, like, at all."

"If it's any consolation, the nastier ones probably don't care about you, anyway," I assured him. "They're only really interested in those of us who can hear them. Or the living they're trying to attach themselves to for whatever reason. People they might've hated with a particular passion or really cared about, too much and too deeply to let go of yet."

"Would you be able to see them?" he asked, a new note of vulnerability to his tone. "Ones like that? Shades that might be clinging to me, for example, because they still care?"

I bit my lip, seeing where this could be going. "Is there anyone in particular you might be looking for?" I asked, gentle.

"My grandmother Laurel," he answered instantly. "My dad's mom. She died of pancreatic cancer, about ten years ago. And she and I . . . we were tight, to say the least. I still miss her, think about her pretty much every day. Makes me wonder if that's because I can still feel her. Whether she might be sticking around in some way, staying close to me."

I had a flash of memory, Rowan's face darkening when I asked him how far green magic could go, what it could heal, the natural limitations it hitched up against. He'd cited cancer as one of them, and this must have been why.

"I'm sorry for your loss, Rowan," I whispered, laying my hand on his chest. "And it's possible that she's still here, if her attachment to you was that strong. Though that would mean she hasn't managed to move on, to whatever comes next for her. Do you still want me to look? Are you sure that's something you want to know?"

He thought about it for a long time, his chest rising and falling beneath my hand. I could feel the mallet of his heart thumping just under my ear. A slow, steady, peaceful cadence, solid and reassuring as the rest of him.

"No," he said, finally. "It wouldn't help. Even if she's here, she's still gone in the ways that matter. It's not like I'm ever gonna get to hold her hand again. Thank you, though. It means a lot, to know you would've done it for me."

"Of course. We used to be called deathspeakers, back in the old world. It's part of our responsibility, to act as the channel between, when someone needs us to be that for them." I stroked his warm skin, running my fingertips over the curves and dips of muscle that bound his chest. "And even if it wasn't, I would've done it for you anyway. Just 'cause I like you."

He caught my hand, brought it to his lips to brush a kiss over my knuckles. Then his mouth stilled against my skin, his grip tightening on my hand.

"Wait a minute," he said slowly. "I just had a thought. You said ghosts with the strongest emotions . . . they're the ones that tend to stick around. Right?"

"Right. And?"

"And we've been treating your gnarly auntie like she doesn't matter, doesn't figure into things because she's dead," Rowan said, impatience and something akin to excitement jostling into his tone. "But what if she *isn't* gone, Issa? Sounds like she had plenty of strong emotions to tie her down and keep her here. Like, say, all that high-key hatred for my family."

I sat up abruptly with the sheets clutched to my chest, my mind racing, my heart catapulting into my throat. Even though the room was warm, the slight breeze wafting from the window drew a trail of goose bumps all the way down my back.

"But she'd be so faded," I murmured to myself, thinking. "So frayed, ancient even for a shade. Barely even able to manifest. Three hundred years is a long time to cling to this mortal plane."

Then a memory surfaced, of Lottie the head chambermaid's careworn face when she'd apparated beside me in The Bitters halls, her talk of the pestering, problematic ghost she referred to as "madam." The one who wouldn't leave, who wouldn't listen to sense, who was frightening the rest of them with her high dudgeon.

Why would she call another spirit "madam"—unless that spirit had once been an Avramov, and the Dread Lady's own sister, no less? And what other kind of shade would have had the strength to infect our demesne that way, twist it with their own singular malevolence?

"Shit," I said, under my breath. "Rowan, I think you might be onto something. We've had a nasty poltergeist problem for over a month now, back at The Bitters—and I guess it *could* be her haunting us. It would make sense that you'd be her target, too, as the Thorn scion. The direct male descendant of her archenemy himself."

"So, could she have cast the curses?" Rowan asked, sitting up himself. "*Can* ghosts cast spells if they were witches back when they were alive? Could she even have come to the orchards, or up to Lady's Lake?"

"That's the thing. I doubt she'd be able to travel that far from The Bitters," I said, shaking my head. "That's usually not how it works; most of them have a locus, a sphere of influence beyond which they can't really tread. And I've never known a ghost capable of casting, no matter how much magic they might've commanded in life. They can wreak plenty of other kinds of telekinetic havoc, sure. But usually their magical abilities die with them. You need a living body, flesh and blood to channel magic."

"Then how would she have pulled it off?" Rowan wondered.

"I'm not sure," I said, biting at a knuckle. "She could have enlisted an accomplice, enticed someone else to her cause. The stronger spirits can sneak into your dreams sometimes, influence you, if you don't know how to protect yourself. Maybe it was something like that."

"Like, possession?"

"No, that's different. It's a possibility, too—though that's much harder to successfully pull off than ghost movies would have you think. Most people have strongly integrated egos, aren't nearly open or vulnerable enough for something like that. And even then, a shade would have to exert a tremendous amount of control to be able to access a possessed witch's magic."

"But it could happen." His face stilled as another thought struck him. "And to cast hexes like the ones that were used . . . wouldn't she have needed one of you? An Avramov? Someone who could handle that kind of heavyweight necromantic magic?"

"Probably." I thought, with a little lurch of fear; I did not like where this was heading, not one bit, and yet it made too much terrible sense. "And if that's the case, then of course she would have used her host's magic to cast her own spells. Avramovs do tend to be a little more susceptible to influence and possession than the average person, too, because of our connection to the other side. But we're trained up to resist it. And that's where our garnets also come in, as another layer of protection."

"But both are still possibilities. What do we do next, to find out which it is we're dealing with?" Rowan asked, tossing off the covers and swinging his feet to the floor, turning over his shoulder to look at me.

"We cast a summoning spell," I said meeting his eyes, my own gaze flinty. "We force her to come to us. But you can't compel a shade out of a living host, not from afar. So if she doesn't come . . . then we'll know we're dealing with possession."

BACK AT THE Bitters, with Rowan's help, I assembled everything I needed for a heavy-duty summoning spell.

When I'd done this off-the-cuff in my attempt to chase off Davara, I hadn't had the luxury of any magical accoutrements. Instead, I'd relied on my own brute strength, fueled by desperate need and panic. This time, Rowan and I sat on the wine cellar's dusty stone with a circle of candles flickering between us, talismanic objects gathered at the center. The kinds of things that would speak to the particular shade I meant to summon through sympathetic magic, all within an ironclad circle that would ensure the shade couldn't budge once we wrenched her here.

Before we began, I'd taken some time to read more of Valentina's biography, and I'd learned a few additional things about her. Like that she kept ravens, preferred the kind of red wine that I always thought tasted like barnyards and leather, and enjoyed long baths under moonlight à la Elizabeth Báthory. Apparently she'd had servants wrestle massive bathtubs outside for her, just so she could soak in rose petals and goat's milk under the full moon.

Good for the skin, I guessed, and also for being insufferably fancy if you chose to live like that. (This also seemed like the kind of uncomfortably sexy detail my great-uncle the biographer hadn't *really* needed to include about one of his own blood relatives, but okay! At least it helped.)

Now, breathing long and slow, I passed my hand over a porcelain bowl of milk—2 percent cow's milk was all I had, and Valentina would just have to deal—swimming with red petals, moving it in slow circles. Then I trailed my fingers over the glossy sheaf of raven feathers I'd pinned down with red jasper and smoky quartz, along with a few other crystals, a collection of stones known as medium's helpers, which best facilitated connection with unruly spirits.

In the middle of it all, a censer burned with a loose blend I'd mixed myself with Valentina in mind. Mugwort, jasmine, frankincense, and henbane, with just a touch of mullein and attar of rose. A perfume that should be irresistible to her, like a compulsion. The heady smell of it was already winding around us like chains, both enchanting and oppressive, as though it had weight as well as scent.

"Shit, this feels heavy," Rowan muttered, his eyelids fluttering. "Good, too, in a way, but . . . *dense*. I've never felt like this during a spell before."

"That's death magic for you," I murmured back. "No cupcakes or unicorns around these parts. You sure you can hang?"

He opened his eyes fully, lifting an eyebrow. "Managed to make it this far, haven't I?" he demanded, with just a little edge. "You won't see me backing out this late in the game."

"In that case," I said, inclining my head, "time to set this baby off."

I picked up the last object in the candlelit circle, a goblet of red wine. I took a long sip, heavy on the tannins and almost gritty on the tongue, then handed it to Rowan. Once he'd drunk from it, too, I intoned the opening words of the strongest, most brutal summoning charm I knew. My magic sang loud inside my veins as it whirled to primal, heady life. A deafening chorale, like a whole host of dread angels, power surging up inside me like welling blood.

This was not the kind of spell you cast while you were still interested in playing nice.

Ectoplasm began gathering all around us like a dark and icy mist, rising in coiled wisps not only from my hands but also from the objects ringed by the candles. As I closed my eyes, a vivid image of Valentina Avramov flared to life behind them.

I'd known what she looked like from the woodcut of her I'd seen in the biography, but this was different. Now I saw her in oversaturated color, as she would've been in life, but even brighter, more textured. The lines of her proud face bold and stark, as if carved by some sculptor's exacting knife. A cruel but dainty mouth with colorless lips, pale as her fair skin. Ice-gray eyes like my own sister's, except long and narrow and tilted up at the corners. A cloud of the same copper hair my mother had inherited, unfurling all around her like a banner.

The way her own shade remembered herself, in what remained of her mind.

Because Valentina *was* on our side of the veil, I realized, my pulse quickening. If she hadn't been, I couldn't have felt her like this.

Darkness ringed her bright silhouette on all sides—like the opposite of an eclipse, a shadow halo—and suspicion played across that feral face. She sensed my call, the lure of all the talismans I'd set out to attract her. And by rights, she shouldn't have been able to resist their siren song—not if she was on this side only in spirit.

I opened my eyes with an effort, looking around the cellar. Rowan and I were hemmed in by ectoplasm, ashen currents of it coursing around our circle. What should have happened next was a coalescing, a forcible apparition of the shade from all the raw material I'd provided. Instead, the sticky darkness began to fold together like batter, and then thin itself out—forming something like a slender river or a floating ribbon, which spooled out of the cellar and led up and away.

"She's not coming, Rowan," I told him, fumbling to my feet. "Which means you were right—she's probably hiding inside someone. But the spell's laying down a trail for us. If we follow it, she'll be on the other end."

26

) ☽ ☽ ● ☾ ☾ (

A Seed Pearl of a Shade

T HE SHADOW TRAIL of the ectoplasm led us down Hyssop Street and straight to the Arcane Emporium—or, more specifically, to the haunted house next door.

"What the actual fuck," I said to Rowan, my entire body surging with shock. "She's *here*?"

"Gotta be hitching a ride, right?" Rowan muttered beside me. "Only way she could have made it this far."

Rowan and I had walked all the way here, over a mile from The Bitters. It would have been too complicated to try to follow my phantom version of the yellow-brick road in a car, and I wasn't totally sure how being in a moving vehicle might have messed with the spell itself. Sometimes magic and technology didn't play so well together, and I'd felt that this was not the moment for experimentation.

Now we were here, the ashen ribbon disappearing through the

hammered metal doors—which were only ajar at all because to-day happened to be the haunted house's soft open.

I sank my nails into my palms, a fresh throb of fear pulsing through me. "No other explanation."

Rowan worked his jaw from side to side, glaring at the open door, the darkness that beckoned from within. Spooky music filtered from inside: faint wailing moans; a discordant, gloomy score; the echo of a low and malevolent laughter. I knew it wasn't real, that it would be only Letha's clever handiwork we found inside, but my skin bunched into goose bumps all the same.

Because somewhere in there lurked an evil that *was* very real—a malevolence that was related to me, torn out of time and ripped from the annals of my own family's violent history.

"Then let's go find her insidious ass," Rowan said, reaching for my hand, mouth setting in a compressed line. "And figure out what the hell her problem is with me."

Together, we slipped inside, past a slack-jawed normie usher so befuddled by the ribbon of ectoplasm running beside him—and the oblivion glamour's persistent efforts to erase his awareness of it—that he barely had a glance to spare for us. We jogged through the narrow candlelit passageway where visitors usually waited in line, when there were enough of them to queue. Right before we ducked through a set of heavy velvet curtains and into the first scene that lay beyond, the heavy fabric rippled and Letha stepped out.

"Issa?" she said, startled, her eyes flicking from me to Rowan. "I was just heading out for food, since everything's going perfect— what are you even doing here? You're supposed to be resting."

"Can't talk right now," I said, yanking Rowan toward the

curtains. "But something—someone—might be in there. Someone dangerous."

Proprietary rage blazed over her face, presumably at the notion of some troll wreaking havoc on her precious handiwork.

"Do we need to go into evacuation mode? Trip the alarms?" she said.

Like every haunted house worth its salt, we had security protocols in place, in the event of all kinds of emergencies—but I couldn't risk tipping Valentina off with alarms.

"No time for that. Rowan and I'll handle it; you just make sure no one else comes in here after us," I tossed over my shoulder as I parted the curtains for us. "Get that usher out of here, and bar the doors."

She gave me a grim nod, jaw clenching, and then Rowan and I plunged into the first room.

"Hot damn," I whispered, impressed in spite of everything by the massive graveyard city that loomed up all around us.

Letha had outdone herself, constructing a maze of elaborate crypts and tombs like something modeled after a New Orleans cemetery, each so spacious you could walk into and explore them, if you wanted. The illusion of a night sky hung above it all, glittering with LED stars and a glowing full moon suspended from the ceiling pipes that disappeared into the dark.

Everything was shrouded by a thin fog-machine mist, and the cemetery dwellers I'd dreamed up prowled all around us.

Some of them stalked close to us, creeping up to whisper sibilant nonsense into our ears before stealing away, flashing malicious smiles over their shoulders. Others crouched around boiling cauldrons, or intoned rituals that animated plastic skeletons, made them dance and jitter. They wore the black and gray scale costumes I'd designed—all billowing capes and leather and metallic studs—but Letha's finishing touches brought them to another level. She'd braided shining shards and tiny fake bones into their tangled hair, and painted their faces with spectral, sexy makeup. Dead-white skin shimmering with silver glitter, eyes swallowed up by sooty liner, lips stained with blue-black or maroon.

An unmistakable necromantic vibe that screamed Avramov, to anyone who even remotely knew what we were.

I could see Rowan noticing it, a brief curious glance cast at me from the corner of his eye before the ectoplasmic ribbon pulled us onward.

In the next scene, shrieks and panic surrounded us as the cemetery dwellers thronged around a massive broken crypt. A black and ragged entity with glowing red eyes billowed up, suspended by invisible strings—the escaped demonic evil that would taint the forest that lay beyond.

Following the ectoplasm, we rushed past the entity before we could hear the voice-over narrating the unfolding chaos, pounding up a set of stairs and into an indoor orchard.

It was exactly like I'd imagined from what Letha had described, like Honeycake Orchards crossed with some faerie realm—a flawless execution of my original vision. We walked through fake trees strung with multicolored globe lights, their branches hung with gorgeous model fruit and trunks embedded with animatronic faces. The forest witches drifted through it all, beatific and beautiful, wreaths on their heads and their gauzy costumes splashed with flowers. Emerald fading into delicate shell pink, like the ombré of green magic itself. Some of them communed with the trees, dancing around them in rings. Others congregated around softly glowing vines, which were set up to look like the witches were helping them grow and bud.

"Wait a minute," Rowan muttered beside me. "Is this supposed to be *Honeycake*? And those people . . . is that meant to be us? My family?"

Before I could reply, the ectoplasmic trail in front of us picked up speed, hurtling like a black comet into the following room. Hurrying after it, we ducked through a low passageway and into another version of the orchards, the one that Letha called the Forest of Perdition.

Here everything grew gnarled and warped, the fruit fallen to the ground, splattered and rotting by the twisted roots. Smoke wisped throughout, and glimpses of that demonic entity taunted us from between the trees, flitting from one to the next. The cemetery dwellers were here, too, battling against it—the space was divided into separate scenes that visitors could dip into, to witness little vignettes of their resistance—but they were also bedeviled by the furious forest witches. Hell-bent on evening the score, punishing the cemetery dwellers for what they'd allowed to escape and seep into their forest.

Even if it meant letting the escaped entity raze everything around them.

And it was clear that the forest witches were taking no prisoners. Some of the cemetery dwellers shrieked helplessly in corners, all bound up in thorny vines or half buried in risen soil, making it look like the ground was swallowing them whole. They thrashed against their bindings, begged for helped, screamed futile explanations—but all of it fell on the deaf ears of their captors.

"So that *would* be us, then," Rowan said, harsh and flat, taking it all in. "Torturing the shit out of *you*, no less."

Caught up in everything that had happened since, I'd somehow managed to forget that my story line sort of hinged on making Rowan's family look like villainous assholes.

"I know it looks bad, but can we talk about it la—"

I stopped dead, all the breath whooshing from my lungs, because in the middle of the forest carnage stood a figure haloed in black. Her hair drifting all around her like a mermaid's mane, unmoving as a standing stone even as a handful of squealing visitors rushed around her, assuming she was part of the act even as they instinctively kept a careful distance.

My sister.

Talia still looked like herself, but I could see another face overlaid across her own, beautiful but vicious. Even her black hair seemed to shimmer copper where the light caught it exactly right. And I'd never seen my sister with an expression anything like that on her face, so brutal and self-satisfied.

Then her terrible eyes landed on me, an incongruous flash of affection sparking in their depths.

"My little vixen of a niece!" she exclaimed, a grin splitting her face, hanging somehow askew on Talia's lips. "Yet again, I find myself in your debt. First you called me up, from the seed pearl of me that still swam deep inside your sister. Then you helped me remember who I once was. Built me back into myself."

"I . . ." My voice died, my mind a grasping muddle of chaos, my heart sinking as I suddenly realized what she meant.

Last Samhain, when Talia had become possessed, the entire family had come together in the courtyard of Castle Camelot to exorcise her, banish the many spirits that had taken up hostile residence inside her body. It had been a torturous, protracted affair that took hours and hours of work; I still remembered the sweat stinging my eyes, the savage power whipping through all of us as we struggled to tear out an entire squatting horde of spirits from inside my sister. By the end of it, she was drained and limp but Talia again, clear-eyed and sane. Safe from any inhabitation.

But maybe—just maybe—a tiny, wily, ancient scrap of a shade had persisted. Hiding inside her, biding her time.

Then, when I called every spirit in The Bitters to assist me in banishing Davara, I must have snared Valentina, too—only my summoning spell would have juiced her up, invigorated her. Given her the jolt she needed to rear up inside Talia, uncoil like a snake.

"But my sister would have fought you," I whispered, bringing a hand to my mouth. "She knows how to fight, how to shield herself."

"And fight she did," the shade said blithely, waving a dismissive hand. "The trick was not to overwhelm her, to never assert myself *too* rudely. To be, at first, only a subtle, complaisant guest. I rose to the fore only when Natalia felt just as I felt. When our intentions aligned, like mirrors of each other, then I would be permitted to take the helm. Afterward, she would not remember, never even know the difference."

But those of us around her *had* known the difference, I realized with a sickening thud of revelation. Even if we hadn't understood what it was we were seeing.

I thought of the harsh, strange, overly aggressive way Talia had behaved at the Crowning right before the shade inside her cast the Misbegotten Curse; the way she'd slammed binders around Elena's office at the mere mention of Rowan; how wound up she'd been in general. Maybe that was what she and Emmy had been fighting about on First Dew, too. Emmy must have noticed some discrepancy, called Talia out for behaving unlike herself.

Valentina/Talia's eyes slid to Rowan, cold and baleful, teeming with the same malignant hatred I'd felt from her spells.

"Like when we first saw *him*, at the Crowning," she hissed, teeth bared and glinting in the dark. Tendrils of fog-machine smoke drifted in front of her face, like clouds passing over the moon. "When you told us what he had done to you, those seven years ago. Quashed you, quelled you, forced you out of where you had *every* right to be. Just as his forefather, Alastair the Bloody-Minded Bastard, so relished in doing to me time and again."

I closed my eyes, heaving a sigh that shuddered through my entire body. At the Crowning, with Talia so affronted by Rowan's treatment of me back at the shelter, Valentina had come surging up—because she had thought she was *avenging* me. I remembered my sister's hollow face, the flat vacancy I'd misread as shock. That had been Valentina pulling the strings from inside her, casting the Misbegotten Curse through my sister's hands. The only reason I hadn't noticed the casting itself was how wrapped up I'd been in Holly's performance, captivated by her spell and then the progress of the curse itself. Oblivious to what was happening right next to me.

And that was why Valentina had stopped when she did, after the spell caught hold of Holly by mistake. That was when I'd grabbed Talia—her hand had been icy cold, the chill of the grave, completely unlike our normal Avramov warmth—and yanked her back to herself. Refocused her on her concern for Emmy.

"Then up on the mountain, we saw you with him again," Valentina spat at us, eyes sparkling. "Pinned by this bone-knitting worm, this *puny* life worshiper. How could you grant him the privilege of your affection—even as he saw fit to judge you so harshly for only being yourself? For practicing the magic that belongs to you by right? A bold and daring magic beside which his own pales, grows so paltry and insignificant."

I remembered that on the mountaintop, it was Talia who'd found us first, Talia who'd been walking her argument with Emmy off before she saw me and Rowan from a distance. Valentina had taken matters into her own hands a second time around, with the Death's Head Hex.

And maybe some submerged part of Talia *did* remember her actions after the fact. Why else would she have felt so racked with misplaced guilt for not having been the one to bring me back to The Bitters, after I'd fought off the hex? She had barely slept while watching over me, Elena had said, and I remembered how pale and peaked she'd been at my bedside, her nails bitten down to the quick.

Because the hex that it had nearly killed me to stop had been one cast through her own hands.

Valentina/Talia sneered at Rowan, her eyes narrowing in a way that made my blood turn to icy slush.

"That is why they *truly* hate us, you know," she said to me, even as she watched him in that crafty reptilian way. "Why Alastair always despised me so. It has only ever been the purest envy, dressed in righteousness. The jealous loathing of the weaker witch. And the revulsion of a craven man who could not stand to watch a woman's strength far overtake his own."

So I'd been right to think that this was part of it—and utterly evil as Valentina clearly was, some piece of me still believed she might have the very tiniest of points.

"Bullshit," Rowan muttered beside me, growling deep in his throat. I caught his hand, gave it a quick, cautioning squeeze. If he said anything to further enrage this demented shade, who knew what she might do to him?

"Why isn't my sister fighting you now?" I demanded. "Can she—can she even hear me?"

"Oh, she can," Valentina confirmed, a silky smile hovering on my sister's stolen lips. "But she cannot respond, not when I hold sway. For that, I have you to thank, again! Your clever little summoning spell, with the wine and feathers, the roses and the milk—it gave me such a strength as I have not known for centuries. It reminded me of myself, of the full breadth of who I was back when my soul and flesh still walked this place entwined."

She glided toward us in a wash of black—and I realized she was airborne, hovering, Talia's toes just dragging on the ground. The kind of fucked-up shit you never needed to see in real life, no matter how hard-core your taste in horror films.

"Now I am so like myself once again," she said, her smile widening, "courtesy of you both. And now that I know what joy it is to wear her fully, why should I *ever* cede this blissful bundle of blood and nerve and sinew back to her again?"

So this was what the hawthorn had felt back at the orchards, this purely selfish malevolence. Valentina might have thought she was protecting me to start, but she *was* old and cold, a thoroughly miserable bitch. And above all a parasite, sending her poison up through my sister's limbs.

And all of this was my fault, I thought, guilt lashing at my insides. It had begun with me, and somehow everything I'd done since had only managed to make it worse, even when I was trying to help.

I guessed this was as good a time as any to start taking some real responsibility.

"Talia!" I called out, taking a few steps toward my sister's hovering body, my stomach snarling up into a tangle of hope and fear.

"*Sestra*, I know you're in there; I know you can hear me. I'm so sorry I made such a mess of this. And I'm sorry for not talking to you more—for not realizing that something like this was even happening. I should have seen it, should have paid more attention . . ."

Valentina/Talia's fingers twitched by her sides, as if she were listening despite herself.

"But maybe I'm just too used to it being you who takes care of me," I went on. "Because you've always taken care of me, my whole life. You take care of all of us—with the French toast, the listening, the revelries. The crazy-good negronis at all hours. The *love*."

A tremor traveled across Valentina/Talia's face, and I thought I saw the glisten of a tear catch at the corner of her eye.

"And you've always been the strong one in our family," I forged on, gaining steam. "The one who never wavers, no matter what. Shit, even Elena relies on you, and you know she pretends like she doesn't need anyone. Remember how hard you fought during the Gauntlet, Talia? How hard you fought for Emmy's love? So I know you can dig your heels in now, and shake off that narcissistic, thieving bitch inside you. I *know* you can. That's what you do. That's who you are."

"I've seen it, too, Talia," Rowan added from beside me, lending his support. "You're a force, a rock. You know what, no—you're an entire fucking *mountain*. I couldn't have had a better partner than you. And I know you can kick this nasty stowaway out of you now."

A rippling shudder passed through my sister's purloined body, like a small, internal earthquake of a seizure, her face contorting in a series of awful little twitches that hurt to watch. Her hands clenched and released by her sides, fingers flaring out rigid and knuckles paling.

Clenched and released.

Clenched and released.

I held my breath, my heart hammering wildly, helplessly watching the power struggle between Valentina and my sister play out in that invisible inner battlefield. Unable to do anything else from all the way out here.

Then my sister's stolen body stilled, her hands uncurling, her face turning placid, a ferocious smile tugging at the corners of her lips.

"What a pleasure to witness such sisterly devotion," Valentina crooned, baring her teeth at me in a shining rictus. "Useless, of course, but it does so warm the heart. Regardless of all your tender feelings for each other, I do rather think I'll stay right where I am."

"Well, that's a bummer," I said, about a thousand times more calmly than I felt. My heart felt like it was shuddering inside my chest instead of beating, every muscle fiber in my body rigid as a cord. But I wasn't about to let this pilfering old bat see any of that fear. "Because you can't have her. Not now, not ever. Not in a million years."

"Oh, is that so?" Valentina/Talia's lips twitched again, her body drawing even closer to us, toes still scraping the floor. "And what do you plan to do about it?"

I considered trying a banishment, but I'd already spent weeks casting those at The Bitters, trying to drive our haunting out. If anything, it was likely Valentina had built up a tolerance to them. Banishments also didn't tend to work as well when a shade had really made themselves at home, become so deeply lodged inside someone's body that they considered it their own. We'd managed to exorcise Talia that first time around at Samhain only as a family effort, and back then the shades hadn't been given the luxury of enough time to settle in.

And even then, with such a colossal flood of magic funneled into the banishment, a persistent little stain of Valentina had managed to stick around.

We were clearly far past that point; it was time to deploy the nuclear option.

"Me?" I shrugged broadly, spreading my hands. "Nothing, actually. That was pretty much all I had. But I *was* thinking I'd phone a friend."

27

The Nuclear Option

I TOOK THREE SWEEPING steps back to make some room between us and lifted my hands, arranging my fingers into a summoning gesture. Then I chanted out the conjuring that called upon Malachus Azaranthinael.

Also known as the Demon Who Didn't Exist, Davara Circlebreaker's stage name.

In a blinding scarlet flash, Davara materialized on her knees, right between me and Valentina/Talia—this time, without even a circle of my will in place. Nothing at all to bind her.

She was naked and stunning, as she'd been the last time I'd seen her, back when all this began, skeins of black silk hair spilling down her back and around her wings. Fine skin agleam, massive golden eyes filled with licking flames and a feral rage, those glistening black claws curled and ready to rend. Clearly my spirit flash mob hadn't done her any lasting damage.

Hey, maybe she'd be inclined to cut me a little slack for that.

"Who the *fuck* is that, Issa?" Rowan hissed, flinging me a wild look. "Is . . . is she . . ."

"*Definitely* a Sagittarius, yes," I muttered, giving him a little push as I backed up farther myself. "And you're going to want to get out of the way."

I held my breath as Davara Circlebreaker got her bearings, turning in a circle as her golden eyes shifted between me and Valentina/Talia, fine nostrils flared and wing tips atwitch. That potent perfume of jasmine and patchouli emanating from her and filling the entire space.

As she tried, presumably, to decide which of the two of us she wanted to go ripshit on first.

On the one hand there was me, the uppity sorceress. The foolish deathspeaker who'd summoned her up all unwittingly and then banished her so sneakily, enlisting an army of rabid shades in her defense. Far be it from me to decipher demonic motivations, but I imagined that, from her perspective, there was probably at least *some* bad blood between us just based on that.

On the other hand, there was a malevolent shade standing *right there*, ripe for the picking. A shade just like the ones who'd recently sent her ignominiously packing to the nether realms.

With a rasping growl building in her chest, Davara made her choice—and lunged for Valentina, likely figuring she could always chase me down once her first target was dispatched.

Valentina/Talia's eyes went wide, lips parting and hands lifting as she considered casting some defensive spell. My many-times-great-aunt had been a battle mage with the kind of ballistic firepower we rarely saw these days, but she'd also been feeling complacent, having just quelled Talia's rebellion inside her, assured of her own triumph. And she hadn't exactly been prepared for a daemonfolk cameo from out of nowhere—especially not an enraged first-tier demon, barreling down on her like a fanged runaway train that had jumped its tracks.

So instead of tossing her lot in with magic, she instinctively took the easy road—which meant abandoning ship. She leapt out of Talia, reappearing in a shimmering dark mist that slowly coalesced into the rough silhouette of my great-aunt's shape.

As soon as she was free of Valentina, Talia collapsed, falling to her knees and then wilting to the floor. Fear clutched at me, gripping me like a fist, but I could see the flicker of her eyelids, the shallow rise and fall of her chest.

She was hurt, but alive . . . and directly in the oncoming demon's path.

Valentina must have been betting on Davara's momentum, on the demon's lunge for Talia being too far gone for the demon to course correct in the last minute. But Davara was first-tier, one of the fallen; her approach to the constraints of physics was whimsical at best.

She froze and pivoted in the blink of an eye, moving in a shuddering judder I could barely track.

One minute she was poised to take down Talia, claws extended and onyx teeth bared. The next, she'd flitted over to where Valentina's shade hovered by one of the fake trees. There, she unhinged her jaw like a snake, and *inhaled*.

If you could even call it that, when the massive intake of breath was closer to the sudden opening of a vacuum, or the roar of a building hurricane. A tremendous sucking I could feel tugging at me even from where I stood a good fifteen feet away. Valentina had just enough time to form an expression of fury-riddled shock, her mouth opening into a silent scream before the demon consumed her, the shade's gray form sucking into the demon's maw in a vaporous little whirlpool, like water circling a drain.

Then Davara snapped her jaws shut and gave her rosy lips a delicate lick, looking supremely satisfied.

"Mmmm," she said, huge eyes fluttering a little, rubbing her smooth belly like a sated child. It should have been funny, but instead it was purely terrifying, unnerving as all the hells. "A toothsome nibble. Thank you for the meal, little deathspeaker. On another day, I would be in your debt."

"You're so welcome!" I hazarded, gritting my teeth and raising my eyebrows. "So, maybe, we could just call it even, then?"

The demon swayed her head in a silky, undulating motion. "Oh, I think not," she finally said, flashing me that noxious inky smile. "The balance still tips in my favor, after what passed between us last time. So I think I will have your soul as well."

Before she could move, the two gnarled fake trees she stood between bent down and seized her, wrapping their branches around her arms and lifting her up, holding her splayed between them.

The demon's eyes went wide, impossibly so. She flung back her head and screamed, a ululating shriek that shook everything around us to its keystones. Her wings thrashed helplessly behind her, like a trapped pigeon beating against a window, but the branches held her taut—though I could already hear them cracking.

We were almost out of time.

"*Run*, Issa," Rowan said through his teeth—because of course he hadn't budged from my side, hadn't moved so much as an inch when I'd asked him to. Now he stood with arms raised, face carved with concentration and green drifting from his hands. "They're not real trees, for the most part—I think there might be just a little actual foliage in there—so they won't hold for long. I can only do so much with them."

"Lucky for us, then," I said, a fierce, reckless grin splitting my face as I reached up to my neck, "that I brought along a little help."

When I'd prepared the ingredients for the summoning spell back at The Bitters, I hadn't known what to expect; what we would be faced with, exactly, or what kind of protection Rowan and I might need. So I'd rummaged through our wooden chest of talismans and added a few choice amulets to the collection of protective runes around my neck.

One of them was a potent banishing spell, and the other the Serpentinus Hex that Lark Thorn had made.

I wrapped my fingers around them, closed my eyes, and triggered both at the same time.

Davara's shriek gained in furious force and octave, rattling the warehouse down to its foundations. Her form began to waver, growing ragged and insubstantial around the edges as the banishment took effect.

But she'd been stronger than the spell the last time that I tried this, and I had no reason to believe a banishment alone would be enough this time around, either.

That was where the snakes of cold breath came into play.

Like last time on Hallows Hill, they materialized in midair, a hissing, writhing tangle of sinuous bodies and black scales, icy vapor streaming from their open jaws. Streaking toward her, they latched on as one, pumping her full of their eldritch venom.

But Davara was a demon, and these snakes had been molded by Lark Thorn's reluctant will; they'd hatched much less malignant and substantial than the ones I'd conjured up in defense of Rowan. On their own, the serpents couldn't have caused her any irreparable harm—but she was also being assailed by a heavy-duty banishment. The last thing she needed to contend with was the stuff of nightmares the snakes were sluicing into her with their fangs. The terror and uncertainty, the all-consuming cold. The creeping suggestion that a hungry, dark abyss gaped just out of sight, and that it readily ate daemonfolk, too.

When it came to the power of bad dreams, not even demons were immune.

"THE DAY WILL COME WHEN I RETURN FOR YOU," she bellowed at me as she lost cohesion, her form growing ever more transparent. "OF THAT YOU CAN BE SURE, YOU BLASTED, DEATHLY NUISANCE OF A WITCH! AND WHEN I DO, YOU WILL COWER, YOU WILL TREMBLE, YOUR ENTIRE BLOODLINE WILL FALL TO THEIR—"

There was a flash of that infernal scarlet light again—and before she could finish, Davara Circlebreaker fled the earthly realm.

Again.

28

Built to Be Both

TALIA AND I had switched places.

Now she was the one in bed, asleep and pale even against her white pillows, the teal of her velvet headboard tinting her face with an even sicklier cast. I'd been watching over her since Rowan and I had gotten her home, three hours ago. Yet again, I'd left poor Letha in charge of the haunted house, overseeing a cleanup of the wreckage that was the Forest of Perdition, then shutting the entire operation down for the day. She'd already called me to check in; the oblivion glamour had swiftly done its work. As far as the normie cast and the visitors were concerned, our special effects had gone a little haywire, but that was all.

Nothing to see here, folks. Definitely no demons or vengeful ghosts.

She'd also informed me that I owed her infinite shots and beers for the whole rest of my entire life, and I was not inclined to disagree.

Once he was sure we were both safe, Rowan had left without a word, simmering with that trademark Taurus anger, quiet but devastating. I had a lot of damage control to do on that front, I knew, but today was not the day for it. Today, my sister needed me.

Today, first and foremost, I owed an explanation to my family.

When my mother came in, I felt rather than heard her. A sweet whiff of Poison stealing in my nose, her hand lightly brushing my shoulder before she moved away.

"I heard from Letha," she said, keeping her voice low as she pulled up a chair beside me. "And now, I'd like to hear from you."

I turned to look at her, tears welling in my eyes.

"It's all my fault," I said, voice splintering into a ragged whisper. "Everything. I fucked up, Elena. I *really* fucked up this time."

She nodded a little, lips pressing together, her cool green gaze snagging on mine.

"Not entirely your fault, I'm guessing, based on what Letha told me," she finally said, tilting her head. "And the part that was, I'm guessing you addressed—the way you've always done with your own messes, ever since you were a little girl. As eager to take responsibility as you were to stir up trouble in the first place. So why don't we start there; tell me about the trouble."

Quietly, tears dripping freely down my face—I'd never really cried in front of my mother before, not like this, but I didn't have it in me to hold back now—I told Elena everything. From the repercussions of my initial, accidental summoning of Davara Circlebreaker, to what had happened at the Crowning, to Rowan and me. Our complicated history, what was growing between us now, the way it had instigated Valentina's rage and misplaced family loyalty. How we'd finally pieced it all together at the haunted house, where I'd exorcised her—very fucking permanently—using Davara herself.

"And good riddance to her. Even if she was our blood, once upon a time," Elena said at that, her lip curling with quiet ferocity. "I knew some of the old rancor from the stories about her, but it sounds like they don't tell the half of it."

"Do you think the Thorns will still want some kind of punishment imposed on us? For what she did, through Talia?"

Elena shook her head, those familiar lines creasing between her brows. "I doubt it, knowing them. I don't think they'd consider it fair, but I suppose we'll see. They'd certainly be justified if they did . . . Mother and Crone, I can't even imagine such a hatred. That it could sustain her for *centuries*."

"I guess it can be unhealthy like that, sometimes," I said, dragging the backs of my hands down my face to wipe away the tears, "when you're too invested in your family, in your own name. In what you think it means."

One of Elena's fine eyebrows flicked up. "I'm sensing a more personal tack here, *lisichka*. What, exactly, do you mean by that?"

"I mean us," I said, trying to keep my breathing tempered, even as my heart threatened to kick up its usual fuss. "Or me, at least. I should have told you about me and Rowan, Elena, I know that. I was just afraid. I've been afraid to tell you a lot of things, lately. Because I . . . I didn't think they fit with what you wanted for me. And *from* me, as your daughter. As an Avramov."

Hurt rippled across her face, lips pursing a little.

"If I'm going to fail you so spectacularly, Isidora," she said, softly, "I'd like at least the opportunity to make such a mistake on my own terms. Without you presuming it for me. Sound fair?"

"Yeah." I breathed a quiet, surprised laugh. "That *does* seem fair."

As night fell beyond the window, a gathering curtain of dark pinholed by stars, I told my mother all my dreams. The designs, the clothes, the way I wanted to break away from the family legacy.

The way I hoped to try out being *me*, separately from being an Avramov witch.

Elena listened keenly, not even nodding, her eyes never leaving my face. Once I wrapped up, my hands twitching in my lap with the suspense, she took a long breath and finally looked away. Staring through the window into the fallen night behind The Bitters, the Witch Woods beckoning just beyond.

"It does hurt," she said, on a slow exhale. "You were right about that. You've been my little mirror, my reflection and my touchstone, ever since I had you. And it will . . . it will be very difficult to come to grips with losing that."

"I'm sorry," I whispered, the words snagging on the rock that had suddenly lodged itself in my throat.

"No," Elena said brusquely, shaking her head. "Do not *ever* apologize for yourself, Isidora. I hope I've taught you, shown you, better than that. That this feels so personal . . . that's *my* problem. My burden to contend with as your parent. Not something for you to grapple with for me. But I am sorry to have made you feel that way—especially because I understand just what it's like, to stand at such a painful crossroads. After all, I did it myself."

"What do you mean?" I asked her, already feeling some of the tension leave me. An almost euphoric feeling of relief that while she was clearly disappointed, she wasn't pushing me away.

In the life I dreamed of for myself, I was maybe going to get to keep my mother, too.

"Back when I started planning the Arcane Emporium, I'd only

just taken over as elder, right after your grandmother's death," she said, her eyes misting with the memory. "The rest of the family . . . well, many of the old guard didn't take kindly to such a plebeian idea, from an upstart whippersnapper such as myself. To, as they saw it, the *cheap commodification* of our abilities."

"They did *not* call you a sellout!"

Her lips quirked, wry. "Oh, but they did. In many of their minds, we were all stuck in amber, fossilized. Still the mighty Avramovs we once were in the Russian mountains, with our strongholds and treasures and dark glory. Not the Avramovs we'd become, the people we were here. Immigrants who had to strive, to carve out new space for ourselves when that old money ran out on us, as it always does."

"I had no idea," I said, hushed and stunned. "You never told us about any of that."

"Because it was such a ridiculous conflict to navigate. And though I knew it at the time, it still hurt. Left a bad taste in my mouth to have to fight that battle against my own, when I was creating something new, something for all our benefit. And I didn't want it tainting the Emporium for you in any way," she added, steel lining her voice. "I wanted you to be able to enjoy it, to love what I built for us. For our family. But what I *don't* want, Isidora, is for it to be a limitation. That was never my intention."

"I *do* love it," I assured her. "And I love the haunted house, too—and I promise Letha will take amazing care of it for us, given the chance. It can be a slow transition, too, if you're okay with that; it's not like I'm leaving town, or anything wild like that."

"And why shouldn't you leave for a while, if you need to?" Elena said, lifting her eyebrows. "I'm assuming you'll have to take at least a class or two on formal design, as well as on the business side of running that kind of operation. Or am I mistaken?"

"No," I said slowly. She was right; I'd never gone to college, but many of the other Thistle Grove witches had, in pursuit of their chosen professions. Rowan had gone to Virginia, Emmy to Chicago, and the Blackmoores often ventured as far as the East Coast for their overpriced educations. Even Talia had taken a finance course over in Carbondale. "But I was thinking I could do that remotely. All online."

"But I have to imagine that working with fabric, the art of design, is best learned in person. And if it is . . ." She gave me a sideways little smile. "Then do your family the honor of not being afraid of leaving, either. Of trusting that we'll be here waiting for you when it's time to come home."

"Thank you," I whispered, biting at my lip to keep the press of tears in check. "I'll . . . I'll think about that. And of course I'd be happy to keep working while I figure that part out, get things off the ground for myself. There's so much I don't know about running a business, doing it all on my own. So much I'll have to learn."

"The learning curve can be daunting," Elena agreed. "To say the least. There were times when the Emporium itself felt like a bane. Like a curse I cast on myself solely to complicate my own existence. But it's so worth it in the end to see your dream come alive, writ so large. And I know it'll be the same for you."

"But what if it isn't?" I whispered, airing this last, most chilling of my doubts. "What if I can't make it work? What if I give up everything I know—everything I'm good at—and then I fail?"

My mother smiled, reaching out to run a lock of my hair through her fingers.

"You've never failed at anything you really thought worth doing," she said, letting her fingertips rest against my cheek for just a moment. "And I'd be shocked if you started now. But if you *did* decide that striking out on your own wasn't what you imagined, then you'll always have the Emporium to fall back on. A family and home that's yours by right, whenever and however you want it."

"And you're *sure* you're not mad," I whispered back, "about, you know, breaking tradition?"

"We're Avramovs, my love," my mother said with a shrug. "We make our tradition; it doesn't make us. Just consider our summoning words. I know you of all people know those by heart."

"'I serve my goddess, my ancestors, and above all, myself,'" I intoned quietly.

"There you have it, then," she said, with a small, satisfied smile. "That's what it means to have our blood. We give our hearts and take them back, as we see fit. We choose our own course, set sail by our own stars. And no one else can ever—*should* ever—hope to master us."

BOTH EMMY AND I were there when Talia woke up the next day, in the golden hour just before sunset.

Emmy had been staying in the adjoining suite next door, taking shifts with me, Elena, and my siblings to sit with Talia, watch over her as she slept. It was strange for me to see Emmy so *normal*, so undone; she'd looked more like a college student pulling an all-nighter than the Victor of the Wreath, swimming in her oversized U of Chicago sweatshirt and baggy joggers, her grown-out bob pulled back into an adorable stumpy ponytail.

When Talia finally opened her eyes, Emmy had just come in to relieve me, so both of us were there to see my sister stirring against her pillow.

"Holy fuck," she said with a wince, slowly moving her head from side to side. "*Everything* feels terrible, like, spiritual-salmonella bad. I feel like I may vomit up my very soul. Unless it comes out the other end."

Emmy and I caught each other's gaze, sharing a profoundly relieved burst of laughter.

"One to ten, is that something Valentina would say?" Emmy asked.

In the many hours we'd spent together before Talia woke, I'd filled Emmy in on exactly what had happened. She'd needed to hear all the details, not just as my sister's girlfriend, but as the Victor of the Wreath, the one who'd ultimately be in charge of decreeing Talia's guilt or innocence, should she and the quorum decide to proceed with a tribunal. But she'd already let me know in confidence that unless the Thorns strongly pushed for one, it would be her obvious preference to put all this behind us more collaboratively, in a restorative rather than punitive way. According to Emmy's communion with the town, even Thistle Grove itself seemed to feel that way.

After all, it wasn't like Talia had consented to being possessed, caused any harm of her own volition. Punishing her, and the Avramovs by extension—holding Talia responsible for our wayward ancestor's sins—would be semi-barbaric not in line with the kind of safe haven Emmy wanted Thistle Grove to be for us all.

On my end, I suspected that much would hinge on Holly, in terms of how willing the Thorns would be to come around to Emmy's way of thinking. And if they persisted, Talia would still have a strong defense, the magical equivalent of a "not guilty by reason of insanity" plea.

"No way," I replied. "That's my *sestra*, alright. Dignified as ever."

Then we both moved to the bedside, to sit on either side of Talia. Emmy ran a hand down my sister's cheek, cupping its curve, her thumb brushing over Talia's broad cheekbone.

"How literally do you mean that, babe?" she said, wrinkling her nose. "Because I've been sitting here twiddling my thumbs for a minute now, waiting around to kiss you. But now I'm having several kinds of second thoughts about it."

Talia's pitch-black eyebrows rose, chapped lips curving. "That so? And here I thought I was still in the doghouse for the other day."

"Yeah, well, you're in luck. Turns out you get an official pass for being a salty bitch when some deranged old biddy with a grudge possesses you."

"How very fair-minded of you, Victor."

"Oh, let's not push it, babe. With the power vested in me by this town, I could always reconsider."

In answer, Talia reached out and slid a hand behind Emmy's neck, drawing her down.

To give them a moment, I looked away, training my gaze on the window, where the giant elm that shaded Talia's room painted us in flickering shadow, letting in lacy patterns of light filigreed in sunset gold. Sparkling motes danced within it like fairy dust.

Peaceful as it was, seeing Emmy and Talia together made my insides feel wrung out. I had no idea where I stood with Rowan, whether he'd be willing to forgive me for the lapse of judgment I'd made with the haunted house. Whether I'd get to kiss him again like this, now that I'd shown him yet another way an Avramov could fail a Thorn.

With the kind of inflexible morality he tended to subscribe to, somehow I suspected things wouldn't go in my favor.

"Hey," Talia said, flicking me lightly on the arm. "Earth to Iss."

I looked back at the two of them, blinking rapidly, banishing Rowan from my thoughts. I could pine for him in private later—but right now my sister deserved my full attention.

"I'm here," I said with a smile. "Just giving you and our esteemed Victor a minute for the obligatory post-possession makeout sesh. Speaking of which—are we a hundred percent in the 'Ding-Dong! The Witch Is Dead' camp, this time around?"

Talia's gray eyes darkened like a storm front, and she suppressed a shiver. Emmy laced her fingers through Talia's, making a small, angry sound low in her throat.

"Positive," Talia said grimly. "I no longer feel like I'm coming down with the worst PMS anyone ever had, for one. And toward the end, when she took the wheel . . . Let's just say full-throttle body-jacking isn't a ride one soon forgets. She's gone, full stop. There's only me in here, thank the Mother and Crone."

"Let's test it out," I said. "Think something shitty about the Thorns. Like, really go for it. Don't hold back."

Talia looked puzzled, but nodded. "Um, okay, how about . . . Rowan Thorn is a condescending muppet whose lips move when he reads? Wait, I can top that. Three bags of moldy dicks in a trench coat?"

"Damn, tell us what you really think," Emmy mumbled, scowling. "Ugh, it's like a First Dew throwback."

So that was what had set off their argument on First Dew; Valentina/Talia had been bitching about the Thorns, and it had rightfully put Emmy's back up. Probably both as the Victor and as someone whose best friend happened to be none other than Linden Thorn.

"I don't mean it this time, I promise," Talia assured her, "and you'll never hear me say anything like that again." She paused, cocking her head. "Well, unless he actually deserves it."

"Kindly don't make me smack a convalescing woman upside her sickly head."

I held my breath, waiting, gaze drifting around the room for any sign of anything untoward. But around us, The Bitters held its peace.

"What was the point of that little exercise, exactly?" Emmy asked, feathers still ruffled.

"We thought we had an infestation here," I explained. "A poltergeist haunting The Bitters. I thought I'd accidentally conjured one up when I whipped all our local shades into a frenzy to drive off Davara. But turns out, we had it backward."

Talia frowned. "What do you mean? We *did* have one. The Cthulhu of poltergeists, essentially."

"Kind of. But it wasn't that we were being haunted," I clarified. "It was that *you* were being haunted, and The Bitters itself—and all the shades that call it home—sensed Valentina and wanted to protect you from her. Our own demesne was trying to oust her, to dislodge her hold on you. Remember how the cabinets rattled in the kitchen that morning, when I was whining to you about how Rowan Thorn had befallen me? The way the door slammed in the bedroom, when you were sitting by me while I was recovering?"

Talia's face cleared with understanding. "Ah. So anytime I had a . . . let's say, *uncouth* thought about the Thorns, it'd bring Valentina rushing to the surface. And The Bitters would feel her, try to send her packing. Do whatever it could to have my back, futile as it was."

"Right. Even the cats didn't want to hang with you, which frankly should have tipped us both off. And it was only when you were away—or at peace, like at the revelry or in the morning of First Dew—that the house was quiet for any length of time."

"Shit," Talia said, massaging her forehead, looking so distressed it made me ache. "It's so obvious, in retrospect. I knew I felt off, just not why. How could I have *missed* that? Just overlooked an entire awful tapeworm of a shade inside me?"

"Do you remember any of it?" Emmy probed gently. "Casting the hexes?"

Talia shook her head, gnawing at her lower lip in frustration. "Nothing. I do remember a flash of rage both times, like a precipitating event. And then, nothing. Like blacking out. One moment of ultimate Hulk-smash fury, immediately followed by the hex playing itself out, with nothing in between."

"Why didn't you mention that to me?" Emmy said. "Losing time like that?"

"I figured it was a migraine thing," Talia replied. "I'd been having them since Samhain—I assumed they were just the aftermath of that gigantic possession. I figured the time loss must be related, a neural lapse like an aura, or maybe just the shock of seeing a curse like that happen at all. And both times, it seemed like only a few seconds had gone by."

She shook her head, then let it fall back against the pillow. "But you're right, I should have questioned it more. Fuck's sake, I'm an Avramov—we're supposed to be able to recognize intrusion, to protect ourselves. I should never have slipped up like that, given her so much control."

"You can't blame yourself," Emmy and I said in unison, then paused to share a smile. Emmy gestured for me to go on, while she nudged Talia to make room for Emmy to curl up next to her on the bed, temple to temple, her arm slung possessively over Talia's chest.

"You really can't," I continued, stifling another pang at the thought of Rowan. That was how we'd lain together at the Honeycake B and B not so many mornings ago, like two nested apostrophes. "Shit, if we're casting blame, why didn't the *rest* of us sniff out something rotten, a whiff of moldering Valentina? After all, we're the ones who know and love you best, who see the real you every day."

"Right," Emmy said ruefully, nuzzling Talia's head. "For example, you'd think I'd have gotten at least an inkling that something was awry, what with you waking up on the wrong side of the damn bed every day for weeks."

"To be fair, the real me isn't known far and wide as a morning person."

"Yeah, but the real you doesn't usually rouse like you want to murder the world, either."

"Valentina said it herself," I said. "She was being purposely subtle, playing the long game. Waiting for the right opportunity to go for broke."

"But when she took it, you were right there," Talia said softly, reaching out to squeeze my hand. "Thank you, Iss. I wasn't strong enough to force her out myself—you saw that much. And I . . . fuck, I was terrified. I really thought I was screwed, that the die was cast and she was going to get to keep me as her flesh puppet. But it helped to hear you talking me through it the way you did. Like you were holding my hand in there, even when she had me caged up."

"Least I could do," I said with a shrug, trying not to give away how much it meant to hear this. "Given that I basically sicced her on you myself."

Talia shrugged. "Yeah, well, maybe. Nobody's perfect. But you know what they say."

I smiled at this unwitting echo of our mother, when she'd told me that wiping the floor with an obstinate man was the best revenge. Adages invented on the fly, served up to suit the moment, were one of the better Avramov traditions.

"What do they say?" I asked, playing along.

"If you're going to have a little sister in the first place," Talia said, cocking her head and giving me a puckish grin, "get you one who can make you feel loved when you're possessed—and also feed your ghostly passenger to a custom-ordered demon from the hells."

"Shit, when you put it that way, I sound halfway like a hero," I said, ducking my head, "instead of the colossal disaster who instigated this entire mess."

"That's the beauty of being an Avramov, sis," Talia said with a wink. "Let the haters talk as they will about us, because we know the truth."

"Oh, boy, here we go," Emmy muttered under her breath, but her lips twitched with a stifled smile. "Let the self-stanning begin."

"Whatever, you know you love us," Talia retorted, turning to Emmy to steal a quick kiss. "Admit it. We're your *favorite*."

"The voice of Thistle Grove plays no favorites," Emmy said primly. "But I will admit you're obnoxiously hot. And charismatic almost to a fault."

"Sounds like you love us to me."

"So you've figured the lot of us out?" I asked Talia wryly, rolling my eyes at both of them. "Go on, lay it on me."

"It's simple. Disaster and hero, monster and martyr, beauty and beast . . ."

She turned away from Emmy to smile at me, eyes bright with a conspiratorial sparkle—and I abruptly didn't feel at all constrained, oppressed by the expectations of our family name. If I shared it with someone like my sister, someone so completely herself, it could never be anything but a beloved legacy.

"Choose your own dichotomy," Talia finished. "Because it doesn't matter. We were always built to be both."

29

New Magic and Black Diamonds

WITH THE HELP of Gabrielle Thorn and my mother, Holly Thorn recovered her magic just in time for Beltane.

Now, with all of us gathered around her, she stood in front of the central bonfire that blazed at the very heart of Honeycake—a circle of inlaid stones we called the May Day hearth—with her arms outstretched, urging it to ever greater heights. It towered into the sky, much taller than any normal fire, a column of crackling orange and scarlet and electric blue, shot through with vivid greens and violets that would never appear inside a natural flame. Its tip stretched so far above us it seemed to disappear, like a blazing spire reaching for the sun before melting into the atmosphere. Golden sparks danced around it like a school of tamed sprites, whirling around the column in a glittering ribbon.

I'd never seen a Beltane bonfire so tall before, so impossibly radiant.

But, then again, those other times, Holly Thorn hadn't been the Queen.

Micah stood beside her, looking incongruously gorgeous with his glossy black hair and dark family robes, a set of twisting horns perched on his head, twined with green leaves and dripping moss. I hadn't even known that Holly and my brother knew each other, but a few days ago, she'd chosen him as her Green Man. The first time an Avramov had partnered a Thorn May Queen.

As it turned out, there hadn't been a trial for Talia, or any punishment. Once the Thorns understood they hadn't been targeted by any *living* Avramov, they'd been eminently gracious about moving forward, just like Emmy and I had hoped they'd be. This choosing of a Green Man from our family felt even more demonstrative, like another step in the right direction.

Maybe, I thought, smiling into my fragrant spring wine, this really did mark a new era for our families.

Or it would, if I could only get Rowan Thorn to talk to me.

I'd caught sight of him a few times earlier, during the parade of festooned floats that rolled through Thistle Grove, its streets crushed with tourists and crisscrossed with floral bunting, to formally kick off the Flower Moon Festival. But we hadn't approached each other then, and now he stood across from me, on the far side of the flame. I could feel him watching me when I wasn't looking, but each time I glanced back, he determinedly flicked his gaze away, that familiar, maddening muscle twitching in his jaw.

What a total fucking Taurus.

Still, fair play; I deserved the cold shoulder, and then some. I'd been racking my brain in the week since he'd left me and Talia at

The Bitters, trying to figure out how to best make amends. An apology wasn't going to cut it, not when I'd been so thoughtless, putting his family on blast the way I had for the sake of *entertainment*.

I'd finally struck on something I thought just might work—though it was entirely possible he wasn't going to see things my way.

"He's not going to hear you scream-thinking lust and yearning at him from over here, sis," Talia said, poking me in the side. She stood next to me with an arm around Emmy's waist, perfectly herself, that sly, sparkling look back in her eyes—which were bright and familiar, unrimmed by chilly evil. Nothing at all like Valentina's. "They're not *actually* telepathic."

"And how do *you* know what I'm thinking, Ghostface Creeper?" I demanded, provoking a snicker from Emmy. At least we were all well on the other side, able to laugh about it now. "I have a plan, okay? Quit trying to salt my game."

"*You* have a plan?" Letha said from my other side, in the same deadpan tone and at the same time as Talia said, "You have *game*?" This time, Emmy doubled over, clutching helplessly at her middle.

"Mother and Crone, grant me patience," I said to the sky, sucking air through my nose. "For I am surrounded by treacherous bitches who somehow allege to be my friends."

"Excuse me, I allege to be your big sister," Talia retorted with a snort. "A totally different privilege."

"And I only ever alleged to be your faithfully treacherous bitch," Letha clarified. "It's in our pact, just check the fine print."

"I'll be your friend!" Emmy chimed in cheerfully. "But I also, *nicely*, think you should go talk to him."

"Fine," I groused into my wine, nerves stirring uneasily in my stomach. Apparently even three glasses of spring wine hadn't been enough to tamp down the anxious buzz that flared up every time

I imagined myself approaching Rowan and being decisively shut down. "I'll go. But if I die of rejection, you'll have only yourselves to blame when my restless shade starts fucking up all your shit."

Talia gave my hair a playful tug, leaning over to whisper into my ear.

"Hey, if that happens, you can always come live in me," she suggested. "I owe you one, anyway, and I bet you'd be a way less pushy roommate. Bodymate? There's gotta be an accurate term for it."

I cackled out loud, shoving her away. "That is *so* vile. And yet, kind of sweet? Thanks for the thought, *sestra*. Why don't we both just hope I live through this next part, instead?"

BY THE TIME I made my way through the increasingly rowdy May Day crowd to the other side of the bonfire, Rowan was gone. But knowing him as I now did, I had a fair idea of where he might have taken himself off to. So I wandered through the orchards until I found myself back among the apple trees, in the space where the Misbegotten Curse had detonated.

Where everything had begun for me and Rowan.

He was there, just like I'd predicted, standing on the coat of new grass, fuzzy and delicate as a baby chick's down, that the Thorns had managed to coax from the blasted soil. But to my surprise, the dead trees were gone, cut down and cleared away. In their place, a series of slim saplings flourished. Brown and green and tender, just about chest height. Something about them tugged at me, that naked vulnerability and fragile potential, the feeling lodging just behind my breastbone.

It was silly, but they looked a little like how I felt. Like an entirely new beginning.

I stopped by his side, my heart beating so hard it throbbed in my ears. "Happy May Day," I said, keeping my gaze on the grass, sneaking only little looks at him. "You regrew, I see. And, uh, replanted."

He nodded, silent, licking his lips. Rolling his eyes just the tiniest bit, like, *Yes, duh, indeed.*

"Weak opener, I know," I said, nodding to myself. "Look, I really hate this, not being able to talk to you. Turns out I've gotten kind of used to you wanting to talk to me."

He huffed through his nose, rolling his shoulders.

"Then maybe you shouldn't have made caricatures out of my family," he retorted, roughly, still not looking at me. "Because we do *not* deserve that shit. Far from it."

"I know," I said quickly, seizing the opening. "I know I fucked up with the haunted house. In my defense, I came up with the idea when we were still butting heads. It felt . . . more appropriate, back then."

"And now?" he demanded, wheeling to face me. "How does it feel now, Issa?"

"Terrible," I said softly, my eyes shifting between his. "The worst kind of wrong—and you know admitting that doesn't come easily to me. So, I went ahead and fixed it."

He cocked his head, eyes narrowed. "Come again?"

"The Forest of Perdition was wrecked anyway," I said with a shrug. "And you're right, it was a garbage idea. Not even true to life, clearly. My family *did* curse yours with an escaped evil, more or less. And you never once retaliated, not even when you had every reason to suspect foul play."

"No," he said tightly. "We didn't. Glad we can agree on that much, at least. So . . . ?"

"So I redesigned that scene, with Letha's help," I said, biting on the inside of my lip, trepidation surging hot inside me. Because this was it, all I had, the last and only ace up my sleeve. "It only needed to be tweaked, anyway. What happens now is, the cemetery dwellers and the forest witches come together to take down the demon. The, uh, hero and heroine make a new kind of magic to fight it, actually. It's possible they also kiss at the end."

"That is . . ." Rowan shook his head, mouth working—then broke into that open, dazzling smile that had come to mean so much to me. "Wow, Issa. *So* fucking corny."

"Excuse me?" My jaw fell open. "I worked hard on that new direction, and on a very tight schedule, I might add, to have it open today. And you're going to mock me for it?"

"Only a little," he said, reaching to grab me by the waist and tug me close, wrapping one arm around me. "Come on, Issa, I *like* corny. Sometimes corny hits exactly the right way. In fact . . ."

He reached out toward one of the saplings, an emerald wash of magic surging from his hand and curling around one of its tiny branches.

"We're letting them grow naturally," he said, as it sprouted a tiny pearl of a fruit. A perfect apple, rendered in miniature. "It's better that way, healthier not to rush them. But when they grow up . . ."

He reached out to pluck the little fruit, offering it to me. It gleamed against the creases of his palm, its stem and leaf achingly small, the skin a glossy, speckled black. I took it carefully, holding it between my thumb and index finger, marveling at it.

"They're going to be Black Diamonds," he said, looking up at me with such a wealth of tenderness that I bit my lip, afraid my own feelings might come spilling out in a gush. "A rare variety of the Hua Niu apple. The Chinese Red Delicious."

"Why?" I whispered. "Why not more Pink Pearls? You loved those trees."

"Well, there's this tower-dwelling sorceress," he said, tilting his forehead until it met mine, his eyes glistening with emotion. "She's really something else, you know? Turns out, I'm falling for her pretty hard. And I thought she might like them, when she came to visit me here. And I was hoping she would, eventually."

I exhaled, a long, shuddering breath, standing up on my tiptoes to press my lips to his.

He kissed me back hard, his hand knotting in my hair, his other sliding up my back to rest warmly between my shoulder blades. The air around us seemed to vibrate, buzzing with the high vibe of Beltane energy, the bright tremor of emotion flooding back and forth between us like a wave.

The sparkling rush of our own made magic, the kind no spellsmith, good or ill, would ever be able to replicate.

"I like them *so* much," I told him, when we paused to take a breath. "As long as you're sure this isn't a bad-apple joke. 'Cause that would maybe sting a bit."

He snorted, rolling his eyes. "Issa. Can you just be romantic with me for a minute, here?"

"Oh, absolutely. And see, I was right! They *do* kiss at the end."

He chuckled through a groan, tossing back his head. "Damn, okay, that may actually be too corny. Even for me."

"I can't help it," I told him, reaching up to cup his face, smiling up into his eyes. "Because the thing is, I'm a Leo—and it's a fact of life and the cosmos that we're naturally dramatic. So you, Rowan Thorn, are going to have to deal."

Acknowledgments

))) ● (((

Second books in a series are often a little scary to write; the pressure! The expectations! The continued building of a world that now actually exists in some known form, so you can *definitely* screw it up this time! But this story took me by complete surprise, by being almost more joyful to write than *Payback's a Witch*. Part of the pleasure was the tremendous support and enthusiasm from the spectacular team at Berkley—also known as Thistle Grove's biggest fans, and the people who allow me to keep writing these witchy books I love so much. Bridget, Elisha, Stephanie, Jessica, Angela, Katie, Julie—thank you so much for everything you do. Thistle Grove would literally not exist without you.

Special thanks to Cindy Hwang for being the editor of my dreams, my safe place to land and the very best idea sounding board. These books are infinitely better for having had your eyes on them. My thanks as well to Anna Boatman at Piatkus, for giving the witches of Thistle Grove a chance to call the UK home, too!

ACKNOWLEDGMENTS

Thank you to Vicki Lester for dreaming up these gorgeous covers, and to Jeremy Carlisle Parker, who narrates the audiobooks so beautifully, for being such a completely wonderful human with an incredible voice. Tremendous thanks as well to Karen Marks for her read, and kind, thoughtful feedback.

As always, huge thanks to Taylor Haggerty and Root Literary, for shepherding these books into the world so gracefully, and with so much patience and enthusiasm. I'm especially grateful to Taylor and Jasmine Brown for their advance reads of *Cursed*. My critique group ladies (Jilly, Chelsea, and Adriana) also always come through for me in early drafts; I know how lucky I am to have your humor and sharp minds in my arsenal.

I'm also especially indebted to Cara and Ramona Watts, for lending me their names for Gabrielle Thorn's family in Virginia. You're both #GOAT in my book, and your support means the world to me.

Thank you so much to my family and wonderful friends; I would be a mess without you (and often am one, even with you, so thanks also for putting up with that)! In particular, my mother and my little lion often have to deal with the oatmeal-brain version of me at the end of a long writing day, and they both still seem to love me regardless, which is a pretty massive win.

Finally, to the readers who loved *Payback* and took the time to reach out and let me know how much Emmy, Talia, and Thistle Grove meant to them, how much they enjoyed the bi love story, and how excited they were for the sequel—you have no idea how profoundly you make my day. Nothing makes me happier than knowing that Thistle Grove is a haven for others, too, and that's why this book (and all the others, really) are for you. Thank you for everything.

From Bad to Cursed

LANA HARPER

Questions for Discussion

))) ● (((

1. When we first meet Isidora Avramov, she's summoning a relatively benign demon—who turns out to be a lot more than she bargained for! We discover that Issa often does risky magic of this nature just to blow off some steam. What do you think of the morality of an outlet that may put others in danger? Did it influence your perception of Issa right off the bat, one way or the other?

2. Issa is deeply conflicted about her position as creative director of the Arcane Emporium's haunted house—a role she once loved, but has since outgrown in favor of other professional aspirations. Can you identify with Issa's guilt and fear of sharing these new desires and goals with her family?

3. Issa and Elena, her mother and the Avramov matriarch, are very close, yet it's also clear that much goes unsaid between them. What do you think of their relationship? Can you identify with the way they relate to each other, or does it mystify you?

4. Issa and Rowan have a somewhat silly "archnemesis-ship," but it's one they both take *very* seriously. What do you think of the way things went down between them at the animal shelter, and how they both contributed to that conflict? Who do you think was more at fault, if anyone?

5. The Thorns and the Avramovs have a long and complicated family history. Do you think they're truly as at odds with one another as they seem? Do you think some of their polar opposite qualities actually intensify Issa and Rowan's attraction to each other? If so, why?

6. Issa is a powerful necromantic sorceress, even stronger than her older sister. Which of her spells did you find most impressive? Which, if any, did you find the most unnerving? What do you think of her necromancy, as it compares to Rowan's green magic and healing?

7. The Thorns have very different family dynamics than the Avramovs, but both families consider themselves tight-knit and devoted to one another. Compare the bonds between Rowan and his cousin Holly and younger sister, Lark, to Issa's relationship with her cousin Letha and the way she interacts with her siblings at the revelry. What differences and similarities do you see?

8. Issa has a history of anxiety and panic attacks, which she does her best to quell and hide from even her closest friends

and family. What do you think of the way she chooses to handle her anxiety, and the way Rowan approaches it?

9. What do you think of the way the Thorn family reacts to repeated attacks against their own—especially ones that seem to be of such trademark Avramov magic? Do you appreciate their restraint, or do you think you might have been more aggressive in their shoes?

10. What do you think of Issa's decision to process her complex feelings by incorporating her unfolding story with Rowan and the mystery of the curse into her new narrative for the haunted house? Was this hitting below the belt, or a legitimate source of inspiration?

11. Talia has a surprising role to play in the mystery of the poltergeist haunting, The Bitters, and the attacks against the Thorns. Were you surprised to discover her connection with Valentina Avramov? Do you think Issa, and even Emmy, are right to blame themselves in not having noticed something awry with Talia? Why do you think they didn't?

12. What lessons on misplaced family values, individual ambition, and even perceptions of misogyny can you draw from Valentina's possession? Do you think she was downright evil . . . or did she occasionally have a valid point to make? By the end of the book, what differences could you see between the ways Valentina and Issa relate to the Thorns, and to their own family legacy?

Keep reading for a preview of the next book in
The Witches of Thistle Grove series by *New York Times*
bestselling author Lana Harper,

Back in a Spell

Coming soon from Jove.

1

Let It Snow

I'VE NEVER BEEN what one might call a *winter person*.

Witches are supposed to feel naturally aligned with the Wheel of the Year, receptive to the charms of every season—and nowhere is that easier than in Thistle Grove, where every type of weather is utterly and gorgeously flamboyant, the most extravagant cosplay version of what it might look like anywhere else. In theory, I could appreciate the extremeness of its contrasts: all that diamond-faceted white, blazing against the blue of windswept skies and the stark black silhouette of Hallows Hill. I could even get behind winter chic, when it came to sleek apres-ski wear. And then there was Yule, with its fragrant wreaths and crackling logs and sea of candlelight. Arguably the most luminous and magical of the solstices.

But in practice? Winter is horribly inelegant and messy, almost impossible to calibrate. One too many layers leaves you sticky and sweltering, while one too few lets the chill sneak into your bones. Your hair turns into kindling, or poufs into a staticky halo immune even to glamour spells. You can't even run properly in winter, unless you're a die-hard marathoner with no self-preservation instincts left intact.

All around cruel and unusual. At least we rarely suffered more than two months or so of yearly punishment in Thistle Grove.

But this year, strangely, winter seemed to suit me. This year, I found every fresh snowfall soothing, almost meditative. There was one raging right now beyond the frost-rimmed window of the Silver Cherry, where I was grin-and-bearing my way through a jewelry-making class. A feathery whirlwind, like being inside a just-shaken snow globe filled with drifting down. It felt hypnotic, a chaotic escapade of white that made it hard to hold on to any single thought for long. Which, these days, was more than fine by me.

These days, my thoughts and I didn't tend to be on the best of terms.

"Sweetheart," Jessa said, in that delicate tone she'd taken to using on me, like one harsh note might topple me over, damage me in some irreparable way. She didn't have to be quite *that* careful with me, but I loved that she wanted to be. "You're doing your depressed mime face again."

The words themselves didn't tend to match up with the spun-sugar tone all that often, and I loved her for that, too.

"What?" I mumbled, finally tearing my eyes from the window. "My . . . *what*?"

"You know." She rearranged her adorable, ringlet-framed features into a dismal expression, drooping puppy-dog eyes and a dramatically downturned mouth like a melancholy bass. "Like you're about to perish of chronic woe. Or possibly planning to re-create that scene from *The Giver*, where the kid and his little brother escape into the snow to die with their emotions."

"It's been a while since middle school English, but even so, I'm *fairly* sure that wasn't supposed to be the takeaway," I told her with a snort. "And hard pass on that cold demise. If I absolutely have to die somewhere with my emotions, I'd rather go all nice and toasty."

Dragging my attention back to my little work tray, strewn with a glittery mishmash of wire and beads, I saw that I'd been half-heartedly tooling around with making earrings before the blizzard got the best of me. Once upon a time, I'd have crafted something gorgeous given an opportunity like this, painstakingly applied myself until I had it just right.

Too bad "once upon a time" felt like several eons and an infinity of wrong turns ago.

"Burn you at the stake, then, noted," Jessa quipped—though, of course, thoroughly normie as she was, my best friend had no idea how close to home that hit. As far as I knew, Jessa had never once seriously considered the notion that our charming postcard of a town really *was* settled by witches, exactly like Thistle Grove legend would have you believe.

To her, I was just Nina. Best friend and partner in crime from our shared law school days, now in-house counsel to my family's extensive business interests. Not Nineve Cliodhna of House Blackmoore, second in line to the most powerful witch dynasty in Thistle Grove.

"Don't worry, buddy," I assured her. "I do still have considerable will to live. Just not, like, enough *zest* to care about these earrings, apparently."

Jessa pooched out her lower lip, abandoning the complicated (and suspiciously BDSM-looking) beaded choker she'd been working on.

"But that's the *point*," she insisted, smooth brow wrinkling with concern. "That's what these classes are for, Nina. We're supposed to be nurturing our creative selves, meeting new people, rediscovering your zest. Unearthing it."

She looked so crestfallen that for the barest moment, I entertained the idea of assembling the pitiful bead hodgepodge into something pretty with a simple transmutation spell of the pumpkin-into-carriage variety, but even more basic. The raw materials were already right in front of me, half-threaded. I could have done it with just a few words, using a single purely distilled thought as a vehicle of my will.

But that wouldn't have been honest or fair, which was part of the reason I never did magic in front of my best friend. For the safety and the continuing preservation of our town, as per the Grimoire—the spellbook that also held sway over the conduct and governance of Thistle Grove's witch community—only long-term partners were permitted access to that secret. And for all that I adored Jessa to pieces, our friendship wasn't the kind of love the founders had had in mind when deciding who should be privy to our magic.

Letting the oblivion glamour that was cast over the town take hold of her, erasing her memory of whatever spell I'd worked, would have felt . . . traitorous. A little gross, even.

And it would have been a cop-out at best. Jessa was the kind of delightful whirlwind of a person who effortlessly transformed strangers into friends—or short-lived partners, as the case may be—wherever she went, and I knew she'd been hoping a little of that joie de vivre might rub off on me. Tonight's event was the fourth hopeful outing of its kind, following a disastrous wine-and-paint night (during which I'd gotten the not-artistically-conducive kind of wasted), an equally catastrophic pottery class that had reminded me of Sydney's love of ceremonial teacups and sent me spinning into a meltdown, and a flower arranging class that had only managed to unearth memories of the dusky-blue-and-rose-gold palette I'd chosen for the flowers at my own wedding.

A wedding that was never going to happen, much like the perfect life with Sydney that had been meant to materialize thereafter. A life that now seemed not just fictional, but so fantastically unbelievable that even I, a flesh-and-blood descendant of the sorceress Morgan le Fay, couldn't conceive of it as a reality.

"You're talking about me like I'm some archeological dig, Jess, and we're sifting for ancient potsherds of joy. What if there's no zest to unearth? What if I'm just a barren wasteland?" I dropped my chin, the familiar, hateful well of tears pressing against my eyes. I was so damn sick of crying at the slightest provocation, like some weepy damsel stuck in a mire of never-ending distress, but I'd apparently won the sob lottery. Team #Leaky4Life over here. "Permanently broken?"

"Everyone's fixable, sweetheart," Jessa assured me, slipping a soft arm around my shoulders and tilting her temple against mine. She favored those subtle skin-musk perfumes that you couldn't detect on yourself—the kind I'd never go for, because what was the point if you couldn't catch indulgent whiffs of it throughout the day?—but that made her smell gorgeous, a vanilla-cedar scent that hit somewhere between gourmand and woody. Being hugged by her felt like free aromatherapy.

"Even that guy you dated with the towering manbun?" I asked thickly.

"You say that like there's only been one . . . which, *would* that that were the truth."

"The one who drank so much Bulletproof coffee it was like he was speaking in fast-forward all the time," I clarified. "And did bicep curls while taking dumps."

"Fuck no, not him." She shuddered delicately against me, sticking out her tongue—which was pierced, something no other estate lawyer I knew could ever have gotten away with. Apparently a deceptively angelic face like Jessa's covered a multitude of sins, even when it came to the most uptight of clients. "Everyone but Chasen, then."

"Of course that was his name. And what about dictators? Or sex cult leaders? Or serial killers?"

"Now you're just being difficult. Allow me to rephrase, counselor." She shifted sideways against me, just enough to boop me on the nose. "*You* are fixable, sweetheart. Eminently so."

"Then why can't I get into even this, the most emotionally undemanding of activities?" I asked her, that relentless ache lurching in my chest again. A panging disorientation that felt almost like homesickness as my gaze skimmed over the dozen or so other people happily crafting beneath the cherry cutouts dangling from the ceiling, the recessed lighting spilling over them in a mellow glow. Mostly clusters of women around Jessa's and my age, along with a few mothers with their tweens in tow.

Even the solitary goth enby with the pentagram neck tattoo—likely a tourist drawn to the Silver Cherry by its affiliation with Lark Thorn, who was not only teaching this class but also selling her line of enchanted jewelry here—looked to be having a more exuberant experience with this mortal coil than I was.

"What kind of mess can't focus on stringing beads together? Or letting loose on a pottery wheel?" I swiped at my eyes, trying in vain to keep from smearing my eyeliner. "It's been a whole year, Jess. How long is this . . . *emotional fugue state* even supposed to last?"

My voice rose enough that on the other side of the room, Lark abruptly straightened from where she'd been instructing one of the tweens. She turned just enough to flick a concerned glance at me over her shoulder, deep brown skin glowing against the vivid turquoise of her scoop-neck sweater, her dark eyes liquid with sympathy. The Thorns were empathically attuned to one another's feelings, and acutely sensitive to others' emotional landscapes, too. Though I doubted she even needed their particular brand of ESP to detect the seismic rumble of my distress.

The Nina I used to be was bulletproof—unshakably sure of herself, vacuum-sealed into her composure. But these days, the old me felt like a fossil, a crumbling memory. These days, I was more of a tempest in a teacup.

A flailing, distractible tempest that just could not seem to get it together.

I twitched my lips into an *Everything's just* peachy *over here* smile, wincing inwardly as she gave me a lingering look before turning away. I wouldn't have agreed to come here tonight at all had I remembered Lark's connection to the studio. Given how the Blackmoores' standing in this town had declined since the debacle of last year's Gauntlet of the Grove—not to mention the fact that my little brother, Gawain, had briefly come under suspicion when one of the Avramovs' dearly departed ancestors cursed the Thorns this past Beltane—the last thing I needed to be doing was signaling weakness in front of a member of one of the other families.

The thought spurred me into taking a breath, stiffening my

spine a little, and leaning away from Jessa as if she weren't, in fact, my load-bearing support column. Trying to act as though I at least remembered who I was supposed to be.

"I don't think heartbreak's an exact science, sweetie. Though I will concur that maybe we've been going about this the wrong way," Jessa concluded thoughtfully, nibbling on her lip. "You know what, why don't we ditch this and grab some drinks instead? Rethink our strategy?"

"But what about your . . ." I gestured vaguely toward the abandoned snarl on her work tray. "Fetishwear-in-progress? It has such promise."

She chuckled through her nose, not bothering to deny it. "I can always take it home. It was going to be for Jordan, anyway . . . *Ooh*, maybe I can make him finish it for me, before he gets to wear it! You know, like a meta-kink moment. Foreplay for the foreplay."

I stared at her for a second, equally confounded by the rigorous intellectual component her most recent bedroom exploits apparently called for, and the fact that her flavor of the week had already earned himself an actual name. By Jessa's standards, that was unusually rapid progress. Most of her conquests went by evocative nicknames the likes of "Old Man Zayn" or "Emo Clark Kent" until they fell out of the rotation; maybe she actually *liked* this guy.

"I do not claim to understand your ways, Jessamyn Singer, but I respect them," I finally said.

"Just the way I like it." She slid the jewelry into a small plastic bag, grinning to herself. "So, where do you want to go? Dive bar? Nice bar? Weird bar?"

"Nice bar," I said automatically, suppressing a sniffle. My spirits rose a little at the idea of delicious craft cocktails and low lighting, the utter relief of not having to funnel any more energy into forcibly enjoying, or pretending to enjoy, yet another form of alleged entertainment.

"See, *there* you are," she said warmly, reaching out to give me another squeeze. "Knew my favorite fancy bitch was in there somewhere."

2

Whimsical Bitches and Trickster Gods

TEN MINUTES LATER, Jessa and I wedged ourselves into an empty booth at Whistler's Fireside, a waft of cold still clinging to us as we shed our layers and stamped our snow-crusted boots under the table, wind-lashed cheeks both numb and glowing.

The Fireside's majestic black walnut booths, with their intricately carved backs and must-and-varnish smell, looked like they'd begun their lives as pews in some medieval abbey. Bare Edison bulbs holding twists of glowing filament swung above each table, and to our right, the bar top gleamed copper from the vintage pennies preserved under its glass slab, fat pillar candles flickering along its length. Even the cool blue cast of early winter dusk drifting through the Victorian windows couldn't chill the aura of warmth. There was no actual hearth to be seen, despite the name—probably the owner's idea of an ironic joke—but the whole ethos of the bar *did* feel like sitting at a fireside.

I loved it here. It reminded me of my favorite New York speak-easies, the ones that had brazenly ridiculous thousand-dollar concoctions tucked into the drink menus like dirty capitalist secrets, and all but demanded a password and secret handshake to get in, even though everyone and their mother knew where to find them. I couldn't help but enjoy that little thrill, the sense of being part of an exclusive club—especially when it wasn't *real* elitism, but just for fun, the way it was at Whistler's.

"What are you thinking?" Jessa asked, once the server had dropped off menus and a complimentary bowl of honey-and-harissa popcorn. Truly, this place was the bomb. "They have the spiked hot chocolate today, and *oooh*, a new buttered rum hot toddy. Shit, but does that even sound good, in reality? Or are they counting on the butter to gaslight us into believing it must be delicious?"

"Hmm, as yet unclear."

I gave the happy hour specials a cursory skim even though I already knew what I wanted, wondering whether I should at least try to be more adventurous. As sometimes happened at moments like this, the Ghost of Sydney Past materialized by my shoulder to whisper in my ear. (Though not, to be clear, her *literal* spirit, as Sydney had been alive and aggravatingly well in Chicago last I'd checked. And in any case, ghost whispering was more the kind of ghastly trick you'd expect to find in the Avramovs' shady repertoire than the magic my family preferred to practice.)

Why do you always have to order the exact same thing, the memory of her voice sniped at me, in that coldly exasperated tone that always used to make my shoulders hunch. *Why not just* try *something new for once, so we can share?*

But I happened to *like* the mulled wine here. And furthermore, I *liked* the tried-and-true reliability, the comfort of an order that you knew for a fact would make you happy. That was one of Syd's and my most well-worn fights—her desire for spontaneity, set against my craving for structure and routine. The core disparity between us that had seemed like a charming opposites-attract deal at first, she the fluttering kite and I the grounded ballast. Together, a rare alchemical balance that would elevate our relationship beyond the sum of its parts and into something golden and enviable.

No such elevation had, in fact, transpired. In hindsight, as happy as much of our relationship had made me, Syd and I had been the very definition of fool's gold.

"I'm sticking with the mulled wine," I decided, banishing the Ghost of Sydney Past with as much firmness as I could muster.

Jessa pursed her lips and squinted at the menu for another moment, the bulb's ruddy light picking out wavering highlights in the rings stacked above and below her knuckles. She had a rose gold manicure this week, too; seriously, what the hell kind of amenable clientele did she even have? "Okay, yup. I'm gonna take a gamble on the hot toddy and see if I live to rue the day."

I huffed a laugh into my handful of popcorn, shaking my head. "As if 'regret' even figures into your vocabulary."

"Just because I choose to look back fondly on most of my mistakes doesn't mean I don't learn from them."

Once our order was in and the menus whisked away, she propped an elbow on the table and rested her chin in the cup of her palm, giving me a frankly assessing stare.

"How worried do I really need to be about you, sweetheart?" she said, matter-of-factly but still in that sweet tone that dissolved anything sharp or accusatory before it could make me shrink into myself. "This two-step of meltdowns and existential malaise is starting to seem like more than you should have to handle on your own. What does Sassy Sue have to say about this situation? Is it time to consider meds?"

Sassy Sue was my much beloved and, yes, profoundly spicy and no-nonsense therapist. WWSSD—What Would Sassy Sue Do— had long been Jessa's and my tough-love code for "Get your shit together and make the right call."

"We've discussed it," I said, wiping popcorn grease off my hands and then folding the napkin into a neat little square before setting it aside. "But she thinks, and I agree, that my issue is more situational. Meds might give me a little boost, sure. But the thing is, I don't actually *feel* the chronic kind of depressed, Jess. I still like my job, and I enjoy working out. I get pretty reliable jollies from retail therapy, just like before."

And I still adored the magic in my life every breathtaking bit as much as I ever had, not that I could share that with Jessa.

"No issues getting out of bed in the morning or motivating," I went on. "So it's not that I've become incapable of producing happy feelings. I'm more or less fine, as long as I don't venture beyond my comfort zone."

Jessa gave a pensive nod, mulling it over. "Got it, I think. So, what is the problem, then? Is it that you still miss her?"

Our drinks arrived, just in time to help choke down the tangle of competing emotions clambering up my throat like climbing vines. I closed my eyes, took a therapeutic inhale of the boozy steam followed by a semi-scalding sip of red wine. Cinnamon and nutmeg and the bright, sweet tang of hot alcohol seeped into my mouth, blunting the thorns in my throat into something more manageable.

"No," I said, fighting the tremble in my voice, even though the real answer was unfortunately still *sometimes*. "It's when I start trying to move forward, to do *anything* new. It makes me feel so lost, Jess. So . . . disjointed, permanently off-balance, somehow. Like I woke up one morning and suddenly found myself a castaway, stranded in the wrong life. I should be *married* right now, to the love of my life. Maybe even starting to think about having kids."

Jessa suppressed a little eye roll, presumably bored stiff by the unforgivably vanilla, spouse-plus-2.5-kids slant of my life goals. I felt a stab of annoyance back at her, for not understanding the way she usually did, with ample empathy. I certainly expended enough of it on her, trying to wrap my brain around the offbeat way she conducted her relationships.

"Look, I'm well aware those aren't your things," I said, just a little sharply, "but they *are* mine. You know that."

Her round face softened immediately, brief chagrin glinting in her brown eyes. "It's not that, Nina. I'm just not sure I'd call Sydney 'Jacqueline-pronounced-Zha-KLEEN' Grant the great love of your life, you know? She did call the wedding off a *week* before you were supposed to get married. Might as well have ditched you the day of, at least let you have your beautifully tragic moment at the altar if you couldn't get your damn deposits back."

I gritted my teeth at the memory of Sydney sobbing in our loft apartment—she'd cried much more than I had at the time, which struck me now as quite a bit of bullshit—as she trailed me from room to room, wringing her hands and pleading for my understanding while I paced back and forth, my entire life dissolving around me like an ice palace under a blowtorch. *I just can't* breathe *when I'm with you, Nina*, she'd said through shimmering tears;

Sydney somehow even cried prettily, like she was creating content for her Instagram reels just by existing. *It's like there's not enough air around you, like you create this vacuum wherever you are. And I . . . I don't want to live the rest of my life that way, so joyless, so arid.*

I can't do that to myself. I won't.

You'd have thought she might've been struck by this tragic revelation at any other, more helpful time in our four years together—before, for instance, proposing to me, and insisting on a December wedding even though she knew how much I hated winter.

Now, instead, *I* had to live the rest of my life knowing I was the kind of "joyless," suffocating person who made other people feel like they'd been vented out of an airlock.

I hadn't told anyone, not even Jessa, the damning details of what Sydney had said to me. The dramatic way things had unfolded, everyone hated her enough as it was, which was fine by me. But what if I went beyond the broad strokes, and it turned out they *agreed* with her? This fragile eggshell version of me couldn't roll with a punch like that. I'd shatter into a mess of shards, and not even Sassy Sue would be able to glue me back together again.

"I just don't understand how things could've gone so wrong," I said instead, a half-truth that at least skimmed the surface of the awfulness iceberg floating just beneath. "And I'm . . . honestly, Jess, I'm a little scared that I'm the problem. That if I try again, with someone new, the same exact thing will happen. But I don't think I know how to fix myself. Or whether I even really *want* to."

"First off, you are brilliant and generous and considerate, and certainly in no need of some kind of personality overhaul," Jessa said, admirably restraining herself from launching into a full-bore Sydney takedown, though I could see the mutiny brewing in her eyes. Even though I'd thrown them together at every opportunity, hoping they'd eventually come around to each other, there had never been much love lost between my partner and my best friend. "Second, your ex-fiancée was an obnoxious, self-centered, *whimsical* bitch with tremendously overblown notions of her own worth. So let us never again refer to that shitty manic pixie gallery girl as the 'love of your life,' 'kay?"

And boom, there came the drag.

I burst out laughing, shaking my head, marveling at how deftly she'd turned a generally positive word into an insult with such bite to it. Sydney *had* been almost methodically quirky, but even still, I'd been charmed by her. Her appeal had never struck me as manufactured. "Whoa, buddy, tell me what you really think. And she *was* a curator, technically."

"Let it be known that I do not give a solitary, last-of-its-kind fuck about Sydney Zha-KLEEN's former job title," Jessa declared, giving the French pronunciation another prissy twist. "The one thoughtful thing she did was clear out in the aftermath and let you have this town to yourself. At least we don't have to look upon her precious wee *Amélie* face ever again."

"To small mercies," I agreed, clinking my glass against hers— though, obviously, I'd thought Sydney was beautiful, and still occasionally stalked her social media when I felt low enough to want to inflict on myself the stiletto-twist pain of seeing her be happy. "Full disclosure, I had no idea you loathed her whole Francophile thing so much."

"Eh, didn't seem like a helpful take at the time," Jessa replied with a shrug. "But boy, am I stoked to talk about it now! Feels downright *cleansing*, like it's clearing out all those years of pent-up shade. Gotta be good for the skin."

"Makes one of us, then." I bit down on the inside of my cheek to stave off the inevitable tears. "Because talking about her just makes me feel hopeless. Like I already had my shot at my dream life, everything the way I wanted it, the way it was *supposed* to be—and I screwed it up just by being myself."

"Oh, sweetie," Jessa exhaled, pert face scrunching up with sympathy. "So that's why there haven't been any second dates."

I'd been cautiously trying to put myself back out there the past few months, at both Jessa's and Sassy Sue's urging. But even the handful of first dates I'd been on made me queasily anxious, and the prospect of a second date flung me into full-blown panic. I ruthlessly overanalyzed myself at every turn, as if each prospective partner might be scrutinizing my every choice and mannerism with Sydney's witheringly critical gaze. The pressure felt buckling, enormous, as though what drink I chose and whether I agreed to taste the other person's tapas could derail my whole future with them before it even began.

So I'd decided, hey, maybe better to just tap out before I proceeded to lose my entire mind.

"That's why," I admitted with a sigh, taking another slug of my wine. "I can't relax enough to even think about letting someone get to know me. The pressure is just untenable."

Jessa rocked her head from side to side, an endearing Machiavellian expression stealing over her face, the one she always slipped into when thinking.

"What if," she said, lifting her eyebrows, "we took the pressure off? Picked someone so unlikely, so obviously not a realistic prospect for you, that you could just chill a little, have fun with it? Go on a date or three, possibly even enjoy a solid bang, as God knows you need one in the direst of ways. Have a shallow-end-of-the-pool experience, you know? Just doggy paddle around a little bit before you go full-on snorkeling."

I knit my brow, trying to parse this tortured metaphor. "So, you want me to pick someone I'm not into? How is that supposed to help?"

"No, duh, of course they still have to be a smoke show. I'm thinking someone super hot, but relatively low investment." She snaked her hand across the table, palm up, and wiggled her fingers at me. "Hand over your phone, and I'll show you what I mean."

"I don't know, Jess," I said slowly, balking. "This feels like a very ill-advised experiment. Or worse, a reality dating show with seriously low production value. Which, as you know, is the opposite of my bag."

"Oh, just try it *once*, Neenie," Jessa wheedled. "One wee little date. Think of it as a change of scenery!"

I tilted my head against the booth's slick back, mulling it over. I knew that I was stagnating; one way or another, it was past time to implement a different strategy. And once upon a time, I used to be a very proficient dater. If I was being honest, the idea of a no-pressure date with some hot yet ludicrously unsuitable individual sounded about a million times less excruciating than the glow-paint-and-goat yoga Jessa was probably planning on foisting on me next.

Sensing my softening, Jessa doubled down, a cunning gleam in her eye. "Aaaand if it's a total catastrophe, I'll owe you a batch of my gourmet pigs in blankets—*and* I'll even throw in a *Lost Girl* marathon."

"Ugh, you know me far too well, friend," I groaned, dropping my face into my hands. Puff pastries of any kind were my bizarre mortal weakness, the savory version of my kryptonite. I probably had my parents' epic dinner parties to thank for that, and all the stealth scavenging my brothers and I had done at them before we'd been allowed to formally attend. For the right kind of flaky hors d'oeuvre—especially one of Jessa's rare homemade treats, and in conjunction with my favorite TV series—there was really troublingly little I wouldn't do.

Lifting my head, I unlocked the phone and plopped it into her palm with a grimace. "Deal, I suppose. But to be clear, the terms of our agreement do *not* extend beyond the one date."

With a gleeful crow, Jessa swiped over to the third screen and pulled up my dating apps. Seeing as she'd created the folder and downloaded them for me in the first place, even wordsmithed my profiles so I couldn't hide behind the excuse of not having the energy to write about myself, she knew exactly where to find them all.

Rolling my empty mug between my palms, I watched her with a mixture of trepidation and the slightest brush of intrigue. It *did* feel just a little refreshing to cede control over this, instead of swiping through prospective partners in the late nights after work, with an eagle eye toward how many of my boxes they checked. Sitting alone in the dark bedroom that sometimes still smelled faintly of Sydney's dainty Un Jardin sur le Toit—for no good reason, given how many scrubbings my loft had gotten since she left—peering into that rectangle of sallow light like it was an exam I badly needed to pass, had felt depressing and lonely and borderline desperate.

This, astonishingly, felt like it might even be fun.

"Too perky . . . too basic . . . *oof, way* too messy," Jessa was muttering under her breath as she swiped through possible candidates with decisive little flicks, nose wrinkled in thought. "Too Aritzia-catalog-model—"

"Excuse me, what? Let me see." I snatched at the phone, but she slapped my hand away.

"Hands to yourself, missy," she ordered, cradling my phone to her chest. "This chick is not the one we're looking for, trust me on this. She's basically brunette you, which means instant disqualification. And might I remind you I'm in charge of Operation Doggy Paddle? You just sit back, relax, and let me do this good work."

"Yes, *ma'am*."

"That's what he said."

Snorting, I flagged down the server for another mug of mulled wine, while Jessa speed-swiped through so many profiles it was like watching a live-action carpal tunnel PSA. Then she paused, lips parted, fingertip hovering over the screen. "Well, *hello* there, sir. Finally, someone with actual promise."

"Sir?" I echoed, my heart sinking a little. "It's a dude?"

I'd been trying to keep my options open in the apps, seeing no reason to throw up any additional obstacles for myself. But while I'd slept with a handful of guys, and briefly dated a trans man back in college, my serious relationships had all been with women. When I could bring myself to imagine the hazy outline of a future partner, my mind always conjured up a woman of its own accord.

Which maybe meant that *not* a woman might be perfect for this absurd experiment.

"Well, maybe not entirely," she corrected, still engrossed in the profile, a tiny reflection of the phone screen glowing blue in her pupils as she flicked through the photos. "Pronouns are he/they, and pan orientation, just like you. TBH, I'm more concerned with this *face*. Here, take a look."

She passed me the phone, still warm from her grip. I reared back a little at the profile picture, my eyebrows rising as I saw what she'd meant. Bright blue eyes glittering like gems against the shadows of black liner, a tousled shock of dark brown hair falling into them. Stubble roughening what was otherwise a clean-cut face, with features so fine they were nearly feminine, closer to pretty than handsome. A lazy, crooked half smile, the "stick with me, I'll show you some things" kind that looked like a gauntlet thrown.

Okay, well. *Maybe.*

Intrigued despite myself, I swiped through more of his photos, defaulting in my mind to the masculine pronoun since he'd listed it first. In one of the pictures, he wore a dramatic corset and midnight-blue lipstick, galactic flares of silver paint and glitter swooping over his cheekbones. A fuchsia feather boa wrapped around his neck and strung across the shoulders of the two grinning, similarly festooned people crowding in on either side to press their cheeks against his. In another, he was shirtless and upside down, suspended in aerial silks, caught in a pose that highlighted the striking definition of his abs and obliques, bright stage lights illuminating waterfalls of technicolor tattoos coursing down his arms. He had the kind of muscle so sleek it looked carven, somehow feline.

Something that I tended to like a whole lot, in women and men and everyone else.

Not all the pictures were quite as flattering. In one, he wore a plaid shirt under suspenders—which, what?—and had his mouth massively open as he prepared to chow down on monstrous-looking burger that appeared to include both chili and a smooshed doughnut. In another selfie, he was giving duckface and flashing the devil horns hand sign, having clearly gotten a makeover from a little kid—his lips a mess of bubblegum pink, yellow eyeshadow indiscriminately smeared all over his upper face.

But in the final photo, he was in Lady's Lake, submerged up to the bridge of his nose, dark hair bristling in waterlogged spikes. Only those mischievous blue eyes were visible, narrowed against sunshine and reflecting the sequined shimmer of the waterline just below them, beads glistening on his forehead and clinging to the defined arches of his eyebrows.

I felt an unexpected little flutter in the depths of my belly, even as I acknowledged that he looked . . . risky. Impulsive, unpredictable. Sydney had been quirky and flighty, yes, but in the most polished, socially acceptable, Zooey Deschanel of ways. More Anthropologie, a lot less Burning Man. Before we fell apart, she and I had had similar values, the same ultimate goals for what we wanted our life to look like.

This person looked like the embodiment of a dare, someone I'd never in a million years have picked for myself.

"So you want me to go out with the trickster god of circus and burlesque," I said to Jessa, looking up to fix her with a flat stare, "is what you're telling me."

"Is that the vibe you're getting here?" She canted her head, considering. "I'm thinking more like *Lord of the Rings* elven, but with just the right dash of black sheep."

"Dash?" I demanded, brandishing the phone at her. "His username is literally 'lowkeyloki,' which, okay, possibly I'm a tiny bit here for that. But *look* at him. He looks like someone who'd get cast to play a sexy chaos demon on *Supernatural.*"

She shrugged, like, *And this is a problem, how?* "A little CW bone structure never hurt nobody."

"That's not the point. He likes dangling upside down at a perilously great distance from the ground, on purpose. He eats heart-attack burgers with freaking *doughnuts* in them, like some kind of carpe diem cliché. He posts terrible pictures of himself of his own free will and not under any obvious duress." I crossed my arms over my chest like, *Rest my case.* "I cannot date this individual."

"You can, and you will—because I picked him for you, and that was the deal, remember? One date. You're not going to go back on your word *now*, are you?"

She grinned hugely, knowing she had me there. No Blackmoore, and certainly not me, ever reneged on an oath once given. Though she wasn't privy to the witchy background behind this code of honor, Jessa certainly knew it to be true based on experience. Once I committed to something, I always followed through, no matter the cost to myself.

Which wasn't to say that being honorable didn't occasionally suck the big one.

"Fine," I groused, slumping back against the booth. "Swipe right it is, then. Maybe we won't even match."

3

A Winter Spell

W E MATCHED.

My phone had pinged with the notification before I'd even gotten home, soon followed by a message from none other than lowkeyloki himself. He'd introduced himself as Morty—even his *name* was somehow uncouth, at such stodgy odds with his whole alternative vibe—told me I was "wicked cute," and then promptly cut to the chase, asking me to grab a drink at the Moon and Scythe the following Saturday.

At least he had the good sense not to want to waste everyone's time by texting for weeks before we actually met up.

But I'd gritted my teeth at the choice of venue. The Moon and Scythe was the closest thing Thistle Grove had to a dive bar—the kind of place one might unironically refer to as a "joint"—and therefore so far from my scene that it wasn't even in the same zip code. But when I texted Jessa in desperation, wanting to know if the laissez-faire nature of this whole arrangement extended to relaxing my standards even as to venue, she'd texted back with Yessssss, bonus points for sticky beer floors, THIS IS PERFECT. To which I'd responded with a whole scroll of cringe emojis, only to get Just think of the pigs in blankets!!! 😄 😄 in response.

Who could argue with that logic? Certainly not me.

And I had to admit, the pressure-valve psychology of it seemed to work, at least as far as getting ready went. I managed not to triple-guess either my outfit, shoes, or choice of perfume—already a minor miracle in itself—and just a single glass of malbec took the edge off what nerves I had. It felt like a marked enough change of pace from my previous attempts to fill me with a swell of hope as I gave myself a final glance in the mirror, feeling only the faintest, creeping tendril of self-doubt.

Maybe this could work. Maybe I could be the real Nina again, sooner rather than later.

I'd given myself so much extra time to get ready that I wound up with more than half an hour before I needed to make an appearance at the tavern. Sitting alone with my thoughts would only leave room for the doubt to claw its way back to the surface, wriggle through my cracks. So I did something I hadn't done in almost a month, not since it had gotten properly cold.

I wound a scarf around my neck and shrugged into my warmest Moncler parka, then portaled up to Lady's Lake.

Portal magic was some of the most demanding spellwork a witch could cast. It required finesse, a vast reservoir of magical strength, and an iron will—the kind of unflagging focus that didn't falter even for a breath. In essence, it allowed you to craft a vessel of magic for your body, a spellbound capsule to whisk you through the fabric of reality itself, without letting all the opposing forces at play shred your flesh and spirit into its most minute component parts. To pull it off, you had to be capable of holding two opposing convictions in your mind, cemented alongside each other—that you were a perfectly cohesive unit, unassailable and self-contained, *and* that you were made of the same fluid, malleable matter as the rest of the universe. Both wave form and particle at once.

An absolute mindfuck, one which also happened to be my specialty. Holding coexisting yet contradictory lines of thought as self-evident truths is exactly the type of mental contortion lawyers do all day, and I was very good at it. Only a handful of other living Blackmoores could pull off a portal, my grandmother Igraine and my mother among them. My little brother, Gawain, had always been too chickenshit to even try, and my older brother, Gareth, could only travel relatively short distances.

But to me, it had always felt like second nature.

Closing my eyes, I lifted my hands and chanted the words to Lightborne Folly, concentrating intently on both my inviolable individuality and my oneness with the cosmos, as ribbons of light with a pearly rainbow sheen shimmered into being, weaving themselves around me. Magic rushed under my skin, a glittering flood, like liquid lightning crackling through my veins, so ecstatic it was almost unbearable. My pulse quickened, thudding in my ears as I wrested the swirl of light into the proper shape around me, and thought myself toward the lake.

For a brief, jarring moment, gravity and direction winked out altogether, and I tumbled through a vast expanse of nothingness.

The bottom of my stomach fell out, the lurching feeling of having missed the final step in a staircase, even as I lost any sense of myself as a physical object anchored in space. The closest analogue to the feeling was falling—but falling *upside down* somehow, like Alice plummeting down the rabbit hole. If you let your focus slip while you went hurtling like a wayward comet through this formless sea of in-between, no part of you would emerge on the other end.

A very powerful motivator to keep your will and mind firmly in check against a rising tide of instinctual terror.

From one heartbeat to the next, the world snapped back into place. A crisp skin of snow crunched under my boots as my feet suddenly found purchase, and a bracing gust of lake wind curled around me like something old and sentient, stealing my breath and combing through my hair.

I stood atop Hallows Hill, with Lady's Lake sparkling in front of me and the lights of Thistle Grove at my back, blinking like fireflies down by the mountain's distant base.

This time of year, the lake somehow looked even more elemental. Like some primordial origin story, the place where winter's cold heart had been born back when everything began. Up here, the sky had a brittle quality to it, a chilly purity so keen it made the abundant slew of stars look nearly sharp, a frozen, milky spill shattered across the glassy sky. The pines ringing the banks looked like darker brushstrokes flicked against the night, their branches etched with white. The black mirror of the water held an emerald waver along the edges, a phantom ripple that echoed the flicker of the northern lights that danced above.

Thistle Grove had spectacular displays of aurora borealis in the winter, despite not being anywhere close to far enough north; another of those beautiful quirks that those of us who lived here simply came to take for granted.

All Thistle Grove witches loved the lake, but I *loved* it. The way you loved something that was only yours, even though of course Lady's Lake belonged to all of us. Maybe to the Harlows most of all, since they were the ones who sieved remarkable magic into something we all could use. But I'd felt connected to the lake ever since I could remember.

Maybe, more than the fact that I loved it, sometimes it felt like the lake loved *me*.

Or maybe that was just the infamous Blackmoore egotism at play, our sense that this town revolved around us just because we happened to be the strongest of the families. I tried not to think like that when I caught myself doing it—being powerful didn't make you *better*, not in any way that mattered—but when it came to the lake, sometimes I let myself slip.

I took a few crunching steps closer, wind lifting my hair as I approached the water's edge, that muffled, wintry silence pressing into my ears. Each exhale turned into a spinning ghost in front of me, tumbling away into the night. It was so cold up here that my eyeballs burned with it, and I could feel a shiver start up even under my heavy-duty parka. Even still, contentment curled in my belly, that sense of pure belonging I only really felt up here. Like I was known, and I was perfect, and I didn't need to be anything beyond what I already was.

I sighed a little, wrapping my arms around myself and closing my eyes, wishing I could feel this untroubled all the time. Wishing I were different, stronger, better . . . that *everything* was different, but in a way that would let me make peace with myself. Discover the version of me that still had it in her to be happy and confident, fully at home in her own skin once again.

The wind died down as if a switch had been flipped, so completely and abruptly my eyes sprang open.

Just in time to see the lake flare white.

It was brief but utterly dazzling, like a colossal flare had gone off somewhere in the depths, a controlled explosion that somehow didn't so much as ripple the water's surface. Then the blinding white seemed to *fracture*, dissolving into a glittering mosaic of silver and platinum, like a shower of falling stars—if stars could fall upside down, rising like bubbles from the bottom of the lake up to its smooth surface.

I stood rooted in place, shading my eyes and gaping as the water finally cleared, shifting back to black and green, a simple reflection of the night. I had *never* seen the lake do anything like that in my whole life, not even during the Gauntlet last fall. It had looked, for all the world, like some kind of enormous spell being cast somewhere deep beneath the water, farther down than anyone had ever reached.

But what kind of spell could that possibly have been?

And who could have cast it, when there was only me up here?

Photo by Gary Alpert, Deafboyphotography

Lana Harper is the *New York Times* bestselling author of *Payback's a Witch*. Writing as Lana Popović, she has also written four YA novels about modern-day witches and historical murderesses. Born in Serbia, Lana grew up in Hungary, Romania, and Bulgaria before moving to the US, where she studied psychology and literature at Yale University, law at Boston University, and publishing at Emerson College. She lives in Chicago with her family.

CONNECT ONLINE

LanaPopovicBooks.com

🐦 LanaPopovicLit

📷 Lanalyte

Ready to find
your next great read?

Let us help.

Visit prh.com/nextread